IRISH WHISKEY

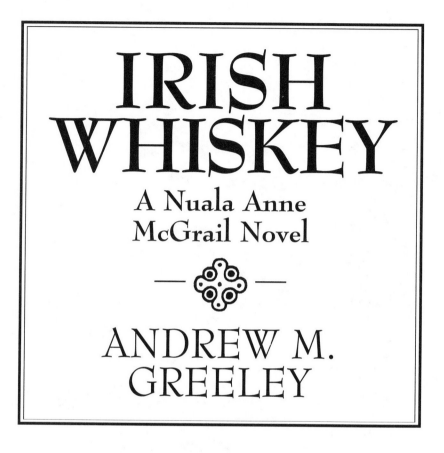

IRISH WHISKEY

A Nuala Anne McGrail Novel

ANDREW M. GREELEY

A TOM DOHERTY ASSOCIATES BOOK
NEW YORK

IRISH WHISKEY

This book is printed on acid-free paper.

A Forge Book
Published by Tom Doherty Associates, Inc.
175 Fifth Avenue
New York, NY 10010

Forge® is a registered trademark of Tom Doherty Associates, Inc.

Library of Congress Cataloging-in-Publication Data

Greeley, Andrew M.
    Irish whiskey : a Nuala Anne McGrail novel / Andrew M. Greeley.—
1st ed.
        p.   cm.
    "A Tom Doherty Associates book."
    ISBN 0-312-85596-6 (acid-free paper)
    I. Title.
PS3557.R358I8   1998
813'.54—dc21   97-4037
                                                            CIP

First edition: March 1998

Printed in the United States of America

0 9 8 7 6 5 4 3 2 1

All the characters in this story are creatures of my imagination. They exist only in my world and have no counterparts in God's world. In particular, none of the lawyers or judges or law-enforcement officers are based on any real people.

For Gail and Terry Goggin in honor of their silver
wedding anniversary: from now on it gets even better!

Whiskey, you're the divil, ye're leading me astray;
Over hills and mountains and to a brighter day;
Ye're sweeter, stronger, spunkier;
Ye're lovelier than tay;
Oh, whiskey ye're me darling; drunk or sober.

—Irish song

Whiskey also Whisky (1705–1715 short for *whis-kybae* <Ir *uisce beatha*, ult. trans. of ML *aqua vitae*, lit., water of life).

IRISH WHISKEY

— 1 —

"THERE'S SOMETHING wrong with that grave," Nuala Anne McGrail informed me. She was pointing an accusing right hand at a large monument with the Sacred Heart and the Blessed Mother presiding over a grave on which the family name "Sullivan" was carved.

I had just helped her off the ground after she had made a sign of the cross to indicate that our period of devotion was over. That she accepted my help was typical of her present mood; normally she would have disdained my assistance and bounded up on her own. Nuala was the bounding kind of young woman.

"Wrong?" I asked, dreading another manifestation of my affianced's notorious psychic intuitions.

"Who was this man James Sullivan who died in 1927?" she demanded.

It was a bleak Sunday in mid-September. Mother Nature had forgotten there ever was such a thing as summer and was settling in for an early and brief autumn, which she would follow with her favorite season in Chicago—endless winter. The lawns of Mount Carmel cemetery were already covered with a carpet of leaves. A chill northeast wind was shaking the trees and adding to the carpet. The dank smell of rain was in the air. A perfect day for a visit to a cemetery—and a perfect day for the dark mood into which the beauteous Nuala seemed to have sunk.

"He was a bootlegger, Nuala. And a very successful one at that. The Italians called him Sweet Rolls Sullivan because he owned a bakery right across from the Cathedral. Where the parking lot is now."

"Whatever in the world was a bootlegger, Dermot Michael?"

Looking like a teenager, she was dressed in the standard utility uniform of young women—jeans, white Nike running shoes, and a dark blue sweatshirt, the last named in this instance representing one of my alma maters, Marquette University (from which at the end of my four years of college I did not depart with a degree). She wore no makeup and her long black hair was tied back in a brisk ponytail. None of these utilitarian measures affected in the least her radiant good looks.

"A bootlegger," I explained, "was a man who smuggled whiskey."

"To escape the tariffs?" She frowned at the offending gravestone.

My beloved was the kind of beautiful woman at whom everyone turned to look, even in a cemetery. She was tall and her body was that of a lithe woman athlete. Her pale skin and glowing blue eyes hinted at an ancient Celtic goddess as did the twinkling of bells over the bogs in her voice. The first time I saw her, I thought of such womanly Celtic deities and came to learn that on occasion she could be at least as imperious as Brigid or Sionna or Bionna or one of those gorgeous and fearsome women. Naturally I promptly fell in love with her.

It turned out that, although she had dismissed me the year before in O'Neill's pub down the street from Trinity College as a friggin' rich Yank, she had also fallen in love with me.

By the way, if you want to pronounce her name correctly, it sounds like "Noola" with the double "o" stretched out and sounding like you had a bit of Dublin fog in your throat.

"No, it was Prohibition time."

Her frown deepened.

"Well, then, whatever was Prohibition?"

Ah, the innocence of the young.

"There was a time, back in the nineteen twenties, when the Protestants in this country passed a constitutional amendment prohibiting the possession or sale of alcoholic beverages."

"You're having me on, Dermot," she insisted, huddling close, her arm around my waist. "There *never* was such a thing as prohibition in this country."

When the Irish say "never" like that they are not so much

denying the existence of the reality in question as they are expressing astonishment that such a reality could ever be.

Naturally, I put my arm around her and held her tightly. In a couple of weeks this woman would be mine—and I would be hers—and I looked forward with passionate eagerness to that union.

In all its manifestations.

She was shivering as though it were December instead of mid-September. It wasn't *that* cold.

"It's true," I said. "Obviously it didn't work. It was a foolish law, which almost everyone violated. The saloons were closed, but speakeasies as we called them opened everywhere. Jazz music came to Chicago to entertain the flappers and their dates while they drank bootlegged booze. The bootleggers made tons of money and of course risked their lives in wars with one another."

"The Untouchables were real people then? I thought it was just a film."

Naturally, being Irish, she pronounced that last word as "fillum."

"Organized crime as we now have it in this country was the result of Prohibition."

"This poor man was born in 1898," she said, cuddling even closer to me. "He lived only twenty-nine years."

"The Italians were the most ruthless of all the bootleggers. They killed off everyone else. Killer Sullivan down there killed some of them, but they got him eventually."

I knew these things only because my parents had told me about them when we passed the Sullivan grave site on our infrequent visits to the family plot at Mount Carmel.

"His wife isn't buried here?" she asked.

The gravestone told of one Marie Kavanaugh who had been born in 1908, but it gave no date of death.

"She's still alive, I guess. She'd be in her late eighties now. They'd been married only a year and a half. I think she had a kid. I don't know whether the kid survives."

"Almost seventy years of widowhood . . . Dermot Michael, don't you ever do that to me."

"I'm not a bootlegger," I said, resting my hand against her breast.

She sighed contentedly.

"Who killed the poor man?"

"Capone."

"Who was he?"

"Nuala Anne, when you hear the name of Chicago of whom do you think?"

"Michael Jordan," she said promptly, going through the required motion of a jump shot. "Who else?"

I didn't say, "whom else?" I had learned a few things about women while courting this one. Probably not enough.

"Well, before that, everyone said 'Al Capone' and made like they were firing an automatic weapon. He was the king of the bootleggers, the most successful because he was the most brutal. A violent and vicious Sicilian.[1]"

"Was he the one the Untouchables sent to prison because he didn't pay his taxes?"

"He was."

"Whatever happened to him?"

"He had contracted syphilis before he went to prison. He died in his middle forties. His brain was so diseased at the end that he would sit in front of a tennis net and lob balls into it."

She shivered again.

"What horrible men!"

"The drug gangs make them look like saints."

"'Tis true," she said with her monumental West of Ireland sigh.

Since our engagement I had begun to wonder whether I had won myself a changeling. Normally an exuberant, not to say mercurial, and a contentious woman, Nuala had become quiet, serious and docile.

"'Tis a sacrament, now isn't it, Dermot Michael? And we should be serious about it."

So that was why we had spent Friday and Saturday and much of Sunday at a retreat house in one of the western suburbs, praying, reflecting, and talking about our marriage.

Nuala's relationship to the Deity was unusual. She "half" didn't believe in Him and professed to think that it was highly unlikely that any deity would care about someone as useless as she was. On the other hand she went to Mass almost every day, in case her agnosticism was wrong. Since our engagement, she had begun to

---

[1] Dermot, often in error but seldom in doubt, is wrong here. Actually, as he certainly should have known, Capone was a Neapolitan and hence ineligible for the Unione Siciliana, the backbone of the Mafia, or Outfit as it is more often called in Chicago.

tilt in the direction of belief. The signal of this tilt was her reference to God with the womanly pronoun.

"Well, hasn't She acted like a good mother to me, Dermot Michael, and Herself sending a gorgeous fella like you to take care of me and love me and maybe fock me once a month or so?"

"It's likely to be more frequent than that, Nuala Anne."

"That will be as may be," she said with a giggle and a pat on my arm.

I must say a word here about Nuala's use of obscenity and scatology. Like all the other Irish, who are superbly skilled at such usage, she meant no harm by it. It was merely one more exercise in Irish poetry and playfulness. And their own language having no such four-letter words! She never used any of the Anglo-Saxon words in the presence of my parents or, heaven save us all, in the presence of her parents or the little bishop. My brother George the Priest was a borderline case. In this story I'll use the verb "to frig" as a substitute for the most favorite of the Irish four-letter words. Much of the time Nuala herself would use the participle "friggin' " as part of her struggle to clean up her language so that she would sound like a "friggin' proper Yank." The reader can choose which times the word is my surrogate and which times it is hers. On some occasions, however, I will revert to the Anglo-Saxon vernacular when it is necessary to convey the full sense of the conversation.

"I knew, Dermot," she had told me in the chapel at the retreat house, "the first moment you sat down across from me in O'Neill's pub that you were the nicest, sweetest, most tender young fella I would ever meet, and yourself a big handsome hunk besides. I said to meself that there's one like me own da and you'd better not let him get away. There were a couple of times when I thought you might get away, but you never did. She wouldn't let you."

Nuala was a conniver and schemer from day one. But that was all right. So was Ma, as we called my grandmother.

I knew that I was supposed to reply to her well-rehearsed candor, but I had no time for preparation. So I had to wing it. Well, there's no point in even pretending to be a writer if you can't wing it.

"Nuala, my love, there was no chance of my ever getting away once I looked into those deep blue eyes of yours and saw twenty centuries of Irish wonder and surprise and heard your voice, in which there lurked the sound of clear bells ringing through the mists and over bogs . . ."

"Aren't you the grand poet." She laughed softly. "Though I think you hesitated until I took off me jacket so I could sing and you could ogle me boobs."

"I was about to say that my highly romantic reaction was confirmed when I saw that you had the figure as well as the face of an Irish goddess."

"That lot were no better than they had to be." She sniffed.

"And then you sang with that wonderful, sweet, pure voice and I was hooked."

"And yourself looking at me lasciviously all the while, but reverently, too."

"And would you ever remember the song that you sang that night?"

"Och, Dermot Michael, don't you know that I'll never forget it?"

And so in that tiny baroque chapel she sang our theme song:

> *In Dublin's fair city,*
> *Where the girls are so pretty*
> *I first set my eyes*
> *On sweet Molly Malone.*
> *She wheeled her wheelbarrow*
> *Through streets broad and narrow,*
> *Crying, "Cockles and mussels*
> *Alive, alive, oh!"*
>
> *Alive, alive oh!*
> *Alive, alive oh!*
> *Crying, "Cockles and mussels*
> *Alive, alive, oh!"*
>
> *She was a fishmonger,*
> *But sure 'twas no wonder,*
> *For so her was her father and mother before*
> *And they both wheeled their barrow*
> *Through streets broad and narrow*
> *Crying, "Cockles and mussels*
> *Alive, alive, oh!"*

Alive, alive, oh!
Alive, alive oh!
Crying, "Cockles and mussels
Alive, alive oh!"

She died of a fever
And no one could relieve her,
And that was the end of sweet Molly Malone,
But her ghost wheels her barrow
Through streets broad and narrow,
Crying, "Cockles and mussels
Alive, alive, oh!"

Alive, alive, oh!
Alive, alive, oh!
Crying, "Cockles and mussels
Alive, alive, oh!"

Tears poured down both our faces as she finished, tears for poor Molly who, God rest her, would be known as long as any Irish were alive in the world, and tears of happiness for our own great grace of being drawn together by Molly's song.

"Sure, didn't your Ma, and meself not even knowing about her yet, whisper in my ear that I should sing that song, and the night thick with fog at that."

There were times, and I presumed there always would be, when I was not sure where Nuala drew the line in her fantasies between metaphor and literal reality. I suspected she wasn't sure either and didn't care. Well, I had wanted mystery and wonder and surprise, had I not?

And that was why, when she had learned that Mount Carmel was only fifteen minutes away from the retreat house, she begged me to take her to the grave of my grandparents. When she was translating Ma's diary, she thought she established some kind of communication with that remarkable firebrand from her own home-town in the Irish-speaking district of the Connemara Peninsula. She took it as a given truth that Ma was looking after both of us.

I was not prepared to argue that Ma would not reach back from the grave—or down from heaven—to meddle in the love affairs of her favorite grandson.

So we had driven over to Mount Carmel—an old cemetery in which there were no more lots available—and knelt on the moist leaves to pray. My prayers were mostly happy. I was dizzily in love with Nuala and had not the slightest doubt that our marriage would be happy, though, to put it mildly, never dull.

Nuala's prayers, under the roof of trees which had lost much of their green but had yet to acquire their funereal robes of red and gold, were intense and serious. She had grave doubts about our union.

"Do you want to postpone it, Nuala?" I said to her. "I don't want to force you into something you're not ready for yet."

After all, had not she been the one who was so confident that I would give her a ring on the Labor Day weekend that she had told the little bishop at the Cathedral (with whom she was as thick as thieves) to pencil in the second Saturday in October for our wedding?

Typical of the male reluctant to make a permanent commitment, I would have waited until spring with little protest.

"Och, no, Dermot, that wouldn't be fair."

I didn't ask what she meant by that. Like I say, I had learned a few things if not about women, at least about this woman.

"Are you having doubts about me?" I asked.

"Ah, go long with you now." She lightly tapped my arm, a sign of mild and affectionate reproof. "Aren't you the grandest man in all the world? And won't you be a brilliant husband? No woman in her right mind would let you get away."

Small chance of that happening.

"Then why are you so worried?"

"Not to say worried, exactly." She sighed. "Just not sure of meself, if you take me meaning."

"Hmm."

That had become one of my favorite expressions in coping with my wondrous if often perplexing bride-to-be. It was a cue to her to explain what she meant without challenging her words. The secret for a man trying to understand a woman is to listen to what she means, not what she says.

Got it?

"I don't think I'll be a very good wife."

I almost argued with her, which would have been a mistake. Instead I said, "Worried about being a good wife, is it now?"

"Oh, Dermot"—she had burst into tears—"I'm a terrible woman altogether, difficult and contentious and argumentative . . ."

"I know that," I had said. "I knew it from that first night in O'Neill's."

She laughed through her tears.

"You'll need the patience of a saint to put up with me for the rest of your life . . . Besides, I don't think I'll be very good in bed. I know you want to make love to me something terrible. That's what a man should feel. And I'll be a terrible disappointment."

In her Dublin manifestation, she would have said "fuck." America and Chicago were ruining her vocabulary.

"And you don't want to fuck with me, woman?"

"Dermot Michael Coyne." She slapped my arm in a more vigorous reprimand. "Such terrible language!"

She giggled through her tears and then sobbed again.

"Don't you?" I demanded.

"Sure I do." She sniffled and began to dab at her eyes. "Don't I want to more than anything else in the world? But I don't know whether I'll be any good at it, do I now?"

So that was it. I could have said that adjusting to marital intimacy requires time and patience and sensitivity. Or I might have said that there was so much passion in her lovely body when she clung to me that I knew she'd explode with desire when we came together. Or I could have tried to reassure her with soothing words.

Instead, wise man in the ways of womankind that I had become, I took her in my arms and held her fervently. The tears had stopped, she relaxed, and looked up at me sheepishly.

"Am I not a terrible friggin' amadon, Dermot Michael?"

"Ah, woman, you are," I had said as I began to kiss her.

And so that tempest had passed—sweetly as far as I was concerned and with temporary reassurance as far as she was concerned. It would recur several times more in different forms.

I should make it clear that we were sufficiently old-fashioned to wait till our wedding night for our lovemaking. Well, I was anyway. Since we never discussed other possibilities, I didn't know what Nuala's feelings were on the matter. But I respected her vulnerability—at the core of her enormous energy and strength—too much even to suggest otherwise to her.

To be honest I was not without some unease as we approached our wedding day and night. I was not afraid of lovemaking, not

even afraid that I lacked the tenderness and sensitivity I needed
to be a good bridegroom. But I was afraid of hurting Nuala.

WELL, ME BUCKO, the Adversary in my head observed, AREN'T
YOU THE SELF-CONFIDENT COCKSMAN?

"I don't like your fake brogue," I told him. "And I don't like
your language."

He laughed loudly at that.

AND WHAT IF YOU COME UP IMPOTENT ON YOUR WEDDING NIGHT?
OR COME OFF IN A MINUTE OR TWO?

"Not a chance. Now go away."

He went.

Obviously the Adversary is part of me, so that thought must have
been banging around, you should excuse the expression, in one of
the subbasements of my soul.

I was also afraid about the loss of my personal privacy. I had
been an Irish bachelor, living in his own pad, for six years, counting
those last two at Marquette after I flunked out of Notre Dame. I
had become selfish and self-centered. How would I cope with a
loud, mercurial, enthusiastic person of the opposite gender who
usually bounded instead of walked, and who would surely want to
remake me and my life, as Irish women always want to do?

But I desired her so much that I figured I could put up with those
minor inconveniences.

At the graveside that day, she said, "I suppose you were hoping
I'd never get one of these experiences again, weren't you, Dermot
Michael? And especially not before our wedding?"

"You are who you are, Nuala. The results of your experiences
have always been interesting."

The fact of the matter is that my true love is fey, psychically
sensitive, whatever you want to call it. She *knows* things that others
don't know, which is why she is such a good detective and I am
reduced to being her spear-carrier when we get involved in a mystery.
Moreover, she picks up psychic vibrations of which almost everyone
else is unaware, like the horrors of the Civil War prison camp at
31st and Cottage Grove in Chicago or of Bealneblah (The Vale of
the Blossoms) where Michael Collins was killed.

Nuala and I keep these traits—fascinating but a little scary—to
ourselves, though my brother George the Priest has some inkling
of them.

"Shall we dig up the grave?" I asked her.

"Certainly not!" she exclaimed. "Well, not yet, anyhow."

So. We were on the edge of another one.

In my experience, young women (especially when they are not quite yet twenty-one) are overwhelmed by the excitement of wedding preparations, an effect reinforced by the high anxiety of their mothers. I assumed that Nuala would be no different from the rest of them.

Wrong again.

Her mother and father were coming over from Ireland a week before the wedding (their first trip to America) and it was most unlikely that her beautiful and serene mother ever suffered from high anxiety anyway. Nuala was content to let my mother (for whom yet another family wedding in which she was responsible for the bride was an unexpected opportunity) and my sister Cindy assume full responsibility.

"That one is remarkable," Mom had said to me. "We walk into the bridal salon, she looks at three dresses, points to the second one and says that's it."

"And it was," Cindy had agreed. "I never heard of such a brief decision-making process about a bridal gown."

"Was it a bad choice?"

"Wonderfully tasteful," Mom had admitted. "Perfect for her. You'll love it."

"But she deprived us," Cindy had said with a touch of sadness, "of a lot of high-quality worry time!"

"She's a strong woman, Dermot," Mom had added, a touch of worry in her voice.

"Tell me about it."

"You'd never know"—my father had shaken his head in amazement—"that the young woman will enter solemn wedlock in a couple of weeks. Totally cool."

"No way," I had said.

I had not, however, tried to explain.

Nuala had kept up her usual routine. By day she went to Mass every morning, ran a couple of miles, worked at Arthur Andersen (which had graciously given her an extended leave for a honeymoon because they wanted her back) sang two nights a week at the Abbey Pub, was faithful to her two voice lessons a week with Madame in the Fine Arts Building on South Michigan Avenue, and even cut her first disc of Irish songs, a copy of which we planned to give to everyone who came to the wedding.

"It's commercial," the agent I had found for her told us. "It will be really big."

"Fine," said Nuala, monumentally unimpressed.

After five minutes of reflection she decided that the Casino Club was too fancy for the reception and chose instead the Grand Ballroom of the Drake and selected the menu.

She deferred to me on both decisions. At first I thought this was merely ceremonial. Then I realized that when she said, "Whatever you think best, Dermot," she meant it.

"Shall our honeymoon be in America or Europe, Nuala Anne? Los Angeles and San Francisco? Or Paris, Florence and Rome?"

"Whatever you think best, Dermot."

"Or maybe do both?"

"Whatever you think best, Dermot."

Whatever had happened to my contentious, argumentative Nuala Anne? The only time the old Nuala returned was when she announced to us, "Isn't my pompous asshole brother Laurence flying in from Pacific Palisades to vet my intended and his family and himself bringing his fat bitch of a wife with him?"

"Dear," Mom said, "we'll be happy to meet your relatives."

Mom adored Ma, but she wasn't anything like that fierce Celtic warrior who brought her into the world. Ma's language would have been worse than Nuala's.

"We won't pass muster," I said happily. "Especially me."

"There's nothing worse than a Galway man who's made a little money," Nuala continued, her jaw tense and her eyes flashing, "and thinks he has friggin' veto rights on everything that someone else in the family does."

"Derm is probably right," my brother George the Priest observed. "What responsible Irish male would want his youngest sister marrying someone like him? A writer, would you believe? No good will ever come of marrying a writer."

George was kidding, not very subtly.

"I'll scratch the friggin' bitch's eyes out," Nuala warned us. "Me ma and me da like Dermot Michael and that's enough for me. I'm not a docile little sister who does what the friggin' amadon wants her to do."

"And probably never were either," I added.

She turned on me, ready to vent her anger on me. If she was angry at her brother, then loyalty demanded that I be, too.

Instead she grinned, "Och, sure, Dermot, won't you talk circles around him now?"

"Or if not, might I not throw him through a plate-glass window?"

I had done that once in Dublin when three toughs tried to teach me a thing or two.

"Good enough for him," Nuala said complacently.

We were to meet the Laurence McGrails at my family's home in River Forest after our retreat and take them to supper at the Oak Park Country Club.

"They won't be impressed by that grand place," Nuala had admonished us. "And himself using an outdoor shit-house for the first twenty years of his life. Sure, if it's not in Pacific Palisades, it isn't any good at all, at all."

"What will he do after he decides that we're not good enough for his little sister?"

"Won't he be calling all his brothers and sisters and telling them what a terrible thing it is and then me poor parents and try to worry them?"

"Does he know," brother George asked, his family loyalty aroused, "who put the phone in your parents' house?"

"And it wasn't himself either. Or that tub of lard he's married to and herself with all them expensive rings she wears? And won't he be thinking that it was irresponsible altogether for you to spend money on a phone they didn't need, the shithead that he is?"

By Irish standards, Nuala's language around my family was relatively free of obscenity and scatology. That she was on a run just now suggested an intense dislike which I had not heard before. Heaven forfend that I ever become the target of such rage. I would dry up and wither away.

So I said, "Nuala Anne Marie McGrail, I'll not be having you use such shocking language when your poor ma and da come to Chicago."

Again warning clouds of rage furrowed her graceful forehead and then were dissipated by her smile—which as always filled the room with radiance.

She hugged me and murmured, "Aren't you the lovely man, Dermot Michael? Grand altogether."

"Bring along a copy of your income tax return, Derm," me, er, my brother the cleric suggested, "and offer it to them at the dinner table."

"The bastards will take it home to look at!" Nuala's ire was returning.

"I couldn't do that."

"Ah, your reverence." Nuala hugged George this time. "Still tis a grand idea, isn't it? Do it, Dermot Michael! Please do it!"

Reluctantly I agreed.

"Can he make serious trouble, Nuala?" I asked her later when I dropped her off at her house on North Southport across from St. Josaphat's Church.

"You mean prevent me from marrying you, Dermot Michael? Och, don't be daft. But he could ruin the wedding for everyone in my family and maybe some in your family."

"Not hardly," I said.

For some reason that escapes me people tend to think of me as a pushover, though I'm built like a linebacker (college not pro). Maybe it's my innocent face, dimple, and longish blond hair. Cute, they seem to think, but hardly anything more than a cream puff, physically and emotionally. Maybe Nuala's brother would have to learn the hard way.

YOU AREN'T THINKING OF BATTERING HIM PHYSICALLY, ARE YOU? the Adversary demanded in pretended disapproval, as I conducted herself up the outside stairs to her apartment. ARE YOU JUST LOOKING FOR ANOTHER OPPORTUNITY TO PLAY THE MACHO HERO?

"Only if necessary," I replied. "Now leave me alone. I'm going to kiss my woman good night."

Which I did with considerable, but appropriate vigor, much to the woman's delight. Mind you I was not invited into the apartment, which I'm sure was just as well.

The apartment was on the second floor of a wooden A-frame house which had once been an elegant home. It was the only house in the neighborhood that had survived the Great Chicago Fire which in that area had spread as far as Fullerton Avenue two blocks north. Nuala had shared the apartment with a crew of greenhorns like herself, though none of them shared her passion for neatness. The first floor was vacant. When the greenhorns were shipped back to Ireland because they were illegal and Nuala was deported though she was legal, I had bought the house at a bargain price and remodeled the second floor temporarily because I was sure she'd be back.

Then I had begun the process of restoring the whole place. It was across the street from a church and a parochial school; the neighborhood was a mix of ethnics (of every hue under heaven) and gentrifying yuppies and boasted a couple of corner groceries and bars. A strip mall over on Clybourn, the nearby Kennedy Expressway, fast public transportation into the Loop, and Lincoln Park and the Lake within walking distance—why not raise one's children here in West Lincoln Park, or DePaul (after the neighborhood university) as real estate people had recently named it?

Mind you, at the time I was making all these prudent choices, there were no children, no wife, no fiancée in the offing. I assumed that I would marry Nuala eventually, some unspecified years into the future. But about that I had no definite plans.

None that I was willing to admit to myself anyway.

So within the month I had bought a ring with which to surprise her on the Labor Day weekend along with a suggestion of a Christmas wedding—only to find that she had already chatted with her buddy, the little bishop.

The groom is always the last to know.

So the following week, I had advanced my notion of living after our marriage in the house on Southport.

I had heard then for the first time, though not the last, "Sure, whatever you think best, Dermot."

"You get a vote."

"Well, I suppose that 'Titia will like the idea of another newly married couple living in her home."

'Titia was Letitia Walsh Murray, Lace Maker, whose narrative had clarified the problem of the alleged Camp Douglas conspiracies and who had received a priceless letter from "A. Lincoln," written on that fateful Good Friday, a couple of hours before he and his wife went over to Ford's Theater to see Our American Cousin.

During the course of our investigating the Camp Douglas matter, Nuala had imagined herself bonding with Ms. Murray, a fearsome woman much like herself. Whether this bonding was metaphorical or literal, I did not know. Nor did I ask because I was sure that the explanation would not be satisfactory.

Some of the Irish, particularly if they are Irish speakers from the West, tend to live in a borderland between various worlds, all of them "real" in one way or another. When one asks them to distinguish among the degrees of real in these worlds, they are incapable of answering the question.

I think.

So, after the emotional exhaustion of the weekend retreat and mortality-reminding experience of praying at my grandparents' grave, I was not eager to face our guests at my family's home.

"You should be ashamed of yourself, Dermot Michael Coyne," Nuala admonished me with total lack of sincerity as we cuddled by the bootlegger's grave. "And yourself molesting a woman in a cemetery."

"Irish comic tradition," I said, alluding to Vivian Mercier's book which argued that for the Irish sex was a way of defying death, of asserting that life was stronger than death.

My hand was now under her sweatshirt and had found its way— on its own initiative of course—to her lace-enclosed breast.

"It would be easier, Nuala Anne, if you didn't put any barriers in my way," I said, as I slipped away the cup and felt the firm flesh and the hard nipple.

"Sure, doesn't it add to the pleasure of your exploration?"

There were two aspects of my love's complex personality that gave me great hope for our marriage. She had an almost infinite capacity to absorb affection, or to give it a more proper name, love. When I first knew her in Dublin's fair city I thought that perhaps she needed such affection because she had been deprived of it as a child. Then, when I met her parents on their pathetic but happy little farm in Galway, I understood that she was a sponge for love because she had been so totally immersed in it for her whole life. She was an actress who slipped from role to role in life depending upon the requirements of a situation, but within the changing masks she wore and her natural shyness (which she shared with most of the Irish-speaking folk) there lurked a solid core of faith in her own worth. Her concern about whether she would be a good wife was a mask, a sincere enough one, but beneath the mask, she had damn well made up her mind that she was going to be a better wife than anyone else.

Moreover, perhaps precisely because she did not doubt her value, Nuala never fended me off when I was kissing and caressing her. "Sure, Dermot me love, wouldn't I be a terrible eejit altogether, if I chose a fella because I knew I could trust him and then didn't trust him?"

So it was left to me to draw the line during our time of, as she once called it at Grand Beach, "half keeping company," and more recently of betrothal. I knew of no other relationship between young people in which that was the case.

So I delicately replaced the lace and with a quick caress of her belly, removed my hand from underneath her sweatshirt.

"You're a grand man, Dermot," she sighed. "Sure, tis meself that can hardly wait to take off all my clothes for you."

Being of my age and gender and with the hormones of my species, my fantasy had been steaming since I had first encountered her with deliciously obscene images of what I might and would and could do to Nuala when I finally got my hands on her. As our wedding night approached, this imagery often took possession of me so that I could think of nothing else. In my (relatively few) sane moments I realized that whatever would happen would be with her and not to her and would be utterly different from my exploitive fantasies. Well, partially different.

Since I'm a writer, I must try to understand the sexual fantasies of women. They hide them pretty well. My editor thinks I do a good job at it. For a man.

So I was intrigued by Nuala's telling me that she could hardly wait to undress for me. There is no law against doing research while you're courting and seducing a woman—and being courted and seduced—is there?

"Do you really imagine such things, Nuala?" I asked cautiously.

"Well, why wouldn't I? Sure, won't it be grand to see the light go on in your eyes?"

"Sounds like you're a bit of an exhibitionist," I said cautiously.

"Sure, aren't all of us that way? Didn't Herself design us to delight men? And so why shouldn't we enjoy it when we do? Even if they'd better enjoy us respectfully?"

"And how long have you delighted in the prospect of delighting me?"

"And yourself doing research for your stories . . . Sure, don't I sometimes think you're marrying me as a research project . . . And don't you already know the answer to that question? Didn't I go back to me room on that rainy night and ask meself if I'd like to undress for you?"

"And you decided?"

"That it would be brilliant fun altogether and that I'd claw the clothes off of you, too, and that you'd probably be more prudish than I am."

"Some women are very prudish," I suggested.

"That's because they're humans and not because they're women."

"So what then is modesty?"

"Modesty means that you insist that men delight in you at the right time and in the right place and in the right way and we dictate what that means . . . Sure, Dermot, you don't have to worry at all at all. You do it right instinctively. Most of the time, anyway. And for the next fifty years or so, I'll edjicate you on the subject."

That was as far as I wanted to go.

"An interesting prospect," I said, patting her rear end lightly. "Maybe we should go back to my mom's."

"Aye," she said. "Still, Dermot, I don't like that grave."

"What do you think is in it?"

"I didn't say that I thought anything is in it. I said that something was wrong with it."

"Indeed you did say just that. What do you think is wrong with it?"

As hard as it is for a man to do so, I must learn the trick of listening carefully to exactly what this woman said.

"I don't know yet, darling boy, but I don't like it. Eventually I'll figure out what is wrong with it and I'll tell you before I tell anyone else."

"Fair enough."

"Now then," she said briskly, "let's go back to your ma's and face my asshole brother and his fat bitch of a wife."

—2—

"THAT ISN'T a Negro family next door, is it now?"
Laurence McGrail asked my father in shocked disbelief
as he looked down his nose at the scene outside on
Lathrop Street.

"They're both colleagues of mine, at the Loyola Medical Center,"
Dad replied, embarrassed by the gaucherie of the question. "She's
a neurologist and he's a neurological surgeon. They belong to our
parish here, of course."

"I suppose the poor people feel better with one of their own
treating them."

Nuala, now dressed in a lavender autumn suit and looking like
a sophisticated woman of the world instead of a casual teen, spat
out a string of angry words in the Irish language, which is hard to
do because it is a very polite language. Her brother ignored her.

"Do you have many Negroes in your community?" Melissa
McGrail demanded. "We don't have any in Pacific Palisades."

"I don't know about Pacific Palisades," I cut in. "But here in
Chicago we call them African-Americans or blacks."

(Subsequent research revealed that there were several African-
American families in the Palisades).

Nuala beamed proudly at my pugnacious remark.

YOU ARE GOING TO HIT HIM BEFORE THE NIGHT IS OVER, the
Adversary complained. YOU'RE WORKING UP A HEAD OF STEAM
ALREADY.

"African-Americans, is it?" Laurence asked in a tone of voice which indicated contemptuous skepticism, a comment and a tone we would hear often in the next several hours.

Nuala's brother looked very much like her father, but like her father might have looked if he were going to seed, same height, same distinguished face, same silver-gray hair, same dark blue eyes. But Laurence McGrail displayed a potbelly, slumped shoulders, and a ravaged face. His dark Armani three-piece suit did not successfully hide his physical deterioration. He was not exactly fat, as my bride-to-be had claimed, but he could afford to lose twenty pounds. He had paid a heavy price for his financial success.

His American-born wife, on the other hand, was on the knife edge which separates overweight from obese. A short woman with a face that must have been sweetly attractive before she had become bloated, she was clad in a dress of autumnal mauve which was perhaps two sizes too small.

As soon as they were seated in our living room (as Ma had insisted it be called), they both reached for their cigarettes.

"I'm sorry," I said, "this is a nonsmoking house."

It was indeed, but these guests were relatives. Mom, Dad, my sister Cindy and her husband Joe were prepared to grant a temporary dispensation. They were shocked by my ukase. Nuala Anne and my brother George the Priest beamed happily, however.

"Nonsmoking, is it?" Laurence said. With a face appropriate for his patron roasting on the gridiron, he returned the cigarettes to his jacket pocket.

They were offered drinks. They both wanted whiskey, straight up. Irish or Scotch or Bourbon or Canadian? I asked. They preferred single malt. We could offer them Bushmill's Single Malt. Laurence assured me that you couldn't buy it in America. You can in Chicago. So I brought the bottle with the green label into the parlor, as well as a bottle of Glenlivet. They wanted the Glenlivet, darkly hinting that the green label could not be authentic. Ostentatiously I poured Bushmill's into Waterford tumblers for Nuala, George the Priest, and myself and two meager glasses of sherry for my parents.

"Thank you, Dermot Michael," herself said as I handed her the tumbler of Irish whiskey. "And would you ever give Melissa a refill?"

To my astonishment Laurence's wife had already drained her

glass of Scotch. I made her wait for a refill, which pleased my true love even more than calling attention to her sister-in-law's compulsive drinking.

Ah, the Irish are great haters when they turn their minds to it, are they not?

"What kind of architecture is this house, Nuala Anne?" Laurence asked her, ignoring my parents whose house, after all, it was.

"Dutch Colonial," I replied promptly. "All of us were raised here."

"Dutch Colonial, is it?"

"How many bedrooms does it have?" Melissa demanded.

"Five," Mom replied, "counting the one on this floor that we use for an office."

"Five, is it?" Laurence said suspiciously.

"We have six in our house in Pacific Palisades," Melissa crowed in triumph.

"Mom isn't counting the coach-house apartment in back, which has two more bedrooms. My grandparents lived there until their deaths. Since I was their favorite grandson, they wanted to be near me."

Nuala was giggling. So was the priest. And even Cindy, who had caught on to the game.

The Irish Americans can be pretty good haters too, when they turn angry. And I was angry now. I would not permit these creeps to mar the wedding for my Nuala and her family.

"Nuala's parents will be staying there when they arrive. I'm sure they'll love it."

Lawrence continued to address his questions to herself and to ignore the rest of us.

"Now, Nuala Anne, where exactly is this wedding supposed to take place? At the local church, I presume?"

The word "wedding" on his lips was heavily layered with disapproval and doubt.

"Actually," I replied, "it will be at the Cathedral. I live in the parish, and my priestly brother is on the staff. He will preside over the Eucharist and officiate at the marriage ceremony. Nuala Anne's good friend, the little bishop, will preach his famous strawberry story. My uncle, the retired bishop of Alton, will give the final blessing. It's only a short walk to the Drake from there."

"The Cathedral, is it? I don't imagine that's a very desirable neighborhood, Nuala, is it now?"

"Highest median income of any parish in the city," I replied triumphantly.

That answer might not have been quite the factual truth. I wasn't sure. Certainly it was among the top ten, which was as near the truth as we needed to get under the circumstances.

"And isn't your man going to preside from his throne?" Nuala said innocently, pure divilment sparkling in her eyes.

"The big fella?" George said in surprise.

"Your man in crimson," Nuala smiled sweetly. "Isn't that nice of him?"

"The bishop didn't get around to telling me that this morning."

"Sure, didn't he call me just before me relatives stepped into the house? And wasn't himself busy conspiring with his sister, so I didn't have a chance to tell him?"

"The Cardinal, is it?" Laurence said incredulously.

"The very same. Didn't I sing Irish songs for him one night at the Cathedral? And didn't he say that they were brilliant?"

The Cardinal's word in fact was "dazzling." One must understand that in Ireland the list of comparative adjectives starts at "grand," progresses through "super," and culminates at "brilliant."

"We are close personal friends of the Monsignor in Pacific Palisades," Melissa said, her voice already slurring from the second "jar" drained. "He is a very important Monsignor, as you might imagine. He worked for our Cardinal for many years."

"Judge in the matrimonial tribunal," I observed.

That should have been a warning to them that I had done some research. They missed it completely.

I raised an eyebrow for my love, asking silently whether I should refill Melissa's jar. She shook her head in a slight but decisive negative motion.

So it went. Laurence would make a supercilious remark to his sister. Someone from our family—they had all caught on by now—would trump his ace and then his tipsy wife would offer an inane remark about the Palisades.

THEY'RE PATHETIC PEOPLE, the Adversary said, feigning disapproval. YOU OUGHT TO BE ASHAMED OF YOURSELF. DUCKS IN A SHOOTING GALLERY.

"Pathetic," I agreed, "but impenetrable. Nothing gets through to them. They are still determined to ruin Nuala's wedding. I don't intend to permit that."

Despite the fun of bantering with Nuala's brother and sister-in-law, I was preoccupied by the "conspiracy," as Nuala Anne who misses nothing had called the conversation between myself and Cindy, while we were awaiting the Laurence McGrails.

—3—

"YOU BEEN over to the Exchange lately, Derm?" asked Cindy.

"I stay away from that place. I'm no good at their game. Why?"

"I bumped into your old friend Jarry Kennedy on LaSalle Street the other day."

"Friend" in the context of Chicago political conversation does not have its usual meaning.

"How's Jarry doing?" I had asked guardedly.

"Same old Jarry. Still your classic borderline personality."

Cindy (short for Cynthia), my oldest sibling, just barely forty, as she would say, is a pert, pretty, intense blond mother of three kids. She looks and acts like a suburban homemaker, which she is. She is also a lawyer and like her husband Joe, a giant (bigger even than I am) with flaming red hair—a fearsomely effective litigator. They are both senior partners in the same prestigious Loop law factory, though currently Cindy telecommutes and works on tax law so she can be with her children. A teenager when I appeared on the scene, Cindy took over as my little mother and had played the role ever since. She had been suspicious about the "girl" I'd met in Ireland, until she met Nuala. Then the two of them made common cause against me, which is what women do.

"Yeah," I said curtly, realizing how much I hate Jarry Kennedy—and fear him.

"He said something about you better not show your face over

there. You know the way he talks, like he has the inside dope on everything."

"He still blames me for Kel's death. Always will."

"He met Nuala at the beach this summer?"

"Yeah. We bumped into him on one of our walks. I had to introduce her."

"He made some comment about her being fat. Tasteless jerk."

"He said she'd better watch out or she might go the way Kel did."

"The word on the street is that he's wearing a wire for the Bureau. Looks like they're trying to go after a few more traders. They never learn. They blew the last effort sky-high."

"I'm not a trader anymore. I never go near the place. And I don't talk to Jared Alphonsus Kennedy. But I take your point."

Her point had been that I should avoid him even more completely than I had in the past.

IF HE APPROACHES YOU, the Adversary had warned me, YOU'D BETTER PULL THE WIRE OFF HIM.

"Exactly what I'll do."

Jared Alphonsus Liguori Kennedy was my bête noire, my implacable enemy, the person who was always lurking in the shadows, plotting ways to get me. He hated me with a fury so pure, so undeviating, so profound that he had become a symbol of evil in my life. I usually dismissed him as a sick and twisted mental case. Yet in the subbasement of my psyche he lurked. Coyote as the Native American saying puts it, is always waiting and he is always hungry.

He hated me more than anyone else because we had always been compared when we were growing up together, most people feeling that he was destined for success and fame and I for failure and mediocrity. It had turned out the other way around and he had persuaded himself that I had stolen his success from him and made it my own.

He also believed that I was responsible for the tragic death of a young woman he loved (though she did not return that love). So I stole his success and killed his woman. There were no rational reasons for either of these convictions. Her parents blamed me for her death, but no one else thought that. However, these obsessions in a mind that was already twisted became a driving force in his life.

Jarry and I had once been friends, close friends. All through the years at St. Luke Grammar School and Fenwick High School we had been inseparable companions. That means we were friends, doesn't it? Or maybe we had never been friends. Maybe we were only rivals, even in early childhood keeping a wary eye on each other.

The Kennedys lived just down Lathrop Street from us, his father a successful real estate broker who had just managed to make it into Oak Park Country Club on the third try, his mother active in every woman's organization that would have her. They were, as Ma said once, just a little bit too vulgar.

Jarry and I walked to school together almost every day during the eight years of grammar school. If there were any competition between us in those days, I was the loser. Jarry was smarter, better-looking, and a better athlete. The girls adored his smile and his dimple and his curly red hair; the priests and the nuns and the lay teachers admired his quickness and wit; the coaches thought that he had the makings of an All-American quarterback even when he was in seventh grade.

I knew that he had one terrible weakness: he was a cheater. He copied his homework from compliant girls, he stole answers in tests from those sitting around him, he lied about why he missed acolyte assignments, he skipped football practices, he was an ever-undiscovered truant.

"Why do you cheat, Jarry?" I had asked him once. "You don't have to."

His face had expanded in his usual infectious grin.

"It's fun, Dermy Boy. There are two ways of doing things—the hard way, which means work, and the easy way, which means being smarter than everyone else. You do it the first way, I do it the second. I have more fun."

As my brother George the Priest would say later, "Jarry Kennedy cheats not because it is in his interest to cheat but because it is in his nature to cheat."

Everyone liked Jarry. I was an oversize, shy oaf. No one seemed to like me. I took the unfavorable comparisons for granted. I was not surprised when I heard a girl say to him, "Why do you hang around with that dweeb?"

"Dermy Boy needs me," he said with a laugh. "Without me, he's nothing."

When we were in eighth grade, I was not sure that I liked him anymore or that I had ever liked him. He was my friend, but he was, as I had told Ma once, kind of twisted.

"Och," she had said, "he'll come to no good, that one."

At Fenwick the balance of power had shifted. I had become a solid hunk of linebacker poise and my shyness through some miracle changed to extroverted wit. I possessed, it turned out much to my surprise, a quick mind and an even quicker tongue.

"Coyne, you talk in paragraphs," a Dominican priest had said to me, making it sound like he was accusing me of a crime.

"Yes, Father," I had replied. "Was that a paragraph?"

Even he had laughed.

At Fenwick some of the glow had worn off Jarry. In the freshman year, he had been caught cheating and was expelled. His father managed to persuade the Dominicans to take him back. He was drunk most of the time on weekends. In seventh and eighth grade he had become adept at getting as much beer as he wanted and consuming it with his buddies, I not among them, in back of the Convent. At Fenwick he turned to the hard stuff. He was thrown off the football team for goofing around, but somehow managed to persuade the coach to take him back. He led the team to the quarterfinals in our senior year (after I had quit the team because I didn't like the coach) but had blown the game because of a hangover, of which, like all his hangovers, he was immensely proud. We still purported to be friends and I guess I had kind of enjoyed basking in the reflections of his glory, even when the glory was becoming tarnished.

He spent much of his time figuring out "angles" and working on "deals."

"He's a charming and gifted kid," I had heard a young Dominican whisper to another. "Too bad he's a sociopath."

He still had virtually everything that a young man might want. But I had one thing he did not have—Kel Morrisey. It should have been clear to me in those days that he wanted her and that he was jealous of me. I guess I was still an innocent and did not understand that his drumbeat of obscenities about her hid his resentment that she hated him.

"He is a faker, a jerk, a dweeb, a nut," she would insist to me. "You should get rid of him."

She had been baptized Kelly Anne Morrisey. In her early teens that became Kellianne. Later it was simply Keli. To me she had always been Kel. She was my first love. I can't remember a time when I didn't know her. Or didn't love her.

Her father and mine had been classmates in medical school. Her mother and my mother had graduated from Trinity High School in River Forest the same year. She was born a month before me, the last of seven and a surprise, a mistake perhaps that became an adored child. I had sensed from the beginning—so far back that I can't remember when the feeling came—that I had lucked out on parents compared to her. Mom and Dad are unfailingly refined and gentle folk. I cannot remember either of them ever being drunk. Her father was a loudmouth braggart even if he is a highly successful urologist. Her mother is a tasteless and overweight bitch, three words that no one could imagine predicating of my mother.

However, Doctor and Mrs. Morrisey were part of the environment into which I was born and in which I was raised. They were as much an element of my personal scenery as St. Mark's Parish, Oak Park Country Club, Lake Geneva and my brother who wanted to be a priest. Only when I was a teen did I realize not only that I didn't like them but that I had never liked them. Later I would discover that my parents didn't like them either.

"If we ever need proof," George said, his quick, wry grin indicating that he was about to be perceptive and harsh, "that our parents are both saints we only have to consider that they put up with those two drunks for thirty-five years."

George doesn't look or act much like my brother. He's five-eight, black-haired instead of blond, with a sharply etched face, thick eyebrows and an animated grin. He is quick, intense, forceful. Epigrams and quotes spin off his lips like bullets from an automatic weapon. When he is talking or thinking or both (which is almost all the time) he strides up and down like a bantamweight boxer before a fight.

"Drunks?"

"You miss things, don't you, Derm? They're both alcoholics. Of course."

He was right about the elder Morriseys. Their heavy drinking had been as much part of the world in which I grew up as their daughter's pale blond hair, light blue eyes, and pretty, pretty face. Just as I had assumed that "Kel"—as she always was to me—would be pretty, so I had always taken for granted that her parents drank a lot and acted kind of silly.

I cannot remember a time when Kel and I were not inseparable friends. Nor can I remember the time when we first kissed, though she probably kissed me. She certainly initiated the kisses in the early years of grammar school and resumed them again in seventh grade, when we boys were no longer ashamed of kissing girls but began to brag about our conquests—I never bragged about kissing her, however.

Kel and I were always together. We made sand castles on the beach at Lake Geneva and splashed each other with water; we walked the side roads and picked wild raspberries; we watched television together, we did our homework together, we threw snowballs at each other sometimes but usually at others, pretending that they had thrown the first snowballs at us.

Every morning in St. Mark's schoolyard my eyes, pretending to be uninterested, would seek her out—and meet hers looking for me. We'd both giggle and turn away, not wanting to admit to anyone else how much we meant to each other.

At parties and dances in high school, I was never at ease till I had spotted Kel—an easy enough task because her effervescent laughter usually told me where to look.

More skillfully perhaps, she kept an eye out for me.

Jarry always trailed along with me, whispering in my ear that everyone knew she "put out" and was a bit of a whore. Amazingly, it never occurred to me to punch him in the mouth for these comments.

"You came at ten after nine," she said accusingly after one such party. "Late."

"Keeping tabs on me?"

"You bet." She hugged me. "Where would I be without you?"

Did she love me more than I loved her? Or was it easier for a young woman to display her love?

I don't know. Maybe both.

In our teen years the kisses turned passionate, and that was my doing, though she did not protest. Our parents had mixed emotions about the two of us. Our affection for each other was "cute" and they thought we'd make an "adorable" marriage. But they worried about whether we were becoming "too involved," by which they meant that they were afraid that adolescent passion might interfere with our careers. My parents never worried very much about me, in part because Ma was always lurking in the background, telling them what a "grand lad" I was. Tom Morrisey, however, was a disappointed man because none of his children had become M.D.s like himself.

"It's the highest profession a man can have," he said once to my father.

"Only if he likes it," my dad replied—one of his cautious little bits of wisdom that Tom never heard.

The problem was not that the Morrisey kids didn't try to be doctors. Alas, they either failed to get into medical school or flunked out, a disgrace far worse than my failure at the Golden Dome. Kel, the last and most golden child, was different. She was number one in everything from kindergarten on—highest marks in the class, class officer, valedictorian, student-council president, Merit scholar semifinalist, prom queen, captain of the volleyball team. . . . You name an honor, she won it. Moreover, unlike Jarry, she worked at success.

"The difference between you and little Kelly Anne," my mother said once, "is that she uses her talents and you don't."

"She's a girl," I protested with notable lack of logic.

"Ah, you noticed that, did you now?" Ma grinned impishly. "Sure, you've always acted like she's one of the guys."

"She's that, too," I said stubbornly. "She's not stuck-up like the other girls."

"The poor child is a nervous wreck," Ma continued, shaking her head sadly, "and her parents pushing her all the time."

She pushed me harder than my parents ever would. I was more afraid of her reaction to my Bs and Cs than I was afraid of Mom's and Dad's. Her fury when I quit the football team was worse than theirs.

"You're stubborn and proud and lazy," she told me bluntly, in the front seat of her Mustang convertible after a date on the Friday night I had walked out of the locker room never to return.

"But you still love me."

"Certainly I still love you." She nuzzled close to me. "But I want to be proud of you, too."

"What about the As I'm getting?" I touched one of her pert young breasts.

She did not pull away from me. She seemed to like to be fondled even more than I liked to fondle her. Our love play was an endlessly interesting sport, one in which I often sensed nervously that I could have gone much farther than I did.

"You'd better keep on getting them." She sighed contentedly. "I'd be awfully lonely at Notre Dame without you."

I dutifully pulled up my average, made it to Notre Dame by the skin of my teeth, and discovered that her father had other plans for her—Yale.

We were an oddly matched pair: Kel was always exuberant, an enthusiastic master of the revels as well as academic and athletic leader. I was the big amadon (a word which was affectionate, more or less, when Ma used it) who tagged along behind her.

She led the songs in the bus on the high-school club picnics, consoled the lonely and unhappy kids in our crowd, organized the double dates, planned the dances, took charge whenever someone was needed to take charge, and even when, strictly speaking, no take-charge person was required. I arranged the chairs and cleaned up afterwards.

How did I balance Kel and Jarry? Even today I'm not sure. In those days it didn't seem to be a problem. We weren't exactly the Three Musketeers, but when we were together, Jarry kept his obscene thoughts to himself and Kel masked her delight. Towards the end of the high-school years, we saw less of Jarry because he spent a lot of his time in bars and at poker games, which he claimed he always won.

I did win a prize or two, poetry and story contests, but who needs a scribbler when they have a prom queen who is also a Merit scholarship winner and a volleyball ace who did not quit in mid-season?

A mild spasm of pride did run briefly through the parish and the school when my prizes were announced, but such awards didn't get you into Notre Dame.

"Sure," Ma announced to the family. "Merit scholars are a dime a dozen, but poets are rare birds."

"Rare birds indeed," said Pa, whose strategy for dealing with his wife's vigorous assertions was to echo her last two words and then add the decisive "indeed," usually with a happy grin which said in effect, "Sure, the woman is a terror, now isn't she?"

Afterwards I often wondered whether Kel and I would have become romantically involved if we had not been friends for so long before the hormones were dumped into our bloodstreams. We were locked into a relationship which we might not have chosen if we had been strangers at fourteen. As it was, adolescent passion trapped us before we had a chance to think, not that either of us minded in those days.

There was a dark side to Kel's sunny, dynamic personality. She drank one or two more cans of beer than she should have and experimented with both marijuana and cocaine, much to my horror.

When I begged her to stop the drugs and cut down the beer, she did so promptly, apologized for causing me to worry, and begged me to forgive her.

"I don't want to lose you, Derm," she said, tears in her eyes. "I don't know how I'd survive without you."

I'd tell her she didn't need me at all and she'd hug me and bury her head in my chest, and say, "Yes I do, Derm. I really do."

When Yale accepted her and "Doctor"—as Tom Morrisey was always called in his family, commanded that she go there instead of Notre Dame, she was unable to refuse. Doctor had beaten me as I always knew he would.

These are all afterthoughts. In those days I thought Kel was the perfect girl and I was the luckiest guy in the world.

Was I brokenhearted when she told me that she "had" to go to Yale?

To tell the truth, as I look back on it, I was not. I consoled her in her tears and argued that maybe absence really did make the heart grow fonder. Looking back on that conversation I wonder if I was not experiencing somewhere deep down inside myself a bit of relief.

As Ma said, "Isn't she the grand young woman now? But, sure, Dermot Michael, isn't she just a little too intense?"

Well, as it turned out I had found an even more intense young woman (according to said young woman at Ma's instigation) but one in whom the gift of laughter had never been and never would be suppressed.

I wouldn't admit then, however, that I felt liberated by Kel's decision to go to Yale. I was besotted with her, dazzled by her wit and energy, captivated by her beauty, astonished by her love for me, enraptured by her superb young body.

Yet she was not quite beautiful, not the way Nuala is beautiful. She was pretty and mildly voluptuous, a young man's fantasy of a woman he'd like to see naked rather than a mature man's image of ideal beauty.

I never did see her completely undressed, although I did have the opportunity.

Some of our friends were certain that we had slept together. We were too close to each other, they said, to have resisted the demands of our bodies. I won't pretend that the idea had not occurred to me. Yet I would never have suggested it to her. How do you proposition your best friend, I wondered.

She offered herself to me the day before her senior prom.

"Do you want to make love with me after the prom, Derm?" she asked with her usual direct candor. "Maybe we ought to be lovers this summer so we will remember each other when we go away to college at the end of August?"

What kind of a young man would say no to such a request?

One that was frightened by the prospect, I suppose.

"I think we're too young, Kel. I respect you too much to do that to you now. And I don't need sex to remember you."

She sighed, disappointed I suppose. "You're right, as always. But, just the same, I'm yours whenever you want me."

"A breathtaking offer, Kel." I wrapped my arms around her. "I won't forget it."

She hanged herself on Father's Day. Wearing her prom dress. In front of a video camera. After she had shouted her hatred for her parents into the camera and damned them to hell for all eternity. Just before she had kicked the chair, she shouted, "I'm sorry, Derm. I love you!"

Her parents blamed me because they had to blame someone. Everyone else blamed them, especially after a TV station managed to get its grimy paws on the tape. My mother, who is a psychiatric nurse—indeed a vice president at her hospital—tried to ease my feelings of guilt.

"There was nothing you or anyone could do, Dermot. Your father and I begged her parents to see that she received counseling. They wouldn't hear of it. It was bound to happen, I'm afraid."

That helped a bit.

"Why did she need help?"

"She's been showing signs of the alternative mood syndrome for the past couple of years. Manic depressive, to use the popular term. She was treatable, I'm sure."

Some of the people in the parish who didn't like the Morriseys complained to the Chancery Office that Kel should not receive Christian burial because it would encourage other young people to commit suicide. But their complaints were overruled.

I had to live with my grief and my guilt and my pain for a long time. I still grieve for the tragic end of her life and still dream that she is alive.

Her parents moved away and did not even send us Christmas cards. In their view I was a killer, perhaps even a murderer. Jarry agreed with them. He spread rumors that I had got her pregnant and had refused to help her have an abortion. Those who knew me laughed it off, sometimes with the cynical comment that I wouldn't know how to impregnate a woman. But still his story had a life of its own.

"Why are you lying about me and Kel?" I had demanded of him one day in the shadow of the golden dome of Notre Dame.

"You killed her," he had sneered at me, "and I'm going to get you if it's the last thing I ever do."

"I didn't kill her," I replied. "She wasn't pregnant and you know that."

"Yeah?" he sneered. "It's still your fault. You should have saved her from her asshole parents."

"How?"

"That's not my problem . . . Don't ever feel safe, Dermy Boy. When you least expect it, I'm going to get you."

I told no one of his threats, no one except Nuala. Preternaturally perceptive as she often was, she had understood in those early weeks in Dublin that I was grieving for a lost love.

"He's a bad 'un, Dermot Michael," she had said gravely when I was finished with the story.

"He's washed up, a has-been."

And so he was. He was thrown off the football team at Notre Dame during his freshman year and out of the school at the beginning of the next year for an attempted sexual assault on a woman student. He was drunk and high on amphetamines when he tried it. Florida State, which seems to have no concerns about such matters, recruited him, but he was bounced from there in a couple of months. He had grown fat and flabby but still talked about all the deals and prospects he had lined up.

I was bounced from Notre Dame at the end of my second year,

because of "academic inadequacies." Without Kel around to drive me, I didn't find classwork very interesting. I went off to Marquette, where I had a wonderful time for two years, reading what I wanted to read and writing what I wanted to write. I didn't fail anything, but at the end of my two years there I was only marginally closer to graduation than I had been at the end of my first year at N.D.

Jarry's parents bought him a seat on the Mercantile Exchange, where he made a lot of money in a hurry. Then lost most of it in an equal hurry. My own parents, facing, with characteristic gentleness, the prospect that their last—and possibly their most gifted—child was not about to be a "success" like his siblings, bought me a seat, too. I arrived just in time to learn that Jarry had been suspended for five years for a violation of professional ethics, the exact nature of which was not altogether clear, though it seemed to have involved trading in his own name with clients' money.

"Professional ethics at the world's biggest gambling den?" George the Priest had murmured. "That's an oxymoron if there ever was one."

I was a failure at the Exchange, too. Except by a dumb mistake I made three million dollars one Friday afternoon. "The angels made you do it, child," Ma told me.

It must have been a good angel who made me sell my seat, give the money and my capital back to Mom and Dad, and invest the rest in municipals and in a trading account that I turned over to the best trader on the floor. Thereupon the same angel persuaded me to retire, to go on the "grand tour" of Europe, and to wander into O'Neill's pub in Dublin, just down the street from T.C.D.—Trinity College Dublin.

Then the angel, having thrust Marie Phinoulah Annagh McGriel into my life, departed, doubtless complacent about her work. Ma didn't live to meet her, alas, but she would have surely said, "Tis about time, young man, that you brought home the proper young woman."

Mom and Dad were pleased. Nuala's charm and goodness overwhelmed them.

"She'll settle him down and make something out of him," I had heard Mom say to George the Priest.

The worthy cleric had exploded in laughter. "Not a chance, Mom. That one likes him the way he is."

"Well, she does seem to be a bit of a handful."

"Like someone's own mother?"

"She doesn't look a bit like Ma."

Which was Mom's way of conceding the point.

Nuala did indeed like me the way I was and forswore all intentions of remaking me. "Don't mess around with your identity, Dermot Michael," she had told me sternly. "It's not healthy."

This from someone whose persona changed with the room she was in and the clothes she wore and the hour of the day.

While my life was looking up, through the combined operations of Lady Luck and my guardian angel, Jarry's was going down. He never did return to the Exchange even when his suspension was over. Rather he hung around the bars at that end of the Loop and talked to traders, always exuding an aura of mystery as a man with many irons in the fire, many deals cooking, many big payoffs in the offing. I saw him occasionally at a distance before I retired, and he looked painfully seedy. I felt sorry for him. I heard that he spent a lot of time at the racetracks and in Vegas and had become a cocaine addict.

Then Nuala and I encountered him the day after I managed to persuade her to take an engagement ring, though she insisted that it was "too big altogether"—not that she was willing to give it back to me so I could buy a smaller one.

We were walking down the beach in the hot and humid Sunday afternoon of the Labor Day weekend. As in every resort across the land, people were trying desperately to squeeze the last fleeting moments of summer out of the three days, a bittersweet and melancholy exercise usually, but not for Nuala or myself. We were engaged now and foolishly we thought it would always be summertime as long as we had each other.

Our stroll was a triumphal procession for Nuala, as women of all ages swarmed to investigate her diamond. Somehow she had managed to learn everyone's name, especially the small-girl contingent to whom she had told stories for much of the summer.

"It's gorgeous, Nuala, simply gorgeous!"

"What a marvelous ring!"

"It's almost as pretty as you are!"

"Isn't it huge?"

"Ah, sure it will do now, won't it?"

Ignored in the celebrations, I felt that they should at least acknowledge that I had paid for it.

"Isn't it too big altogether?" I would say. "But she won't let me take it back for a smaller one."

Some would laugh. Others would simply ignore me. I had better get used to being odd person out for the next couple of months. Years. Decades.

"Aren't you Yanks terrible fat?" she said as we progressed along the beach. It was stated as an interrogatory sentence, but, like so many Irish questions, it was a declarative statement of fact. When Nuala liked something about the United States she always said, "we Americans." When she was displeased with us, she would begin with "You Yanks" and sometimes "You friggin' Yanks."

"Are we now?"

"And don't you eat too much altogether? Would you ever see so much obesity on an Irish beach?"

"Would I not?"

"Isn't the trouble that you eat too much and drink too much and don't exercise at all at all?"

"'Tis," I said with a sigh.

Note that I had followed all the rules of Irish conversation in that exchange.

Then I added, "There's a genetic basis for obesity, Nuala Anne."

"Sure, Dermot Michael, aren't the genes here the same as at Bull Island or the Forty Foot or Salt Hill? Besides, aren't you well enough educated to know that in most cases genetic propensities interact with environment? No one is fated to be fat. Not even me asshole brother's asshole wife Melissa."

If I had ever learned anything about genes and environment, I had forgotten it. I wasn't sure where Melissa and her husband fit into the family tree of the McGriels of Carraroe, but I knew they were the only ones about whom Nuala had strongly negative views.

"'Tis true," I sighed, signaling that once more I had been routed in a discussion, although I had in this case taken a politically correct position.

As we walked, I was pondering the latest wisdom served up by George the Priest. "God is not merely love," he would say. "God is forgiving love. Men and women have to remember that. Love IS forgiveness. When husband and wife forgive one another, they mirror God to each other. They mirror God all the time of course in their passion for one another, but especially in forgiveness, and most especially in passionate forgiveness."

This *fervorino* was not explicitly intended for meself and herself and was part of his Saturday afternoon homily on the dune during his vacation. But since George rarely misses an opportunity to lecture me, I knew that he had us in mind even if we were not yet formally engaged.

"Brill, your rivrence," Nuala Anne had informed him after Mass. "Sure, won't me husband, assuming I'm lucky enough to find one, have to play God a lot of the time?"

"Brill" is short for "brilliant" in Irish, as in "dead friggin' brill." This in a stage whisper so I could hear her.

"The man will need the patience of a saint," I observed.

"Too bad there are no saints around."

Down in flames again.

The couple ahead of us as we ambled along the sand were perhaps in their late thirties, both attractive and in good condition. As I watched them the husband extended his arm around his wife's shoulders, cautiously and tentatively, I thought. For a moment she did not respond. Then she wrapped her arm around his waist and patted his back affectionately. Finally she snuggled closer to him. I was probably the only one who noticed their little byplay.

This was what George the Priest had been talking about, a small, undemonstrative exchange of affection in which all the power of forgiving love had exploded. God probably was the only other one besides me and the two lovers who saw it happen, not counting any lurking angels. If George were right, God enjoyed it even more than I did.

YOU JUST WANT TO SLIP YOUR HAND UNDER HER SWIMSUIT, PLAY WITH HER TITS AND THEN FUCK HER, the Adversary sneered at me.

"That would certainly be nice," I replied piously. "But I'll let him do it. I have a woman of me own."

MY OWN, he corrected me. YOU'RE ALREADY TALKING LIKE SHE DOES.

To defy him, I stretched out my left arm around Nuala's waist and permitted my fingers to press ever so lightly against her rock-hard belly muscles. She responded in kind and snuggled closer to me.

"Wasn't I wondering when you were going to do that?" she murmured. "Aren't we engaged now?"

"Woman"—I sighed loudly—"we are indeed. But that makes me wonder . . ."

"Wonder what, Dermot me love?"

"Whether a woman who is already spoken for should be lollygagging down the beach in such a revealing outfit."

She stiffened in our semiembrace and turned towards me, chin in the air, eyes glinting fire, ready for a fight.

"Och, Derm, aren't you having me on? And fair play to you, too! Usually I'm the one that starts the argument for the pure fun of it . . . Besides I'm just practicing for Cocacabana if you take me there on me . . . our honeymoon."

"You would be overdressed in Brazil . . . Do you want go there on your honeymoon?"

Then I heard for the same refrain which would recur constantly in the weeks ahead.

"Whatever you think best, Dermot."

Then she added. "Couldn't I buy one of them sinful Brazilian things and wear it here?"

"You could indeed, Nuala Anne, and cause a riot."

She giggled.

"Wouldn't that be fun now?"

I tightened the pressure of my fingers against her belly. She sighed contentedly.

Then we met Jarry. I almost didn't recognize him. Not quite fat enough to merit Nuala's strictures on obesity, he was still seriously overweight, no longer the lean, slick quarterback. His face was pasty, his eyes bloodshot, his red hair unkempt, his smile crooked, his skin red from too much sun. He smelled of beer and sweat and was carrying a can of Red Dog in his hand.

"Dermy Boy," he said, extending his hand in my direction. "What's happening? Who's the babe?"

In the euphoria of having won my woman, I removed my arm from Nuala and shook his hand.

"Good to see you again, Jarry . . . Nuala this is Jarry Kennedy. I went to school with him . . . Jarry, this is Nuala Anne McGrail, my fiancée."

"Hi," herself said with notable lack of enthusiasm.

"Yeah," he replied with a barely civil nod.

"What are you doing these days, Jarry?" I asked him.

"Usual stuff. Making tons of money here and there. Not much time to spend it."

"Not back on the floor of the Exchange?"

"Nah. That's for peasants; too much work . . . Hear you've turned to writing storybooks? Not much money in that, is there?"

"It depends . . . A lot of work, but I like it better than the floor."

"Yeah . . . I imagine you would. You sure lucked out . . . If it were luck."

His sneer turned ominous on that last phrase.

"Luck it was."

"So *you* say. Ever get over there?"

"Avoid it totally."

"Yeah, well be on your best behavior. The feds don't like people who make a lot of money on mistakes with other people's money."

Although temporarily not in physical contact with my affianced, I could sense her muscles tightening next to me.

"It was all on my own mistake," I said, remembering with a shiver the terror and emptiness I had felt when I realized my mistake.

"Yeah, well, that's what you say . . . Anyway stay away from the feds, know what I mean?"

"I'm not afraid of them, Jarry."

"Yeah, well, we'll see what happens . . . You take care, kid"— he sneered again at Nuala—"this guy is bad news for babes."

My love's lips had tightened as had her eyebrows, warning of an approaching thunderstorm.

"Fock you," she whispered softly. "Me Dermot is too nice a man to do anything to you. If you try to hurt him, you'll be sorry for the rest of your life, which might not be very long."

Jarry recoiled in terror, as though her words had been a tempered steel blade thrust into his gut.

"I don't know what you're talking about," he said, gulping his Red Dog and staggering away. "You're as nutty as he is."

"Nuttier," she called after him, her voice icy. "And far more dangerous."

This was a Nuala persona that I rarely saw, the deadly alley fighter *cum* wicked witch.

"He's a bad 'un, Dermot Michael," she said, still sounding deadly. "But don't worry about him. I won't let him take you away from me."

"I think you scared the hell out of him, Nuala."

She smiled complacently. "I hope I did."

We continued our stroll down the beach. I went over the "mistake" that had earned me three million dollars. By mistake I had sold when I had intended to buy on a client's account. The client never complained because he got his contracts at the price he had ordered. He congratulated me on my good fortune, though he said he was not sure he'd give me an order again.

The CFTC was all over me, as they often are when a minor and unimportant trader makes a huge gain. After looking over my paper trail, they concluded that I had been damn lucky, which was an understatement; as one of their lawyers said, I probably wasn't smart enough to cheat everyone.

A tax lawyer in Cindy's firm dealt with the IRS under stern injunction from my sibling and myself to play it straight. The Service went over everything with a fine-tooth comb and refunded twenty-five thousand dollars.

I had committed no crime. I was clean. But a lot of people hate commodity traders because they seem to make so much money so easily. Coyote could be lurking out there in the jungle waiting for me. Jarry's warning made me feel guilty and unclean.

The sky was still cloudless. However, as Nuala and I continued our victorious parade down the beach, I felt a dismal cloud edge over my life. Jarry would certainly try to ruin my life, probably before our wedding.

My mistake was not to take Nuala's threat to Jarry seriously.

Like the man who said to Grace O'Malley, "What do you mean, you're going to capture my castle before nightfall?"

— 4 —

"YOUR RIVRENCE, I'm a nine-fingered shite hawk!" Nuala turned around in the front seat of my Benz 190 (one of the last of its breed but still a Benz and still in excellent shape) and accused herself to George the Priest. For reasons that escaped me, she treated him like he was forty years older than I am and not a little less than ten. He was the source of wisdom (though not as much as his boss, the little bishop) and I was not to be trusted in serious religious matters.

"It's a bird I'm not familiar with," George replied easily. "Can you describe it to me?"

"I've never seen one meself," I observed—and was ignored by both of them.

"It's the kind of bird who lets two assholes ruin a perfectly good Sunday afternoon and a nice weekend retreat."

We were on our way to Oak Park Country Club for the second act of our "September Song" drama. Joe and Cindy were riding in their own car, and my parents and the Laurence McGrails were coming in my dad's seven-year-old Lincoln Town Car.

"A seven-year-old Lincoln, is it now, Nuala?" her brother had said as we had approached the cars. "And an ancient Mercedes?"

"Both classics," I had replied in a barefaced lie. "Dad's car is already worth more than he paid for it."

"At least the Bears won," I said as Nuala continued her consultation with George the Priest on our way to the club.

"I don't think the afternoon was wasted at all," George replied. "I thought our victory was total."

"They're both too friggin' thick to know that they lost. They're trouble, your rivrence. Won't they be on the phone before the day is over, telling all the family what terrible folks the Coynes are? They spoiled my sister Nessa's wedding and they'll spoil mine if they can. Fockmall! I won't let them do it."

The one-word sentence does not refer to a shopping mall but is a contraction of "Frig'em all!"

"Will they pay any attention?" I asked as I turned onto Thatcher Road.

"They might," she said sadly. "I'm supposed to be the wild, crazy one in the family.

"There are some members of the clan, myself certainly included, who would be proud of the charge. Wasn't there once a sign in a bar on North Avenue which said, 'No Coynes allowed?' "

Nuala giggled.

"Can't I believe that!"

"There's no reason to be afraid of them," George continued in the fullness of his priestly wisdom.

"How did they spoil Nessa's wedding?" I asked.

Nuala turned back to face me, acknowledging again that her fiancé was driving the car.

"The wedding was in Carraroe, though both Timmy and Nessa live in Boston. They're both strong on the Irish language and culture. Didn't your man go around complaining to everyone about how crude the ceremony and the dinner were and how much they were embarrassing their Yank friends? Wasn't poor Nessa in tears the whole day long?"

"Nessa is a warm and tender-hearted woman."

"Isn't she the sweetest girl in all the world? . . . And I'm not, God knows that's true. But they'll find ways to get at me, just like they have today."

"Not twice," I said grimly.

Laurence and Melissa were crude caricatures of themselves. Yet I knew enough Irish-Americans who with much less excuse were every bit as bad. Some of them lived on our own block.

"If you got into a fight with them at the wedding, that would make their day."

"They're sad, pathetic people, Nuala Anne," I reassured her. "They only have power over us if we give it to them."

"'Tis true . . . Sure, Dermot, aren't you right all the time?"

Thereupon she patted my arm affectionately.

"Occasionally," I murmured contentedly.

"What will they say in their phone calls?" the priest asked.

"Won't they call everyone and say that they are advising against the wedding? As though they had any right to give advice." Her voice rose in rage. "Or we have an obligation to listen to their advice! It'll upset me ma and me da something terrible. And on a phone line you pay for, Dermot!"

"Will your parents believe Laurence?"

"They respect his opinion because they think he's a great friggin' success. But they love you, Dermot Michael, they really do!"

"We'll work it out," I assured.

"You can count on that, Nuala," the priest said. "Today is just practice."

I had attended far too many Irish weddings where there was open warfare between the families. That would be fun, but it wouldn't help much.

We turned into the country club, the attendant took my car, and we waited for the rest of the entourage. I had prepared for Laurence McGrail with more care than I had told Nuala. If my tactics did not smash into his thick skull, nothing would.

"A nice little club, Nuala," he said as he glanced around, "not especially elegant, but the course looks to be challenging in its own small way . . . Does your young man play golf?"

"A little, now and then," I said modestly.

"His handicap is three," Nuala lied.

"Three is it?" Her brother's eyebrow shot up.

"Our club in the Palisades is much larger," Melissa commented.

Actually my handicap is down to five. Golf is my kind of game. It does not require much physical effort, only steady or, even better, lethargic nerves. My brothers and brothers-in-law insist that I win the family tournament every year because I don't give a damn whether I win or not.

Too true.

At the dinner table, fortified by more drinks, Laurence McGrail settled down to the main issue at hand—money.

"What exactly does your young man do, Nuala Anne?" he asked in a somber tone, like a prosecuting attorney beginning to question a witness.

"I don't do anything exactly at all," I answered for her. "I'm retired."

"Retired, is it?" he said with a heavy frown.

"Right! I made a lot of money in the grain markets and live off my earnings. It's a great life. That's why my handicap is almost down to two."

"Dermot writes," Nuala said, rising to my defense.

"Writes, does he now?"

"Isn't he having a novel published just before our wedding?"

"There can't be much money in that," he said, shaking his head in disapproval.

George the Priest took over my defense.

"That depends on a lot of factors, Larry. They gave the kid a two-hundred-thousand-dollar advance on his novel and are printing a hundred thousand copies. Then there's all the subsidiary rights . . ."

"'Tis true?" Nuala whispered in my ear.

"Would the holy priest lie?"

Nuala's brother winced at "Larry." So from then on he was "Larry" to all of us. The Coynes can be pretty nasty people themselves when they make up their minds to be. It's a wonder that they didn't put the sign from the North Avenue bar on the club.

"But he can't expect that kind of income every year from writing, can he now Nuala Anne?"

"Whatever it is, Larry," Cindy joined in, "it's a nice supplement to the regular income from his investments."

As we worked our way through dinner, Larry continued to talk to Nuala and we continued to answer his questions. Melissa was out of the loop because she was now thoroughly looped out.

"He really doesn't have steady work, though, does he? He doesn't go to his office every day?"

"Dermot doesn't have an office," Mom said proudly, though she had been frightened more than anyone by my haphazard career. "He telecommutes from his apartment in the John Hancock Center."

That was her standard answer to matrons of her generation who pretended to worry about "where is Dermot working now?"

"Doesn't sound like a very stable life to me."

"Maybe not," I agreed. "But it sure is a lot of fun. Anyway, Nuala will bring stability to the marriage. She has a grand job at Arthur Andersen and makes her pin money by singing at the Abbey Pub. The one here, that is, and recording."

That remark caused everyone at the table, except our guests, to struggle against laughter.

"Singing in a pub?" Larry said in horror. "And recording?"

"Och, Larry, won't we have a copy of me first disc as a present for everyone who's coming to the wedding? And won't I sing the 'Ave' meself at the Eucharist and won't I sing a few songs at the reception?"

This was all news to me.

"Sing at your own wedding!" Larry said, as he wiped his lips with his napkin and then placed the napkin on the table in a sweeping gesture of disapproval and dismay.

"Why not?" I said, pretending to be privy to these plans. "She's better than anyone we could hire. And she comes free."

Nuala did dissolve in laughter at that one.

"'Tis not the original cost, me love, tis the long-term maintenance, if you take me meaning. Your singing brides don't come cheap."

General laughter, except from Larry and the sloshed Melissa.

"Isn't commodity trading a very unstable business?"

Larry never gave up, absolutely never.

"There's some that think real estate is even more unstable," I observed grandly. "I'm told that in your part of the world, many people are forfeiting their mortgages because it's cheaper than selling the property."

This was, or at least should have been, hitting pretty close to home, Larry's home that is. I knew from certain private research that he had engaged in some risky investments in the last couple of years. While his back wasn't against the whitewashed wall yet, he was pretty close to getting his carefully tailored suit marked by the whitewash.

He went on as though he had not heard me. He really was thick and hence more dangerous. We were having fun with him, but we weren't getting anywhere.

"I'm told that most commodity brokers eventually lose all their money."

"That's not altogether true." My dad, Jim Coyne, the sound, sober, self-disciplined family practice physician, was not about to let the game pass him by. "All horseplayers may die broke, but not all traders, by any means. I have a lot of them as patients, so I ought to know. If they die younger, the reason is that the Exchange closes at 1:00 every day and they play all afternoon. Too much of the drink is taken, if you don't mind my saying so. Our Dermot, of course, doesn't trade anymore because he doesn't like the lifestyle. He'd rather not work the whole day, instead of just the afternoon. He hardly drinks anything."

Well, I do have this weakness for good wine, like the Rothschild I had ordered for supper.

As we turned to dessert—ice cream cake for me, nothing for my bride-to-be, who had understandably lost her appetite—I realized that Larry had beaten us. Nothing had penetrated his thick skull.

As we waited for our cars in the fading September light, the chill of autumn and the smell of rain in the air, Larry took his sister aside, dragging his stumbling wife along with him.

"I really must advise against this match, Nuala Anne," he said to her, loudly enough for me to hear. "Your young man is unstable and irresponsible. His family is obviously in serious financial disarray and in any event seems quite disorganized, if you take my meaning. I can only regret that I was not consulted before you went so far as to accept a ring and set a date for the marriage. You will simply have to cancel it, that's all there is to it."

He spoke as one who had the authority to make such a decision and the power to enforce it.

Nuala replied in Irish, in the same frigid tones she had used with Jarry Kennedy. Like Jarry, her brother recoiled in surprise.

"If you don't mind, Larry, I'd like a word with you." I dragged him to the end of the walk. He abandoned his wife, who would have collapsed if Cindy had not caught her. Nuala tagged along. Not much of a chance of keeping her out of the conversation.

"Larry," I said softly, "I have here in my coat pocket a number of documents you may find interesting. Basically, they are my tax returns for the last three years and estimates of my net worth. You might want to consider them very carefully before you bother Nuala's parents—on a line I pay for incidentally, not you—with charges that I am not financially responsible."

"That's not the point," he tried to cut me off.

"'Tis the point. If you make such charges, they are, I would remind you, defamatory. Should I hear that you are making them, I will mail these documents to all the members of your family."

I pushed the papers into his trembling hand.

"That doesn't make any difference," he said, trying to tug away from me.

"Ah, but it does, Larry. I also have here an estimate of your net worth. Never mind how I got it. I think you will find it pretty accurate, though it may underestimate the financial troubles you are having just now. Should I feel constrained to mail around my other documents, I might just send this along, too. Is that clear?"

"I don't know what you're talking about," he said nervously as he glanced at my estimate of his net worth.

"Yes, you do."

He tried to force the papers back into my hand. I stuffed them into his jacket pocket.

Nuala was watching the exchange, silent and wide-eyed.

"Now take your fat and drunken wife and both of you get the hell off the grounds of my country club."

The cab we had called to take them back to their hotel at the airport had pulled up. I ushered him firmly to the car. Cindy helped his wife in beside him.

"Is he really in trouble?" Nuala asked me softly. "Poor man."

"Nothing he shouldn't be able to get out of if he uses what little intelligence he has left. But right now the ice under him is kind of thin."

She took my arm in hers. "You're a desperate man, Dermot Michael Coyne. Desperate altogether."

That's a compliment in Irish English.

"Maybe we were made for each other, Nuala Anne McGrail."

She grinned, recovering some of her good spirits.

"That will be as may be."

"The Lord made us and the divil matched us."

"Didn't he ever."

But on our way back to the house on Southport, we both grew silent. It had begun to rain, the kind of patented Chicago drizzle which hangs on for weeks. I turned on the windshield wipers.

"What did you say to him, Nuala Anne?"

"I won't tell you."

"Fair play to you."

"I have to tell you, don't I?"

"No."

"I do too. I can't hide anything from my husband."

"Yes you can. And I'm not your husband yet, worse luck for me on this rainy Sunday night in September."

"I cursed him."

"You never did!"

"I did so. I had my fingers crossed. And anyway God doesn't listen to curses, though I don't suppose She likes them very much either."

"What did you say?"

She took a deep breath. "I said, 'May the devil damn you to the stone of dirges and to the well of ashes seven miles below hell; and may the devil break all your bones. May calamity and harm and misfortune for a whole year be upon you. And after you're dead may you roast in hellfire for all eternity.' "

"A powerful curse, Nuala Anne."

"Aren't we Irish the great ones for cursing? I didn't mean it. Not exactly. But he made me so mad with his friggin' presumption and himself embarrassing me in front of your family."

"We didn't do any good, did we?"

"You mean did we knock him off his friggin' high horse? I don't think so, Dermot. In a few days he'll forget about my curse and about the papers you had and start making the calls."

"So I shouldn't send my dossier around?"

"Only the papers about you. It won't stop him, but it will reassure the rest of the family that he's wrong again. No one will say that, though, because we can't admit that our oldest is not the success he pretends to be but a damn fool!"

"So the fight will go on even at the wedding. That is if we invite him."

"We have to invite him, Dermot. He's my brother."

I was not about to challenge family loyalty.

"Anyway, I'm not Nessa, and no one is going to make me cry on my wedding day. I'll just ignore him."

"That won't be easy."

"And I won't curse him again; well at least I won't damn him to hellfire for all eternity . . . But we're a fair pair of gobshites when we're crossed, aren't we, Dermot Michael?"

"We are that."

I turned the wiper knob up.

"I'll never curse you."

"I hope not."

"Except maybe with my fingers crossed."

If Nuala wanted to invite her crazy brother and his drunken wife to our wedding, that was her right. And it was my right to cook up schemes to keep him away. Little did I realize on that September Sunday that there would be a good chance I wouldn't make it to the wedding.

I turned off the Kennedy Expressway at Fullerton and then down Southport.

"I know what was wrong with that grave, Dermot," she said, breaking the gloomy silence.

I shivered, as I usually do when I have to face Nuala's second sight . . . Or whatever it should be called.

"What was wrong with it?"

"He isn't in it. Your man Sweet Rolls Sullivan isn't buried in his own tomb."

"Then who is?"

"No one. The coffin is empty. Some stones in it make it seem heavy."

"Are you sure?"

"I see it, Dermot."

"As I remember he was gunned down by Capone's men in the bakery on a Friday afternoon. Before the eyes of his customers. The police ambulance took his body away to the morgue. If he isn't in the tomb, then where is he?"

"I don't know, Dermot. I don't know."

"He must be buried somewhere else."

"If he was ever buried. He was born in 1898, that would mean he would be . . ."

"Ninety-eight years old now. You don't think he's still alive, do you?"

I thought about turning on the heater. But it wouldn't make my chill go away.

"I don't think he was dead when they buried him."

"You want me to try to get the casket dug up?"

"No need for that, Dermot. We know he's not there, don't we now?"

"We do indeed."

"Would you ever see if you could find out more about him? For some reason I think we are meant to get to know him better."

"I'll see what I can dig up at the Historical Society. They panic when I appear there. They are afraid that ghosts are going to crawl out of their files."

"You don't have to do it right away."

Which meant I'd better do it the first thing in the morning.

"I don't have much else to do tomorrow. But then I never have much to do on Monday morning. Or any other morning, for that matter."

She chuckled and leaned her head against my shoulder.

"I'm the only one who isn't worried that you don't have a steady job. Well, I don't think it bothers the holy priest much, but he keeps quiet on the subject."

"Maybe if I rented a big office in the Loop and put my name on the directory as Dermot Michael Coyne, Writer, it would satisfy my family and yours."

"Don't you dare waste the money!"

I stopped in front of her house, our house really, ducked around in the rain, opened the trunk, and pulled out an umbrella.

"Don't slip on the stairs," I warned her as I escorted her up to the second-floor entrance of the old wooden place.

"I'll try not to . . ."

At the landing, I hugged her as passionately as I could with an umbrella in my hand. She leaned against me in contented surrender.

"I'm crazy in love with you, Dermot Michael."

"And I with you, Nuala Anne."

"Just a few more weeks."

"Right. Two weeks from Friday."

I opened the door for her.

Just before she closed it, she said, "Och, Dermot, you won't have to worry about getting into me on our wedding night. Didn't I injure meself at hurling with the lads when I was a kid?"

She disappeared before I could reply.

Well, that was useful information.

Foolishly I expected pleasant dreams after my weekend retreat. Instead, as I was trying to bed my wife on our wedding night, three men tried to take her away from me—her brother, Jarry Kennedy, and a red-haired guy in a double-breasted suit who seemed to be Sweet Rolls Sullivan.

—5—

"YOUR MAN had an interesting life," I informed herself. "If anyone could climb out of the grave and go on living after they buried him, he was the one who could do it."

"I didn't say he climbed out. I don't think he was ever there to begin with."

We were having a nightcap at a neighborhood bar at the corner of Webster and Southport—two Bailey's on ice, an order which did not surprise the comely young woman with Slavic features who was tending bar. Doubtless she had learned how to distinguish the yuppies from the natives.

Her name was Sonia and she was already on a first-name basis with my date.

The aforementioned date, clad in jeans and one of those of knit tops which are designed to reveal several inches of midriff, was weary and a bit somber. It had been a hard day, she told me listlessly, at Arthur Andersen, Madame was upset with her because she had not practiced her breathing over the weekend, and the crowd at the Abbey was less responsive than usual.

September, I told her, is a hard month.

"'Tis." She sighed.

"You need a vacation, a long vacation."

"If it is a honeymoon you mean, sure, I won't say no to it at all, at all."

She placed her hand gently over my hand.

"You won't have to worry about your job or about Madame or the Abbey. Only about me."

"Ah, you're no bother, Dermot Michael."

"Your brother hasn't been calling yet, has he?"

"Didn't he wake up me ma and me da in the middle of the night to complain about you?"

The miserable bastard!

"Not responsible? Not stable? No class?"

"And no visible employment . . . Sure, didn't I know the amadon would? So I called them first thing this morning."

"I hope he didn't call them collect?"

She grinned faintly. "No, but I bet he thought about it."

"And what did your parents say?"

"You know what we Irish speakers are like, Dermot Michael. We don't like to argue or fight. So they just listened and said what a sweet young man you were."

"Older Irish speakers."

She squeezed my hand.

"Some of us younger ones revert to type after we're married."

"Did they seem worried?"

"About you? No, but about Laurence and what else he might do."

I didn't ask for a replay of the conversation, because I knew it would involve intricate Celtic circumlocutions and indirections.

"Enough to upset them?"

"And make them troubled, the friggin' eejit. But let's not talk about him anymore. Let's talk about your man the baker. I can see by the look in your eyes, you have another one of your professorial lectures all prepared."

"I don't want to bore you, Nuala," I said, hurt that she was making fun of my habit of occasional background lectures on her new country.

"Och, Dermot," she said, her hand squeezing mine, "if you stop being a writer, wouldn't you make a wonderful teacher, and wouldn't that keep my eejit brother quiet for a while."

"Well," I said, mollified by her flattery and her smile, "you must think of the first bootleggers as being not unlike the black and Hispanic drug gangs today."

Not unlike! That was pompous and professorial and from a guy who hated classrooms, which is why he flunked out of Notre Dame.

"Uh-huh." She gazed at me with rapt adoration, which I did not deserve.

"They were people at the low end of the economic ladder, often without much prospect of getting up it. Suddenly a new market appears and they gingerly test the waters. They are astonished at how much money they can make in a short period of time. At first the only people to fear are the law-enforcement types who are either overwhelmed by the amount of criminal activity or corrupted by it. Then as their greed expands, they begin to fear one another. The next step is killing, first of all, as they justify it, to protect their turf, and after a while to take over someone else's turf to which they figure they have a right. It gets dangerous, kill or be killed. Kill them before they kill you. These are all young men, still in their twenties and not troubled, any of them, by much in the way of conscience. They are, in other words, a new generation of American entrepreneurs on the way up. They tell themselves that they are no worse than the rich Protestants who are already ripping off the country or the hypocritical cops who are extorting payoffs from them. They are simply businessmen who are providing a public service, selling goods that people want."

"Do they really believe that, Dermot love?"

"Hard to say, Nuala. Up to a point they do. And despite movies like *The Godfather*, they weren't all Italians. There were Irish gangs and German gangs and an occasional Polish or WASP gang. The Italians, however, had a couple of advantages. Like the blacks today they were the poorest of the poor, they brought the Mafia tradition of secret societies with them, and they were the most ruthless of any of the gangs. Capone was no brighter than anyone else. His secret of success was that he was the most ruthless of them all. He killed without hesitation and without guilt."

She shivered. "One of your borderline personalities, was he now?"

"He used to like inviting someone who had offended him to dinner, then have his guys suspend the victim from the ceiling, and beat him to death with a sawed off baseball bat . . . When he came to Chicago, he went to work for a man named Big Jim Colosimo, a major bootlegger and 'speak' owner. A 'speak' was a 'speakeasy,' a saloon which was technically illegal but paid off the cops and provided big-time jazz music as well as booze. They called it a 'speakeasy,' it is said, because you had to speak softly when you entered the club. Capone and his friend Johnny Torrio killed Colosimo because he stood in the way of the expansion of the liquor trade."

"Ugh."

"Originally, the Mafia was a kind of vigilante group which in effect became an alternative government in the old Kingdom of Naples. It enforced the law and order and kept the peace and meted out justice, all of which the corrupt administration in Naples could not do, much like the IRA does in some places in Northern Ireland, and Ribbon Men and the White Boys before them."

"You know more Irish history than I do, Dermot."

"That's because no one forced me to study it . . . Anyway, it was only a slight change for them to apply the same rules, along with the same secret oaths and the other rituals, to the situation in this country. They were only another government, less hypocritical than the legal one as they saw it, protecting their own interests in a chaotic situation."

"So Capone was kind of Sicilian warlord?"

"He probably thought of himself as kind of warlord and protector of his people, but I just learned he wasn't Sicilian. His family was from Naples, which was a bit of a problem for him at first. Then he killed so many people that it didn't matter where he came from. You gotta remember, Nuala, that these were not the wise old men you see in the films and TV, the dons who have survived a long life of crime. There were no dons in those days, only the wild and half-crazy young punks who believed they were immortal. Capone ruled Chicago by the time he was thirty."

"So very much like the street gangs today?"

"Even up to the drive-by shootings. Capone's guys would drive by a speak that was buying someone else's booze and spray it with their Thompson submachine guns—tommy guns as they called them. If the owner of the speak survived, he changed his mind about who he would buy from."

"And they thought they were just businessmen?"

"So they said. And very successful businessmen at that. If some of the drug kings survive for another twenty years, they may become old wise guys as did the few Italians who survived Prohibition and turned to gambling and vice, extortion, and eventually drugs to make their money. Crime, they had discovered, any kind of crime, was too easy a way to make money for them to give up. They also branched out into legitimate or quasi-legitimate business—movie theaters, unions, laundries, liquor stores, real estate, auto dealers, even banks. Eventually, their criminal activities and their legitimate

ones became so intertwined that they probably couldn't keep them
straight in their own heads. They were always willing to use violence
in their legitimate business, too. Scare off a rival laundry or racetrack
tip sheet by wrecking some equipment and maybe killing a couple
of people, if you really had to. Many of the major banks in Chicago
appointed a vice president in charge of dealing with the Outfit.
They still had their gang wars, they still killed, but they had learned
the ways of prudence. You killed only when you had to, not for
the sheer fun of it."

"So that's what the Mafia is today?"

"We don't use that word much here in Chicago. Nor do we ever
use 'La Cosa Nostra'—Italian for 'Our Thing'—which is mostly a
media word. We call them the Mob, or the Outfit or the Boys,
sometimes the Boys on the West Side. They usually don't try to fight
the street gangs these days, because they think it's too dangerous a
way to make money."

"OK, I think I understand so far."

"They were not and are not nice people, Nuala Anne. The
novels and the movies glorify them but they are nothing more than
sociopaths, evil men without conscience and without morals."

"Some of them still live in River Forest, don't they? Do any of
them belong to the country club?"

"No, we don't let them in, any more than the WASPs let the
Irish in a half century ago. Some of their kids maybe, especially a
daughter that married out of the Mob. We don't draw the line on
the bankers or the politicians or the 'legitimate' businessmen that
deal with them . . . But this gets us ahead of the story. No one was
thinking country club in those days nor new business ventures.
They were only a crowd of ruthless young guys out to make a lot
of money in a hurry. American society had provided them with a
perfect opportunity."

"Just like you Yanks do for the drug gangs today."

"Arguably, as your friend the little bishop would say. At first
they bring in a truckload from Canada to help a friend at a speak
out who was running short. Then maybe a couple of truckloads.
Then they discover there were guys like themselves all over town
doing the same thing, guys from the North Side and the West Side
and the South Side and from Northern Indiana and Italians and
Irish and Jews and, like I say, a few Poles. So they join forces with
some of them to drive others out of business with threats and an

occasional salutary murder. They use their combined resources to buy off cops and public officials and open or reopen breweries in Chicago. Capone eventually owns the working-class suburb we call Cicero and practically owned Chicago. So primitive capitalism turns into economic oligarchy and eventually, as Capone kills off more and more rival gangs, a virtual monopoly. There was only one guy in town who was as tough as Capone, as ruthless, as ready to kill."

"And that was Sweet Rolls Sullivan?"

"You got it. He'd been a killer for an even longer time than Scarface Al. And murder no more troubled him than it troubled Capone. They were the perfect match in that respect. In every other way, however, they were as unlike as two men could be."

"And isn't that an article about him that you're holding there in your hand?"

"'Tis," I said, imitating her sigh.

"And you'd be expecting me to read it before the evening is over?"

"Before we leave here."

She grinned at me, took the article, and called to the bar person, "Sonia, your man wants two more Bailey's on the rocks. Make those double Bailey's."

(Chicago History, Spring 1970)
SWEET ROLLS SULLIVAN:
THE LAST OF THE IRISH GANGSTERS
By Timothy Patrick McCarthy

The Italian bootleggers called him "Sweet Rolls" because he owned a bakery in the 700 block on North State Street. His own men called him "Red" or sometimes "The Little Fella." His wife called him "Jimmy Dear." Chicago cops called him "Killer Sullivan" or sometimes, half-admiringly, "Dago Killer," because he had wiped out so many of Scarface Capone's hired guns. On the day of his funeral, the largest till then in Chicago gangland history, Federal cops called him the last man who might have stopped Capone's drive to dominate Chicago crime, and for all practical purposes Chicago itself.

"We all thought the redhead was as tough as Capone and a lot smarter too," a reporter for the *Chicago Tribune* remarked as the funeral cortège pulled away from Immaculate Conception

Church on North Park Avenue on that gray September day in 1927. "Marriage must have softened him up. Too bad."

Cops, reporters, habitués of the most expensive speakeasies in the city, and the other hangers-on in the demimonde between the bootleggers and what remained of law-abiding society were placing bets on who would kill whom first. The smart money was betting on Sweet Rolls Sullivan, the wish perhaps being, as Sullivan himself might have said, the father of the thought. Sweet Rolls killed with no more scruples than Scarface did. But he wasn't crazy. If he had taken over from Capone, the rest of the Prohibition era in Chicago would have been relatively peaceful.

The bets were not unrealistic. Only three weeks before forty-five caliber bullets tore gaping holes in James Xavier Sullivan's chest, gunners allegedly from his gang gunned down three of Capone's henchmen as they came out of the Lexington Hotel on South Michigan Avenue, which was Capone's headquarters. With characteristic sorrow for the death of his soldiers, a horrified Capone said to reporters, "It might have been me."

As it turned out, Sullivan signed his own death warrant when he failed to follow up the "Lexington Hotel Massacre" with the killing of Scarface himself. To this day no one is sure why he didn't take advantage of the temporary disarray in the Capone gang.

Popular history has it that, long before Prohibition, the Chicago Irish made their money in politics and government jobs, in which activities they were not averse to making a dishonest buck. While it is true that the Irish did not need Prohibition to become successful Americans, it is not true there were no Irish criminal gangs. Long before the Italians came to America, Irish gangs flourished in this country.

The legendary Spike O'Donnell was probably the first Chicago bootlegger. Long before the Outfit, as Chicagoans call the crime syndicate, moved into the sale of illegal liquor, indeed before there was an outfit, O'Donnell saw the possibility that the Volstead Act had created. A two-bit gang of burglars and fixers, O'Donnell's mob quickly became wealthy beyond their dreams. When Capone's tommy guns silenced several of his allies, O'Donnell saw the wisdom of early retirement. The Irish made lots of money off what President Hoover would later call the "Noble Experiment" of Prohibition, but they made it as recipients of bribes from the bootleggers. However, this neat paradigm leaves out the enigmatic and fascinating Sweet Rolls Sullivan who gathered together the remnants of the O'Donnell gang, added his own followers, and fought Scarface to the end.

He was an equal-opportunity employer, too: his gang included members of most of Chicago's ethnic groups, blacks, Mexicans, and two northern Italians who despised any "monkey" from south of Rome.

Sullivan was a Democrat and Capone was a Republican, though they paid off candidates and office holders from both parties. Like the good Republican he was, Scarface favored the continuation of Prohibition, a policy which was assuredly good for his business. Sweet Rolls was a "wet." Prohibition, he told reporters, was an attempt by Protestant Americans to enforce virtue on the rest of us. "We're going to have to pay a heavy price for that in the years and decades to come."

Asked what he would do if the bootlegging business dried up, he replied, "Work full-time in my bakeshop."

No one was sure whether he meant it. The redhead loved to joke and rarely said what he meant or meant what he said. Still he did lay claim to both civic and religious virtue. He went to Mass every Sunday, was married by a priest, contributed heavily to Catholic causes, especially St. Mary's Training School in DesPlaines, and supported the Chicago Symphony and the Chicago Opera Company. In his role at the Opera Company he occasionally would bump into the Company's great patron, utility magnate Samuel Insull. Chicago legend has it that Insull once arranged a private dinner for himself, Sullivan, and crusty George William Mundelein at the Archbishop's house on North State Parkway. Nothing came of this odd ménage à trois, because, while Mundelein did not like Italian criminals he saw little difference between them and Irish criminals, even if, as one of the Archbishop's staff later would comment, the Irish crooks at least knew how to use knives and forks.

When Sullivan was gunned down, spilling his blood on a large birthday cake he had made for his wife Marie, Mundelein denied him a Mass at Holy Name Cathedral, across the street from his bakery, and Catholic burial. The pastor of the little church on North Park, a man of such advanced age that he did not fear the Archbishop, agreed to say the Requiem Mass in his church, though, in deference to the Cardinal, he did not accompany the body to Mount Carmel Cemetery. Such defiance of an Archbishop, especially such a lordly, would-be Renaissance prince, was most infrequent in those days.

Legend has it that the gravediggers at Mount Carmel threw dirt from a section of the cemetery which had not been blessed into Sullivan's grave to honor the rule which forbade the burial of criminals in "consecrated" ground.

"Tis true, Dermot Michael, about the unconsecrated ground?"

"True enough, I fear."

"Didn't it bother your grandparents that their grave would be next to this Sullivan person?"

"They thought it was funny."

"Did they know him?"

"They were vague about that. They did say once that he was not the worst of them."

"Maybe," Nuala suggested, "they knew his body wasn't in the ground, at all, at all."

"Maybe."

Details about Sullivan's past are hard to find. He claimed to come from County Cork, from a town just outside of the city, and to have worked as a lad in a bakery in Cork. His death certificate lists Cork as his place of birth. Those who remember hearing him talk, however, say that he lost the rich Cork brogue if he ever had it. The files containing his marriage records have disappeared mysteriously from Immaculate Conception Church on North Park. There is no evidence that he ever became an American citizen or that he entered the United States with a valid passport. There are four bakeries in Cork with Sullivan as a name. Only two of them date back to the first decades of this century. At one of them there is no family memory of a Jim Sullivan, if that were his real name, who migrated to America. At the other bakery, there is a vague recollection of a cute kid with red hair named Jimmy, Jimmy Ahern to be precise, who worked there during the years before the Great War.

"Ah, wasn't he a cute little darling," said an elderly woman, whose family kept the public house across the street. "Always smiling and eager to please? And didn't he work terrible hard and didn't they say he was a great baker, whatever that means? But his name wasn't Sullivan, though it was Sullivan's Bakery all right. And weren't they terrible hard on him, making him work eighteen and even twenty hours a day and never letting him go to school."

Why was he treated so harshly? The thin memories of the past say that he was an illegitimate child, son of a young woman who was "no better than she had to be and her kind never had to be to very good at all, at all."

When the woman died, Jimmy was only seven years old according to the legend. The Sullivans were relatives of his mother in Cork City to whose care she had committed her son. That must have been about 1905.

Did he ever learn to read and write? He must have because there was no doubt about his ability to read in Chicago two decades later. He gave the impression of being a well-educated man, though one whose choice of words suggested that he was an autodidact. Perhaps his mother taught him to read before she died, though if that be the case she must have been something more than a common trollop.

The vague Cork memories say that he enlisted in the British Army in 1914 just after the war started. Doubtless he lied about his age as many young Irishmen did in those days, figuring that life was easier in the trenches of Flanders than in the poorhouses of Ireland. There is a record of a man in London named James Sullivan from Cork who enlisted in December of 1914 and served as a baker. At first.

The Cork legend says nothing more about him, save for dubious rumors that he was some kind of hero. The army record indicates that James Sullivan served in France for four years until the very end of the war, at first as a baker and then as an infantry noncom and then as an officer. With the exceptions of an occasional leave to go "home," wherever that might have been, he seems to have spent most of those four years in the trenches. He won just about every medal England had to give him, except the Victoria Cross, and he seems to have been recommended even for that after the massacre at the Somme (or Paschendale, as the English call it). He was seriously wounded on the third day of the battle, but survived to lead a company in the final battles of the war. Apparently they didn't give the V.C. to Micks. He was demobilized almost four years to the day after his enlistment as Major James P. Sullivan, D.S.O. He was twenty-three years old according to the English records and only twenty if one believes he was truly born in 1898.

Then he disappears from sight until 1922 when a small bakery named "Sullivan's Bakeshop" opened on Clark Street just north of Armitage. Within the year he had assembled a crowd of Irish toughs to help him run whiskey across the Canadian border. He also became a "silent partner" in several modest speakeasies. Where did he get the money? Perhaps he had saved a nest egg from his army pay during the war years.

Sweet Rolls was secretive about his past. He would summarize his youth concisely and always in the same words, "Sure, wasn't I a poor kid from West Cork who learned how to be a baker and then joined the English army and came home after the war and got involved in a mild sort of way in the 'troubles' that were happening there."

Legends about this "mild involvement" in the Irish War for Independence and the Irish Civil War which followed it spread through the Irish community in Chicago during his brief five years of glory before the end came in his new and enlarged bakery shop across from Holy Name Cathedral. At the height of his popularity, when it seemed that he might indeed be the one to block Capone, these legends seeped into the Chicago papers. One story has it that he was a member of Michael Collins's "flying squad" which assassinated British intelligence agents. Another says he was involved in the murder of Sir Henry Maitland, the Chief of the Imperial General Staff, in a London park. He was supposed to have turned against Collins during the Civil War, joined the "Irregulars" in the war against the "Free Staters" and left, when the former won their inevitable victory, with a price on his head. Another story holds that he killed so many Irregulars to avenge Collins (who was a scant seven years older) that even the hard-liner Kevin O'Higgins, who became the backbone of the Free State after "The Big Fella's" death, warned him to leave because it would be difficult to protect him.

Yet another story claims that he had served in the hated

Black and Tans, the English auxiliary force which terrorized Ireland during the last days of its imperialist reign over the twenty-six counties which would emerge as a barely independent Ireland.

Sullivan must have heard all these stories. He may have told some of them himself. "There's all kinds of good stories about me," he is supposed to have said to the Chief of Detectives of the Chicago Police Department, who was his employee.

"Did you serve in the English Army during the Great War?"

"If I did, I wouldn't have been the only Irishman that did so, would I now? And sure, it wasn't the only army I served in, was it?"

Thus one pieces together a story: a child of an unwed mother comes to Cork City at the age of seven after the death of his mother. He becomes a virtual slave of his relatives who owned the bakery. He is, however, charming and hardworking, wins the admiration of the neighbors, and earns the reputation of being an excellent baker. He survives four years in the trenches—a rare feat indeed—and becomes a hero, perhaps because he no longer cared whether he lived or died.

Then, with the horror of the trenches forever locked in his head, he comes back to Ireland and, on one side or the other, engages in more killing. When the "troubles" end, he migrates to America, probably entering illegally across the Canadian border, settles in Chicago, opens a bakery, organizes his own gang, and enters the bootlegger business and the bootlegger wars. His reputation for ruthlessness is matched only by that of Scarface Al.

That is about as much detail as we will ever have about Sweet Rolls Sullivan. It seems likely, however, that he had done a lot of killing before he appeared in Chicago. If he was truly the Lt. James Sullivan who was wounded in Flanders, the killings in Chicago must have seemed penny ante.

When he married Marie Kavanagh, a year before his death, he was asked whether his parents would "come over" from Ireland. "Not very likely," he said with a bitter laugh. Those who heard the response were surprised. "Red" usually gave no hint of bitterness.

But then he usually gave no hints at all.

A reporter for the *Chicago Herald* summed him up the week

before his wedding: "James 'Sweet Rolls' Sullivan is a charming, witty, quick-talking Irishman. He could as well be a politician or a doctor or even a priest. Until you look at his pale blue eyes, which seem utterly unrelated to the joke he's just told or the quick answer with which he has just fended off a reporter. They are cold, hard eyes, unblinking, unfeeling, without a trace of mercy or compassion. Young Marie Kavanagh should take a close look at those eyes before she marches down the aisle of Immaculate Conception Church to enter holy wedlock with this handsome, but deadly man."

Without any realization, however, that Jimmy Sullivan was approaching the denouement of his life, Marie did not look into his deadly eyes and see misery and suffering in her future.

"Your man loves his French words, doesn't he?" Nuala pointed at the photocopy of his article.

"Doesn't he now?"

"His eyes were not as pretty as yours, Dermot Michael, not at all, at all. No way."

"You never saw his."

"I don't have to . . . Would he have been any better than Capone if he had won?"

"Probably not, Nuala Anne. Capone was fat and ugly and crude. Sullivan was slender and handsome and seemed civilized. Prohibition would have run its deadly course anyway."

"Wouldn't the right-thinking people of America hated him just as much as they hated Capone?"

"The right-thinking people of America turned Capone into a folk hero. That's what Prohibition did to us."

"Is Sullivan a hero?"

"He was not a good guy, Nuala. The point in the article and in his life is that, as well as a gangster, he was a romantic and tragic figure, far more than Capone was."

She nodded.

"Ireland has had more than its share of them kind . . . And, Dermot Michael, go easy on that Bailey's. You're not going to get another, and yourself driving home."

"If I had a third, I might sleep at your house."

"It's not my house and much good you'd be to me with three of them things under your belt."

I sighed.

"'Tis true."

"Sure, don't I sound like an awful Irish matriarch now? You mustn't let me be that way after we're married, do you understand?"

"It won't be easy."

"It's not SUPPOSED to be easy . . . But wasn't this one a strange man altogether?"

"He was all of that, Nuala Anne. He must have loved danger. Couldn't do without it."

"Still you'd think that after all his experience of battle, he wouldn't have been alone in his bakeshop in the middle of a gang war. Does your man ask that question?"

"Only indirectly. But read on."

"Speaking of strange men, what do you hear about your old friend, Jared Kennedy?"

A question like that might simply have been a chance. But with Nuala I could never be sure whether she might not have a sense of the worries which Cindy had stirred up the day before.

"I hear on the street that he's wearing a wire for the Bureau, uh, a tape recorder for the FBI."

"What street?"

"LaSalle Street: that's where you hear all the rumors."

"I thought you didn't go over there."

"I don't. Hearing it on the street is a kind of a figure of speech. I heard it from Cindy, who heard it somewhere."

"So that's what you were talking about Sunday, was it now?"

"It was."

Never, never try to hide a worry from Nuala.

"If people on the street know that he's wearing a wire, what good does it do to wear the wire?"

"To catch the people who never hear anything on the street, the little, not-very-bright people who have no business in the game anyway. The big guys know about a wire as soon as it goes on and avoid the guy that's wearing it as if he's got typhoid fever. They'd avoid Jarry even if he wasn't wearing a wire. All the Bureau ever picks up in these much-publicized 'stings' is a few minor operators and a lot of publicity."

"Are you sure you're safe?"

"Sure I'm sure. I don't work over there anymore. I never see

Jarry, thank heaven. And I've never done anything wrong. I'm probably not smart enough to."

"Uhm," she said, and went back to her reading.

Yet I was scared. My troubles with the CFTC and IRS had made me feel guilty, though neither agency had found any wrongdoing. Suspicion had been enough to scare me.

Not a very good hardball player.

Marie Elizabeth Kavanagh was a flapper, a typical young woman of the twenties, one who thought she was a liberated spirit. She was a Catholic flapper, however, a product of the Convent of the Sacred Heart, so she was a conservative flapper, not that there were all that many Chicago flappers in those days who were all that radical. Her father, Henry Kavanagh, a chief auditor for the Pullman Company (ticket receipts) with an office on Michigan Avenue, was on the upper crust of the Irish middle class, sufficiently affluent that he could afford the tuition the Sacred Heart nuns charged and the costs of a coming-out party at the family home on Marine Drive. The Chicago papers delighted in calling her a debutante, as in the headline in the Hearst paper, "Gorgeous Debutante to Wed Hood!"

She was indeed gorgeous, to judge from the pictures of her at the time of her betrothal and marriage, a tall willowy blonde with a lovely body and a bright smile. Apparently there was not much behind the smile. The papers deftly hinted that she was not very bright.

As one can imagine, Henry Kavanagh was less than enthused at the prospect of his eighteen-year-old daughter's wedding to a criminal. Under pressure from his wife, who seems to have been as empty-headed as their daughter, he compromised. He granted his daughter permission to marry, authorized his wife to spend money on the wedding, and announced his intention not to attend the wedding. The *Examiner*'s gossip columnist reported breathlessly that he had asked Archbishop Mundelein to intervene to prevent the marriage.

"Deb's Father Asks Church's Help to Prevent Marriage," the headline had said.

"Oh, Daddy will give in and be there. He's really a cream puff," Marie had said in response to the rumor.

Her prediction was accurate. Her father did indeed attend

the wedding and, according to observers, looked decidedly uncomfortable in the presence of the lords of the demimonde. Naturally Scarface Al—Al Brown as he sometimes liked to call himself—was there in his finest and most expensive—and most vulgar—duds. Bugs Moran, head of a rival North Side gang was not invited; as Jimmy Sullivan was claiming possession of his bride in the Honeymoon Suite of the new Drake Hotel, three of Moran's gang were gunned down in front of Moran's speakeasy on Armitage.

Capone was blamed for the killings. He always pleaded innocent, a rare claim for Scarface. Later he hinted that maybe Sweet Rolls Sullivan was responsible for the assassination. Sweet Rolls was dead and couldn't defend himself. A year and a half later, Capone finished off the Moran gang in the notorious St. Valentine's Day massacre. If Sullivan was indeed to blame for having three men murdered on his wedding night, he was merely doing Capone a favor.

Ten months after the wedding, Marie Kavanagh Sullivan presented her husband with a baby girl who was baptized—in their little church on North Park—Margaret Ellen. Newspaper pictures showed Sweet Rolls beaming over his new daughter. Four months later he would be dead, though not before impregnating his wife for a second time. Marie and Margaret dropped completely from sight soon after the funeral. The present researcher could find no trace of them in the usual records. Relatives of the Kavanagh family refused to discuss them. Even contacts in organized crime shrugged. It was a long time ago, they would say. No one cares about them anymore. At this time Marie Sullivan, born in 1909, would be just over sixty years old. Her children would both be in their forties.

If any of them are still alive.

"Och," Nuala announced to me, "she'd be in her middle eighties now and they'd be in their sixties."

"Something like that."

"Ah, she'd have stories to tell, wouldn't she?"

"She would indeed . . . But your man was a dogged researcher. If he couldn't find anything, there was probably nothing to find."

"Unless someone made him an offer he couldn't refuse."

She picked up the article again and began to read it, her eyes narrowed in intense concentration.

"Such as?"

"Such as, if you want to keep living, you'll forget about Marie and Peggy and young Jimmy."

"Peggy, is it?"

"Of course it is, what else would it be?"

What else indeed?

Nuala was on the hunt. Quick, Dermot Michael, the game's afoot and we haven't a second to lose.

Right, Holmes.

James Sullivan, if that were truly his name, was a man with everything for which to live—money, power, a beautiful wife, a child of whom he was proud. Why did he not get out of the illegal trade in liquor and settle down to enjoy life? Perhaps open a chain of bakeshops, as he liked to call them?

There is no clear answer to that question. Perhaps he loved the danger and excitement. Perhaps he could not be happy unless there was violence in his life. Perhaps he wanted total power.

Then why not go after Capone, not just his gang, but Scarface himself? Why not finish off "Al Brown" and win the gratitude of all right-thinking people in America?

Of which there were very few when it came to Prohibition.

Everyone realized that there could be only one bootlegger in Chicago, either Sullivan or Capone—though poor Bugs Moran thought he was still in the game, as did the sinister Genna brothers. During the year after Sullivan's marriage, the killings continued. So too did the pictures of Marie Sullivan in the society pages, engaged in all kinds of virtuous activity. There are many pictures also of her and her husband, expensively and tastefully, at Orchestra Hall and various Chicago theaters.

In the skirmishing that year, Capone seemed to be losing—along with the remnants of other gangs, small businessmen trying to fight the duopoly that was emerging.

Someone had to go. Either Capone or Sullivan. The question remains even today as to why Capone survived. Scarface Al was ruthless and cunning. But he was not as ruthless and not as shrewd as Sweet Rolls Jimmy.

The two sides engaged in chess moves. A Capone convoy of

trucks was ambushed outside of International Falls, Minnesota, the booze smashed on the road, the trucks burned, the drivers and shotgun riders bound and left in the winter cold. A classy speak, in which Sweet Rolls was a silent partner, burned to the ground on a Saturday night. No one died in these ventures, but they well might have.

"Why don't they go after each other?" they asked in Chicago. And sometimes, "Why doesn't Sully kill that cheap Sicilian pimp?"

Then they began to go after one another's soldiers. As in all wars, there was argument about who started it. A Sullivan man disappeared from the face of the earth. Rumor had it that he was dumped off of Navy Pier into an icy lake. Within a week two of Capone's tommy gunners went up in flames when the touring car in which they were preparing for a raid blew up. The battle dragged on through the winter into spring and summer. Safe houses in the country belonging to both sides were torched. The windows of Sullivan's bakeshop were smashed and a firebomb thrown inside. Fortunately it did not ignite. Then a car sideswiped Marie Sullivan's car when she was eight and a half months pregnant. Fortunately she was not injured. Then there was the exchange of gunfire in front of the Lexington Hotel, after which Scarface complained that it could have been him.

In the meantime a citizens committee had been established to end the warfare between the "bootlegger titans." Editorial writers denounced the "random and senseless violence" as editorial writers always do. Sweet Rolls smiled benignly and told reporters that apparently there were some "business differences" between a couple of criminal groups.

Scarface growled that nobody killed his people.

The obvious answer was that someone had.

Despite the publicity and the public outrage, anyone who knew anything about Chicago was aware that more hobo drunks died every winter night on West Madison Street in the winter than gunmen of the two gangs killed in the battles between Sullivan and Capone. They also knew that the police and the city officials could stop the war anytime they wanted to, which was anytime they were willing to give up the fat envelopes of greenbacks which mysteriously appeared on their desk every Tuesday afternoon, just before the end of the working day.

The most puzzling question, then and now, is why Sullivan, having failed to nail Capone after the shoot-out in front of the Lexington Hotel, did not strike again quickly before Capone got him. After his death, many wondered why he stood waiting, without a bodyguard, for the killers to come.

And come they did at 4:30 in the afternoon. Jimmy Sullivan was showing two of his women employees the sumptuous cake he had just fashioned for his wife's twentieth birthday—chocolate cake with vanilla frosting and silver decorations including a giant Roman "XX." A black Packard pulled up in front of the bakery and three men emerged. It was a lovely autumn day and across the street from the bakeshop the sun glowed on the white bricks of Holy Name Cathedral set against the clear blue sky. Men and women entered and left the church for their "visit to the Blessed Sacrament" on the way home from work.

"It was like a medieval painting of quiet devotion," someone said afterwards.

"Get out the back door," Sullivan snapped at the women, as he drew his gun. As they ran by the brand-new ovens at the rear of the store, they heard the crash of glass and the bark of guns, revolvers this time and not tommy guns. They dove under the ovens, listened to the shots, and prayed for their boss.

Outside on State Street scores of people dove for cover as the fusillade continued, for what, one woman later said, "seemed like ages." Bullets caromed all around; a ricochet allegedly wounded slightly a fourteen-year-old boy who was a student at Mundelein Cathedral High. The Archbishop himself had emerged from the Chancery next door to the Cathedral (once the home of the University of St. Mary of the Lake) and was walking briskly down the steps from the second-floor entrance when the shooting began. Like everyone else, he fell to the ground. The injury to his archepiscopal dignity was intolerable. "No one who shoots at him can expect Christian burial," a priest said with a chuckle.

Then the shooting stopped. There was silence for a moment. No one dared to rise from the ground. One of the three men on the outside leaned against the car, apparently wounded. The other two men, wearing long black topcoats, black fedoras, and masks, gingerly picked their way through the shattered window. There were four quick shots. Then, as calmly as if they were dropping into the Cathedral to say a prayer, they emerged from the shop, helped their wounded and bleeding companion into the Packard, and calmly drove away, their day's work done.

For a moment the scene in front of the Cathedral remained frozen. Then as women screamed and men shouted, the crowd in front of the Cathedral scrambled to their feet and quickly emptied the street. Father Joseph Curran, a curate from the Cathedral, reported that the street was virtually empty (his boss had been carried off in his long limousine) when he dashed across the street to send Jimmy Sullivan off to his maker. The only sound he heard was the distant roar of police sirens, as the Chicago Avenue Police Station came alive.

"Jim was spread out over the ruins of his wife's birthday cake," he later told reporters. "He had been wounded several times, a half dozen at least. His blood had turned the frosting on the cake red. His guns were on the counter in front of him. The women in the kitchen were wailing like banshees. All I could think of was that I would have to tell his wife and what a terrible waste Jimmy's death was. God rest his generous soul."

"Now wasn't that a strange thing to say?" Nuala asked me.
"How so?"
"Your man didn't say that he anointed the poor fella. Or gave him absolution. Or imparted the papal blessing for the end of life. Isn't that odd?"
"Now that you mention it."
"The poor priest must be dead by now."
"I'm sure he is."
"But there must be priests alive who knew him as he grew older. I'm sure he told the story over and over again."
"Priests like to tell stories," I agreed.
"So you'll ask his rivrence the names of such priests?"
"Woman, I will," I said meekly.
"And then interview those priests."
"Woman, I will."
"Good. But you won't get another drop of whiskey."
"May I have another sip of Bailey's?"

"All right." She sighed. "Sonia, another drop of Bailey's, I do mean a drop, for your man."

"Thank you, Holmes."

She squeezed my arm and smiled affectionately at me. I might almost have said "adoringly."

"Aren't you proud of me for not ordering another whiskey for meself?

"I'd have to carry you home."

"If that were a promise, I just might do it."

Then she returned to the article.

Whatever became of his soul, the cops took James Sullivan's body to the County Morgue over at Cook County Hospital, where to no one's surprise he was pronounced dead on arrival. Then he was brought back to Carroll's funeral home at the corner of State and Superior Streets, a half block away from Sullivan's Bakeshop and kitty-corner from the Cathedral, where the late Sweet Rolls Sullivan had already been banned by an irate Archbishop.

The funeral was hailed as the largest funeral in Chicago gangland history with twenty-five flower cars, including a whole car with flowers from "Al Brown."

Marie Sullivan did not appear at the three-night wake. Shrouded in black, her face hidden behind a veil, she appeared at the funeral, leaning on her father's arm. She also was present at Mount Carmel Cemetery when her husband's bullet-ridden body was lowered into the ground. Then she disappeared from sight. All attempts to locate her for this article failed.

They will show you pockmarks on the Cathedral steps which, it is alleged, had been caused by Jim Sullivan's last gunfight, just before, as they will say, his luck finally ran out

His luck certainly ran out that afternoon.

While researching the story of Sweet Rolls Sullivan, I spoke with an elderly reporter, long since retired from the journalistic fray. He had been a young reporter at the time of the shooting. He was sitting in Billy Goat's having his first drink after breakfast—vodka, straight up. It would not be his last drink of the day. Nor would he leave Billy Goat's till late at night.

"Why didn't he kill Capone before Capone killed him?"

"Jimmy liked the game, you see. He loved danger. Probably

couldn't live without it. Some folks back then said that he didn't
have to stay in the bootleg business. That was true. He had
plenty of money. But he needed the game. Had to have it. He
liked the game to be fair. He didn't get Capone in front of the
hotel. Now it was Scarface's turn."

"But he didn't have any bodyguards with him?"

"That was the way it was with Jimmy. He liked to think he
was afraid of nothing. Invulnerable. He had escaped death so
often, he thought he was immune to it."

"Like Michael Collins?"

"The Big Fella had never really been shot at before the bullet
that killed him. Jimmy had been shot at hundreds, thousands
of times."

"Bravado?"

"Something like that . . . I don't know if Chicago would be
a better place if Jimmy had lived. Your Italians would have
taken over the game eventually. But it would have been a better
world without Capone."

I waited while he ordered his second drink. His wife would
join him at noon and drink with him the rest of the day.

"There were some that said he didn't want to live any longer.
That he was tired of the game. That there was too much killing.
Or that he had cancer and figured that this was a quick way
to die. Or that Marie was sleeping with someone else, which
might have been true, heaven knows. She was nothing more
than a spoiled, crazy kid. Great looker, but nothing inside."

"So we'll never know why he died?"

"Who's going to tell us? God knows, but we've never been
able to get an interview with him."

I waited again.

"Strange story," he went on. "He came with mystery behind
him and left with mystery. I figure that's the way he wanted
it . . . Odd, some people thought he was still alive and would
come back later to get Capone. Closed casket at the wake started
that story. Kind of like King Arthur sleeping on Avalon until
Britain needed him again. But he never did come back. Not yet
anyway."

"If he were still alive, he'd be seventy-two years old."

"If he were really sleeping in a place like Avalon, he wouldn't
have aged."

I dismissed this Celtic folklore as the result of vodka and Irish imagination. In equal parts.

Yet it is not a bad way to end the story of James "Sweet Rolls" Sullivan. He was a Gaelic warrior of a sort, a legend on his own battlefields just as Arthur was. A gangster, a war-lover, a killer (though perhaps only in self-defense, certainly not a hero).

Yet nonetheless a legend.

There's no epigraph on the splendid tombstone which marks his grave in Mount Carmel Cemetery, just his name and his years and his wife's name without a date of death. Her grave, the management at Mount Carmel tells me, remains empty.

But a fitting inscription might well be "All Irish Heroes Die Young!"

—6—

NUALA SHUDDERED as she put the manuscript aside. "Well, we know that both graves are empty. Do you think he could have faked it all?"

"Is that possible? Could he have bribed enough people to fake the shooting and his burial? Sure it's possible, but extremely unlikely. Eventually someone would have talked and the secret would be out. Your article was written a quarter century ago. A lot of people would have read it. Surely the whole story would have come out then."

"Maybe." She frowned, deep in thought.

"Don't frown that way, Nuala Anne," I said, erasing the frown line from her forehead. "You're so much prettier when you're smiling."

"Go long wid ya," she said as she thumped my arm. "Aren't you grand with the blarney?"

"We'd better walk you home now. You'll sleep well and yourself with two jars of the creature in your belly."

"Sonia," she said as we got up, "your man is making me leave early and himself such a short hitter?"

"Are you all ready for the wedding, Nuala?"

"Ah, I'm way ahead of the game . . . You'll be coming, won't you now?"

"Wouldn't miss it for the world."

It was a quiet, comfortable evening, no wind, gentle air, warm without being hot. A lover's evening.

I wrapped my arm around her waist. She snuggled close to me.

"These tops that you women are wearing today are a serious temptation to a fella."

"That's what they're supposed to be. But, sure, you shouldn't be looking at me all evening like you want to tear it off."

"Shouldn't I?"

"Well of course you should. That's the whole idea, isn't it now? But you shouldn't be so obvious."

"I shouldn't reveal my fantasies to you?"

"I don't mind them at all, at all. But you embarrass me when others see what you're thinking."

I didn't believe a word of it. Instead of arguing, I tickled her.

"Stop that, Dermot Michael." She giggled, squirming in my arm. She did not, however, try to escape.

"You'd better get used to it, Nuala Anne, because starting on the second Friday in October, that's likely to happen every day."

"I suppose I'll have to resign myself to it," she said with a loud sigh. "Till you get tired of me."

"That will never happen."

We were under an old oak tree, shielded from the streetlights. I took her in my arms—or maybe she took me in her arms—and threw myself into a wildly passionate embrace and kiss.

"We're out in public, Dermot," she said before I silenced her with my lips.

She didn't seem to mind at all. At all.

We clung to each other, caressing and kissing, for what might have been only a few moments or might have been eternity.

"Do you promise," she asked, as we drew away, "that you're going to assault me like that every day?"

"I think I was the one assaulted, but, sure, every day. At least once."

"Well, then." She sighed her sigh of contentment which was different from a sigh of self-pity. "I suppose I might just show up for the wedding."

We held hands as we walked up Southport.

"Would it be terrible unromantic of me to want to talk about the article?"

"Anything you do is romantic, Nuala. And enchanting."

"Well, didn't you get the impression that your man was not telling us the whole story, not even all that he knew?"

"What evidence is there of that?" I asked, knowing that was my assigned line.

"Well, he didn't wonder about what the priest told the journalists, did he? He was obviously a Catholic and Father Curran's words were kind of strange. He might have been alive in 1970. Yet your man doesn't say he tried to interview him. Nor does he seemed to have followed up on herself. He simply avoids the subject. He does tell us the King Arthur legend, but then rejects it without any further discussion. I think he knows a lot more than he's telling us. Is he still alive, Dermot?"

"I still see his articles. He teaches history, I think, at Loyola. I'll see if I can find him . . . But why would he not tell us all he knew?"

"Because it might have been very dangerous to do so."

"After all those years? Even today?"

"Maybe, Derm. But don't we know that both graves out there at your Mount Carmel place are empty?"

"We do," I said, unwilling to challenge her second sight.

"Maybe that gives us a whole different perspective."

"I suppose it does. If he's not in the grave, then there's a major part of the story missing. You might think someone's covering something up. But it doesn't make sense. Why disappear that way when it would be so much less complicated simply to get out of town?"

"Don't you know us Irish well enough to know that we love complexity?"

"I've suspected that for some time," I said. "But still the plot you suggest is too elaborate by half. There must be something we're missing."

"Maybe, if people knew he were alive, wouldn't they try to get him to come back? Maybe he had to go to Glastonbury Tor to escape from crime."

"Maybe."

We had come to the steps leading to the second-floor entry to her house—our house.

"Aren't you going to walk up the steps to our house and kiss me good night, Dermot Michael?"

"I just might."

"Grand," she said, leaning her head against my shoulder.

"Should we keep the stairway here when the house is finished?"

"Och, Dermot love, I'll leave that to you. Don't you know what's best?"

Once again she was the pliant, passive, shy child, ready to surrender to me in all things. That was close as I would ever get to the ur-Nuala, the vulnerable kid from Carraroe. I was overwhelmed by my love for her.

"Just a simple good-night kiss, Dermot Michael," she begged. "Mind you, nothing like your previous assault."

"Just a simple good-night kiss," I agreed.

I meant that when I said it. But she caressed my face with a silk-like touch. Then when our lips touched, my passionate love for her turned into a firestorm of longing to which she was instantly responsive. We clung together in ecstasy as time stood still and all the love in the world flowed through our bodies.

"Dermot," she gasped finally, "you've destroyed me altogether."

She did not, however, try to extinguish the fire which had enveloped us.

Somehow her clothes were in disarray. She was naked to her waist, her breasts glowing in moonlight, as I devoured them with my lips, her nipples hard against my tongue. I exulted in her submission and my conquest. My brain exploded in love, desire, and pride. I would prolong this moment of joy forever.

I really wasn't doing this was I?

Yeah, I was. I'd better stop.

So I did.

She rested her head against my chest. I gently caressed her bare back.

"Och, Dermot . . .We're outside, aren't we?"

"Woman, we are."

"You're a terrible desperate man."

"Woman, I am."

"I'm a desperate woman, too."

"Terrible."

"Do you really love me that much?"

For some reason tears stung my eyes . . .

"That was only a hint of how much I want you and love you."

She sighed, her contented, complacent sigh.

"I'm yours, Dermot. Yours for now and forever. All yours."

"And I'm yours, Nuala."

"Tis different but tis the same."

"Two weeks from Friday seems like a long time."

"It does that . . . Are we really outside?"

"We are." With great reluctance I began to rearrange her clothes.

She giggled at my clumsiness as I tried to put together the hooks of her bra.

"Did anyone see us?"

"The street is empty."

"You know what I suspect about you, Dermot Michael Coyne?"

"No, what?"

"That you're the kind of friggin' eejit who thinks that a man can fuck a woman outdoors if he wants to."

"As long as she also wants to."

"Shocking, outrageous, disgusting, degenerate . . . So I guess that's one more reason for showing up at the Cathedral for that ceremony you're talking about."

"That might be a nice idea."

"Promise me one thing?"

"And what's that?"

I had finished my ministrations. Now she leaned against the door to the house. She took my hands and pressed them against her now well-covered breasts.

"That we'll make love outdoors during our honeymoon."

"First week."

"I'll hold you to that promise, Dermot Michael."

"And I won't let you change your mind, even though you'll try to."

She released my hands just in time or we would have started over again.

She sighed. "Probably . . . Do I look awful disheveled?"

"Delightfully so."

Then my conscience, silent through the whole ecstatic interlude, finally caught up with me.

"I'm sorry, Nuala Anne, I'm afraid I was carried away. I shouldn't have . . ."

"Tis nothing wrong with us preparing for our ultimate intimacy, if you take me meaning."

"I'm afraid I was pretty brutal."

"You're an amadon." She brushed her lips against mine. "But a nice amadon. Now, Dermot Michael, I'm going into my apartment. I'm going to take a nice cold shower and then I'm going to bed."

"Yes ma'am."

"And I'm going to count the nights till the second Friday in October as I go to sleep."

"Twenty," I said as I opened the door for her.

"And isn't it all your fault for making me drink that second jar?" She closed the door before I could answer.

I walked down the stairs and strolled back to Clyborn to catch a cab.

I SUPPOSE the Adversary murmured, THAT YOU FEEL VERY PROUD OF YOURSELF.

"As a matter of fact I do."

YOU THINK YOU OVERWHELMED THAT POOR SHY CHILD.

"You got it."

YOU ARE SO DUMB THAT YOU DIDN'T NOTICE THAT SHE OVER-WHELMED YOU.

"Not true."

YOU'RE A TOTAL EEJIT.

I considered his charge. Maybe he was right.

"Well, if she did start it all, then so much the better for me."

SO YOU THINK YOU'RE HOT SHIT NOW THAT YOU HAVE BEEN THE OBJECT OF LUST.

"Love," I insisted. "Passionate love."

SHE'LL GET TIRED OF YOU WHEN SHE FINDS OUT WHAT A DUD YOU ARE.

My worst fear. How did he know about it?

I flagged down a cab.

"I wasn't a dud tonight," I replied.

The Adversary laughed cynically.

He did not get in the cab with me however.

As I drifted into sleep in my apartment, I remembered tenderly, the demanding warmth of her lips, the linenlike softness of her skin, and the defiant firmness of her breasts. I dreamed of manic, playful love with her under the stars.

— 7 —

NEW FBI STING
Operation Full Platter
Targets Traders

Informed sources revealed yesterday that the FBI is continuing its investigation of the Chicago commodity exchanges. A new sting, dubbed "Operation Full Platter" will soon produce, according to these sources, massive indictments against commodity traders.

"We're tired of these guys ripping off their clients," the source said. "This time we're going to nail them good."

The source refused to confirm that the Bureau is continuing its tactic of using informants wired with tape recorders in its investigation. Those who have followed FBI methods in recent years, however, assume that they have yet another "wired informant."

"That's the only way they can get indictments these days," one observer commented. "This one had better come up with solid evidence against some big fish. Their last effort was a fiasco."

The source in the U.S. Attorney's office insisted that this time the Bureau would indeed bring in "big fish." "People's eyes are going to pop when they find out who's in our net this time. Some real celebrities."

Joel Redmond, President of the Chicago Board of Trade, said that he objected to another sting operation. "Our commodity markets are the biggest in the world and critically important to the economy of Chicago. I can't understand why the federal government is so interested in harassing us and trying to destroy us. We do a pretty good job policing ourselves. On the basis of their past performance I'd say that they are not going to catch anyone whom we haven't caught already or will catch eventually, except maybe some clumsy novices who haven't caught on to the rules yet. I can't understand why the feds spend so much time on us and so little on the drug gangs."

Indictments are expected to be handed down within the next two weeks.

I threw the paper aside in disgust and returned to my morning cup of tea. Redmond had them cold. Their elaborate scams might pick up a few goofs and a few innocents. They wouldn't get any of the big crooks because the big crooks were too smart to say anything to anyone, much less Jarry Kennedy. The Bureau must be hard up if they were using a crazy like him as their wire.

Why bother?

Well, because their investigations and indictments would get them lots of publicity, and the dismissals and acquittals would appear in small paragraphs on the inside pages of the papers and would not rate a clip on the five o'clock or ten o'clock news. Moreover, they could create the impression that they had "reformed" the commodity exchanges among those citizens who didn't know how the exchanges worked. If they went after the drug gangs, they would fool no one as long as the drive-by shootings continued.

Justice American style.

Well, I could breathe a sigh of relief. The "source" had promised a celebrity. I certainly wasn't a celebrity.

Was I?

Prominent Chicago Writer Indicted

I wasn't a prominent writer, even if I had published a handful of short stories and my first novel would appear just before our wedding. That wouldn't make me famous, would it?

In the world of headline writers that would be enough.

I discovered that sweat was pouring out of my body.

Well, I told myself glumly, the publicity might help the book.

Then, as I turned on the shower, I told myself that I was acting like a damn fool. Not even the Bureau would be crazy enough to think I was a big fish.

I had awakened in great good spirits. Nuala was as passionately in love with me as I with her. Moreover, I would surely be a good lover for her and she for me.

You knew that all along, the Adversary, who had somehow slipped into my apartment, grumbled after I had tossed the morning papers aside.

"There's a difference between knowing it and experiencing it," I insisted. "That's why it was a religious experience for me."

Playing with a woman's tits is religious? he sneered.

"Yes, but you wouldn't understand it."

I'm not sure I did either, but I knew that I had crossed a major barrier. No more fear of the wedding night.

Well, not much anyway.

Content with myself and my male skills, I was in no mood to begin my day's chores. The ringing telephone stirred me out of my complacent fantasies.

"Dermot Coyne."

"Good day to you, Dermot. This is Annie."

A West of Ireland accent. But did I know any Annie from the West of Ireland?

"Good morning, Annie," I said.

"How you keeping, Dermot."

"Couldn't be happier," I said bravely, despite the article in the paper.

"And herself?"

"She's just brilliant."

"Grand, glad to hear it. Gerry and I thought we'd give you a ring."

"I'm glad you did."

"Everything's coming along fine for the wedding, is it now? The child isn't skittish, is she?"

Then I knew who it was. Annagh McGriel, herself's mom. And Gerry was her father Gerroid.

It would be a long, indirect and obscure conversation, on my meter (since I was paying for their phone) and at the end I wouldn't know any more about what they wanted to say than I did at the beginning.

"Not that one, Annie," the name seemed disrespectful, but I'd been trapped into using it. "We're looking forward to seeing you the week before the wedding."

"Och, aren't the two of us frightened about the trip, and ourselves never being to America and never even flying in one of them airplane things?"

She did sound like her youngest daughter. I had been a ninny not to recognize her voice.

"You'll love every second of it. Wait till you see the wedding dress!"

"Have you seen it now?"

" 'Course not, but it has been described to me at great length."

"You're sure herself is keeping well?"

I must listen to what the woman means, not the words she's saying.

"She's working hard at her job and at her singing, but she's in grand shape."

"Shape" might not have been the best choice of words.

"Sure, aren't we both glad to hear that?"

Now I got it. Their eldest son had stirred up worry. Bastard.

"We had a grand time with Larry and his wife on Sunday," I said, making the Yank mistake of trying to force the issue. That never worked with an Irish person, especially an Irish woman.

"Isn't that grand? And isn't Larry a terrible successful man?"

"He is that."

"Doesn't he take a kind of paternal interest in all the younger children?"

"And don't younger children often resent that kind of interest from an older brother or sister?"

A rich laugh, so much like herself's that it was almost scary. I had said the right words.

"Don't they ever, Dermot Michael? Still and all don't the older ones sometimes know what they're talking about?"

"Occasionally my older siblings do have a good insight or two."

"Sometimes they see problems that you younger folk don't see."

"That's true."

"And then sometimes they don't."

"Usually."

Again she laughed happily.

"I suppose that's true, Dermot. Still they have to say what they think, don't they now?"

"Very carefully and very cautiously and usually not at all."

Yet another laugh.

"Och, Dermot, aren't we both terrible happy that you and Nuala found each other. You're a grand pair altogether."

"Thank you very much, Annie. I know I'm awfully lucky. I'm not sure that Nuala is."

"Go long with you now, Dermot Michael, isn't that one lucky to have found someone who will put up with her."

We both laughed and promised to see each other soon and hung up.

Now what the hell was that all about?

I decided I'd call Nuala and find out. However, the delivery room knocked at my door. Two packages. Brochures for our honeymoon and the first jacket for Nuala's disc. The artwork was perfect: herself in her minimal white knit summer dress with the spaghetti straps, strumming her harp. Her eyes were deep, deep blue with a faraway mystical look. They grabbed your attention immediately, even if the rest of her didn't. In pseudo Celtic letters, the only words on the cover were NUALA ANNE! It was a real grabber. Any person of Irish origin who came upon the disc would not be able to resist it.

Before I called herself, I phoned Prester George and arranged to meet him in front of the Cathedral at 10:30. Then with some trepidation, I dialed her office number at Arthur's.

"Marie McGrail," said this Yank voice.

"I must have the wrong number. I'm looking for Nuala McGrail."

"You're not supposed to call me at work," she said primly, the brogue returning.

She did not sound too unhappy, however.

"Except in an emergency."

"What's the emergency?" she asked anxiously.

"I had a phone call from your mother. The way she talks makes your most convoluted discourse look crystalline."

"Ah, won't you ever have a hard time understanding that one, and you a poor Irish-American who doesn't have the Irish language . . . What did she say?"

As best as I could remember the conversation, I recounted it.

"Isn't she saying that they don't give a good fock about the bullshite that me asshole brother is spreading in the family?"

"That's what she's saying?"

"Depend on it, Dermot. They love you, like I said they do. Still and all, they're a bit worried about what your man will do next . . . Now I have to get back to me work."

"You have a lesson with Madame tonight?"

"I do."

"We could see *Horseman on the Roof* afterwards. Then I could take you to Grappa for a bowl of pasta."

"Only a small bowl. If I get fat, I won't fit in my wedding dress."

"With yourself running every morning, there's small chance of that happening. Besides I have the first jacket for your disc."

"I don't want to see it!"

"Up to you. I won't bring it along."

"Don't you dare not bring it along! . . . Now I'm going back to work."

"Yes ma'am."

I fantasized about her for a few moments and then dashed into the shower so as not to be late for my meeting with the Priest. In the shower I realized that Laurence McGrail was hell-bent on making trouble. What if the feds really went after me?

The phone rang. No towel, no robe. I need a woman to keep my house in order. I dashed out of the shower and grabbed the phone.

"Dermot Coyne."

"You waited long enough to answer it," herself told me.

"I was in the shower."

"Sure, you shouldn't be talking to a woman with none of your clothes on . . . Dermot Michael, I'm sorry I was curt with you when you called before. I'm really glad you're taking me to the movie and to Grappa. I want to see you every day for the rest of me life. Thank you. Good-bye, Dermot Michael."

She hung up.

My face was warm and I was grinning when I went back to shower. I was still grinning as I dressed and walked over to the Cathedral.

"You worried about the upcoming nuptials?" George greeted me.

George has, as much as I hate to admit it, an absolutely first-rate mind. He was wearing tan slacks and a white knit shirt with some sort of weird animal above the pocket, rather different than the clothes Joe Curran must have worn in front of the Cathedral. It didn't seem to bother the folks coming out of church who smiled and greeted him with the same words that their predecessors greeted Father Curran.

"Good morning, Father."

Pure adoration for the smart and zealous young priest.

"Only worried," I replied to his question, "that two weeks and two days are too long a time."

"No fears?" he asked, examining my face with his shrewd eyes.

"Why should I be afraid?"

"No reason. A lot of men tend to lose their nerve as the big day draws close. We've had two cancellations the last two months."

"Why?"

"They keep telling the bride how nervous they are and finally she says well, if you're so nervous, let's put it off. The guy jumps for joy because he's hoping that's what she'll say."

"Kids?"

"Nah, yuppies, late twenties, early thirties, been living together for a while or at least sleeping together a lot."

"So what's to be afraid of?"

"Loss of privacy, marital sex, conflicts, failure, commitment, mostly the latter. Typical male reaction. One of the negatives of living together. No mystery left."

"What do you tell them?"

"It's obvious. The real mystery only begins after commitment. Big macho bums can't figure out what that means."

"It seems clear enough to me."

"Yeah, little bro, you lucked out with that one, not that it will always be perfect. There'll be ebbs and flows, ups and downs."

"With Nuala that happens every half hour."

He laughed. "Yeah, I imagine it does . . . Well, what's on your mind this morning."

"I want to see the bullet holes on the steps."

"Herself into another one of her psychic things? Well here's one and here's another. I don't think I believe in any of that stuff about the shoot-out in the hardware shop across the street, where the parking lot is now."

The whole city block across from the Cathedral had been cleared and was now a parking lot. It ought to be, I often thought, a plaza. Cathedrals ought to have plazas. Park the cars underground. Only trouble is that it would cost tons of money.

"Bakeshop, big bro. George William Mundelein had to fall on the steps of the old Chancery, which was right here where the school is now."

"Really? I guess I knew that . . . about the Chancery. Never knew about Mundelein falling down the steps . . . He was not a nice man, little bro."

"I guess not."

"Nuala?"

"Yep."

"Oh, oh! Does she think it is important?"

"Doesn't she always?"

"Where's the famous cornerstone?"

"Over here."

I looked at the weathered stone.

> Every knee should bend
> heaven and
> on earth

"It's from St. Paul to the Philippians," George observed. "The reference is to the Holy Name of Jesus. The legend is that 'those in' on the second line were chipped off by a ricochet and 'those' in the last line by another bullet. But most likely the only word missing is an 'in' from the second line. And weather or slush from street salt could have done that or vibrations from construction on the State Street Subway fifty years ago."

"No one around here remembers anything?"

"Little bro, that was seventy years ago. We're Americans; we don't remember last year."

"Yeah."

"What am I supposed to do?" he asked.

"Do you remember a priest named Joe Curran?"

"Curran? . . . I don't think so. There are a couple of Currans around but no Joe Curran."

"1927?"

"THAT Joe Curran. He was one of my predecessors, seventy years ago. A great character. A legend. Died maybe twenty-five years ago. Can't Nuala reach him across the boundary?"

"She doesn't do that kind of thing. I want to talk to a priest that might have known him."

"Let me see . . . Yeah, Leo Nolan up at St. Mary's by the Brook is the curator of the legend. He was with him on his first assignment out at St. Bart's. Knows all the stories."

"Would you give him a ring for me? I want to talk to him."

"Sure."

"Now."

George raised his eyebrows, but led me into the rectory and made the phone call. Father Nolan would see me at 1:30.

"I'm not supposed to ask what this is all about, little bro?"

"Not yet."

"Is it dangerous?"

"I don't see how it could be."

"Be careful."

"I'm not taking any chances just before my wedding," I said as I walked towards the door of the rectory.

"Yeah . . . What was the name of the guy they shot across the street?"

"Sullivan. Sweet Rolls Sullivan."

"The guy that's buried next to Ma and Pa?"

"The same."

"Hold it, little bro, let me think . . . They knew him, you know?"

"I didn't know . . . How well?"

"Pa was moving up in the real estate business back then, working hard, getting ahead, doing well. Some bad guys tried to muscle in. He called Sullivan, who was well-known for helping greenhorns."

"He was little more than that himself."

"Sullivan warned them off. Pa never had any more trouble."

"How come I never heard any of this?"

"Ma told us about it when she was dying. She wanted us to know that Sullivan was not a totally bad man. She did not mind being buried next to him. She kind of laughed and said something like, 'not to say that he's really there.' "

"Fascinating . . . I'd better go. I've got a couple of errands before I drive up to Brookside."

I left Prester George looking totally befuddled. Thank heaven he didn't ask for any more information.

I walked out on Wabash Avenue. It was a pleasant early-autumn day, low seventies, hazy, wisps of clouds slowly slipping over the city towards the Lake. Not many days like this left.

My fingers were trembling. Goose bumps moved up and down my arms. What was going on? Were Ma and Nuala at it again? Would this happen often during our marriage? Was I about to drift into the Twilight Zone?

I hailed a cab and told the driver I wanted the County Building, Clark Street side. The offices of the County Clerk are on the east side of a massive block square, pseudoclassical building which had been built just before Prohibition. City Hall is in the LaSalle Street half of the building, Cook County Government in the Clark Street half. A long, low, dimly lit catacomb-like lobby ran through the middle of the building, connecting Clark with LaSalle. Both governments are reasonably clean some of the time these days. Yet when you saw the groups of men and women talking to each other by the pillars and in front of the elevators, you felt that there were deals going on, fixes being put in, favors being exchanged.

"I need a favor," I said, with my most charming shanty Irish smile, to the pleasant African-American woman at the reception desk of the Office of Vital Statistics. When dealing with bureaucrats you always start out with charm.

"Honey, everyone does! What kind of favor do you want?"

"Just to look at the death certificates for 1927."

She grinned at me. "You're not some kind of detective are you?"

"Do I look like one?"

"You surely don't!"

"What do I look like?"

"Honey, you look like a real nice gentleman . . . I'll get you the microfiche. You can go over there to the reader . . . Which month?"

"September."

As I searched for the date of Jimmy Sullivan's death, a distraction slipped into my imagination—Nuala's imagining me naked—or maybe actually seeing me that way. Why was I embarrassed? Or was I delighted? I had fantasies about her, tons of them. Did she have fantasies about me? Wasn't that wonderful!

I was so delighted by such pleasant fantasies that I passed the date of Sweet Rolls's death. As I flicked back to it I realized that our Sunday at the cemetery was the sixty-eighth anniversary of his death.

I shivered again. This was too much. Too much altogether.

I steadied my nerves and tried to concentrate on the microfiche. My daydreaming was getting in the way of my work. Ninety-five people died that day, each death a tragedy in one way or another. My name would be on a microfiche someday. Nuala's too. Well, love was as strong as death as the Song of Songs says. That's strong enough.

I went through the list four times, fighting off the distractions. No dice. Jimmy Sullivan did not die that day, not, if one is to believe the records of the Office of Vital Statistics of the City of Chicago. Nor any day in the week before or the week after.

But scores of witnesses had seen his body on State Street. Hadn't they? Weren't there photographs in the article of him hanging over Marie's twentieth-birthday cake?

I brought the fiche back to the clerk.

"Thank you very much, ma'am; you've been very helpful."

"You look like you've seen a ghost, honey."

"No, ma'am. That's exactly what I didn't see . . . have a nice day."

I walked out on Clark Street and down towards Adams Street, where I was going to meet a reporter who had been a classmate of mine at Marquette and now worked for *The Chicago Law Bulletin* on the crime beat. As I crossed Monroe I glanced over at the building where herself worked. Was she up there in her cubby-hole fantasizing about my bod?

Well, if she were, fair play to her.

I arrived at Berghof's a few minutes before my friend. Two lawyer types were at the next table. I eavesdropped because that's where writers pick up dialogue.

"You ask me, Joel Redmond is right. The Bureau is never going to nail the big fellas over there. They're too smart. If the Bureau guys were that smart, they'd be working on the floor, too."

"Yeah, they sweep up some small fry and won't get convictions against most of them. The man must be desperate for headlines. Even the media assholes are laughing at them."

"I hear that Dale Quade threatened to make him stop banging her if he didn't let her go ahead with the indictment."

"I wouldn't mind banging her; she's a nice piece of ass."

"Might as well bang the ice on the United Center floor. Used to be a nice woman, idealistic, you know, and concerned about civil rights. Then that asshole husband walked out on her . . . Did you hear the quote they leaked from their wire this morning?"

"No. What did the poor jerk say?"

"On September 4 he is supposed to have said 'I screwed them left and right, took all their money and they didn't even have the sense to complain.'"

"That's not worth shit. But if the guy doesn't have any money to fight them, he'll have to plea bargain like Danny Rostenkowski did, and he'll do time. Not much time, but a little time."

"I agree. Unless they have paper, that won't be enough to get a conviction in a jury trial."

"Is the Service involved?"

"I hear not. They won't touch it."

"The guys over there are usually assholes. Now the women are trying to outasshole the guys."

They both laughed and then went on to a clinical discussion of what engaging in sexual intercourse with Dale Quade, a Senior Assistant United States Attorney, might be like. Apparently there was an extensive folklore on the subject.

Men in their late thirties talking like teenagers in a locker room and loud enough so an observant storyteller might hear them.

I stood up to shake hands with my friend, a little more at ease about the Jarry Kennedy caper. I hadn't talked to him on September 4. That was the day after Labor Day. I had seen him on Labor Day. Moreover, I had never said anything like that in my life to him or anyone else. If they claimed I did, I wouldn't have to plea bargain and we'd beat them in a jury trial. Still, the whole business seemed scary.

My buddy, a certain Sean Cassidy, who had devoured books on organized crime when we were at Marquette, told me that he thought he'd died and gone to heaven. They were paying good money to cover a beat that he would have covered for nothing. He had heard I was engaged and congratulated me. I showed him the picture of Nuala on the jacket of her disc that I was carrying in my attaché case. Sean whistled and congratulated me again. He'd like to meet her someday. I took down his address and assured him we'd send him an invitation to the wedding. Hell, she was inviting everyone in the city. No, he wasn't dating anyone special. Too busy on the job. Lots of gorgeous women in Chicago, though, a lot better than in Green Bay. None as nice as my fiancée, however.

Then I asked him about Sweet Rolls Sullivan. His eyes lit up. Yeah, he knew all about him. He recycled the story for me. Most colorful of all the bootleggers and no one had ever written a book about him.

"Did he really die?" I inquired.

"Sure he died. Capone's hit men, Anselmi and Scalise, gunned him down in his bakery in front of scores of people, including the Cardinal. There was no one more dead than a guy Scarface killed in those days."

"From now on this is a personal confidence between friends?"

"Absolutely. You know what I think of guys like Joe Klein."

"There's no death certificate."

"What?"

"Or burial certificate at his parish church."

I didn't know that for sure. I'd have George check on it. But I was willing to bet on it.

"You gotta be kidding. It was the biggest of all the gang funerals. Scarface sent a whole car of flowers. From Al Brown, which is what he called himself when he was being fancy."

"There is no record of anyone seeing the body after they took it out of the bakeshop. I have reason to believe it is not in the grave."

Sean stopped eating his zweibelfleiche, took a long swallow of his Red Dog beer, and asked, "You sure."

"Yep. I can't tell you how, but I'm sure."

"Wow!"

"Marie, his ditsy wife, disappeared. No one knows where she is or the two kids she had. You read the old story in *Chicago History?*"

"Got it in my files."

"Go back and read it again with that perspective."

Sean thought for a moment. "You know, I felt that there was something missing in that article but I couldn't quite put my finger on it. Why would he choose to disappear that way?"

"He was Irish, and they like things complicated."

"I read a book by a guy named David Tracy who says that the Irish spiritual experience is simple nature mysticism but because they are such playful people they love to tell elaborate stories about the experience, the *Book of Kells* and Joyce for example . . . Hey, is this gorgeous woman of yours—let me see her picture again—is she playful?"

I showed him the picture.

"That's a good one-word description of her."

"You lucky bastard . . . Anyway, maybe Sweet Rolls liked a playful escape. Or maybe he had so many enemies that this was the only way to go. Start a whole new life somewhere . . . But, hey, Capone would have had to cooperate."

"I never thought of that."

We both were silent for a moment. Sean finished off his Red Dog and signaled for a refill.

"You know, Dermot, now that you mention it there's a kind of mystery about him that lingers. None of the older guys on the crime beat were around in his day, but when his name comes up at the Ale House, they act like the whole story about him hasn't been told."

"Some pieces missing?"

"Something like that . . . They don't know what the pieces are, not exactly. Let me poke around and try to find out."

"Don't mention my name."

"No way, Dermot, no way."

I'm sure he didn't mention my name. However, I must have talked to too many people in the next few days to keep my interest a secret, especially since I was about to become big-time news. Our interest wasn't secret anymore. The results were scary.

— 8 —

 "SURE I remember Joe Curran," the Pastor of St. Mary's by the Brook said with a marvelous laugh. "Who could ever forget him?"

Father Nolan was in his middle sixties, a man of enthusiasm and wit, relaxed, confident, and dedicated. He had thin black hair, wore glasses, and smiled more than half the time. The fires of zeal burned in him like he had just been ordained. We were talking in the "counseling room," which once had been the parlor of a bungalow before it became a rectory.

"In what way, Father?" I asked.

"He was a working pastor back in the middle nineteen fifties when a pastor didn't have to work because there were plenty of curates around. That has changed a lot as your brother has probably told you. Curates are a vanishing breed. You can't push them around anymore, thank God. Joe took his turn on calls and at the 6:30 Mass. Went to every wake, showed up at every wedding, visited every sick person in the hospital. He had his fatal heart attack while he was blessing a newborn baby. His last words were, 'It's a good thing I'm dying in a hospital. It won't upset the guys back at the rectory.' That's the kind of guy he was."

"A good priest."

"One of the best. Maybe the most radical priest in the Archdiocese. Long before the Vatican Council he figured out the same things that the Council did. His motto, and I quote, was 'Fuck the rules! We're here to serve the people.' He saw nothing wrong with birth control and granted dispensations and annulments in his office. The Chancery was all over him, but it didn't stop him. Everyone in the Archdiocese thought he was a saint."

"Tell a lot of stories?"

"How did you know that? He had a limitless supply of stories about the twenties and thirties. I was with him five wonderful years at St. Henry the Pious and he repeated stories only a couple of times. He loved to tell them and we, priests and people, loved to hear them. He had a favorite that we heard pretty often, usually in a different form each time."

"About Jimmy Sweet Rolls Sullivan?"

"Your brother George didn't say you were psychic. He's, by the way, an impressive young priest. We need more like him. Have you ever thought about following him?"

"On occasion. I'm marrying on the second Friday of next month. To a Galway woman."

"From where?"

"Carraroe."

"Irish speaker?"

"Indeed."

"There's a lot of dark ones from out there."

"Tell me about it."

I showed him the CD jacket.

"Galway woman, all right . . . Do you think she'd give a concert out here for the parish benefit drive? We'll pay her rate."

"Once she finds out that your family is from Galway, it's a done deal. Free . . . It's the Sweet Rolls story I'm interested in. Did Father Curran ever say in so many words that he anointed Jimmy in the bakeshop?"

Father Nolan's face went blank.

"You sound like a dark one, too."

"Believe me, I'm not."

"Now that you mention it, I can't remember him ever saying anything about administering the sacraments in the bakeshop. I never thought it strange until you asked. He talked a lot about Jimmy's past—orphan in Cork City, English Army at the Somme, Irregulars in the Irish Civil War, left half his money to his wife and the other half to Maryville, St. Mary's Training School then, first-rate mind, self-educated—all that kind of stuff. The high point of the story was his comic description of George Cardinal Mundelein falling on his face in front of the Chancery. Not a word about anointing the corpse ... Strange, Joe usually talked about the sacraments. He was a liturgist before the word was invented."

I remained silent, waiting for the priest's memories to flood back.

"Or about Marie Sullivan, Jimmy's wife?" I said finally.

"I was just thinking about her. Joe was fond of her. Admitted he had a kind of crush on her. He said she had a first-rate mind and was a good influence on Jimmy."

"Ever say where she went after the funeral?"

"I don't think so ... Someone asked once whether she was still alive. He just smiled, and said something like, 'Ah that would be telling, wouldn't it now?' "

"As far as I can tell Sullivan's family vanished from the face of the earth."

"Put down?"

"I don't think so."

Father Nolan frowned, searching again for memories.

"In the middle nineteen fifties," I continued, "she would have been in her late forties or early fifties. Did a woman ever come to see him, tall, handsome, hair still red?"

His eyes flickered.

"Dermot, you scare me."

"The dark one scares me, too."

"That's the way of it, is it ... Lovely woman, they'd chat for a half hour after the nine o'clock Mass in the rectory office, oh, maybe a couple of times a year. He never introduced us. He'd laugh and say that she was the mysterious Madam S. ... For Sullivan, do you think?"

"Probably ... Did he say where she was from?"

"As best as I can remember, he said she spent part of the year on the West Coast and part in Chicago. One of her kids was at the University of Chicago Law School. Probably twenty-three or so then."

Twenty-three from fifty-five? The kid would have been born five years after Sweet Rolls's death!

"When did Sullivan die?" he went on. "Late twenties?"

"Right."

"So she must have married again."

"Or Jimmy wasn't really dead."

"That's the way of it, is it?"

"Maybe."

He rested his jaw on his thumbs and crossed his fingers in front of his mouth—a man in deep thought.

"It's strange, Dermot," he said slowly. "As I remember the way he told the story, it was kind of like part of the Arthurian saga, funny, sad, but not tragic. Occasionally, he'd say that among some of the people from that time—the ones that survived and later went straight—there was a legend that Jimmy would come back someday. Jimmy, Joe would say with a chuckle, never expected when he was growing up in Cork and stealing whatever he could, that he'd become a mythological figure."

"Mythological was Father Curran's word?"

"Oh yeah, he was a great reader. The guys in the rectory said that he had read everything . . . Is that what you're interested in?"

"Professional secret?"

"Absolutely."

"The dark one says there's no body in his grave."

Father Nolan shivered for a moment.

"You're not afraid to marry someone like that?"

"She's as wonderful a human being as she is a beautiful woman."

"So Sweet Rolls is still alive somewhere? Where?"

"Avalon maybe . . . but only if he is ninety-nine years old."

"So why are you interested in his story? What difference does it make today?"

"My lovely dark one insists that we should be interested. You don't argue with Irish women, Father Leo. You surely know that."

"Fascinating story . . . Tell you what: I'll talk to some of the guys that lived with Jolly Joe, as they called him. Get at it indirectly. Won't mention you at all. Fair enough?"

"More than fair . . . And, oh yes, we'll send you a copy of the CD, and I'm sure herself will be happy to sing for you when we come back from our honeymoon."

He wished us happiness in our marriage and prayed that God would bless the two of us, "especially Dermot who may need Your help."

"I will indeed need the help, Father. Life with herself will never be dull."

"She's from Galway, isn't she?"

We both laughed and shook hands and I left.

My next stop was at the Old Town Ale House on North Avenue, where I was to meet a veteran reporter who also covered the crime beat. Prester George had set up that interview for me. I had not told Sean about him and I would not tell him about Sean.

I entered the dark and, I suspect deliberately, dirty tavern which smelled like a men's washroom that hadn't been cleaned in weeks. A little bald man in a shabby suit stood up and signaled me over to his table in the corner. For a moment I thought I had entered the world of Timothy Patrick McCarthy, except the reporter across the pockmarked wooden table from me probably had not consumed quite as many shots of vodka as had McCarthy's informant. However, he had already put away quite a few.

"Whadya want to drink?"

"Irish, straight up."

"Any preferences?"

"Jameson's or Bushmill's."

"They got both."

"Bushmill's."

"A shot of Jameson's straight up for my friend?"

"On the rocks?" the bartender asked.

"Blasphemy."

They both laughed.

Only one. No way would I go on a date with herself tonight with more than one under my belt.

"So you want to know more about Jimmy Sullivan?" he asked genially, as he sipped slowly and lovingly from the vodka glass.

"Let me tell you what I already know: there is no death certificate; no burial certificate from Immaculate Conception Parish; his body was never taken to the morgue; the ambulance which picked him up doubled back and brought him to Carroll's funeral home; the casket was not open; even then a few of the guys were saying that Jimmy wasn't dead and that someday he'd come back."

The only assertions of which I was sure were the ones about the death certificate and the closed casket. The rest was the seanachie, the storyteller, at work. They were the scenario I had made up on the spur of the moment to explain the empty tomb, a reality which I dare not deny any longer, not even to myself.

The reporter put the glass back on the table, steadied it so it wouldn't spill, and rocked back on his chair.

"Damn good work. Really DAMN good work. Nice going."

"Thank you."

"Mind telling me how you dug up all that stuff?" he asked carefully, as though it were only a matter of academic interest.

"Gotta protect my sources. People are worried about what happened that day, though it was seventy years ago."

"They sure are," he said with a sigh. "They sure are. And with reason."

"So I understand."

I certainly did not understand that. Had herself communicated some of her fey intuitions to me?

"You read Tim McCarthy's article?"

"Of course."

"What did you think?"

"He was pulling a lot of punches."

"He sure was. He was scared shitless."

"I figured as much."

"Of course," he said as he stared into his drink, "that was a quarter century ago."

"Probably Jimmy was alive then. He'd be ninety-nine if he were alive today."

The journalist glanced around nervously.

"When you say things like that, say them in whispers," he warned me. "Better never say them at all. Better don't even think them."

"What I don't understand," I said, playing tough, "is why he chose such an elaborate scam to disappear."

"Look, I don't know much about it, only what I heard from a friend of mine on his deathbed. I didn't believe him, but I snooped around and found out a little more. I wish he hadn't told me. Don't ever quote me on any of this stuff. All right?"

He continued to stare moodily at his drink.

"Deep background."

"Yeah . . . Look, it's a lot less dangerous to mess around about Jimmy Sullivan now than it was a quarter century ago. But it's still a mystery that you want to leave alone. Some people are still alive, get me?"

"Marie."

"I'm NOT saying that."

"She got a bum rap from your predecessors. She was, or more likely is, anything but an empty-headed fool."

"You going to write a novel about this?"

"I'm not planning to at the present."

"You could probably get away with it if you changed the city and changed the people and if you just speculated about how it was done, instead of trying to find out, get me?"

"You mean if no one could figure out that I meant Jimmy Sullivan?"

"Yeah, though you'd be better off if you waited five or six more years."

"To tell the truth, I doubt that any publisher would be interested in a novel about a bootlegger everyone has forgotten, subplot maybe, but not the whole story."

"Then why you so interested?"

"I like puzzles."

"Even puzzles that might be dangerous?"

"That makes them more interesting."

Those who know me will immediately realize that was a barefaced lie. I was slipping into Nuala's trick of identifying with temporary roles. Mistake.

"I'll tell you what I know, so long as you don't quote me. Ever. But my advice is to leave the story alone. What does it matter? Seventy years is a long, long time. What does the Old Testament say? Let the dead bury their dead."

"Jesus, actually."

"Yeah . . . Well, whoever, but you get it?"

"Sure. I have no desire to ruin people's lives, if that's what you mean, and no desire to put myself at unnecessary risk either. Like I say, I have no intention of writing it up now. I probably never will."

"That's a sound idea. Very sound. Don't touch it for now. Why the interest anyway?"

I could hardly tell him because my black-haired, blue-eyed affianced was one of the dark ones, could I?

"Curiosity."

"Remember what it did to the cat?"

"Cats have nine lives."

What was I doing sounding so tough?

"OK. I've warned you. One thing you should remember, however: McCarthy did publish his article. Yeah, he pulled punches. But even a quarter century ago, he avoided serious trouble because he stayed away from certain speculations. Got it?"

"Absolutely."

"OK. I'll tell you what I know, which isn't much, but you don't tell anyone you talked to me. I don't think anyone else knows what I know."

"Fair enough."

"There were a couple of guys who knew what went down. Figured it out like you did, though a lot closer to the actual events. They asked some of the individuals who they suspected were involved. These individuals warned them to keep their mouths shut. They said that if certain other individuals found out what they knew, they might be in serious danger. The guys who had done the figuring, not being fools, kept their mouths shut, most of the time. Still the story kind of hung around in the atmosphere, so to speak. A lot of guys had their suspicions, but kept it to themselves, get it?"

"Urban folklore?"

"Yeah, that's it. So the King Arthur story comes out, mostly among the Irish guys when they have too much to drink."

He winked and raised the glass in salute to me.

I sipped the whiskey cautiously. It did indeed clear the sinuses.

"Nothing you can do to kill a myth."

"Right. It makes the individuals who were mainly responsible uneasy, but they let it go, because no one really believes in myths, get it?"

Actually people do believe in myths, but that was irrelevant to our discussion.

"Yeah."

He drained his vodka in a single gulp and waved for another.

"You want another?"

"Nope."

"No one ever had all the details about how it went down, see? A lot of speculation, I was told, and some comparing of notes and maybe an indirect question here or there. But no one knows for sure that Jimmy is not out there in his grave at Queen of Heaven Cemetery."

"Mount Carmel, actually."

"Whatever . . . the point is that there's not a shred of evidence to prove that Scarface's gunmen, Scalise and Anselmi, didn't put him down that day. The only way you could begin to prove there was a plot would be to dig up the grave. Believe me, that isn't going down. No way."

There was another way to know that he wasn't in his grave, but we weren't going to talk about that. No way.

"So guys had their suspicions, but no proof. And no way of getting proof. The people who could give them proof didn't dare talk. And the individuals on top were sworn to keeping the secret."

"If there was one. You see we can't be sure there was a secret . . . These individuals were and are heavy into this honor shit. You swear a solemn oath of honor and you never break it, not unless you want a bullet in the back of your head or a baseball bat beating you to death, get it?"

"They break their oaths occasionally, don't they?"

"Yeah, and spend the rest of their lives looking over their shoulders, even if they're in a fed program."

"Witness protection program?"

"There's some people the feds just can't protect."

"But these individuals have been dead a long time now."

"The oaths get passed on to their heirs. Believe me, if Tim McCarthy had been poking around when the first generation was alive, they'd never have found his body. Now we're into the third generation and they're more relaxed about it. Yeah, there's an oath all right, but it doesn't bind the way it use to. Get it?"

I nodded.

"So they have a word with McCarthy and that straightens him out."

"Why did Jimmy want to get out that way?"

"Your myth doesn't say. It says he was clean. The feds never went after him on tax evasion, like they did Scarface. No one was thinking of that in those days. He was one damn clever Irishman though."

"That he was. That he sure was . . . Why did the individuals you refer to help him out?"

"Beats me. Jimmy was a charmer by all accounts. Maybe he charmed them?"

"Charmed Capone?"

"He was a lot more complicated a guy than they make him out to be in the movies. But who knows why? And who knows whether this is any more than dreams, get me? Nothing to back it up and there never will be unless someone digs up the grave, and, like I say, no way that's gonna happen."

I paid for the drinks.

"Thanks for the information."

"Remember, I don't know anything about this matter and I never talked to you."

"I promise."

I walked over to Clark to catch a cab down to the Fine Arts Building, which once had been a carriage factory. It was a charm-ingly ugly old rabbit warren with artist's and musician's studios on the upper floor and decrepit theaters on the first floor. Madame—Nuala's voice coach—presided in one of the studios. I would have walked the three miles, but if I were not there promptly, I'd be in trouble with herself.

He had not told me much, except that this might be a dangerous exploration. He had, however, confirmed, albeit indirectly, the main lines of the story. As he said, it was the stuff of dreams. There was no way we could ever prove it, even if we wanted to.

I would tell Nuala that and strongly urge that we forget about the whole thing.

I didn't think that would go down at all.

At all.

—9—

IN THE lobby of the Fine Arts Building, a gorgeous woman enveloped me in a radiant smile that turned my legs to water. Then she hugged me, caressed my face, and kissed me. My brain stopped working.

"I'm so happy to see you, Dermot Michael. I've missed you something terrible!"

It was herself, I realized, slowly recapturing my sanity. She was dressed in a rather tight-fitting black suit, with the miniest of miniskirts, and a V neck with a swath of lace providing either modesty or invitation depending on your perspective. Her scent made me dizzy again. She didn't seem to want to let me go, which was all right with me.

"Are you going to take off my clothes now?" I asked her.

" 'Course not. Not just yet . . . Madame let me out a few minutes early. Didn't she say that I was improving rapidly in me breathing? . . . And you shouldn't worry anymore about my obsession with punctuality. Isn't that immature? Shouldn't a married woman be mature?"

A new persona was emerging: Nuala, the sexy, mature wife. Who was I to fight it?

"Shall we see the movie?" I asked weakly.

"Haven't I bought the tickets already? You can buy the popcorn. Large for me."

"Won't it spoil your supper?"

"Sure, won't I starve to death before then?"

I bought the popcorn and the natural water.

"I think Ma and Pa were involved with the Sullivans." I said as we—or more precisely my bride-to-be—selected our seats in the back corner of the main theater.

"Well, why wouldn't they have been? And herself telling me about the empty grave? And isn't she the one who insists that we should solve this mystery?"

"Ah," I said. "Do you remember anything from Ma's diary?"

"I don't but then I wasn't looking for it. Don't you have the whole translation in your apartment?"

"I'll look for it tomorrow morning."

"Good." She patted my arm. "Now let's enjoy the fillum and worry about our mystery after it's over."

Attending a "fillum" with Nuala Anne is a vigorous experience. She laughs, cries, grabs one's arm, shouts in protest, demands that one do something about what is happening, and intermittently cheers enthusiastically. This time, however, she engaged in another activity. During those interludes when she was sitting in relative repose, her hand found its way to my knee and thigh.

Well.

So I began my own explorations, a quest facilitated by her mini-skirt. I did not proceed very far, but far enough to make her gasp in surprise and, I thought, pleasure. At any rate she didn't try to stop me.

"Weren't you just a little fresh in there," she said, after she had led a standing ovation at the end of the film.

"You started it."

"'Tis true . . . I don't suppose you'll be interested in doing that at the fillums after we're married?"

"Don't you now?"

She laughed happily, linked her arm in mine, and more or less dragged me up Michigan Avenue in the soft autumn twilight.

"Do you want me to report my adventures during the day?"

"Och, Dermot Michael, aren't you terrible unromantic altogether this evening?"

"Am I now?"

"Well," she said feigning resignation, "I suppose I have to listen."

I finished my report as we passed the Chicago Cultural Center and neared the River. Nuala's exuberance had disappeared. She was serious, solemn, thoughtful.

"Well at least you don't think I'm crazy anymore."

"I never thought you were crazy, Nuala Anne. Now I know that all the evidence we have fits your model."

"You certainly tricked that poor reporter."

"I'm pretty good in the Watson role . . . I still can't figure out why Sullivan wanted to disappear, especially that way. Or why Capone wanted to help him. He couldn't have done it without Al Brown's help."

She nodded.

"Or why, after all these years, it's such a terrible dark secret. Dark and dangerous."

"Maybe we should stop searching."

That was my thought, too.

"If you want."

"Yet I know that it is important for us to do it and that it's not really dangerous."

"What will happen if we don't do it?"

She paused, perhaps consulting the *fairie* folk or the angels or whoever was whispering in her ear.

"Well, won't a good thing not happen for us?"

"You're sure of that?"

"Yes," she said. "Very sure."

"I see no reason why I shouldn't poke around a little more—check Ma's diary, talk to Tim McCarthy, see what my friend Sean and Father Leo come up with."

"You'll do that tomorrow?"

"I will."

"Then we can talk about it tomorrow night . . . Where are we going to eat tomorrow night, Dermot Michael?"

"Am I taking you out for supper tomorrow night?"

"Naturally! Don't I want to eat supper with you every night for the rest of me life?"

"Well, why don't I take you some place where you can dress up in your finest clothes and astonish everyone in the dining room?"

"What you really mean is wear practically nothing at all so you can ogle me all night long?"

"That's the general idea."

"Well, I don't think I'd mind that at all, at all . . . So long as the food is good, mind you."

"Absolutely."

"I have to go for me last fitting for me bridal dress. Actually I don't have to go at all, but if I don't, I'll spoil the day for your ma and your sis. And they'll want to talk about the flowers again and meeting people at the airport and all that stuff."

Well, she didn't say "all that shite."

"Seven-thirty at Gordon."

"Isn't that terrible expensive?"

"Won't I use all the money I saved because you paid for the movie?"

"Go long wid ya!" she said, snuggling even closer to me in the failing light.

Even in the encroaching darkness people still took a second and third look at her. As well they might.

"What's your man up to now?"

Her arm stiffened in mine.

"I'm not going to lose my temper, Dermot Michael. I'm NOT! I will not blow my top because of that friggin' gobshite!"

"I'm glad to hear that."

"Didn't I get three calls today, and meself at work, from Michael and Pedar and Nessa? And themselves all worried about what he had told them on the phone? And wouldn't I have heard from Fionna, too, but she won't talk to him?"

"And that was?"

"That your family lacked quality and that you were unstable!"

And didn't I laugh at that?

And then didn't I become very angry?

"They believed him?"

"Not to say believe. None of us ever exactly believe Laurence, if you take my meaning. He upsets us. We half wonder whether he's right. We have to reassure ourselves that he isn't."

"And you told them?"

"That he was full of shite and that I wouldn't discuss the matter and that they should see for themselves when they come to the wedding and that I'd marry you even if you were the poorest man in Chicago and yourself being far from that anyway!"

"But the luckiest."

"Because you made a little money?"

"No."

"Then why?"

"Because the most beautiful and most wonderful woman in the world wants to drag me into bed with her!"

"Dermot! Aren't you a desperate man!"

Right there on the bridge over the Chicago River, didn't she kiss me?

A respectable kiss, mind you, because weren't we in public?

"Should I mail my statements of net worth and my tax returns to everyone?"

"Ah, no, Derm. Wouldn't that be too direct altogether if you're dealing with the Irish?"

"Is there anything we can do?"

She thought for a moment as we bore down on the Water Tower. "Couldn't I send just your statement of net worth meself, without a word of comment?"

"In a Federal Express envelope?"

Why that would be less direct than my suggestion escaped me. But I would spend the rest of my life trying to learn the rules.

"Wouldn't that be a good idea now?"

"Tell you what: I have the statements and the FedEx materials. I'll drop them off tomorrow morning at the counter in my building with your name as the sender. That way they'd have them on Thursday or Friday at the latest . . ."

"Aren't you the brilliant man?" She kissed me again.

I was assaulted only twice more before we arrived at Grappa.

"Oh, Dermot," she said after the last exchange of affection, "I want you so bad."

"And I can't believe my good fortune."

"Go long wid ya!"

She very carefully removed the lipstick from my face.

"You can't go into that nice restaurant looking like you've been walking down your Magnificent Mile with an abandoned woman."

"Nothing better in the world than an abandoned woman."

She merely giggled.

We ordered a bottle of Chianti Classico and ravioli with meat sauce and settled down to our dinner conversation.

"You just chose a booth so you could feel me up again," she said with mock horror. "And made me sit in the corner, so I can't escape your machinations."

"I hadn't thought of it, but now that you mention it . . ."

"Don't you dare! Not in public!"

I was sure she was insincere, but we had other matters at hand.

I opened my attaché case.

"We have three issues to face, Nuala Anne. First of all . . ."

"I don't want to see the jacket for me disc. Not at all, at all."

"All right, we'll cross that off the list . . ."

"Give it to me!" she demanded, pulling the folder I had removed from the case away from me.

"That's honeymoon options."

She pushed it away.

"I don't care how bad it is, I want to see it!"

She was laughing at herself, but also, as Ma would have said, half fun and full earnest.

"Just a moment now." I pushed her hand away. "I'm not going to eat it . . . Ah, here it is."

I held up the sample jacket.

She examined it from a distance, frown on her face; then, now very gently, removed it from my hand and examined it up close, examined it critically.

"Well, now, it isn't so bad after all, is it?"

"I never said it was."

"Me eyes don't look that way . . ."

"Woman, they do!"

She ignored me.

"But it will attract attention, won't it, because I look so Irish and with all them designs from the *Book of Kells*?"

"It might."

"Och, no, Dermot, it will. Sure, isn't it what they call a commercial cover?"

"Some might even say a beautiful cover."

She ignored me again.

"May I take it along with me?"

She put it in her purse, just to make sure I wouldn't take it away from her.

"You certainly may . . . A couple of hundred early discs will show up at your house on Monday for the wedding guests and anyone else we might want to give it to."

"Won't that be grand," she said softly, as though she were in deep reflection. "Have I told you, Dermot Michael, what me next disc will be?"

"You have not."

This was the same woman who had argued vociferously that she was NOT a singer and that she would NEVER take voice lessons and that she would NOT, repeat NOT cut even a trial disc.

"Won't I be calling it Nuala Anne Goes to Church! And won't I sing Irish songs and American songs and songs in English and songs in Irish and songs in Latin and maybe even some songs I'll write meself?"

"And won't God be delighted that you've at last made peace with Her?"

"She loves me a lot, Dermot, or She wouldn't have sent you into me life. Wasn't it Her that gave me the idea for the album? And won't I be standing in one of the old monasteries, one they've rebuilt, with the stained glass behind me and meself in front of the altar and dressed in some sort of white robe like I'm a monk or maybe even a priesteen?"

What does one say to that?

What I said, "Nuala, that's dead focking brill!"

"Go long wid ya!"

But she thought it was, too. She would always surprise me. And that was dead focking brill, too.

"Now there's the matter of the honeymoon . . ."

"People only have them things when they're married," she replied, her eyes twinkling with mischief.

"So I am told . . . I see three options . . ."

"Only three?"

Her hand found its way to my knee again.

I ignored this distraction.

"Well, within those three options there are of course suboptions."

"Are there now?" She moved her hand slowly up and down my thigh, stopping only when our wine was poured.

"There are," I said. "Europe, America, and a combination of both."

"They all sound nice."

"What I would suggest is the combination."

"That sounds nice."

"We could spend two weeks on the beach in San Diego, which has the nicest climate in this country, swimming and soaking up sun . . ."

"Lovely," she interjected.

"Then we could go to Italy and spend a week in Rome and a week in Florence and maybe a few days in Ireland on the way back."

"Lovely," she said again.

"But we don't have to do it that way."

She removed her hand from my knee and wrapped my hand in both of hers.

"Whatever you think best, Dermot Michael."

"Hey, it's your honeymoon, as well as mine."

"Dermot, have you forgotten that I was never out of the County Galway until I went up to the University? And never out of Ireland till I got off the plane at your O'Hare Airport? I never expected to leave Ireland. What do I know about all these grand places? Why shouldn't I follow your suggestions?"

It was all very reasonable. But it wasn't like Nuala. Well it was yet another persona—and an appealing one at that.

"Then we'll do that. No fair complaining if you don't like these places."

"If you like them, Dermot love"—she squeezed my hand—"I'm sure I'll like them, too. All that matters is that you'll be there with me."

Tears glistened in her eyes.

"The third matter is a delicate one."

"Is it now?" she said with a wicked grin. "I bet it has to do with focking!"

"In a manner of speaking . . . We, uh, have yet to determine where we will spend our wedding night."

"That IS an important question," she said, her hand returning to my knee.

"We could reserve the honeymoon suite at the Drake. I don't imagine it's taken on Friday night."

At least I hoped not. I had delayed too long in raising this issue.

"We could."

"Or I could reserve a suite at the Four Seasons across the street. It's one of the best hotels in the world."

"That would be nice."

"Or we could go up to your house on Southport . . ."

"Our house."

"Right. Our house."

"Whatever you think best, Dermot Michael."

"Woman, it's your wedding night."

"Tis."

"You decide."

"Do I have to?"

"You do."

"Well," she said, her eyes down, and then paused. "Well, if it's all the same to you . . . Sure, wouldn't I like it to be in the house where Letitia and her man lived and where we're going to live and raise our children? Isn't it kind of like our cottage, even if there are no bogs around, but only your Chicago River?"

"We'll have to make our own breakfast."

"Ah, no, Dermot, you'll have to make our breakfast!" She laughed happily. "Won't it be wonderful altogether?"

"I'll have a king-size bed sent up there. I don't want to have to sleep in your cot."

"You'll have a hard time catching me in a bed that big."

"Woman, I will not."

We were both giggling, a little bit embarrassed and very happy. We toasted each other in the Chianti and started to work on our Portobello mushrooms.

"I can hardly believe it, Dermot."

"What can you hardly believe?"

"That I'll be sleeping with you a week from Friday night. Or early Saturday morning."

"You will be, Nuala," I said.

It was my turn to take her elegant hand into my huge paws.

"Didn't that first night in the pub, I say to meself I want to sleep with that man? But I never thought I would. And now a year later won't I be doing just that?"

"You said that to yourself?"

"I did. And wasn't that awful of me?"

"Terrible altogether, and yourself pretending not to want to talk to me."

We waited for the pasta to be served. Then Nuala continued, the soft burr still in her voice, but now in simple declarative sentences.

"I'd had crushes on fellas before, but nothing like this one. I couldn't sleep the night when I rode my bicycle away from you in the fog. I told myself that I was a dirty-minded slut. That didn't do any good at all. Then I said I would never see you again. Still I couldn't think of anything but you. I imagined you playing with me and teasing me and hugging me and kissing me and taking off my clothes and thrusting into me and I thought I'd go mad with joy. Then you found me, like I knew you would. And you were not only beautiful, you were kind and sweet and respectful. You adored me and cherished me like I was a rare and fragile piece of crystal. You took care of me. I hid behind my banter and kept you at a distance. I said to myself that I was too young to fall in love and I was going to be an accountant and stay in Galway and not immigrate and that there was no room for a big, gorgeous rich Yank like you in my life. But I knew in my heart that I belonged to you, Dermot Michael Coyne, and always would. Do I shock you, my love?"

We had begun to eat our pasta.

"You must tell me in full detail what those fantasies were like so I can make them real."

Our laughter broke the ice.

"Not quite yet, Dermot, except to say that I imagined you as very determined and very tender, which is what you are anyway . . . Am I saying too much about meself?"

"You're the most fascinating subject in all my world, Nuala. Please go on."

"You have to remember how shy and inexperienced I was—and still am, as far as that goes. I was hopelessly in love with you and terrified of you and of my own desires. I wanted you and I wanted to run away from you and I didn't do either. Then, when you were sick at Dublin Airport, poor man, and broke up with me, I told myself that I was relieved and happy. At last you were out of my life. My crush on you . . . I still called it that . . . wouldn't go away. So, shameless woman that I am, I came after you and have been making a fool of myself over you ever since. I don't care. I still want you and soon I'll have you!"

What does one say to a woman who makes herself so vulnerable? What one doesn't say is that my emotions had been parallel to hers all along. Or that one doesn't merit such affection and desire.

"You were in love with me, Nuala," was all I could manage.

"Was I ever! . . . It's been a terrible year and a wonderful year. I learned so much about meself and about men and about you. Maybe I've matured a little . . . Do you think I've grown up, Dermot, just a little bit? Am I something more than a shy child?"

"We're both shy children, my love, and always will be, thank God. 'Mature' isn't the word I'd use."

"And what word would you use?" she asked with a shy child smile.

Desperately I searched for the right word.

"More self-possessed, more secure in your own identity—and more outrageous!"

"Outrageous, is it? Well, I like that word!"

"You have found some inkling of who Nuala Anne really is and, despite yourself, you kind of like her and in all her different manifestations. So you like being Nuala Anne. A year ago, even a month or two ago, you wouldn't have revealed so much of yourself to me. If you want to call that maturity, it's all right with me, but that doesn't even begin to tell the whole story."

Her hand returned to its place on my knee, a position I suspect it would often occupy in the years ahead.

"I'm not an accountant, Dermot. I'm a singer and an actress and a good one, good enough that a lot of people will actually pay money to hear me sing. Folks like me, your whole family likes me. The more outrageous I am, to use your word, the more they like me. So I don't have to change, I just have to be me. If it weren't for your love, as solid and as firm as that lovely body of yours, I would not have learned who I am so quickly, maybe not ever. I owe you everything, Dermot Michael, everything."

Tears formed quickly in her eyes and flowed down her face.

"Maybe not quite everything, but we'll let that stand."

She grabbed a tissue from her purse and dabbed at her eyes, in the process abandoning my thigh for the moment.

"I don't care that I'm crying," she said. "I don't care at all, at all. I'm in love and I'm going to have my man so I should cry."

It was my hand's turn to search for a thigh in which it was likely to revel for a half century or more. It was, I noted not for the first time, a substantial thigh, nothing soft and yielding about it. At all, at all.

"Dermot!" she gasped. "You're a desperate man and taking advantage of my vulnerability!"

"I plan to do that for a half century and more; and yourself wearing a skirt that makes it easy."

Laughter replaced her tears. I explored a bit closer to my ultimate target, but still stayed safely away. Having instinctively—and luckily—played the courting rituals pretty well thus far, I was not about to mess up the game at this late stage.

YOU SHOULD MAKE LOVE TO HER TONIGHT, the Adversary intruded. SHE'S READY FOR IT AND SO ARE YOU.

"Go away," I told him. "You've been wrong all along and you're wrong now. Besides I didn't invite you to dinner."

Grudgingly he slipped away, but he lurked in the background, sneering at my delicacy. She was, however, my bride, not his. Delicacy now was good practice for what would be a life of delicacy towards a woman who would always be fragile crystal and a shy child.

"Sure, why else would a woman wear a miniskirt, except to make men look at her legs?"

"Seems reasonable to me."

"One last thing, Dermot Michael Coyne. I may be more self-confident, as you say . . ."

"Self-possessed. There's a difference."

"Fair play to you, Derm me love. Fair play to you. Anyway, that doesn't mean I'm going to change."

"If you ever try, I'll ask the Church for an annulment."

"You'd never dare!"

We returned to the remnants of our pasta and then ordered dessert, chocolate mousse cake.

"Isn't it strange," she said, returning to her self-revelation, "how desire and love get mixed up? I want you, Dermot Michael Coyne, and I love you, and I can't tell the difference."

"If Prester George is to be believed, that's the way God made us to give us a hint what She's like. We're not supposed to be able to untangle them. Love renews desire and desire renews love. It really is kind of ingenious, isn't it?"

She sniffed. "Good enough for him. He probably heard it from the little bishop, but the Church doesn't say that often enough."

"We're the Church, too, Nuala Anne."

"Doesn't it follow, me beloved bridegroom, that the Church should urge the married laity to fock as often as they possibly can so they'll be more like God . . . No, I don't mean that. What I mean is make love as often as they can?"

"I'd vote for it, my beloved bride!"

"Well," she said happily, "that settles that."

Fair play to you, Dermot Michael Coyne. You're likely to have a busy couple of months ahead of you. And a busy life.

"Would you be driving me home?" she asked as our coffee was served.

"If you don't mind, I'll take you home in a cab. I don't want to drive after a half bottle of wine."

"Then could we ever have a small jar of Jameson's to celebrate?"

"Woman, we could . . . What are we celebrating?"

"Me spiritual undressing . . ."

"Well worth celebrating!"

So we celebrated and I took her home, kissed her forcefully on the top steps of her apartment, and returned to the John Hancock Center. The Adversary left me alone on the ride home. I marveled until sleep replaced my thought with images that a woman actually desired me physically. I must always treasure that desire.

I was a very happy young man on that pleasant autumn evening.

Just before I drifted into the deepest sleep I heard thunder. Clouds must have gathered without my noticing it.

Other clouds were gathering, too. If I had known about them, my happiness would have been blighted.

—10—

1926

My Bill came home sad from work last night to our flat here at Austin and Washington and myself having a hard day with the little ones. I could tell that something was wrong, so I kept my complaints to myself and listened to him.

His first big project was in trouble. He's been putting up these lovely homes in North Oak Park which wouldn't we be lucky if one of them was for us. A grand architect designed them and there's a waiting list of people who want to buy them. The project seemed certain to be a big success. Bill would show everyone that a greenhorn from Ireland could make it in this crazy American world.

"They want me to pay protection," he said to me with a loud sigh.

"Who wants you to pay protection from what?"

"A man they call Klondike O'Donnell. Protection from accidents on the project."

"But don't you have insurance?" says I, pouring him a jar of whisky, which I do only when he needs one and ought to have it. Naturally, I poured myself one too, since it's not good for a man to drink by himself.

"Not against delays caused to the project."

"Well, you haven't had any accidents yet, have you?"

"If I don't pay this man a thousand dollars a week, won't I have accidents?"

"You mean he'd make accidents happen?" I said, ready for a fight with this Klondike O'Donnell.

"He's a criminal, Nell Pat," says my man, putting his arm around me, "A bootlegger and an extortionist. It's what they call a protection racket."

"Can't you go to the police?"

"He pays off the police with ten percent of what he collects from the people he's protecting."

"What did you tell him, me love?"

"I told him to fock off!"

"Well good for you!"

But last night, as I was sleeping in his strong arms, I was worried. Something bad, I knew, was about to happen.

Well, like I knew it would, something bad happened. Two of Bill's trucks were burned last night and the walls of one of his houses torn down. That Klondike O'Donnell is a mean and nasty man.

"What are you going to do?" I says to him.

"I guess we'll have to pay him his money. Everyone else does it. There's no other way of staying in business in this country."

"It's as bad as home was under the English!"

"Not quite, me love," he says kissing me, "we can still have our own home and our own money and our own business."

"With that gombeen man taking half your profit!"

"I don't know what else we can do."

"'Tis true," I said, weeping in his arms for the terrible disappointment he was feeling.

"There's one other thing I might do."

"What's that?"

"There's a man I know from the troubles that lives in Chicago now. They say he's a lot more powerful than Klondike. Maybe if I go to see him, he'll stop the extorting."

"He's a criminal too?"

"One of the biggest bootleggers in town."

"How will he stop your man?"

"Warn him off. He's so powerful that Klondike wouldn't dare resist him."

"Do we want to deal with a man like that?"

"They say he's a perfect gentleman and likes to take care of greenhorns like himself."

"Well, then, shouldn't we go see him?"

"We?"

"If you think, Bill Ready, that I'm going to let you talk to a man like Al Capone without meself being along to protect you, then you have another think coming!"

"He's not a bit like Capone."

"I don't care."

Bill says, "We'll see."

That means I'll go with him.

Well, wasn't your bootlegger the nicest man in the world! Doesn't he live in a gorgeous big apartment near Lincoln Park and the Lake with beautiful furniture and rugs and paintings and even one of them phonograph things that play music. He's a baker as well as a bootlegger and he made the pastries we ate at tea. His fiancée was there, a lovely young American woman with red hair just like mine. She's a smart one, too, terrible smart. I think they're sleeping together, though wouldn't I be a fine one to criticize that? But she's a nice young woman and she and I hit it off real well.

We're dressed in our finest clothes and seem to fit right in to her living room, even if we had ridden on the L train and the streetcar instead of driving in a fancy Packard or something like that. My Bill and I are pretty good at pretending that we're classy people, even if we are peasants from the Gaeltacht. Bill says the reason is that I'm so beautiful and elegant. That's not true, but it is nice of him to say it, isn't it now?

Bill and her fiancé have a long talk about the Troubles, though I'm not sure which side your man was on. They both lament the death of the Big Fella, though Bill doesn't tell him what we know about that.

Your man explains that this Prohibition is a terrible thing and that the bootleggers are just businessmen who are supplying a product that everyone wants and should be able to get. He says the violence is caused by a few greedy men who will not abide by the rules, men like Klondike, who might just get himself killed if he isn't careful.

I sort of shiver when he says that.

Then he says that Mr. Capone is a frightening man sometimes, especially when he loses his temper, but other times he's a nice and very generous man. He says that it's a shame that people like Klondike don't abide by the rules Mr. Capone makes because they're sensible rules.

I don't know what to make of any of that. But I notice his woman frowns. She's not convinced, I think to myself.

"You have to understand," your man says, "that people like Klondike are petty criminals, clumsy thugs, cheap crooks. They make plenty of money providing beer for the marketplace. But they cannot resist the temptation to engage in other activities like robbery and extortion more or less for the fun of it."

"'Tis true," my Bill agrees.

"Well, you need not worry about them. I can promise you that they will not interfere with your enterprise in the future. I will have a word with Klondike first thing in the morning."

"That's very kind of you," Bill says. "Nell Pat and I are very grateful."

"We are indeed," says I, not being one to keep my mouth shut.

"Not at all," your man says. "You're the kind of Irish immigrant who is a credit to our homeland and to our new country."

"Thank you, sir," my man says. "We owe you a favor."

"I'll remember," says the bootlegger, with a flash of his fine white teeth. "Someday I may need a favor."

Then he invites us to join him and his woman at their "club" over on Wells Street. Bill seems a little shy because neither of us have ever been in a speakeasy in all our lives. But I think it will be fun to do it just once. So I says, "That's very generous of you, sir."

Bill smiles because he knows there's no sense arguing with me.

So his chauffeur drives the four of us over to the "club." A man in a tuxedo greets us at the door, opens the door, and then leads us down a long narrow hallway. He opens another door and we enter this big room, which is the most fancy place I've ever seen. A Negro band is playing jazz music, the people are all wearing fancy clothes, the waiters are in tuxedos, the lights are soft and low, and some couples are dancing. At first I'm a little scared because I think it's sinful altogether. Then I realize that me man and I must act like we're just as refined as the rest of them and probably more. So I walk in like I belong there and maybe have been to better places. I'm not a flapper at all, at all — and meself the mother of two children even if I am only twenty-four. But if I want to pretend that I'm a flapper, I can pretend with the best of them. The men and women stare at me, which happens sometimes when I get all dressed up. A few of the men look at me like they want to take my clothes off. I just stick my nose higher in the air and ignore them. Bill smiles like he's very proud of me.

Well we have a jar of Irish whisky and, to be honest, a second one, which I never do, and we dance and me man holds me very close and I feel happy in his arms.

Then Bill tells your man that we should really get home to our kiddies. He asks about the kiddies and I let Bill do the bragging. Then doesn't he insist that his chauffeur drive us home. Bill says that isn't necessary at all at all. But I cut him off and say wouldn't we be terrible grateful altogether and meself not sure I can walk a straight line after the two jars.

When we are home again in our snug little flat and the kiddies in bed, Bill says it's been a long day and maybe we should get some sleep, I agree with him, though I know it's not sleep he wants.

We don't have to worry about Klondike anymore, but I wonder about the poor bootlegger man and his nice young fiancée. They don't seem very happy.

Well, aren't we invited to the wedding! Bill says he doesn't think we ought to go because the criminal element will be there. And I says that, sure, we'll never get a chance to see them again. Won't it be nice to be able to tell our children about them when they've grown up. He says that he'll make up his mind about it later. That always means that he's going to do what I want him to do — like he always does.

Well, we went to the wedding and met Al Capone, who is a big, greasy man in fancy clothes — spats and all — with hard eyes, a charming smile, and a fat cigar in his mouth. He looks at me like I'm a piece of Fanny Mae candy to be swallowed in a single bite and I get away from him in a hurry. I admit to me man that he was probably right: we don't belong at this wedding with all the crooked bootleggers, and crooked politicians and crooked police. We stay at the party at their club only long enough to congratulate your man and his wife and then we get out of there in a hurry.

The bride looks happy, as brides should. But I can tell by her eyes that she doesn't like the crowd any more than I do and that she's afraid of Mr. Capone just like I am.

"Pray for us, Nell Pat," she says to me. "Pray for us every day."

And don't I promise her that I will.

"Isn't that the craziest idea I've ever heard in all me life?" I says to himself when he tells me what we're going to do for our friend the bootlegger man and his wife.

"Tis," he says.

"I suppose we have to do it."

"Woman, we do."

"And crazy as it is, it isn't dangerous?"

"Not very."

"We do owe him a favor," I say.

"We do . . . Tis a strange kind of favor, isn't it, Nell Pat, me love."

"Tis," I say with me loudest sigh.

"And yourself pregnant."

"That has nothing to do with it," I insist.

So we're going to help them. Your man says that we're the only ones he can trust to keep the secret. That may be true enough, but I can't for the life of me understand why he wants to do things this way.

That's none of our business, says me man. As usual, he's right.

It's done now. And it wasn't a bit dangerous. Nothing like what happened out in Connemara when we tracked down the man responsible for the death of the Big Fella. Aren't me and Bill glad it's all over? And don't we own a grave site out at Mount Carmel, not that either of us are planning to use it for a long time?

Someday won't we be in the ground with everyone else that has gone before us? And ourselves in heaven with God who, Bill says, loves us even more than we love one another.

I hope the two of them find happiness.

And wasn't it clever of them to ask us for help? No one in all the world would suspect the greenhorn contractor and his pregnant wife of getting involved in such a crazy scheme.

It will always be a secret. Bill and I won't dare to tell anyone else. Neither will the others who were involved. I understand why it was necessary.

— 11 —

I PONDERED the sheets I had copied out of the files which contained Ma's diary. Only when I searched for entries which fit the story we already knew, did those selections fit together.

There was no way that Nuala could have seen the pattern when she was translating the diaries or that I would have recognized it when I was editing the translations. What would have happened, I wondered, if I had decided to include those passages in the published edition? Would anyone have figured out what they meant? Would the people that were still interested in protecting the empty grave have read them? If they had, what would they have done?

And exactly what had Ma and Pa done?

I had awakened while it was still dark, made copies of my statement of net worth, addressed the FedEx envelopes to her four siblings, and dropped them off at the still-unopened FedEx counter on the fourteenth floor of the John Hancock Center. Then I dashed back to the apartment to read through Ma's diaries for 1926 and 1927.

The whole story was there. Nuala had been right from the beginning. Naturally. The grave was empty. Ma and Pa had been involved in the plot to keep it empty. Moreover our family grave site had been a reward for cooperation in the plot.

Jimmy "Sweet Rolls" Sullivan was buried somewhere else. So was Marie Kavanagh Sullivan, if she were dead. Somehow I thought she was probably still alive.

Would we meet her before the story was over? Somehow I wouldn't be surprised if we did.

I was also impressed again by how much Ma was like Nuala. Different in many ways, of course, and not at all fey; but the same courage, the same determination, the same ability to play whatever role she thought fit the occasion. The old saw is that a man falls in love with a wife who will be like his mother. In my case it would be a wife who is like my grandmother.

As soon as I figured herself would be in her office, I called.

"Nuala Anne McGrail," she said brightly.

"Wasn't I looking for Marie McGrail?"

"That woman is no longer with us!"

"I kind of liked her."

"She was a bit of a creep."

"She had lovely breasts."

"Dermot Michael Coyne! At this hour of the morning!"

Not a word about bothering her at her work! Another soul transplant.

"I found the parts in Ma's diary about the Sullivans."

"What does she say?"

"I'll bring them along tonight. Briefly, they were involved in the plot, just as you said they were."

"Didn't I know that!"

"Woman, you did . . . The entries are charming. They re-create the era. They were brave young people."

"Didn't we know that!"

"And one thing we didn't know: our family grave site was a gift from Sullivan for helping them."

"YOU didn't know that."

"Did you?"

Silence.

"Och, Dermot, do I have to know *everything?*"

Still the imp, the woman leprechaun. I was glad she was. I didn't want her ever to become a complete adult.

We agreed I'd pick her up at 7:00 for dinner at Gordon.

"Gordon's, is it?"

"Woman, it is not. Gordon. No s."

"Humpf," she snorted.

Then she added. "I'm crazy in love with you, Dermot Michael Coyne. Worse every day."

"And I with you, Nuala Anne McGrail."

"I'd better be getting back to work."

"I'm sorry Marie McGrail isn't there," I said. "She's not psychic at all, but, like I say, her breasts are gorgeous, especially when they're naked."

She hung up on me.

I sat in my massive easy chair, daydreaming about this remarkable woman who would soon be my wife.

The reveries were ended, as most good reveries are, by the ringing telephone.

"Dermot Michael Coyne," I told the phone.

"Cindy."

"Ah?"

"Dale Quade has handed me a subpoena for your financial records for the last three years."

A lump of dry ice manifested itself in the pit of my stomach.

"My accountant has them. There's nothing in them, Cindy. The CFTC and the IRS both went through them with a microscope."

"I know that, Derm. I told her that. She sneered."

"I'm a target?"

"I asked her that. She laughed and said that it was too early to answer that question. My hunch is that she's on a fishing expedition. She'll try to tie whatever she can find with whatever your old buddy Jarry Kennedy has on his wire."

"I've not talked to Jarry, except at the beach on Labor Day. He wasn't wearing a wire and we didn't talk about the Exchange."

"I know that, too. It's all fake. He's taped some kind of baloney. That's why we will win. But it will take time and effort."

"What kind of a woman is she? Why will she buy something that Jarry has cooked up?"

"She's not a very good lawyer, Dermot. She's dangerous because she's not like the other people over there, Derm. For her it's not just a game. She's a true believer."

"What do you mean?"

"Most of the other assistant prosecutors, either there or out at 26th and California are playing a game. All right, they might bankrupt an innocent person, ruin his life, suborn perjury, and force a plea bargain on him because they have bottomless pockets and he doesn't—the way their buddies in Washington did to Danny Rostenkowski—but they're not on any personal moral crusade.

They add the scalp of a celebrity to their belt and it means a better job in a law firm when they switch sides so they can make some money. That's what lawyers do. Dale, however, was brainwashed by the nuns where she went to college. She's determined to eliminate evil and corruption from the world, especially white male evil and corruption. She was a good person, honest, upright, fair until her husband, who was a jerk, left her. Since then she's left the rest of her religion behind and is sleeping with her boss, but she's still on her campaign to send bad people to jail."

"And I'm a white male bad person."

"A white male bad commodity broker . . . Don't worry about her, Derm. We'll beat her and probably go after her for malicious prosecution. Maybe get her disbarred. I hope so. But I'm sorry it has to happen at this point in your life."

"We'll be all right, Cindy."

"I know you will."

I would have to tell herself at supper. How would she react to the news?

She'd don her Grace O'Malley persona. Poor Dale Quade.

"When will this go down?" I asked Cindy.

"She's on a fishing expedition and will be in no hurry. They'll go over your papers looking for something, anything, which will confirm whatever they have from Jarry's wire. Unless something happens, it'll take months before she goes to a grand jury. She's in no hurry and she's got unlimited funds, like they always do. They spent twelve million dollars putting Rosty in jail for giving away rocking chairs."

"So I live under a cloud . . . Will there really be an indictment?"

"I hate to say it, Dermot, but I think so. Maybe the United States Attorney, whom she has burned a couple of times by her zeal, won't think there's enough for an indictment. Maybe the Justice Department will veto it. Maybe she'll go after some other victim. But she's got this phony interview with you from Jarry's wire. Don't worry. Unless we're very unlucky in the judge we end up with, we'll get the charges dismissed. Then we go after her to get her disbarred. There's a lot of people who would like that."

I was not reassured, but I thanked my sister. I already had had one fight with an ambitious prosecutor and a stupid judge who wanted to send Nuala home as an "illegal alien." I did not want another tangle with a justice system which had become corrupt. I was a young man about to marry a wife; I had paid my taxes; now my government was trying to make my life miserable.

The phone rang again. Father Leo.

"I talked to a priest who was with Joe Curran after I was. He said he remembered a handsome woman, maybe in her late forties, who came to see him about the time Kennedy was assassinated. Dressed in black and weeping. Talked to Joe a long time in the office. Joe wasn't himself for days. Ring any bells?"

"It might, Father. Thanks a lot. I'll stay in touch."

I was about to leave my apartment for my appointment with Tim McCarthy when Nuala was back on the phone.

"Dermot Coyne."

"Isn't me eejit brother making trouble again?"

Not a good morning.

"What now?"

"Hasn't he flown all the way to Boston and himself upsetting me brother Pedar?"

"Pedar called you?"

"He's a good soul, Dermot Michael, not like Laurence at all. Pedar's a lot like me da, though he doesn't laugh as much. Laurence told him that you were shiftless and lazy and didn't have an office or a job and that your family lived in neighborhood filled with Negroes. He said the family had to intervene to protect me."

"Does Pedar agree?"

"He doesn't know what to think. He told me that he'd never seen Laurence so upset."

"And you told him."

"I told him that I didn't give a good shite what the family thought and that I was going to marry you no matter what they did and that the whole lot of them could go to hell as far as I was concerned."

"Nuala Anne!"

"I lost it, Derm, I lost it altogether."

"That won't help."

"It helped me . . . Dermot, you have a lot of money and are very generous with it, but that's not the point."

"And the point is?"

"That I'd marry you if you didn't have a penny and I had to support you for the rest of me life with me singing."

My shy child was crying. I clenched my fist. I would settle with Laurence McGrail.

"That's a grand idea," I said. "I'll never write another word."

Her tears turned to a giggle.

"He'll try to spoil everything." She sighed.

"Did you tell Pedar that I was sending a statement of my net worth?"

"I did NOT! I don't care! FOCKMALL!"

More tears.

"Should I talk to Pedar in a day or two?"

"That'd be super, Derm. He's such a nice man."

"See you tonight."

"Thanks for listening to a hysterical woman."

"Who interrupts me when I'm at work."

"Go long wid ya!"

What will happen, I wondered, when Laurence finds out that I'm about to be indicted for fraud.

I encountered my neighbor Mike Casey on the elevator.

"Annie and I are looking forward to the wedding," he said.

Mike, who Nuala says looks like Sean Connery, is an artist and a former police superintendent. He and his wife own a fashionable gallery over on Oak Street. He also presides over Reliable Security, an organization which enables moonlighting cops to do what they would do on the job if they were not busy filling out forms.

"If there is one," I said glumly.

I told him about Dale Quade's investigation.

His steel blue eyes flickered.

"Tell you what, Derm: Let me talk to a few people and see what the wicked witch is up to this time. I'll also ask around about this Jarry Kennedy punk. He's got a reputation."

"Fine."

"Stay in touch," he said, as we left the elevator.

Outside it was another glorious late-September day, soft, mellow and peaceful. It challenged my somber mood and lost.

I crossed Michigan Avenue, walked a block to the Water Tower Park, and turned a half block to the right. Lewis Towers, the downtown center of Loyola University, was a nineteen-twenties skyscraper, the only old building left around the Water Tower square except the Tower itself.

Professor McCarthy, a tall, elegant man with silver hair and a black mustache, was waiting for me in his office. In shirtsleeves and suspenders he looked more like a witty bartender than an academic. A genial and popular teacher, Timothy McCarthy had produced solid work on the history of Chicago and had been engaged for ten years in a definitive history of Chicago crime.

"Nice to meet you, Dermot," he said, as he rose to shake hands with me. "I like your stories. You're an authentic seanachie."

"Irish-American variety," I said.

He laughed. "Nothing wrong with that."

He moved a stack of books off a chair and pointed at it.

"Typical professor's office I guess. Still, you can't beat the view. A cup of tea?"

"I'll never say no to that."

His view revealed the Water Tower, the ugly Museum of Contemporary Art (it looked like a fortress on the Siegfried line) and the Lake beyond.

Tim McCarthy was a nice man. I felt guilty because I intended to play a bit of a trick on him.

"Black?"

"Like I said, I'm Irish-American. My fiancée is from the West. She says that only savages drink tea without milk."

"Irish-speaking?"

"She sure is."

"Congratulations to both of you."

"Thank you."

He poured the tea, from a pot on a warmer (which herself would have thought sacrilegious) into a maroon Loyola University mug.

"So you're thinking of writing a novel about Al Capone?"

"Sort of turning the idea over in my head. He was a brute, but an interesting brute."

"All of that," he said, leaning back in his chair. "You have to understand that he took over from Johnny Torrio in 1925 when Johnny had enough of the violence and danger and by 1930 was already under indictment by the feds. He ran the Outfit for only five years and yet became a world celebrity in an era when that was a lot harder than it is now and without any PR assistance at that. He was the first Chicago celebrity. All over the world, his name became synonymous for Chicago."

"Until Michael came along . . . How did he do it?"

"Style mostly. He wore elegant clothes and talked a fascinating line. He was just a businessman, providing the public with something they wanted. He deplored the violence which Prohibition caused and denounced the corruption of law enforcement. He probably half believed what he said, more than half when he saw how eagerly the press bought it. He was right about the corruption, you know. He and his allies spent a million dollars a week on bribes. Government paid its Prohibition agents $2500 a year, the Outfit paid them a thousand dollars a week. Chicago was wide-open. The bootleggers' problem was not finding customers, so much as finding and making the product."

"Did he enjoy killing?"

Professor McCarthy twisted on his chair.

"He had a terrible temper. He never hesitated to remove someone who got in his way. So he and Torrio called in Frankie Yale from Brooklyn, where Capone was born, to dispose of Big Jim Colosimo, who had been head of the outfit and stood in the way of expansion of the bootlegger trade. Later he returned the favor by eliminating one of Yale's Irish rivals. Still later he had Yale eliminated because he found out that he was scheming to do the same to him. His two favorite gunmen were Al Anselmi and John Scalise—they did the St. Valentine's Day massacre. He found out that they were turning against him and he beat them to death with a sawed-off baseball bat after a big dinner in their honor. I'm sure he enjoyed getting those who were plotting to get him."

"Nice man."

"In principle, however, he deplored the violence because it was bad for business. He thought of himself as a businessman and not a crook. He once said, 'I can't change conditions. I just meet them without backing up.'"

"A solid business principle."

"You have to understand, Dermot, that Chicago was a lawless town from the very beginning. It grew too quickly for the law to catch up. It was a raw frontier town like those you see in the movies, but before anyone knew it there were a million and then two million people here and it was the busiest port in the world and the railroad center of the country. The police and the government were always corrupt. Criminals always flourished. Reformers never had the votes, not for more than one election. The tide has turned against crime and corruption only in this century and only since the election of the first Mayor Daley. Even he had to tolerate a lot of stuff that he didn't like."

"Worse than the other big cities?"

"New York is probably worse. In Chicago, however, it has always been more open. Gangs fought one another for turf from the beginning of the city. Extortion, vice, gambling were their cut of the expanding city. Capone and Torrio's contribution was to attempt to organize it to, 'systematize' it, to use their word, from an Italian word which meant what our professors of business administration mean when they say 'rationalize.' Capone tried to 'restructure' crime in Chicago. His principle was that there was enough money for everyone, so why kill one another? He failed to convince the others for very long. Hence the killings and especially the Saint Valentine's Day massacre. The men who took over while he was in Alcatraz and his brain was deteriorating were more successful. Crime in Chicago is mostly 'systematized,' though even today there are still gang wars. Nothing like the battles between Capone and Bugs Moran or Sweet Rolls Sullivan."

"Why did Capone fail to persuade them to lay off the killing?"

"Most of the bootleggers were punks, small-time racketeers and extortionists. They were too dumb to realize that there was indeed plenty of money for everyone and too greedy to pass up an opportunity to make an extra buck. Capone called meetings, everyone agreed to the division of territory he imposed, they all shook hands and promised lifelong friendship. The next thing you know they were shooting at each other again."

He rose from his chair and refilled my teacup.

"So Scarface was more than a thug and a punk?"

"He was the first criminal businessman. He believed in finding the best possible resources and using them. He discovered the Thompson submachine gun, he bought the fastest cars and the largest trucks, he imported the best booze, he hired the most skillful killers. He also believed in planning. He organized everything. He even planned murders carefully. None of this pulling a gun on a rival in a speak. He'd order his guys to stake out sites in buildings, discover the victim's regular routines, disguise themselves as cops, block the street with cars, and execute their victims quickly and cleanly, unless he thought they were traitors. So when Bugs Moran said after the St. Valentine's Day massacre that only

Capone killed that way, he wasn't referring to the brutality but to the careful organization . . . Bugs was lucky he came to work late that day."

"Just a businessman?"

"Look, Dermot, he was a crook and a killer, though maybe he was no worse than the Carnegies and the Rockefellers and the other business titans. My point is that he was a lot more than a crook and a killer. Beyond the boundaries of his 'business' he was a law-abiding citizen. He never killed a cop, he never resisted arrest, he was generous to charities, and acted like a good father, and by his lights, a good husband. Mae, his wife—and she was Irish-American by the way—was loyal to him to the bitter end. Al Capone was a complicated and very interesting man."

"And the feds got him on tax evasion."

"He had poor lawyers. Today a judge would have dismissed the charges."

"What happened between him and Sweet Rolls?"

"You read my article?"

I nodded.

"It's hard to figure out. Jimmy Sullivan knew there was enough money to go around and that there was no point in his fighting Capone. I think the Genna brothers out in Little Italy, real crazies, deliberately stirred up trouble by killing some of Jimmy's guys and blaming Capone. Then Jimmy fought back and the war was on."

"Like most wars, neither side really wanted it?"

"Capone especially. There was something just a little kinky about Sweet Rolls. He didn't like to start the killing, but once he was into it, he seemed to enjoy the battle. Scarface never did that."

"Yet Sullivan didn't get Capone before Capone got him?"

Tim McCarthy shrugged his shoulders.

"That's the biggest mystery of that whole decade. Jimmy was a decorated military officer, a brilliant tactician and wise strategist. Why did he wait there in his precious bakeshop for McGurn, Scalise, and Anselmi?"

"Machine Gun Jack?"

"Actually McGurn normally used a thirty-eight . . . Capone really admired Sweet Rolls. He knew that the Irishman was brighter, quicker, and more polished, even if he had almost no education. He didn't want to put him down. Jimmy didn't leave him much choice after that attack in front of the Lexington—ten cars with two tommy guns in each one of them. Somebody said it was like the battle of the Somme."

"And just as successful."

"Yeah ... They say that Capone actually wept at Jimmy's funeral."

It was time to spring my trap.

"Even though he knew that Sullivan's body wasn't in the casket?"

McCarthy put down his teacup, sat up straight in his chair, and stared at me.

"What do you mean, Dermot?"

"I mean that we both know that the body of James 'Sweet Rolls' Sullivan is not in that grave out at Mount Carmel. His murder was a carefully staged act over which he and Scarface must have had quite a chuckle."

He picked up a thick fountain pen from his desk and examined it carefully before he replied.

"I can't comment on that, Dermot," he said slowly, avoiding my eyes, but apparently not angry at my trick.

"You pulled a few punches in your article?"

"I may have. If I did, I had good reason ... If I were you, I'd leave it alone. For a couple more years."

"Till Marie is dead?"

"I didn't say that." He replaced the pen on the desk.

"You did say that Capone liked Sweet Rolls?"

"Respected him enormously."

"Enough to do him a really big favor?"

He still would not look at me.

"If Al liked you and you were straight with him, there was no favor too big he'd not try to do for you."

"I guess that answers my question."

"Dermot," he said with a rueful smile, "it's a great story. It really is. You're obviously a very good detective. But the story will keep. Our friends out on the West Side are men of honor in the sense that they keep their promises. The promise on this one will run out soon. The story will keep."

"I understand," I said, rising from my chair and putting my empty Loyola mug back on his cabinet. "I take your point. I'm not going to write anything about it now. I probably never would. I became interested in it because Sullivan's alleged grave site is next to our family tomb out at Mount Carmel."

When I tried later to figure out who had tipped "our friends on the West Side" (as the Outfit is often called in Chicago) to my poking around, I ruled out Tim McCarthy. If he had mentioned the grave sites to the "interested individuals," that would have changed everything.

—12—

"I FOUND out two interesting items today," Sean said to me tentatively, "which I thought I'd pass on to you."

We were sitting in a bar on the top of the John Hancock Center drinking Irish whiskey and watching the shadows of the buildings on the Drive, long and eager fingers, creep out on the deep blue Lake. He had phoned me after lunch to say that he wanted to talk to me "urgently."

"Fire away," I said.

"First of all, as far as I can get it from people who know more than I do, it would seem that your friends out on the West Side have inherited an oath, a very solemn oath, to protect the secret of the death of Sweet Rolls Sullivan. There are some oaths in their world that are passed on from generation to generation."

I counted on my fingers. "That would be four generations, wouldn't it?"

"Three. Capone's contemporaries to Acardo's and then Acardo's generation to Albergetti's."

Anthony Acardo, known variously as "Tough Tony" and "Big Tuna" had presided over the Outfit in the seventies and eighties. Angelo "The Angel" Albergetti, who lived two blocks away from us in River Forest, was the current "don." Unlike Capone who led the Mob when he was still in his twenties, the subsequent leadership had all been old men.

"So The Angel is bound by Scarface's vow?"

"That's what I hear."

I was not about to ask him for his source.

"Permanent vow?"

"Binding all subsequent generations? I gather there's a limit to it. My source says with a wink and a nod that there's a time limit on it and that it might expire soon. He was more indirect than that of course."

Elderly Irish cop, I'd bet.

Second hint today that the statute of limitations on the secret was running out.

"They don't know I'm interested, do they?"

"My source sure didn't, either before or after I talked to him."

"I'm inclined to leave it alone for a while. I've got other things on my mind. Like a wedding."

I sipped cautiously on my "jar." Two hours remained before I was obliged to collect herself at her house. Our house. I wouldn't want to seem to be under the influence, as she would say, of the drink taken. I must therefore make the jar last through our whole conversation.

"I got an invitation today. By messenger. With a prayer in a foreign language on the back. Irish, I presume. Your young woman works fast."

"Now that you mention it, I've noticed that, too."

We both laughed.

"Now your second item."

He shifted uneasily and studied the amber liquid in his glass. "Have you heard that Dale Quade is planning to indict you?"

"It would seem that she has something like that in mind. She subpoenaed my records today. I'm told by my lawyer that it's a fishing expedition. She won't find anything. The CFTC and the IRS have already gone over them."

"Dale always finds something. Not enough for a conviction, but enough for a plea if the target doesn't have the money for a trial."

"Lawyers in my family would love to get her disbarred. And, unlike me, they love fights."

"Someone ought to put a stop to her. We use her leaks, of course, but even the press thinks she's a dangerous person."

"Then she must really be dangerous."

"Apparently they've wired some guy to whom you talked?"

"Allegedly talked, Sean."

"All right, 'allegedly.' "

"I mean that I haven't talked to the guy in years, save for one conversation at the beach on Labor Day. I saw no sign of a wire. But even if he was wearing one, we didn't talk about anything that might interest a grand jury."

"A guy named Jarry Kennedy. An old friend of yours."

"So I understand. A certifiable psychopath."

"Our guys think so, too. She's teasing them with excerpts from the conversation. Apparently they are incriminating."

"It's a fake, Sean . . . This conversation is totally confidential?"

"It sure is."

"Don't get involved in writing the story. My legal relatives will jump on everyone with a suit as soon as this phony conversation is leaked. I don't want you to be a target."

He considered my advice very carefully.

"The Federal Courts are not my beat. But it sounds to me like there's another story lurking around. Like conspiracy to commit fraud?"

"Might be."

"Do you mind if I poke around on this Jarry Kennedy guy? Maybe get a story ready when you folks sue? I won't go with it until you consent."

"Be my guest . . . Tell me more about this Quade woman."

"Sad case. She met her husband during their first year in law school. Married at the end of the first year. She dropped out to get a job at a pizza parlor so she could support the two of them and the kid they had. He was law bulletin and then graduated. Big job offers from around the country. Took one in New York and dumped her. She went to school at night, graduated, and went to work over there at the Dirksen Building. Worked her way up quickly. Sleeps with boss—and lots of other people, too. Hates men, perhaps with good reason. Takes big risks and loses a lot of them."

"The guy dumped her when he got his degree," I commented. "I didn't think stories like that happened anymore in this feminist age."

"You'd be surprised. Even feminists can be fools when they think they're in love."

"She's close to the Bureau?" I asked.

"To one faction over there. The Special Agent-in-Charge hates her guts. The Bureau has enough trouble these days without looking foolish in court with a bad case. There's a lot of infighting in the Bureau between the Agent-in-Charge and the Deputy Agent-in-

Charge. The Deputy has clout inside the Beltway, so he gets to do some things on his own. He's in Quade's corner if not in other regions."

"Let me guess, Sean. My friend Jarry is working for the Deputy."

"You got it . . . And the Agent-in-Charge is away in Bosnia helping them set up their own Bureau."

"What's the Deputy's name?"

"Joe Dever . . . He's a total asshole. Thinks he's an investigative genius. Most agents can't stand him."

"So I'm up against a bitter, reckless woman and a guy on the make?"

"Looks like it, Dermot. Sorry."

"And some of your colleagues are looking for blood?"

"They're out there, too."

"Coyote is always out there, and he's always hungry," I said, finishing my jar.

"Huh?"

"Native American saying . . ."

"If it's a fake, they won't get away with it."

"At first they will," I said with a sigh almost as loud as Nuala's.

"I suppose so," he admitted.

"Want another drink?"

"No thanks. I might have a date tonight . . . I'll be looking forward to meeting herself. She sounds like something else altogether."

"You can't imagine," I agreed.

I decided in my apartment that I had better swim before I encountered herself at 7:30.

As I plowed back and forth in the pool, still feeling sorry for myself, I realized I was in a much better position than the usual targets of the Bureau and the United States Attorney. I had a first-rate lawyer in my family and the resources to fight back. I wouldn't be forced into a plea bargain, as Danny Rostenkowski had been when his lawyers had consumed his three million dollars long before a trial. Even if I lost the money I had won at the Exchange, I could still count on a reasonably steady income from my writing. Maybe I would be more industrious in my work if I lost all my money.

All of which was an exercise in self-pity. Cindy and her friends would eat them alive long before a trial.

If the wheel at the Federal Courthouse spun out a good judge.

—13—

NUALA HAD chosen a simple sheath with a low neck-line and the usual miniskirt for her evening dress. The color of the dress was anything but simple, however. It was bright, bright red. She created more than the usual sensation as we entered Gordon at 500 North Clark Street. Her ring and the diamond necklace I had given her in the cab on the way down from Southport glittered dangerously.

"Woman," I said, "you're radiant tonight."

"I'm about to marry a man I love," she replied with her most glorious smile; "Sure, what better reason to shock all them eejits who are staring at me?"

There was a rigorous logic somewhere in that comment which escaped me.

Nuala loved her engagement ring and her necklace, but the dress, charming as it was, had doubtless been purchased off the rack at a markdown sale or at an outlet store. It was approved behavior for me to spend money on her, but it was wrong for her to spend money on herself. "Good taste," she had once said to me with a sniff, "makes up for a lack of money."

"Well," she said after she had arranged herself at the table, "what reactions do you have to me emotional undressing last night?"

"If taking off your clothes is as much fun, I'll be deliriously happy for the rest of my life."

"Go long wid ya, Dermot Michael Coyne," she said, tapping my arm with substantial force. "I'm serious."

In truth, she was on so much of a high she was only half-serious.

I was not ready for the question. I tried to improvise, not too successfully.

"You're a woman and a half, Nuala Anne, a constant challenge. I've had to grow up, too, during the last year. I've learned more about women than I did in all the other years of my life put together. I still have a lot to learn, so you're going to have to be patient with me."

"Go long wid ya," she said again, her eyes soft with affection. "Don't I like you just the way you are?"

This time her tap on my arm was as soft as a baby's and the pressure of her knee under the table as inviting as the first day of summer, a promise of warmth and comfort and joy.

I think I gulped.

"Did I say last night," she continued, "that you'll have to put up for the rest of your life with me blather, and me contentiousness, and me loud Irish mouth and me crazy visions?"

"I don't recall that you did, but I assume that to be the case."

"Do you now?"

"Woman, I do. Should there be a change in those conditions, I will trade you in on a new model."

"Don't even think of it!"

So we ordered our dinner, or rather I ordered it because herself threw up her hands at the menu—salmon gravlas, wine-marinated pears with Stilton cheese and poached skate for the main course.

"Isn't this a fancy place and meself never hearing of skate before," she said, her hand managing to find my knee.

"Tis."

We chatted happily of our future together: love, sex, children, growing old together. Much of our chatter was about sex; Nuala had been reading books on the subject and was filled with questions, indirect and roundabout, most of which I could not answer.

"Would you ever want to do this to me?" she'd say after alluding to some Ming Dynasty trick.

"Woman, I've never thought about that, but I'm sure I'd like it if you would."

"Well," she'd reply thoughtfully, "not at the very beginning anyway."

We were engaged in one such obscure, if erotic, discussion when the little bishop appeared.

"There was so much crimson over here," he said with his usual sigh, "that I thought it might be the Cardinal himself . . . I note with approval the new necklace."

Flustered, Nuala turned as crimson as her dress.

"Your rivrence! Isn't it meself that's glad to see you and your man wanting to talk about nothing but sex? Isn't it terrible altogether that he has nothing else on his mind and himself about to receive a sacrament?"

"God looks like sex," the bishop said.

"What?" I gulped.

"Is not the Trinity an intimate, ecstatic, and permanent union between two persons which generates a third person? Is not therefore married love an excellent metaphor and indeed a reflection of the most inner and personal activity of the deity?"

"That's beautiful!" I exclaimed.

"Och, the Church doesn't say that to people."

"It just did."

"Sure, you never hear it from the altar, do you now?"

"I have just heard it from the esteemed Father Barron . . . Should I mount the Cathedral pulpit next year on the Feast of the Holy Trinity and preach this metaphor, you may be sure that letters would go off to the Congregation for the Defense of the Faith before the day was over."

"So you won't do it?" I asked.

"Oh, no. I will most certainly do it, Herself granting me life till then," he replied, and drifted away in his usual bemused style, as though he were unsure of where he was or where he ought to be going.

Following the immemorial Irish custom, we finished our dinner and turned to business only over dessert, in this case flourless chocolate cake with espresso ice cream.

"Here are the pertinent excerpts from Ma's diary," I said, removing them from my jacket pocket and handing them across the table to her.

She read the pages silently and then, as was her wont, read them for a second time.

"They got themselves into something dangerous, didn't they?" she said.

"I thought so, too."

"And herself loving it all the time."

"We don't know, Nuala, exactly what it was or why they were needed or why Sweet Rolls Sullivan chose that way to disappear."

She nodded thoughtfully, her forehead creased in a puzzled frown.

I reported on my conversations with Tim McCarthy and with Sean, though I left out the second part of the latter conversation.

"So," I said, summing up, "we know most of the story. Jimmy Sullivan was tired of the danger and the violence. He wanted to get out of the racket, disappear completely. He persuaded Capone to help him stage his vanishing act. Ma and Pa provided some kind of indispensable assistance. Capone swore an oath which was passed on to his successors. They buried the empty casket at Mount Carmel. A couple of months later Marie Sullivan disappeared. Jimmy has been dead for some time. Marie is still alive. The oath dies when she dies . . . Don't we know enough now, Nuala?"

"I don't think so, Dermot me love," she said as she finished off the last tiny piece of her cake and looked around as if she were wondering whether it would be "too much altogether" if she ordered another piece.

"What else do we have to find out?"

"I don't know. Isn't it all surmise? Doesn't it all rest on me vision, if you want to call it that, of the empty grave and ourselves not having the slightest idea why James Sullivan chose to disappear that way and why Al Capone cooperated in such a scheme, if he did. Maybe Sullivan died the week after his apparent murder. Maybe Marie has been dead a long time. We don't have any proof of anything, do we now, me darling man?"

"'Tis true," I agreed.

"We don't know enough of the story, not yet."

She pushed the cake plate aside reluctantly.

"And what do we do now?"

"We wait. Something more has to happen."

"We just wait?"

"We just wait . . . And now, Dermot Michael Coyne, tell me the bad news you've been saving to the end."

I ought not to have been surprised that she knew there would be bad news. Nuala had been seeing right through me since the night we met at O'Neill's pub in Dublin's fair city.

I told her about Dale Quade and Joe Dever and about the indictment which was almost certain to be handed down against me.

"Under the circumstances, Nuala, it might not be a bad idea if
we think about postponing . . ."

A firm hand on my mouth shut off the rest of the sentence.

"Don't you dare say it, Dermot Michael Coyne! Don't you dare
even think it! I'll marry you on our wedding day even if I have to
go to jail to do it."

"I'm not likely to be in jail. Nothing will happen for a couple
of weeks, maybe a couple of months. But the media will have a
great time with it, even though they know that Kennedy and Quade
and Dever are all crooks."

"You feel sorry for yourself, don't you, Dermot?" she said accusingly.

"I guess so. I haven't done anything wrong. Yet my reputation
will be ruined and most of my money spent, even if Cindy won't
charge me."

"'Tis your worst fault," she informed me. "And yourself not having
many of them."

"What's my worst fault?" I demanded.

"You don't get angry when you should. You should be furious at
these terrible people. I've seen you when you're angry and aren't
you brilliant? But it takes you a long time to, as you Yanks say, get
your Irish up."

"The Irish are a peace-loving and gentle people," I said. "Well,
most of the time."

"I saw you jump your man with the knife in front of me house
and I read in the Dublin papers about the three thugs you tossed
through the window on Upper Baggot Street. You have to become
that wild Irishman against them gobshites."

"They were attacking me physically and I fought back physically.
This is different . . ."

"'Tis not, not at all at all."

She was right. If I were to fight back effectively I would have to
bestir myself out of my placid self-pity. It was fortunate that Nuala
had reminded me of that. The course of the next couple of days
would have been different if she had not.

"We'll not let them spoil our happiness," she said, taking my
hand. "Will we, Dermot Michael?"

"Woman, we will not."

We ordered a cup of tea; I told herself what Cindy had promised for our enemies after we had our day in court.

"Good enough for them shite hawks."

"A drink for you and the young woman," our waiter said, placing two brandy snifters on the table, "from Mr. Dever."

Ah, the enemy was among us.

"Who is Mr. Dever?"

"He's the gentleman over there with Ms. Quade," the waiter said. "He's the head of the FBI in Chicago."

At their table across the room, the enemy raised their glasses in mock salute.

"Deputy head," I said to the waiter.

"Pissant gobshites," Nuala murmured.

I rose from the table, took one snifter in each hand, and ambled over to their table. They smiled uncertainly as they watched my progress. Joe Dever was in his late thirties, plump, cherubic, kind of like the films of Winston Churchill you see on A&E. Dale Quade had the haggard look of an addicted runner, a stern, self-tormenting nun who was sacrificing her dark, natural beauty for her vocation of ascetic self-discipline.

I was of a mind to throw the brandy in their faces. That, however, could be interpreted as disorderly conduct. Instead I poured the liquid into their half-empty water glasses.

"Gobshites," I murmured with my most pleasant smile, turned and walked away.

Just before I turned away, however, I saw a look of astonishment, tinged with fear, flit across their faces.

Good enough for them.

"Good enough for them," Nuala Anne said approvingly as I sat down next to her. "You scared the living shite out of them."

"Did I?"

"They know they have a fight on their hands now!" she said triumphantly.

We walked, hand in hand, from the restaurant to the garage of the John Hancock Center. Nuala assaulted me with passionate kisses in the Water Tower Park, in the garage, in the car at the stoplight at Clark and Armitage, and at the door to her apartment.

"I'll never stop loving you, me darlin' man," she'd say, pausing for breath, "Never!"

"Woman, you'd better not."

Instead of anxious nightmares about the Office of the United States Attorney and the Federal Bureau of Investigation, I had glorious dreams about Nuala. My Nuala.

— 14 —

A BELL rang at a great distance. I struggled for it, but could not find it. It continued to ring. I was in the deepest sleep of the night, in the splendid, surrealistic world of vivid images, manic passion, and a beautiful woman, a world so much more pleasurable than the ordinary world that I refused to leave it. Here was reality. The ordinary world was a dream.

The bell continued to ring.

I groped for my phone.

"Dermot Coyne," I mumbled.

The dial tone did not seem to be interested in that fact.

Still the bell rang.

House phone.

I stumbled out of bed, stubbed my toe, and struggled towards the door of the apartment.

I picked up the phone.

"Yes?"

"Mr. Coyne," the doorman said, "there are some people on their way up to see you. They say they're from the FBI."

Confused and still longing for my dreams, I stumbled back to my bed, sat on the edge, and turned on the lamp. The clock said 3:10 A.M.

FBI? Why were they looking for me? Why were they using their Gestapo techniques on me?

I should call someone. Who? I glanced at the phone on the bed stand. A business card next to it, tossed there thoughtlessly when I was undressing. Whose card?

Michael P.V. Casey. Business number. I flipped the card. Home number. I punched it in.

Lawyer, artist, president of a security company, former superintendent of police, friend and shirttail relative of the little bishop, helper on the art gallery case.

"Casey." He sounded wide-awake. Making love? Sorry, Mike.

"Dermot. The FBI are riding up on the elevators."

"In their storm-trooper jackboots, no doubt. Don't let them in the door until I get there."

Reluctantly I gave up my hope that I could slip back into the dream with Nuala and pulled on a sweat suit.

As I was rinsing my mouth—can't greet the FBI with bad breath— I heard a fierce knocking on my door.

"FBI! Open up!"

I let them knock while I combed my hair.

"We know you're in there, Coyne! Open up!"

It was my apartment. Where the hell else would I be?

I sauntered to the door, now wide-awake and remembering that I was, courtesy me woman, in me fighting mode.

"Who's there?" I asked sleepily.

Angry pounding on the door.

"Federal Bureau of Investigation. We want to question you and the woman."

"Go way. It's the middle of the night."

Yet more pounding.

"Let us in. We must speak to you and the woman!"

"Do you have a search warrant!"

The knocking now turned angry.

"We will charge you with resisting arrest."

"Do you have a warrant for my arrest?"

"We want to speak to your girlfriend!"

No warrants. Maybe I should not have poured Joe Dever's brandy into his water glass.

"There's no woman in my apartment."

"We know she's there. You've just committed perjury by lying to a government agent. You're under arrest."

"There's no woman here, and you're engaging in disorderly conduct."

Arrests in the small hours of the morning were now a standard trick of the Bureau, learned from the KGB and the Gestapo. Usually the woman of the house answers the door. The paladins of American justice demand to see her husband. She says that he's not home. They arrest her for perjury, cuff her, and in her nightclothes they drag her down to one of their cars, and threaten to take her to their "office." The man of the house appears and he is arrested, too. In the confusion of such an arrest and a midnight ride to the Dirksen Federal Building, people have been known to make incriminating admissions. The media and the American Civil Liberties Union take no heed of such violations of due process of the law.

"You can open the door, Dermot," Mike Casey's voice said.

The FBI agents spilled into my apartment. They both looked like teenagers—a little guy with freckles and dark hair and a pretty girl with vacant eyes. Both were extremely nervous. Dever had gone to his bench. I was an exhibition game and he was using his third string.

Mike Casey, in neatly pressed light blue pajamas—which matched his eyes—and a dark blue robe eased in behind them. His hair was perfectly combed, the collar of the pajamas neatly tucked in over the robe.

"You're under arrest, Coyne," the kid sputtered, pulling cuffs out of his pocket.

"Just a minute, son," Mike Casey said softly. "What's your name, first of all?"

"Who are you?" the kid demanded, trying to sound tough.

"I'm Michael Patrick Vincent Casey. I am an attorney at law among other things. I am acting for Mr. Coyne here, got that, MISTER Coyne? And I am MISTER Casey, understand? I want to know your names and then I want to see your FBI warrant card, and finally I want to see your warrant for Mr. Coyne's arrest."

"You better tell him, David," the girl said. "He's the man who wrote the book. He used to be Superintendent of Police."

"What book?"

"The one on the practice of criminal investigations," Mike Casey said, the rules of which you two tyros have already violated massively. "Again I ask you your name."

David fumbled with his wallet and flashed his card.

"I'm Special Agent David McAuliffe of the Federal Bureau of Investigation," he said bravely. "My colleague is Special Agent Martha Regan."

The young woman displayed her card.

"All right, Special Agent," Mike said smoothly. "Now let's see your warrant for Mr. Coyne's arrest."

"We don't need a warrant. In the course of our investigation we observed Mr. Coyne violating the laws against perjury by lying to a federal investigator."

Mr. McAuliffe was sputtering again and spittle was forming on his lower lip. Ms. Regan inched away from him as if to say that she wanted no part of this craziness.

Sound instinct.

"Who was the federal investigator, and what was Mr. Coyne's perjured statement?"

"I am the federal investigator. Mr. Coyne denied that his girl-friend was in the apartment. We happen to know that she was and is."

"I see. Do you happen to know the name of the woman you allege is present in this apartment?"

He glanced at the young woman.

"Ah, Anne Grail, I think."

"Do you know anyone with that name, Mr. Coyne?"

"My fiancée is a certain Nuala Anne McGrail," I said, turning on all my charm. "Short for Marie Phinoulah Annagh McGriel. However, she is certainly not present in my apartment. As a point of fact, she never spends the night in my apartment. We are old-fashioned Irish Catholics."

"We have certain information that she is here," McAuliffe insisted.

"You know as well as I do, son, that you can't get away with that unless you tell us the source of your information."

"Mr. Joseph Dever, Acting Special Agent-in-Charge," the FBI man replied triumphantly. His colleague winced.

"Very interesting." Mike smiled graciously. "How does the presence or absence of Ms. McGrail impinge on your investigation?"

"We don't have to reveal the purpose of our investigation."

"Indeed you don't, son. Yet a visit at this hour of the night is a little unusual, isn't it?"

"I'm going to take Mr. Coyne into custody now." He fiddled with the cuffs.

"There is no legitimate presumption of crime here. You have no right to take him into custody. Should you do so, you open yourself to serious charges of false arrest."

The kid hesitated. This was probably his first arrest. He wasn't too bright. Mike Casey scared him.

"I demand to search this apartment to ascertain the presence of Ms. Grail."

"McGrail," I said genially.

"Not without a search warrant, son."

Just then two of Chicago's finest, one of each gender and both of African-American ethnic background, appeared at the door.

"Good evening, Superintendent," they said in unison.

"Good evening, Pete, Jill."

"Is there a problem, sir?"

"These two individuals, claiming to be Special Agents of the Federal Bureau of Investigation, have forced themselves into Mr. Coyne's apartment and are at this moment engaged in something which might be considered disorderly conduct. I thought it would be useful to have witnesses."

Special Agent Regan turned pale and backed away from her colleague.

"You are resisting arrest, Mr. Coyne," McAuliffe barked in a squeaky voice.

"On the advice of counsel," I said brightly.

"Then, sir, I am taking you in by force." He drew a thirty-eight from inside his jacket.

"I'd be careful with that, son. It is a loaded gun. You could hurt someone with it, including yourself."

The kid was breathing rapidly and swallowing hard. He hesitated, realizing at last that he had better cover his ass quickly.

"I demand to search the apartment," he said again.

"Not without a search warrant."

Mike raised an eyebrow in my direction.

"If you put that cannon away, Mr. McAuliffe," I said, "I might as a personal favor let you look around."

Mike smiled his approval.

The punk now had his chance. If he would accept my offer, he could apologize and beat a somewhat graceful retreat. An experienced agent, if one had been so foolish to get involved in such a caper, would have bought in.

Alas, Special Agent David McAuliffe was not an experienced agent.

"I am going to search this apartment now. Special Agent Regan, you look in the bedroom."

"No way," she said flatly, thus guaranteeing herself a future in the Bureau, especially after Mike talked to her boss.

"Very well, I charge you with insubordination. I will make the search myself."

"Officers," Mike said sadly, "I'm afraid I'll have to ask you to take this young man into custody. He's clearly engaging in disorderly conduct. You should remove him to the Chicago Avenue Station and charge him."

"Yes sir."

"Don't come near me! I am a Special Agent of the Federal Bureau of Investigation conducting a legitimate inquiry."

"You are, son, a young man who has obtained illegal entry into the home of a citizen of our republic and you have threatened him and his lawyer and two Chicago police officers with a loaded weapon. Don't make matters worse for yourself. Give that weapon to Officer Clyde."

Confused and threatened, he hesitated. A dumb man with a gun in his hand is very dangerous. The two Chicago cops, hands on their own weapons, watched him intently with narrow, hard eyes.

"Give him the gun, asshole," Martha Regan snapped. "You could kill someone with that."

Mike and the two cops were tense, indeed frightened. I was too dumb and too inexperienced to be scared. I was, indeed, having the time of my life.

McAuliffe's twitching eyes flickered around the room.

"Give the gun to Officer Clyde, son," Mike begged gently.

The policewoman held out her hand.

We stood there in a frozen tableau at the entrance to my apartment. My grandfather clock ticked away the anxious seconds. Everyone was holding their breath.

Finally, Special Agent McAuliffe folded his hand. He handed the weapon, muzzle pointing outward, to Officer Clyde. Gingerly she shifted the grip into her hand.

"Nine-millimeter Beretta, sir. Safety on."

"Cuff him, take him in and book him," Mike ordered. Disorderly conduct and resisting arrest."

"The young woman?" Officer Clyde asked.

Mike raised an eyebrow at me.

I shook my head in the negative.

Mike tilted his head in agreement.

"I don't think that's necessary, Officer. Perhaps you could, however, escort Special Agent Regan around the apartment to search for Ms. McGrail, as Mr. Coyne invited Special Agent McAuliffe to do some moments ago."

"Yes, sir," the cop said.

"That won't be necessary," Special Agent Regan said.

"Young woman, believe me, it is necessary."

The child grinned. "Yes sir, I take your point."

The two of them returned after a brief interlude.

"No young woman, Special Agent?"

"No, sir."

"Officer Clyde?"

"No, sir."

"Good, then we can safely say that Ms. McGrail's good name was falsely impugned?"

Both women nodded solemnly.

"Special Agent Regan," I asked, "would you deliver a direct quote from me to Acting Special Agent-in-Charge Dever?"

"Certainly, sir," she said, barely suppressing an outrageous grin.

"Tell him the next time he wants to play Heinrich Himmler with me he should not send a boy to do a man's job."

"Yes, sir," she said, now having regained control of her face. ". . . Who was Heinrich Himmler?"

"The head of the Gestapo."

The four law-enforcement officers left. Mike and I stood at the doorway, satisfied with ourselves.

"She won't have a chance to talk to Dever. He'll be out of here on the first plane in the morning . . ." Mike said. "Nice going, Dermot, you're getting good at this thing. This nutty raid will be a major plus for your side."

"They are incredibly sloppy over there."

"That's what comes with playing this new kind of game. Kids that age should be out hunting down gang leaders and drug lords. They'd learn a lot quickly. But the Bureau prefers stinging celebrities."

"I'm not a celebrity."

"Quade and Dever think so . . . You should call your sister and have her call your sister-in-law Traci. You want to put your side's spin on this news."

"Right away . . . Thanks much, Mike. I hope I didn't interrupt anything."

"Nothing," he said with a small smile, "that can't be renewed."

As I reached for the phone to call Cindy, it rang and almost jumped into my hands.

Before I could announce my presence, herself weighed in.

"Dermot, what the hell is happening over there?"

$$-15-$$

COPS ARREST FBI AGENTS

(City News Bureau)

Police from the Chicago Avenue Station arrested two FBI agents early this morning at the John Hancock Center apartment of commodity broker and novelist Dermot Coyne. Special Agent David McAuliffe was charged with disorderly conduct and resisting arrest. Special Agent Martha Regan was released without charge. According to Watch Commander Arthur Washington, the two Federal officers attempted to force their way into Coyne's apartment without either an arrest warrant or a search warrant. Coyne has been mentioned as a possible target in an ongoing investigation of commodity trading at the Chicago exchanges.

RADIO NEWS

There has been a major shakeup at the Chicago Office of the FBI. A spokeswoman said this morning that Special Agent David McAuliffe has been placed on administrative leave with pay pending the resolution of charges against him filed by Chicago police. She declined to confirm reports that Deputy Special Agent-in-Charge Joseph R. Dever has been reassigned to the Bureau's Washington Headquarters.

NOON TV NEWS

Anchor: A conflict has arisen between Chicago police and the FBI. Raisa Jefferson has the story at the Dirksen Federal Building.

RJ: FBI officials remain silent, DeeDee, on the case of Special Agent David McAuliffe, who was arrested last night by Chicago police after neighbors summoned them because of noise at the apartment of Chicago novelist Dermot Coyne. The police charged McAuliffe with disorderly conduct and resisting arrest. Apparently McAuliffe and Agent Martha Regan attempted to force their way into Coyne's apartment without warrants. Sources here at the Dirksen Building tell Channel 6 that McAuliffe and Regan had not been authorized to search Coyne's apartment. Cynthia Hurley, Coyne's attorney, said that Coyne would prosecute McAuliffe to the fullest extent of the law.

CH: These two agents, acting on explicit instruction of Joseph R. Dever, Deputy Special Agent-in-Charge, attempted to raid my client's apartment last night. During this Gestapo-like raid, Mr. McAuliffe drew his revolver and threatened my client, putting his life at risk as well as the lives of one of his neighbors and two Chicago police officers. We intend to bring Mr. McAuliffe to trial and to file charges against Mr. Dever. I am also seeking a restraining order against the United States Attorney and the Federal Bureau of Investigation to prevent them from further harassing my client.

RJ: Isn't your client guilty of fraud in the commodities market?

CH: He hasn't even been charged. But the way the federal prosecutor in this city seems to operate is that you are convicted by news leak and remain guilty until you're proven innocent, even if you are never indicted.

RJ: Sources here at the Dirksen Building tell Channel 6 that Coyne has been implicated in the current FBI sting, Operation Full Platter.

4:30 TELEVISION (LIVE)

(Dermot Coyne exits from the Hancock Building. He wears light blue slacks, dark blue jacket and appears calm, cool, and charming. A swarm of vultures with microphones in their hands surround them. Coyne seems astonished by their interest.)

First Vulture: Dermot, are you going to be indicted in the Full Platter sting?

Second Vulture: Was your fiancée in the apartment when the FBI raided it?

Third Vulture: Do you really expect the courts to convict the agents who raided your apartment?

Fourth Vulture: Are you going to cancel your wedding?

Dermot (most engaging smile): Give me a chance to respond. (Vultures calm down.)

Dermot: I don't know whether I'm going to be indicted or not. I have never discussed my trading practices with Jared Kennedy, who is their informant. If I am indicted, we will charge the Office of the United States Attorney with malicious prosescution and probably criminal fraud. My fiancée sleeps at her own home, not at my apartment, and we will continue this practice till we are married. I fully expect Agent McAuliffe to plead guilty to the charges against him. Finally, even if I wanted to delay our wedding, which I do not, my young woman would not tolerate it. Now, if you'll excuse me. . . ."

(Dermot forces his way through vultures and enters cab.)

Third Vulture: (jamming mike through open window of cab): Are your publishers disturbed by the bad publicity this scandal is causing?

Dermot: On the contrary they are delighted, so long as the title of the book is mentioned: *Irish Love!*

(Cab pulls away.)

10:00 TV NEWS

Anchor: Channel 3 has obtained excerpts from a highly incriminating conversation between novelist and commodity trader Dermot Coyne and an undercover agent of the Federal Bureau of Investigation. Our investigative reporter, Rick Reams, has the full story.

RR: (an overweight man with an unconvincing toupee and a voice which conveys perpetual shock at the criminal behavior of Chicagoans): Jenny, last night, controversial Chicago novelist Dermot Coyne arranged for the arrest of two FBI agents. Tonight Coyne himself stands charged with fraud in his commodity-trading practices before he retired at the age of twenty-four to write steamy romances. In a conversation with an FBI informant who is part of Operation Full Platter, Coyne admitted that his retirement was made possible by cheating his customers on the floor of the Chicago Board of Trade. Channel 3 has obtained excerpts of that conversation.

(Typed transcripts appear on the screen. RR reads from them.)

Agent: You sure were lucky when you made all that money.

Coyne: Luck had nothing to do with it. I bought shares on a client's account. Then the market suddenly collapsed. I knew it would bound back and shoot up again on Monday morning and the client would make millions. So I switched the purchase to my own account and told the client that it had been too late to make the purchase. First thing Monday I made enough to keep me in drinks and women for the rest of my life.

Agent: You (blanked) your client then?

Coyne: You bet I did, inside and out, backwards and forwards, real good. And he was too dumb to know what was going on.

RR: So it does not look good for Dermot Coyne tonight. It looks much better for the FBI agent whose arrest Coyne caused last night. Jennifer?

Anchor: Rick, is there any comment from Coyne or his lawyers about this development?

RR: (voice loaded with skepticism) His lawyer, who is also his *sister,* says that the conversation never occurred.

—16—

"I'VE BEEN over it before a thousand times," I pleaded with Cindy. "It sounds worse every time I tell it."

"I want to hear it once more," she insisted, jabbing her finger at me like a homeroom teacher who had caught me sleeping.

Cindy always jabbed her finger at me.

Cindy was an Assistant States Attorney for Rich Daley and Cecil Partee when the Cook County Prosecutor's Office was nonpolitical. After she was eased out because she was, like all our family, a fanatical Democrat, she joined the elite law firm of Winthrop, McClaren, Donovan, and Epstein and turned to estate law so that she could telecommute and spend more time with the kids. She misses the courtroom, however, and would doubtless revel in the confrontations that my case was likely to produce.

Moreover as the oldest child and a girl at that, she had assumed at the age of fourteen responsibility for the oversize, clumsy, but pleasant boy child that Mom had brought home from the hospital. Ever since then she has played the role of a surrogate mother, a role she now shared as a coconspirator with me young woman.

"OK, if you insist . . . The last time the stock market decided to take a plunge, there I was standing in the S and P pit bemused and confused. Some of my friends were making tons of money and some of them were losing tons of money and I wasn't doing anything, because I had no idea what was happening. On Friday the market started to rally and everyone was buying like mad, hoping to ride up the index as it soared. One of my few clients called in a buy order—three hundred contracts . . .' "

"He thought the rally would last so he was going long?"

"I did two things wrong. I was also going to buy a little bit on my own as well as buy on his account. My head was pounding as it usually was when the pit was hopping and my stomach churning somehow I got confused and sold three hundred cars . . . and somehow three hundred more on my own account."

"Went short instead of long? And on your own account, too? Not very swift, Dermot."

She jabbed her finger again. She *always* said that when I told the story of how I became a millionaire.

"That's what I thought on Saturday morning when I went down to the Exchange to catch up on paperwork. I was down six hundred cars, the three hundred he wanted me to buy and the three hundred I had sold on my own. Millions of dollars that I didn't have."

"Why did you do that?"

"Sell on my own? . . . I didn't realize what I was doing. I must have given the wrong signal."

She sighed impatiently.

All right, it was a dumb thing to do. I didn't belong there. I shivered at the recollection. It was a terrible weekend, saved only by the Bear victory that Sunday afternoon.

"So what happened then?"

"So I went in on Monday morning, expecting the worst. I'd try to buy immediately before the market went up any more."

"And it fell?" She started to walk again, beginning to understand my story.

"Like a rock. I watched it go down all day. I bought just before the closing bell."

"And you made a fortune!"

"Just a little over three million dollars, not that I deserved any of it. I had made two dumb mistakes and was very lucky."

"So then what did you do?"

"I sold my seat, returned the money and the capital to my father, paid my income tax, invested everything else in tax-exempt municipals and a conservative commodity account and retired."

She tapped her pen on the yellow, legal-sized notepad without which lawyers cannot think.

"Fortunately for us, the records from your clearing house confirm

what you did. So does your client, who rejoices in your success—
though I don't think he would have ever given you another order
if you'd stayed in the business. The CFTC went after you like our
golden retriever after a stick and found nothing wrong, though they
thought you were dumb, too. The IRS wrung you out and ended
up paying us money."

"So why are we worried?"

"We are worried because you don't look or talk that dumb. People
hear the story and they don't believe it."

"Should I try to act dumb?"

She waved that away. "It would only make matters worse."

"Oh."

"Dale can get an indictment by confusing the grand jury, which
probably doesn't like traders anyway. I don't see how she thinks
she can win a trial. Probably figures you'll plead."

"Why would I do that?"

"To save money, to avoid a couple of years of litigation, to get
on with your life . . . Same reason Danny pled when his attorneys
had used up all his money."

"She can drag it out that long?"

"Maybe not. Your little game last night has forced them to react.
You'll probably be dragged before the grand jury next week and
indicted before the week is out. We'll ask for a dismissal of the
charges. They're so absurd that if we get the right judge, they'll be
thrown out."

"And if we don't?"

She shrugged. "Then we'll do battle."

"We won't plead?"

"No way. Not even if she doesn't want you to do time. That's
improbable. Dale always wants her victims to do time."

"That isn't fair!" I protested.

"Who ever said fair, Dermot? They can indict anyone they want
and force the person to choose between bankruptcy and jail. Of
course it's not fair, but it's the way justice works in this land of the
free and home of the brave."

"She'll be using my papers to hunt for confirmation of what I
am supposed to have told Jarry?"

"Right . . . His testimony and his tape are her only solid weapons."

"But I never had that conversation!"

"I know that, Dermot. And that's our ace in the hole. They're going to have to give us the tape at some point. We'll do a voice analysis and go in for a motion to dismiss. If it's not granted—and only a truly dumb judge could turn us down—we'll go up to the Seventh Circuit and be home free."

"So we have to get the tape?"

"And they'll stall before they turn it over to us."

"Why, Cindy? Because they know it's fake?"

"They don't know it's fake, Dermot. They believe Jarry, though they should have been much more careful. No, they'll stall because they're mean."

"You don't want me to try to act dumb? As dumb as I really was?"

"Nope! It wouldn't work. Besides, you're not dumb. You just didn't belong on the trading floor . . . How's herself holding up?"

"Grace O'Malley? She's fine. Spoiling for an alley fight with someone. Will not discuss postponing the wedding."

" 'Course not . . . You called her first thing this morning, didn't you? To tell her about what happened?"

"She phoned me just after the cops dragged those two agents over to Chicago Avenue. Wanted to know what was going on."

"She *knew*?" Cindy asked with a shiver.

"Naturally she knew. She's fey."

"Can she put hexes on people? Maybe she could . . . No, that wouldn't be ethical."

"She pronounced a solemn curse on her brother last Sunday . . ."

"That jerk."

"Only she didn't mean it, so it doesn't count. It scared the hell out of him. I'm not sure she can do the real thing. Or even would if she could."

"But if she could scare an Assistant United States Attorney . . . She does look a little like a Druid witch, doesn't she, Dermot? Gorgeous and just a little dangerous?"

"Druid goddess!"

"Objection sustained . . . Tell her not to worry about any of this. We're going to win."

She rose from her chair, dismissing her charming but helpless little brother.

I stood up, too.

"She doesn't doubt it for a moment."

"Oh, one more thing, Derm," she said as I was about to leave the office. "I almost forgot it. I assume they will leak some of the text of Jarry's wire to the media. I further assume that they will use it without due diligence to determine its authenticity. That's patently actionable."

Cindy was smiling. Dangerously. Nuala Anne wasn't the only dangerous woman in the crowd that was circling the wagons around poor Dermot.

"Which means?"

"Which means, I'm already drafting our complaint. Tomorrow afternoon I'll go into Cook County Court and file six defamation suits—against the four TV channels and the two papers!"

Cindy looked liked she'd died and gone to heaven.

"That will give everyone something to talk about, won't it?"

"It sure will." She laughed happily.

"I suppose you'll be coordinating it all with Traci."

Traci was our sister-in-law and the senior partner of a PR firm.

"Naturally."

"Remind her that the novel is called *Irish Love* and that it is available at all bookstores."

"I'll tell her to emphasize the line that all Irish men are closet lovers."

"You do that."

I caught up with herself at the Abbey that evening. She was wearing jeans and a white knit top which reminded me of the white sweatshirt at O'Neill's the night I had first encountered her, the night we both had fallen incurably and permanently in love. She embraced me with her radiant smile as I drifted in.

She was, it seemed, singing nothing but lullabies that night. Mostly in Irish, some translated into English—her own translations naturally.

"Now, if you don't mind, I'm going to sing a sexy lullaby. It pretends to be for a boy baby, but if you knew the Irish implications, the lad is a baby only in the sense that all men are babies."

Laughter.

"Once you know that, then all the lyrics make sense. Tradition has it that a bride sings it to her husband on their wedding night. I won't be translating this one. Wouldn't the police close us down if I did?"

She looked straight at me as she sang it. Or I thought she did. No one in the pub turned to look at me, so maybe I was fantasizing.

I had no doubt, however, that I would hear it on our first night together in our house on Southport.

"Did you like me sexy lullaby?" she asked as I drove her home. A mixture of light rain and drizzle was falling. I turned on the windshield wipers. Their breathless sighs seemed very Irish.

"I thought you could translate it. You Irish speakers are pretty indirect about everything. I bet there isn't a single dirty word in the whole song."

"Go long wid ya, Dermot Michael. We Irish speakers can write erotic poems without using dirty language. And can't we be very direct even when we're indirect?"

Her hand captured my knee. I tried to concentrate on my driving.

"I've noticed that . . . I want to hear a translation, just the same."

"Well," she said, pretending to ponder the implication of that. "Won't I just think about doing that?"

"I suspect I may hear it on my wedding night?"

"Och, sure, won't you be so destroyed altogether by the time I get around to singing it that you wouldn't understand it in English or Irish?"

"And wouldn't I like to hear a song when I'm taking off your clothes and sort of teasing your breasts?"

She gasped at the thought.

"Dermot, me darlin' man, I won't be able to sing then, not at all, at all!"

"We'll see."

She hugged me fiercely, making my driving task all the more difficult.

"Shall we stop at our own pub?" I asked.

"Don't I have to hear all the exciting things which happened today?"

"I'm not sure how exciting they are."

We found a parking place on Clybourn and ducked into the pub under an umbrella I kept in the car for "soft" nights like this one— an Irish rain is "soft" if there's no hail.

"A jar of the regular for me, Sonia," Nuala began, "and a glass of Bailey's on ice for your man."

"You were great on TV tonight, Mr. Coyne. Really told those bitches off."

"They have to earn their living like the rest of us, Sonia," I said. "And I'm still Dermot."

"And we will continue this practice till we are married!" Sonia quoted me. "Good on you, Dermot."

Nuala sniffed. "He'd better say that."

After our drinks were served, she said softly. "So tell me all about it, Dermot Michael, all about it."

I went through the news of the day, from the ringing house phone to the ten o'clock news with quotes from the alleged interview. She listened quietly, nodding sympathetically.

"So tomorrow Cindy files her defamation suits and we regain the lead in the media war?"

"I guess so."

"We'll win, Dermot. You know we will."

"I guess we will. It couldn't come at a worse time."

"We'll both survive, me darlin' man, and so will our love."

Grace O'Malley had become St. Brigid, everyone's mother.

"Wait till your brother gets wind of this mess."

"Och, doesn't the friggin' eejit know about it already? Wasn't he on the phone just before I went over to the Abbey telling me that I would be a family disgrace if I married a convicted criminal."

"And you said?"

"Sure, Dermot, wouldn't you have been proud of me? Didn't I say, real quiet and controlled like, that you hadn't even been indicted and that if you were you wouldn't be convicted and that I didn't care whether the family thought I was a disgrace or not?"

"Is that what you said?"

"I answer with the questions," she said with her best leprechaun grin. "You don't!"

"And then what did your man do?"

"Didn't he huff and puff and didn't I tell him that I had to go over to the Abbey and sing and hang up on him very gentle like?"

"Fair play to you Nuala Anne . . . will your record, after Nuala Anne Goes to Church, be Nuala Anne Sings Lullabies?"

"Wouldn't that depend now on whether your singer has a little Nell Pat in her arms to sing to?"

"Will it be a girl?"

"Sure it will . . . And we will name her Mary Anne after your grandma, won't we Dermot?" Her hand touched mine pleadingly. "Won't we?"

"Och, woman, would we have any choice?"

She had predicted the gender of my sister-in-law's child (yet to be born) before the child's mother knew she was pregnant. Why not the gender of a child yet to be conceived?

"Did you hear anything from anyone about Jimmy Sullivan today?" she asked, still holding my hand.

"I had a call from my friend Sean—who by the way has found a date to bring to the wedding, a colleague of yours who called him about going to the wedding together."

"Sure, wait till your man gets a look at her. She's totally gorgeous. If he's a nice fella like you say, she'll go after him, because she wants to get married the worst way."

"You're behind this?"

"Who else? Now what did he say about our puzzle?"

"He said that there was another disagreement between Sweet Rolls and Scarface that hadn't made most of the articles. Capone approved plans for his thugs to take control of unions. Sullivan resisted. He protected workingmen, especially if they were Irish, from crooked leaders and mob infiltration."

"Just like he protected your grand da."

"The interesting point is that long after Sullivan had died or vanished or whatever, the Outfit left those unions alone."

Nuala frowned, as if her psyche was on overload.

"It makes sense, Dermot Michael, but it doesn't make sense at all, at all. There's a big piece of the story missing."

"There is indeed . . . So what do we do?"

"We wait."

"No hints, no voices, no hunches?"

"None at all, at all . . . We should enjoy the weekend and ignore the odd way people look at us."

There would be plenty of that. Tomorrow night (Friday) there would be a farewell party for herself at Arthur's at which she would distribute the first copies of her CD. Technically she would be going on a leave, but her bosses were pretty sure that they were losing a high-quality accountant. So much did they like her that they didn't want to cut the tie completely.

The next day we would venture to South Bend, Indiana, to witness the defense of the Catholic faith by the Fighting Black Baptists of Notre Dame against the perfidious Longhorns of Texas. On Sunday Nuala would be treated to her first American bridal shower.

(I had rejected all plans for a bachelor party. I considered such events to be vulgar and disgusting, as did my brothers . . . with the possible exception of Prester George, who defended their male-bonding function mostly to make trouble.)

Folks would indeed stare at us through these celebrations and perhaps give us their sympathy much as they would at a wake. We would dismiss the investigation as absurd and repeat constantly the mantra that Cindy had endorsed:

"I never participated in such a conversation."

We'd show them!

We'd show Dale Quade that she was destined for the same trash can as her friend Joe Dever.

Nuala and I held hands and sipped our drinks silently, confident now of our own strength.

Well, I was confident of her own quiet strength. Nuala had put on the persona of the "strong woman" of the Book of Wisdom in the Bible and found that it fit.

"How did you know that something was going down at my apartment last night?" I asked her.

She shrugged as if that were an irrelevant question.

"Why wouldn't I know?"

"At the risk of sounding like a rigid American empiricist, Nuala Anne, you weren't there and I hadn't called you, though I would have if you'd given me a chance."

"Sure, Dermot, I just knew. That's all."

"You woke up knowing that something was wrong with me."

"Not to say wrong exactly." She chose her words carefully. "I knew you were all right but that something was happening."

"You were worried?"

"Not to say worried exactly," she repeated herself. "When you wake up in the middle of the night with one of them things, it takes you a while to sort them out. So I didn't bother to sort it out. I just called you on the phone."

"I'll probably never figure it out, not that I have."

"I can't figure it out either, me darlin' man. Mind you, I've never tried. These things have happened to me all me life and they seem perfectly normal. Didn't I know that something special was going to happen to me when I woke up in the morning the day you walked into O'Neill's pub?"

"I almost didn't go in that night."

"Ah, but Dermot Michael, the point is that you did!"

Point was pronounced "pint," a custom which might have caused some confusion if she had said, for example, "The point is that I want another pint of Guinness."

"You see, Dermot," she continued, "in Ireland, especially in the West, we see halos around every bird and flower."

"Really!"

"Not literally, except sometimes a little bit. I mean I see faint halos occasionally. Me ma sees them more often but they're nothing big."

You see auras around people and it's nothing big. Right? Right!

"What color is mine?"

"Oh, Dermot, it's the most lovely color of blue . . . But that's not what I meant."

"What did you mean?"

"One of our poets says that she sees the mountain behind the mountain . . . That's no help at all, at all, is it now?"

"I'm listening."

"Well"—she leaned forward as if she were imparting a big secret—"we see the sky and the ocean and the mountains and the birds and the rivers and the flowers and we also see something behind them that is like them only different . . . "

"Platonic cave?"

"Shite, Dermot Michael, Platonists are the last thing we Irish speakers are. When I say that we see the mountain behind the mountain, don't I mean that we see a reality behind the reality, a beauty behind the beauty, but what we see is every bit as concrete and solid as the mountain itself."

"Irish mysticism is nature mysticism?"

"Och, Dermot Michael, isn't that what the textbooks say? And they're not wrong, exactly but they're not right either. Didn't we know that the world was sacred long before your Christian missionaries showed up? Sure, didn't we let them in only because they seemed to understand that, too?"

"Uh-huh.

"So God is in all the creatures of nature?" I said, trying my best to understand.

"I'm no mystic, Derm, I'm just one of the remnants of the old Irish-speaking world. We knew the Holy was everywhere, only we didn't call it the 'Holy' like your man did and we didn't call it God either, though that's not a bad name."

"I see."

Which was total untruth.

Tears formed in her eyes as she tried desperately to explain to me.

"When I was growing up, I loved the flowers and the animals and the sea and the mountains. When I would look at them, I'd see the tiny edge of light at the end of them and know that's where the angels were. Sometimes I'd slip into the light and see things the way they saw them, if you take my meaning, Dermot Michael?"

"Light," I said solemnly.

"Now you have it," she said enthusiastically. "Isn't it wonderful altogether?"

"'Tis indeed."

I didn't really have it, of course. But, as she would have said herself, under other circumstances, I half had it.

"The light faded away when I went to Dublin, mostly because I didn't want to see it. Somehow it didn't seem right to see it if one was a university girl. Though your man saw it, didn't he?"

"Me man?"

"Him with the wife," she said with a laugh.

James Joyce.

"And your man with the prize, doesn't he see it, out of the corner of his eye, like?"

Seamus Heaney.

"You don't see the light in Chicago?"

"Och, Dermot Michael, how can you miss the point of what I've been trying to say? Isn't the light everywhere in this city? In the lake and the skyline and the River and Southport Avenue and"— she squeezed my hand—"wherever you are!"

Aha.

"I do understand, Nuala Anne," I said slowly.

"Sure, isn't the whole problem your friggin' principle of contradiction!"

"'Tis," I said with a sigh.

"So naturally I know when you're in trouble. I kind of peek into the light and see you, in a manner of speaking. Not all the time, but sometimes, if you take my meaning."

"I do, Nuala, kind of. I hope that's enough."

She beamed happily.

"Isn't that more than enough . . . Sonia, I'll be needing another small jar, because I'm so nervous about sleeping with this eejit for the rest of me life. I suppose he can have another drop of Bailey's for him, but, mind you, only a drop."

Later I walked with her to her house, oops, our house, on the sacred way called Southport Avenue. We kissed tenderly and affectionately. I walked back to my car and pondered the whole conversation.

YOU DIDN'T UNDERSTAND ONE WORD, the Adversary told me. THE WOMAN IS AROUND THE BEND ALTOGETHER, OFF THE WALL, OVER THE TOP.

"She's an accountant and a singer and a very bright young woman. It's not her fault she's from the Gaeltacht."

TOTALLY CRAZY . . . THE LIGHT AT THE END OF THINGS WHERE THE ANGELS ARE. ON SOUTHPORT? YOU GOTTA BE KIDDING!

"Maybe it's here, but I don't see it."

SOUTHPORT BEHIND SOUTHPORT BEHIND SOUTHPORT, he sneered. TOO MUCH CELTIC TWILIGHT. NOW YOU'RE STUCK WITH HER.

"It was your idea," I told him. "And I'm lucky."

THE FRIGGIN' PRINCIPLE OF CONTRADICTION! he crowed.

I told him to go away and turned on the ignition.

I had read all this stuff before I met Nuala. It sounded fine, but I never believed that anyone that I was likely to meet was a throwback to Celtic antiquity. There were, I realized, no beautiful women walking out of the twilight to weave their spells and enchant me.

Now it turned out that I was about to marry one such. One who had weaved a spell around me and had enchanted me.

One who, in the finest traditions of down-to-earth Irish mysticism, had fabulous taste in clothes, a quick, practical mind, and loved my kisses and caresses and delighted in sharing herself with me.

Could she, as Cindy wondered, also whip up some minor curses to rout our enemies?

— 17 —

 ON FRIDAY, while I was wrapping the CDs we intended to give away at the wedding dinner, a fierce rain beat against the windows and the Hancock Center creaked and groaned in the wind, Cindy phoned me.

"Good news, Dermot."

"I need some of that."

"She's issued a subpoena for you to appear before the grand jury on next Monday."

"Monday!"

"Right! . . . Isn't that wonderful!"

"Explain to me why it's wonderful, sis."

"It means that they didn't have time to go through your papers. She hopes to do that after she gets her indictment. All she has is Jarry's tape."

"So?"

"Don't you see? She's panicked. The little show at your apartment the other night, the removal of her buddy Joe Dever, her stupid leaking of the interview and my reaction with the suits against all the media—they've scared the hell out of her. She's trying to regain her balance. Our job is to keep her off-balance."

"So what do we do next?"

"You knock the grand jury dead. She'll have to push to get an indictment. That won't look good when a judge asks to see the record of the grand jury proceedings. And she'll know it. She's living on the wire. Maybe we can make her fall off it."

"I see."

I understood Cindy's tactics about as well as I understood Nuala's description of light and angels and the mountain behind the mountain.

"We've already got the media lawyers terrified. Two of them called to ask, very nervously, whether this was a real suit or merely a media counterploy."

"And you said?"

"I told them that they should find out how due was the diligence with which their editors and reporters checked the authenticity of the tape. That petrified them. It will also plant some doubts in the minds of the businessmen who own the papers and the TV stations. They'll start pushing for documentation. Dale will find out and really go over the top."

"Great," I said with as much enthusiasm as I could muster.

I was caught in the crossfire between two Irish women warriors. One of whom was on the edge and the other of whom was eager to push her over.

Great, indeed.

I continued my mindless task of slipping the discs into their jewel boxes and then into the white wrappings which had been prepared for them. Good work for the groom as the wedding closed in. While I worked, I thought about Nuala. Naturally.

However, I was not indulging in erotic fantasies. Well, only some of the time. Mostly, I was thinking about our conversation the night before. The light where the angels are! The mountain behind the mountain!

Yeah.

The Adversary did not try to argue with me. I think he was as confused as I was.

How often did she see a halo around me? When did I find my way into the edge of light where the angels are? Would there be angels in our bedroom on the wedding night?

That might not be a bad idea. I might need their help.

Men angels or women angels?

Dumb question.

Women angels, of course.

I knew she was different when I fell in love with her. I was certainly not about to fall out of love with her now. Not that I could have even if I wanted to. I had not realized how different she really was.

I didn't realize that troops of the little folk followed her around every day.

Well, she hadn't said that they did, but I was willing to bet on it.

I hardly noticed the phone when it rang and picked it up automatically, as I peered into the rain to see if the little folk were lurking outside my window. I was Irish, too, wasn't I? Couldn't I see the rainstorm beyond the rain?

"Hello," I said glumly.

"'Tis yourself?"

"'Tis."

"It doesn't sound like you, does it now?"

"Maybe it isn't me."

"Go long wid ya."

"I think the little folk are outside my window. They're hiding in the rain and spying on me."

She laughed joyously.

"Och, Dermot me darlin', aren't you the funny man?"

"I am."

"The *shee* didn't come to Chicago. Poor little things, isn't life hard enough for them in Ireland?"

Shee was another name for the Irish fairie, the little people, the gentry, or often simply "they."

"Couldn't they survive here?"

"They barely survive in Ireland," she said briskly. "How are you keeping today?"

"I'm in great form," I replied with the proper answer to that question.

"Are you sure now?"

"I am."

"I hope I didn't confuse you too much with all me West of Ireland blather?"

"It was fascinating, Nuala Anne. I can't claim that I completely understood it all."

"Ah, well, won't that take time? At least you didn't have me arrested as a flaming eejit."

"I don't think you're an eejit, Nuala me, ah, my love."

"Wasn't herself grand on the telly?"

"Herself?"

"Your sis. When she filed her complaints against all them bad fellas in the media."

"I'm afraid I didn't watch it today."

"She was brilliant. They try to make fun of her but she has them on the run . . . You remember what you're supposed to say?"

"Yes, ma'am. I am supposed to say that I never participated in such a conversation."

"And what will you say when them bitches corner you at the door of your building and ask you what you're going to do with the twenty-five million that Cindy wants from them?"

"Uh . . ."

I was still lingering in the Celtic twilight and not thinking about unimportant things.

"You'd better have an answer, Dermot Michael."

"I'm going to build myself a castle in the West of Ireland."

"You'll say no such thing!"

"They'll settle for a lot less than twenty-five million."

"That's not a good answer."

My intellect, which had become a vestigial organ lately because of my fascination with my bride-to-be, kicked in.

"I'll give it all to the schools I attended—St. Luke, Fenwick, Notre Dame, and Marquette?"

"Super!"

I was glad I had passed the test.

"You won't forget about the party down here, will you now?"

"Not a chance."

"See you then, me darlin' man."

I neglected to tell her that I loved her.

Dummy.

You aren't going to be much of a husband, the Adversary had crept in.

"Get out of here," I told him.

The last call before I left for Arthur Andersen was from a man who had been a classmate at Fenwick, the scion of a large cleaning and drying firm.

"Hey, Dermot," he began enthusiastically, "it's Geno."

Just like we talked on the phone every day.

"Hey, Geno. Nice to hear from you."

"Say, congratulations on your upcoming marriage. Is she is as beautiful as that picture in the *Trib*?"

"More beautiful."

"You always were a lucky guy!"

That wasn't the way I remembered it.

Long pause.

"You know, Dermot, there's this individual who's a friend of a friend of ours. He'd like to talk to you. It's no big deal. I swear it isn't. Just a very brief conversation. Something like that."

"Yeah?"

"Like, are you gonna be around tomorrow?"

"I'm taking my fiancée to the Notre Dame game."

"Hey, great! . . . What about Sunday, like maybe Sunday morning, something like that?"

"We go to the ten o'clock Mass at Old St. Patrick's."

"It'll only take a couple of minutes. This individual wants to know whether you would be willing to talk to another individual."

Friend of some friends. "Individual" representing another "individual?" Four layers. And the Irish are supposed to be indirect.

"He's a good friend, Geno?" I asked, deciding that there was no point in not playing the game. They didn't drag you into cars and blindfold you anymore.

"He's a real good friend of some real good friends. It's no big deal, Dermot, I guarantee you that."

That guarantee and a buck and a half would get me a ride on Rich Daley's subway.

"Maybe I could talk to him about 8:30, say in the lobby of my apartment building?"

"Yeah. Maybe you could meet him outside. Take a little walk around the block. Something like that. He'll know you."

"Fine, Geno. I'll be looking forward to it. Give my best to your family."

"Yeah. And you do to yours. Lots of luck with the wedding."

"Thanks, Geno. She'll need it more than I do."

Why the hell did I say that?

The dry-cleaning firm was "legit," though it had not always been "legit." Geno's family was "legit" too. More or less.

We weren't about to be taken for a ride. Just the same, I'd mention the conversation to Prester George.

Just in case we disappeared.

Or something like that.

There were three more calls before I left for the party at the Italian Village.

The first was from the agent in charge of Nuala's recording. It was selling very well, and the producers were already making a second pressing. Would she be interested in another album after our honeymoon? I admitted that she might and I would ask her to call him.

The second was from my editor. There were two good prepublication reviews, though one thought that I might not have given enough attention to Irish Puritanism. As if Cromwell's Puritans had not committed genocide in Ireland. The publicity was helping sales. We were already on a couple of best-seller lists.

Normally these two pieces of good news would have made me very happy. But I was back in my self-pitying modality and I didn't care about success.

Then it occurred to me that the experience of being hounded by a Federal prosecutor would make a very good story. I'd better start taking notes.

I revived enough of my energy to call Nuala and tell her about the good news.

"Grand! Super! Brilliant!" she bellowed. "That'll show all of them!"

I agreed, though I wasn't sure who "all of them" were.

The third call was from me friend Annie, me future mother-in-law. She would make my future wife look transparent.

"How you keeping, Annie?"

"Sure, aren't we both in rare form. And yourself now, Dermot love?"

"Just brilliant, Annie. My novel and herself's album are on their way to being big successes. So we'll start off our marriage with even more confidence about the future."

Having said it aloud, I began to be more confident.

"Isn't that grand now? Sure, are there two young people in all the world who deserve it more?"

"We'll be looking forward to seeing you next week, Annie. I think you'll love Chicago."

"Won't we now? Though I'm not so sure I'll be liking that airplane thing."

"Five minutes into the air and you'll be loving it."

"That's what himself says, as if he's ever spent more than a day or two outside of Galway."

"You should spend some time touring this country of ours."

"Well, haven't we thought of that and ourselves not getting any younger? So doesn't your man say that we should spend a month in America? And, like I had as little sense as he, don't I agree?"

"Wonderful! I'm glad to hear it."

"It's hard arguing with herself, isn't it now?"

"Tell me about it!"

Nuala was certainly paying for it. Good for her. I'd praise her tonight and she'd dismiss it as being unimportant, but would nonetheless be pleased.

"Well, just so long as nothing interferes with your happiness. Don't I always say that the main thing about a wedding is the happiness of the bride and groom?"

"And how right you are. Don't worry, Annie, nothing will interfere with our happiness that day. No one will take it away from us."

"Doesn't it make me terrible happy to hear you say that? . . . Sure, don't I cry every time I think of you two?"

"My mother does, too."

She had asked her question and I had given my answer.

She adjured me to hug "the daughter" for her because "Sure, I don't dare call her at work."

I agreed to do so.

I wondered after I had hung up how she and himself would feel when they arrived in Chicago in the midst of the media coverage of an indictment, especially with Larry moaning about family disgrace.

My fists tightened. I still wanted to slug Larry.

Despite their roundabout rhetoric, Annie and Gerry were tough people. They had to be to wrest a living from their little patch of ground in the desolate regions of Connemara. They could take whatever would happen. It was a shame that they had to.

The vultures were waiting for me outside the lobby of the Hancock Center.

"Why are you suing the Chicago media, Dermot?"

"Because they defamed me."

"How did they do that?"

"By attributing to me a conversation which never occurred."

"Are you saying that the FBI is lying about you?"

"No. I am merely saying that the conversation never happened."

"You don't expect to win the suit, do you?"

Broad grin from the charming ex-linebacker. "Not a doubt about it . . . You guys should check your sources with due diligence."

"If you win, what will you do with all the money?"

"Donate it to Catholic schools, especially the ones I attended—St. Luke Grammar School, Fenwick High School, and Notre Dame and Marquette Universities."

"Will they take tainted money?"

I slipped into the taxi which my friend Mr. Woods had parked at the door.

"If the money is tainted, it won't be by me."

You're beginning to enjoy this, the Adversary warned me. Start writing in your notebook.

"I didn't bring my notebook."

Sure you did. I reminded you.

It was indeed in my jacket pocket.

He must be the Adversary behind the Adversary. Or the one in the edge of light. The Adversary with a halo.

— 18 —

EDITORIAL

FREEDOM OF THE PRESS UNDER ASSAULT

A free society requires a free press. When journalists are inhibited from reporting on cases of wanton corruption, the free press is shackled. When reckless defamation suits are filed to protect those accused of crime, freedom of the press is suppressed. Lawyers, one supposes, will do whatever is necessary to protect their clients, but when they attempt to take away from the press its rightful freedom, then they conspire to destroy all that is good in this country.

Regardless of whether we are the target of such legal machinations, we deplore them. When we are the target of such trickery as unleashed this past week by Cynthia Coyne Hurley, the sister of Desmond Coyne, a target of the Justice Department's "Full Platter" probe, we must resolutely decry such behavior and with equal resolution promise that we will not submit to such legal blackmail.

Coyne has been accused in documents obtained by all Chicago media of massive theft from his clients, indeed accused in his own words. To attempt to deprive us of the right to report such accusations is an outrage. Obviously Coyne is innocent till he is proven guilty, though the evidence against him seems to be massive. We reserve the right to report the charges and leave to a jury of his peers the question of his guilt.

We will not, however, be intimidated by Ms. Hurley's disgraceful legal tactics.

EDITORIAL

WHAT IS DUE DILIGENCE?

Since we are not a target of the complaint filed by lawyers for Michael Coyne, an alleged victim of the latest inept FBI sting, charmingly called "Operation Full Platter," it might seem gratuitous for us to comment on this affair. However, lawyers for the trader-turned-novelist have caught the usual conspirators in the tactic of conviction by prosecutorial leak in the middle of their conspiracy. The media take it for granted that they have the right to print as fact any rumor which oozes out of the office of a prosecuting attorney. Prosecutors also take it for granted that they have the right to leak anything and everything which would ruin a defendant's reputation, deny him the possibility of a fair trial, and force him into an unfavorable plea bargain.

We submit that this is not justice as the term has normally been used in the United States.

Mr. Coyne's lawyers have pounced on the coconspirators in a particularly egregious assault on the assumption that an American is innocent till proven guilty. The United States Attorney has seen fit to turn over to the Chicago media (ourselves included) a transcript of a conversation that is alleged to have occurred between Mr. Coyne and an FBI informant. Mr. Coyne vigorously denies that the conversation ever occurred.

Let us suppose for a moment that this talented young man is telling the truth. Let us suppose that he can prove that he is telling the truth and that the charges against him are faked, perhaps by an overzealous informant and an uncautious Assistant United States Attorney. Stranger things have happened.

Should these contingencies fall into place, the Chicago media will surely seem to have been guilty of lack of due diligence. Mr. Coyne's attorneys will have a field day. The schools which Mr. Coyne attended will profit greatly. And journalistic sleaze will be exposed for what it is.

When we showed our own lawyers the leaked transcript, they asked us one question: how do we know that Mr. Coyne really participated in that conversation? We thought about it and said we did not know that for a fact. They threw up their hands and said if we printed it under such circumstances, we could be in deep trouble. We will watch with interest the development of this fascinating case.

Column Note:

Ace Fed prosecutor **Dale Quade** is about to add another scalp to her belt. Sources tell this column that the flurry of activity by the lawyers of Dermot Coyne, a commodity broker turned author of steamy novels, is a tactic to win him a generous plea bargain. Neither the arrest of two FBI agents by Chicago police, friendly to Coyne, nor the suits filed in county court by his sister are likely to fend off Quade. Moreover those who know this stern legal beagle think that these smoke screens will earn Coyne more rather than less time in prison.

RADIO EDITORIAL

Management of this station has felt for some time that commodity markets in this city are the biggest gambling casinos and that many of the men and women who scream at each other in the "pits" of these exchanges are not much better than members of the Mafia. So we're delighted to hear that the United States Attorney has trapped a young punk from those exchanges in his own words. We hope that this upcoming indictment won't give undue publicity to his potboiler novel. We expect he'll have leisure time behind the bars of a federal correctional institution to work on his next novel.

Conversation heard on LaSalle Street

Trader A: I hear the Feds are going to get Dermot Coyne. A guy with a wire got him to admit that he cheated a customer.

Trader B: No one cheats customers.

Trader C: Some dumb guys try.

Trader A: Do you think Dermot was dumb enough to try?

Trader B: Poor Dermot was a nice kid. Never belonged on the floor. He was so dumb that he couldn't cheat anyone if he wanted to try.

—19—

THE PARTY at the Italian Village was Nuala's. The Notre Dame game was my party, indeed my class's fifth reunion. So naturally I was the leading figure in the Arthur Andersen party, and she stole the stage in the shadow of the Golden Dome.

Figures.

At her party she wore the shy child from the West of Ireland mask, the demure bride with her arm around the astonishing man whose love she had managed to win through no merit of her own. At Notre Dame she was the exuberant hoyden who led the singing and the cheering. I might just as well have not been there, save for the formalities of introducing her to my classmates and friends and handing in the tickets as we entered the stadium.

Figures.

Which Nuala was the real one? Both of them, of course. Both were equally attractive, and both sent my hormones racing. The shy child, however, was closer to the ur-Nuala, the little girl that raced barefoot down the unpaved lanes and along the rocky beaches of Carraroe.

In both venues I had become something of a folk hero for taking on the media. I had forgotten how much the average American hates journalists, especially good-looking and empty-headed television journalists.

"Go get 'em, Dermot!"

"Take 'em for all they're worth!"

"About time someone said they're a pack of liars."

"Dermot, I hope you get every penny."

Prester George had told me that this would happen, but what did he know?

"Dermot, they'll forget you never graduated. Just watch the Holy Cross priests flock around you. Nothing changes the memory of college administrators like the smell of a large gift."

I saw no reason to tell Nuala about the call from my old friend Geno until I talked to the friend of his friends before Mass on Sunday. Doubtless this man would be a messenger for a certain "individual" who was a friend of friends of his. How did they keep all those links straight?

As we were leaving the Italian Village and I was waiting for Nuala to emerge from the women's room, I overheard a conversation between her and one of her (women) coworkers, not unlike one I had heard at the beach earlier in the summer.

"No, we're not living together, and we're not sleeping together either."

"Why not?"

None of her damn business.

"Because he never asked me."

"Would you if he asked?"

The Adversary, who had appeared from nowhere, told me that I should not eavesdrop. I ignored him.

"I knew he'd never ask so I never had to worry about it."

"He sounds a little weird."

"I don't think it's weird at all, at all. He respects me and cherishes me and I like that."

The last was said with considerable vigor and a return of the strong West of Ireland brogue. Good enough for the witch who was asking such personal questions.

"See!" I said to the Adversary.

I did tell her about the conversation with her mother as I drove her home from the party. The rain had cleared away and a sly moon crescent was winking at us in the sky above Southport Avenue, as if to say I know what the two of you are thinking about.

"Och, aren't they all worried sick about us," Nuala replied to my account of the phone call from the Gaeltacht. "That amadon Laurence is calling everyone every day. He is determined to stop our marriage. He's not going to do it, but he upset everyone."

"He should be concentrating on his own business which needs

full-time attention now, instead of running up long-distance phone bills."

"Doesn't he call everyone collect?"

"He calls collect?"

"Doesn't he say that the whole family should share the costs of preventing this disgrace? Me brother Pedar won't accept the charges anymore."

"Why is he doing this, Nuala?"

"Sure, he hates me. He was the admired prince of the family until the little demon came along at the end of the line and got all the attention."

"Which she deserved."

"Well, the poor little thing didn't have much choice, did she now? . . . Don't worry about me ma. I'll call her before we leave for the game tomorrow. We'll have a nice long talk in Irish which will calm her down for a while."

She dressed the part for The Game, tight white jeans, a somewhat less tight blue-and-gold Notre Dame sweatshirt, and a blue baseball cap with the word "Irish" emblazoned on the front. Truth in advertising. She had tied her hair back with a blue-and-gold ribbon and carried a blue-and-gold bag over her shoulder in lieu of a purse.

"You mean to tell me, Dermot Michael, they really can't have a small jar inside the stadium, not even to wash down their sandwiches?"

"Woman, they cannot. There was too much of the drink taken in ages past."

"Won't they perish with the thirst?"

"Some of them have been known to lace their Cokes with the contents of an airline miniature."

"Aren't they the clever ones?"

Nuala knew all about American football and about Notre Dame. Weren't the home games carried live on Irish TV from the NBC satellite channel? And wasn't there a summary of the NFL games on RTE every Monday? She had obviously studied the Chicago sports pages for the previous week because she knew about the players and the problems and the relative strengths of the Fighting Black Baptists and the hated Longhorns. In fact, she knew more about these matters than I did.

"You're not reading the sports pages like you should, Dermot Michael and yourself with nothing important on your mind."

"I begin to read them and then I'm distracted by images of myself on top of a beautiful and totally naked woman."

"Are you now? Sure, why wouldn't herself be on top of you?"

"Fair play to you, Nuala Anne, but either way it would be distracting."

She hugged me. "I'm the lucky one because I never have such daydreams at all, at all."

She reveled in the festival atmosphere of Notre Dame on a brisk early-autumn afternoon with lazy clouds drifting aimlessly across the light blue sky—the excitement of the students, the pride of parents visiting their son or daughter, the nostalgia of the alumni marveling at how everyone else in the class had changed, the sound of the band practicing, the glow on the Golden Dome, the hint of autumn colors on the campus foliage, lovers of every age holding hands as they wandered about the campus.

"Sure, isn't it all grand, Dermot?"

"Woman, tis."

"Almost as grand as the All Ireland finals in Croak Park."

That put me in my place.

She reveled in the N.D. autumn rituals more than I did. I had never been happy at the school and didn't much care whether the team lost or won. My classmates whom I encountered were mostly overweight and unmarried and considered my upcoming marriage, even to one as lovely as Nuala, to be a betrayal of the bachelor class.

Still even someone as cynical as I am on the subject of the Golden Dome cannot remain immune to the excitement of a Saturday football afternoon on the outskirts of South Bend. It is, I suppose, a festival of life and a renewal of life. It matters terribly that the "Irish" win and it really doesn't matter at all. At all.

"Isn't it a grand university altogether?" she asked me as we walked out of the Sacred Heart Chapel.

"It's lovely this time of the year, Nuala, but from November 1 to early May all the greenery vanishes, the snow falls, the wind blows, and you think winter will never end."

"But the education is good, isn't it?"

"It's a fine undergraduate college," I admitted, "and it's on its way at long last to becoming a great university."

"But didn't you leave it?"

"Woman, I did not. They threw me out because I had this bad habit of failing me courses, mostly because I didn't study."

"And why didn't you study?"

"I'd get interested in something else. Like in my European history class, I got interested in Napoleon and read twenty-five books on him. There were no questions about him on the final exam, so I earned meself an F."

"That means failure?"

"It does."

She pondered my bad habit for a moment.

"You were mourning for the girl, too, poor child that she was."

"Yeah . . . Still I guess I'm not the classroom type."

"There's nothing wrong with that, so long as you educate yourself, which you certainly have!"

I have been absolved and given a plenary indulgence besides.

"That's what I kept telling myself."

"And wasn't it fair play to you, Dermot, when you told yourself that?"

Then the bad penny appeared in the person of Father McAteer, my hall rector during my last semester. As a young priest, he had hung out with the Berrigan brothers for a while, and pictured himself a social radical. In fact he was an authoritarian and couldn't help himself.

"Well, Dermot," he said brusquely, "I hardly expected you to appear for your class's reunion."

His lean and ascetic face and his grizzled gray hair suggested hard-won wisdom. In fact, he was, not to put too fine an edge on things, an asshole. The Berrigan image required khaki slacks, a sweatshirt and a gray windbreaker. In fact, he was an incurable clericalist.

I introduced Nuala to him as my fiancée.

"You a St. Mary's girl?" he asked.

In his world "Smick Chicks" were less than human.

"T.C.D." she replied.

"I'm afraid I don't know that hall."

"Trinity College, Dublin, Father," I explained.

"Well, I hope you at least graduated, unlike some people I know."

The familiar thunderhead began to gather on her forehead. Careful, Father, it's Queen Maeve you're offending.

He turned to me, "Well, I hear you published a novel, Dermot."

"Thank you, Father."

"I haven't read it and won't. There is too much injustice in the world for me to waste my time on trash. From what intelligent critics here at the university say, I'm sure it will be very successful. You will be a novelist who is Catholic, Dermot. That's more than any of us would have expected, though not much more. But you'll never be a Catholic novelist. You'll make a lot of money, but you'll never be a Graham Greene."

Duck. She looks like a sweet young Catholic woman, but . . .

"Wouldn't you know that a gobshite of a priest would speak such nonsense? He'll never be a James Joyce or a Seamus Heaney either, but why does he have to be? Isn't it enough that he's a Dermot Michael Coyne who went to your university? Shouldn't you be proud of him for producing a novel when all his classmates are producing nothing more than beer bellies? If you weren't such an asshole, Father, wouldn't you be encouraging him instead of putting him down? Isn't that what you priests do all the time? Don't you try to destroy anyone who is a little different?"

Father McAteer gulped once and then turned on his heel and strode away. He knew better than to try to match words with Grace O'Malley.

"Did I embarrass you something awful, Dermot Michael?" she asked as the priest disappeared around the corner of the university book store.

"Woman, you delighted me . . . I didn't know you were such an anticlerical."

"He's just like some of the priests back home . . . Back in my other home."

"Oh."

"But," she said, cooling off, "aren't there wonderful priests in America like his rivrence and the little bishop and your uncle and your man in crimson?"

"Every profession has its assholes, Nuala Anne."

"Tis true, but some priests enjoy being assholes."

After our stroll through campus, we joined the tailgate party of the Grand Beach crowd. A man who had yet to meet Nuala asked her if she were truly Irish. She responded by singing a rowdy and probably bawdy (though indirectly so) song in Irish. That opened the floodgates of song. She sang all through the lunch, returning frequently to a tune that proclaimed "Whiskey, you're the divil, drunk or sober!"

During the game it turned out that she knew not only the "Victory March" in all its stanzas but even the "Alma Mater," which almost no one knows.

"Isn't it grand, Dermot?" she said at least a thousand times.

"Brilliant, Nuala," I would reply.

I asked her during the revelries at the tailgate party if there was a Golden Dome behind the Golden Dome.

"Sure," she said, a mischievous twinkle in her deep blue eyes. "Why wouldn't there be?"

"And angels on the edge?"

"Who else, and this a university in honor of their queen?"

She was having me on.

Wasn't she?

Just as the tailgate party was winding down for a recess during the game, a TV reporter and cameraperson appeared in our midst. I became aware of their presence when the reporter, a tiny young woman with a pinched face, shoved a mike into my face.

"How are you able to enjoy the game, Dermot, with what's hanging over you?"

Our friends drew back sullenly. The dark, warning frown appeared again on Nuala's face.

"All that's hanging over me," I said easily, "is my wedding week after next and that prospect makes the game even more enjoyable."

"But you're going to be indicted next week."

"That's news to me."

"Haven't you been subpoenaed by the Full Platter grand jury?"

"I believe I have."

"Doesn't that mean you'll be indicted?"

"I have no worries about any of those matters."

Lie, but, oh, so plausibly spoken.

"Aren't you afraid you'll be in jail for the first Notre Dame home game next year?"

"Those who should worry about that are those who have conspired to bring false charges against me and those who report about these charges without due diligence."

Cheers from the tailgate party, even from Cindy, who had just arrived and who in more prudent moments might have thought I had gone too far.

The reporter did not give up easily.

"Isn't it unfair, Dermot, to expect a woman to marry you with a jail term hanging over your head?"

Then a woman's voice began to sing,

"Whiskey, you're the divil, ye're leading me astray;
Over hills and mountains and to a brighter day;
Ye're sweeter, stronger, spunkier;
Ye're lovelier than tay;
Oh, whiskey ye're me darling; drunk or sober.

"Oh, now brave boys were off to town;
We're off to Portugal and Spain;
The drums are beatin'; banners 're flying;
The divil will take you home one night.

"Lord, fare thee well.
With me titlle-de-idum dum-dah,
Me tittle-de-idum dum-doo-lay;
Me, right foot, toor-ah-laree,
Oh, there's whiskey in the jar.

"Said the mother to me boldy;
'Don't take me daughter from me;
For eff you do, I will torment you;
And after death me ghost 'll haint you.'

"'Lord, fare thee well.
With me tittle-de-idum-dum-dah,
Me tittle-de-idum dum doo lay;
Me, right foot toor-ah-laree,
Oh, there's whiskey in the jar!'

"Whiskey, you're the divil, ye're leading me astray;
Over hills and mountains and to a brighter day;
Ye're sweeter, stronger, spunkier;
Ye're lovelier than tay;
Oh, whiskey ye're me darling; drunk or sober."

"Can't you make them stop singing during my interview?" the newsperson pleaded.

"Nope," I said.

"That's not fair!"

"Enjoy the game," I said to her and turned my back on her.

She and her cameraman gave up and drifted away. The singers, proud of themselves, applauded their own efforts.

Cindy rushed over and hugged me.

"Great, Dermot! That will scare them tonight."

"Are they scared?"

"Scared stiff, just like the media lawyers. I hear they're really working over your good friend Jarry Kennedy to make sure he's on the level with them."

Points for our side.

"Jerry is such a sociopath that by now he probably thinks he is."

"Aren't you proud of my bro?" Cindy asked the mistress of song.

"Sure, isn't he me darlin' man?"

"Did you put a curse on her, Nuala?" I asked as we struggled towards our seats in the stadium.

"Och, I'd never do that, would I now, Dermot? . . . Sure, I might scare her a little bit by pretending. I'm pretty good at pretending."

Tell me about it.

"She has to do her job," I said piously.

"I'm tired of hearing that," Cindy snapped. "It's a miserable job."

"Like taking shit from one latrine to another," Nuala agreed.

I found myself wishing during the game that Cindy wasn't enjoying the legal battle quite as much as she was.

The "Irish" routed the hated Longhorns and thus the timeless faith of the Church of Rome was preserved for another autumn week.

Nuala lived every minute of the game just like she lived every minute of a "fillum." She cheered, she shouted, she groaned, she protested decisions of the officials, she booed the hapless Longhorns, she demanded touchdowns and defense, she led the crowd around us (who were charmed by her energy) in singing both the fight song and the "Alma Mater." Well, she sang the latter all by herself.

"You are going to marry her, aren't you, young man?" the woman next to me whispered in my ear.

"In thirteen days," I replied.

"Lucky you."

"Tell me about it."

My future bride was exhausted after the game.

"Sure, wasn't that a terrible workout?"

"You certainly threw yourself into the game, Nuala."

"Well, don't you have to? Otherwise, the team won't win."

Of course.

After the postgame tailgate party we drove back to Grand Beach to swim in the heated pool at my parents' home, a recuperation which herself had insisted was essential.

"Sure, Dermot, won't we have to swim off all the drink taken during the game?"

Her "drink taken" was exactly two beers, one more than I had consumed.

Cindy and Joe were driving straight home to Oak Brook and their children. We would have the pool and the house to ourselves.

"Now don't you be getting any ideas, Dermot Michael Coyne."

"I'll get plenty of ideas, but I won't act on them."

"Sure," she said, holding on to my arm, "aren't you the good and kind man?"

"Sometimes."

"All the time."

The pool is enclosed by a fence (lest we be sued for presenting to the public an attractive nuisance) so Nuala and I reveled in the fantasy that we were all alone in the world.

We turned on the hot tub and jumped into the pool, which was still heated and would be till Columbus Day, which Prester George insisted was the true end of summer.

After a vigorous swim we huddled in robes on the edge of the pool and finished the sandwiches Nuala had made for us, Irish sandwiches with thin slices of meat and crusts trimmed off.

"Now for the hot tub and another swim," she announced.

"Woman, you'll be the death of me!"

"I doubt it!"

She tossed aside the top of her bikini as we climbed into the hot tub.

"Won't I pretend that we're on the French Riviera?" she informed me.

"You've never been to the French Riviera," I reminded her.

"Haven't I seen pictures?"

"I have been there, Nuala Anne. No woman on the Riviera is as beautiful as you are."

"Go long wid ya, Dermot Michael Coyne," she said as she snuggled close to me. "Sure, didn't you swallow the stone at Blarney Castle?"

She gripped my hair and pulled my face down to her breasts. The idea, I gathered, was that I should kiss them. So I did, at great and tender length. She sighed contentedly and often.

"Didn't I start imagining this the day after I met you at O'Neill's pub?"

"It took you that long?"

"I never thought it would happen."

"And yourself thinking about it at Mass."

She pulled up my head so she could examine my face.

"How did you know that?"

"You're not the only one who's fey?"

"I'm not fey?" she said, drawing my lips back to her breast, "I just know a few things now and then."

"Do you now?"

"I do."

She released my head and buried her own against my chest.

"Promise me that you'll always do that to me, Dermot."

Now I knew one fantasy anyway.

"All night?" I said.

"You know I don't mean that. I mean all our life together, even when I'm old and you're tired of me."

"Is your da tired of your ma?"

"Certainly not."

"Then why should I ever be tired of you?"

"Me ma is a sweet and wonderful woman. I'm not."

"You are, too."

"She doesn't have a big mouth like I do."

"I bet she does, too."

Nuala giggled.

"Well sometimes . . . Isn't it a terrible mystery, Dermot?"

"'Tis," I agreed, not having any idea what I was agreeing to.

"We think we're in love with each other and always will be. Doesn't everyone think that when they're about to get married? And yet so many divorces in this country and now in Ireland, too, with divorce being legal."

"Almost half here."

"All of those couples," she continued, "said 'until death do us part' and meant it."

"If you try to run away on me," I warned her, "I'll drag you back by your long black hair."

"Don't let me ever run away, Dermot Michael. If I look like I'm going to do that, the reason will be that I'm frightened."

A strange conversation, I said to myself. What odd mood had taken possession of my adopted Golden Domer?

As the sun slipped away in the west and coated us with a sheen of gold, I tried to respond.

"It won't happen, Nuala Anne."

"I know that, Dermot Michael. It's just like worrying that Notre Dame might lose. Don't you have to worry so that they won't lose?"

I did not understand the logic, but I had heard it often enough. Irish women are genetically programmed to engage in such hedges.

"Come on, woman, let's do the pool again and then go home."

And so we did

SHE's WORRIED, the Adversary said, AND YOU'RE NOT WORRIED AT ALL, AT ALL.

"The hell I'm not."

—20—

THE MAN in the dark gray, carefully tailored three-piece suit was waiting for me. With his razor-cut hair, his prim face, and his worried eyes behind rimless glasses, he looked like a banker who was worried about a loan. Maybe he was a banker.

"So nice of you to agree to see me, Mr. Coyne," he said softly.

"A friend of mine," I said, "told me that you're a friend of a friend of his. So naturally I would talk to you."

"Friends are really important," he whispered again.

"And friends of friends."

"Precisely."

If he caught the hint of satire in my pieties, he gave no sign of it.

"You see, Mr. Coyne," he began as he led me on a stroll around the Hancock Center, "There's a certain individual who would like to have a little talk with you and your fiancée about a mutual problem about which he is concerned."

The words were mild and there was no hint of a threat in them. I decided to take them as a threat.

"Is that individual threatening us?"

"No, no, no," the man sputtered and looked around anxiously to make sure there was no one listening, though that stretch of the Magnificent Mile was deserted at such an early hour. "That's the last impression this individual wants to create. Just a friendly conversation over tea at his house this afternoon."

"Who is this individual?" I asked bluntly, though I knew for certain who he was.

"Mr. Albergetti. Angelo Albergetti. He's a neighbor of your father and mother, same parish I believe."

Angelo "The Angel" Albergetti was the current senior "godfather" or "don" or "*Capo dei Tutti Capi*" of the Chicago Outfit, though those terms were not used in Chicago. Locally he was known simply as the Boss.

"I went to grammar school and high school with his grandson Pete."

"A fine young man. An excellent architect, I believe."

Also a very shy kid who bore the burden of his background as a heavy cross.

"So I'm told."

"We could pick you up in a limo after Mass," he said tentatively.

"That won't do, I'm afraid. There's a shower at my mother's house in River Forest for my fiancée. We could drive down to Mr. Albergetti's home after the shower if that would be all right. Say about four o'clock?"

My companion responded with ecstatic happiness.

"That will be wonderful! Thank you very much, Mr. Coyne. Thank you very much. Mr. Albergetti will be delighted. I'm so happy you have seen your way clear to have this little talk with him. This is very gratifying indeed."

"Would you do me a very big favor?"

"Certainly, Mr. Coyne! Certainly! Anything you want! Anything! Just name it!"

"Would you please tell Mr. Albergetti that Ms. McGrail and I have no intention of doing anything which might cause embarrassment, much less pain, to anyone."

Just a bit of insurance.

"I will be very happy to do that, Mr. Coyne. Very happy indeed. I'm sure Mr. Albergetti will be glad to hear that. Very glad indeed."

He shook my hand enthusiastically and hopped into a very long and very dark limo which had cruised up from nowhere.

Fascinating, I told myself. A confrontation between the Angel and my angel would be fun to watch.

I picked up the aforementioned angel in front of her house. She was wearing a tailored burnt orange dress and a matching hat and looked thoroughly elegant, not to say resplendent, in the bright autumn sunshine.

"Looking for a ride, Miss?"

"Depends on who's driving the car . . . And the make of the car. Isn't your Mercedes a trifle superannuated?"

"You mean old?" I jumped out of the car and opened the door for her.

"Well, since my real date has not come along yet, I suppose I might as well ride with you," she said as she eased her way into the car, being careful not to disarrange her hat.

"That's a lovely hat on your lovely head," I said as I entered on the other side.

"Thank you, Dermot Michael . . . You don't think it is too much, do you?"

"On many another woman it would be. On you it's perfect."

"Go long wid ya!" she tapped my arm, pleased with my approval.

Our life together should always be so easy.

"Well," she said as I turned west on Fullerton to pick up the Kennedy Expressway, "it would appear that your novel is on its way to becoming a best-seller."

"*Irish Love?*"

"The very same. Hasn't everyone in me family bought a copy?"

"Oh," I said cautiously. "Because your man insisted that they buy it?"

"The very same . . . I don't know whether he bought it or borrowed it from someone or read it in a bookstore."

"And his verdict?"

"What would you be thinking that would be, Dermot me darlin' man? His favorite word on the subject is 'degenerate.' "

"Oh boy!"

"He thinks the Church should condemn it as a threat to the morals of the young."

"That would make my publisher's day!"

"Didn't I tell him that!"

"He says that everyone in our family will be humiliated if I marry you, that they will never be able to look their friends in the eye again, and that I'd be a disgrace to the Irish race."

"And you said?"

"I said that I'd be no more a disgrace than Nora Barnacle!"

"Wasn't that going a little far?"

"Well, you're not a fall-down drunk like your man was."

"The others?"

"You know how cautious and careful our kind can be, and them-selves never wanting to take a stand when they can avoid it?"

"I do."

"So didn't me ma say that she read it all last night and that now himself was reading it and that she had to take it away from him so they could go to Mass?"

"Fairly solid endorsement."

"I don't think me brothers and sisters have read it yet. But they will, thanks to your man, they all will."

"And if they don't like it?"

"Sure, no one ever said that all the Irish have good taste, did they?"

"How did a copy of the book get to Ireland?"

"Didn't your man send it over to them by air express?"

"Collect?"

"How else?"

As we left the expressway at Monroe Street, I told her about my early-morning visitor.

"Well, we stirred them up, didn't we now, Dermot?"

"We did that."

"They're going to have to tell us more than we know."

"Maybe."

"You're not afraid of this Angel person, are you? You don't think he'll try to take us for a ride?"

"Not very likely, but I phoned Prester George on the way up to your house to tell him. And Mike Casey."

She nodded thoughtfully.

"Reliable will have someone outside the house?"

"They will."

"And if your man doesn't like it?"

"Too bad for him."

"Brilliant!" she exclaimed.

I thought she was enjoying it entirely too much.

Nuala and I belonged to three parishes. I lived at the Cathedral, and that's where we would be married because that was George's parish, too. She lived in St. Josephat's, an old Polish national parish across the street from our house on Southport, and went to Mass there every day. On Sunday, however, we went like many other Chicago yuppies to Old St. Pat's. It was the place for all unmarried and would-be married young adults to show up, because the liturgy was good, the homilies were superb, and "everyone else" would be there. Moreover, during one of our estrangements in the summer Nuala had joined the choir. Indeed this morning she was to sing one of her Irish songs during the offering of gifts.

It had occurred to me—though I would never dare say it—that if every Catholic parish in the country had a Nuala Anne to sing at their offering of the gifts, the financial problems of the Catholic Church would vanish.

This unacceptable notion returned to my mind when she was actually singing the hymn as the bread and wine were brought to the altar. Since the hymn was in Irish, few if any of the congregation knew what the hymn was about. Indeed it might have been a barroom ballad. But the faith and the hope and the joy of the singer filled every corner of the old church and reduced the men and women and even the kids to reverential awe.

There were several moments of respectful silence when she was finished and then thunderous applause, which I thought inappropriate, as, I suspected, the singer did, too. She had been singing for the God in whom she now half believed and not for an audience.

I wondered why the aforementioned deity had chosen me to protect this shy child. It was not a very good choice I suggested respectfully.

Too LATE NOW, the Adversary informed me. THERE'S NO WAY YOU'LL BE ABLE TO ESCAPE MARRYING HER NOW, EVEN IF YOU ARE LOSING YOUR NERVE.

"I'm not losing my nerve."

YES, YOU ARE.

I refused to permit him to distract my prayers.

"Boring?" I said to herself later in the day when she joined me in front of my parents' house in River Forest.

"Totally boring," she replied. "Wasn't everyone very generous and very gracious and wasn't your mom wonderful?"

"And you don't like all-women gatherings?"

"Not at all, Dermot Michael, not at all, at all . . . and everyone having read these things and wondering what I thought about them."

She handed me two clippings from gossip columns:

QUICK INDICTMENT
FOR COYNE?

Sources at the Dirksen Building report that top fed prosecutor **Dale Quade** intends to make quick work of **Dermot Coyne,** the first big fish to be caught in the net of Operation Full Platter. Coyne will be questioned by the grand jury tomorrow, indicted on Tuesday, arraigned on Wednesday and will plea bargain before the week is over. Quade has yet to decide whether to grant Coyne time for his wedding to **Nell McGrail,** scheduled in the near future before sending him off to the federal pen. Quade, our sources say, would be much more tolerant of Coyne if his sister **Cynthia Hurley** had not filed suits against Chicago media outlets which challenge the integrity of FBI informants. Coyne, they say, is his own worst enemy and Hurley is as destructive to his case as he is.

FEDS ANGRY AT COYNE

We hear that the feds are furious at budding novelist **Dermot Coyne,** whom they have trapped in their Operation Full Platter sting. Ace federal prosecutor **Dale Quade** is determined to punish Coyne for his suits against Chicago media which impugn the veracity of fed informant **Jared Kennedy.** Ms. Quade views Coyne as an incompetent crook who may be disposed of quickly so her team might get on to the bigger fish that Kennedy has hooked. Coyne's lawyer (and sister) feisty **Cindi Hurley** replies that if anyone goes to jail it will be Quade and Kennedy, an accusation not likely to dispose the feds to cut a plea deal with her brother.

"Nell, is it now?" I said, as I gave the clippings back to her. "Save these for our scrapbook."

"And your sister is Cindi with an 'I.' "

"At least we've smoked Jarry out."

"They write as if you are already convicted."

"I am, Nuala," I said as I opened the car door for her, "by the media rules. To be the target of investigation is evidence of guilt. An indictment merely confirms guilt. They know that most people can't afford the costs of a trial and will have to work out a plea bargain deal. All the action is in the maneuvering before a case comes to trial."

"This Quade woman"—Nuala spat out the name in disgust—"is behind the columns?"

I started the car for the three-block trip to the Albergetti house.

"Sure. She's been a good source for these columnists, so she's calling in some of her markers. It is the most brazen use of media leaks I have ever seen and a violation of the federal rules. No one enforces the rules anymore. Cindy will say it shows how frightened she is by our counterattack. Maybe that's true or maybe Dale Quade has finally gone over the top. We'll have to wait and see."

"Can she really stop our marriage?"

"I doubt it."

"I won't let her," Nuala said firmly.

"No curses, Nuala Anne."

"We'll see about that."

We had arrived at the vast and forbidding Queen Anne fortress, hidden behind trees turning red and gold, in which The Angel lived, protected by a high iron fence and, it was alleged, numerous television cameras and monitors. I shivered slightly. The house was totally scary. When I was a kid we always crossed to the other side of the street so that The Angel's gunmen would not confuse us with an enemy.

"That car down the street," Nuala said as I helped her out of the Mercedes, "is Reliable Security?"

"Doubtless."

"The folks inside will know that?"

"Probably."

"Will they be angry?"

"More likely impressed."

I pushed the bell at the gate of the fence.

We waited a long time, almost as long as if we had rung the front doorbell of a Catholic rectory.

Finally we were buzzed in.

"Scared, Nuala Anne?"

"Certainly not!"

The wait after I rang the doorbell was somewhat shorter.

"Yes?" said the handsome Italian woman, in her late fifties, who opened the door, her eyes hard with suspicion.

"Mr. Coyne and Ms. McGrail to see Mr. Albergetti."

"Come this way."

We were ushered into a dark parlor with thick drapes, heavy furniture from the nineteen twenties, and a plush, plum-colored carpet.

"Can you imagine what me brother would think if he knew that there was a place like this in your home parish and ourselves inside it!"

"We could make up wonderful tales, couldn't we, Nuala?"

"We might not have to make them up."

Again we had to wait—probably a routine psychological trick in this house.

Finally a muscular young man in a perfectly fitting navy blue suit appeared. He was supposed to intimidate us by his size and cold eyes. I sized him up and decided that, while not a cream puff, he would be no match for me should I get my Irish up.

That reaction, I admit, was a macho, testosterone-driven male response.

"Mr. Albergetti will see you now," he said icily.

"Thank you very much," Nuala responded politely.

If it came to a fight, she'd grab a lamp or a chair and go after him as quickly as I would.

We were ushered into a sunroom, a bright and airy place with brightly colored furniture and tasteful prints on the wall, a replica perhaps of a room in a summer villa somewhere in Calabria or Sicily.

"Dermot!" The Angel rose from a straight-backed chair next to a table. "So nice to see you again. I talked to Peter this morning and he says I should give you his very best . . . And this is your lovely fiancée. I'm delighted to meet you. Sit down, sit down. We can have a little tea and a little chat. I promise I won't keep you long."

He settled back in his chair with obvious relief.

The Angel was a man in his early eighties, frail perhaps, but lively and charming. He wore a beige sports jacket, brown slacks, and an expensive tie with a flower print. His hair was snow-white and carefully groomed, his face sallow parchment, and his jewels worth a small fortune.

Marlon Brando he was not.

"Mario," he said to the thug, "you may bring the tea."

"Yes, Mr. Albergetti . . . And the sherry?"

"Will you join me?" The Angel asked us.

"We will," herself answered for both of us.

"Yes, Mario, bring the sherry, too."

Of course the thug's name was Mario.

"Before we have our little talk, Dermot, I wonder if you'd mind autographing a copy of your book for me? I said to one of my associates the other day that it was a great honor for our parish that a young man who grew up here would publish a novel, and a very good one and a very successful one at that."

"I'd be delighted, Mr. Albergetti."

What had the Outfit come to?

I inscribed the book to "Mr. Angelo Albergetti, with affection and respect, Dermot Michael Coyne."

The woman peered over my shoulder to make sure I'd done it right. She tilted her head forward in approval.

"That's very nice of you, Dermot," the old man said, apparently quite pleased. "Very nice indeed."

He laid the book reverently on the little desk near his chair, a desk which was empty except for a very expensive fountain pen.

"While I was waiting for you," he said with a sigh, "I was sitting here looking out the window and remembering you walking past the house when you were going to St. Luke's school, a big, blond, good-natured kid who was always nice to my grandson. I said to my wife, who is in heaven now, I said, Dr. Coyne's son is going to amount to something. I'm happy that God has given me enough life to see that."

Was there a tear in the old crook's eye? I forced myself to remember that he had come into the mob as muscle for Frank "The Enforcer" Nitti when Capone was locked way on Alcatraz.

"Is he still that good-natured, my dear? I'm sure he is."

"Och, isn't he the sweetest boy in all the world!"

Nuala had decided on the persona of the nice young immigrant from the West of Ireland. For the moment.

"I knew that!" The Angel beamed approval on both of us, almost like a real angel.

He had never been convicted of anything. Yet how many contracts had he put out? That was perhaps not a relevant question for us.

Mario appeared with tea and cookies and a bottle of sherry, a relatively frugal tea by Irish standards, though the sherry cost at least two hundred dollars a bottle. Wholesale.

"Would you do us the honors, my dear?" The Angel asked her.

"I'd be happy to."

This was getting a little too thick for me. Maybe I ought to slug Mario and stir up a little action. He was a bit too fat to be all that good in a fight.

Nuala Anne poured the tea and gave each of us an Irish crystal glass with a few drops of sherry in it.

Maybe we should have asked for Irish whiskey.

Oh, whiskey ye're me darling; drunk or sober.

"And you were a great football player for Fenwick too," The Angel said, continuing down the nostalgia road. "Peter really admired you for quitting the team because the coach was too brutal."

Maybe Pete had, and maybe he hadn't. But The Angel was showing that he knew all about me.

"I didn't think football was about hurting other people."

"And you're so right, so right. There's too much brutality in sports these days, I always say."

We paused to nibble on cookies, freshly baked chocolate chip cookies. Herself had put three of them on my plate.

"Before we have our discussion, I wanted to say that if you'd like we could have a little talk with the individual Jared Kennedy and straighten him out. It's not a good thing he's doing. He's not a good boy, I'm afraid. Peter told me that a long time ago."

Aha, he was offering us a *quid* before he asked for a *quo*.

"That's very good of you, sir. In the long run we may need that help, but right now and despite the lies in the media, we think we can take care of him ourselves."

"Good, good!" he said with an approving nod. "The media are terrible these days, aren't they? No respect for anyone . . . There's something wrong with that Jared Kennedy individual. He comes from such a good family. These days parents sometimes cannot control what their children do, can they?"

Nuala and I agreed that this was a shame.

"Well," he said with a sigh, "I suppose we should talk a little bit about poor Jimmy Sullivan, if that's all right with you."

"Naturally," I said. "I'd simply like to repeat what I said to your friend who talked to me this morning . . ."

"Friend of a friend."

"Of course . . . We are interested in him because his grave is next to our family plot and because we have discovered in my grandmother's diary that he gave them our plot . . ."

"Did he?" The Angel's eyes flickered in surprise. "I was not aware of that. He was a very generous individual."

He seemed now more uneasy than he had been before. We might know more than he thought we knew.

"However, it is not our intention to cause any trouble or pain for anyone as a result of our interest. I'm not about to base a novel on his story . . . In fact, I think my next novel will be about a United States Attorney."

The Angel laughed, more with relief than amusement.

"I'm very glad to hear that from your own lips, Dermot. It's a source of great happiness to me. I always say that there's no point in digging up the past. Many of the things that have happened in the past are better forgotten. Why hurt people who were not even alive then?"

"Absolutely," I said, as I gobbled down the third cookie.

"This Jimmy Sullivan individual was a very talented and brave man. Perhaps just a little bit too brave. Now he's dead and buried and in his tomb. The best thing to do would be to leave him there."

"But he's not in his grave at Mount Carmel, Mr. Albergetti," my Nuala said demurely. "If he's dead and buried now—and he probably is—then his body is somewhere else."

The Angel picked up his sherry glass for the first time and sipped from it.

"I'm sure that's not true, my dear."

"It is true, Mr. Albergetti," Nuala sighed, as though she regretted having to spring her trap. "I've seen the inside of his casket."

The boss of all bosses sipped from his sherry glass again. Twice. I figured that Dermot Michael Coyne had better sit the rest of this conversation out.

"You've had him dug up? . . . I heard nothing of this!"

"I didn't have to dig it up to see the inside of the casket. There's nine stones in it, which are exactly his weight before he died."

"Holy Mother of God," Angelo exclaimed, making the sign of the cross.

"My fiancée is one of the dark ones, Mr. Albergetti," I said. "She sees things."

Nuala nodded agreement. "Not things I want to see, sir, not things I'd like to see, but things I should see."

"Holy Mother of God," The Angel exclaimed again, and made the sign of the cross again.

"Dermot Michael spoke the truth, sir. We are not going to make any trouble for anyone. We're certainly not going to the media with what we know. He will not write a novel about it. But we both feel that there's more we should know. If you say that you will not let us find that out, then we will wait to another day. But we hope you won't make us wait."

Angelo Albergetti had turned ashen. He coughed a couple of times.

Mario rushed into the room.

"Are you all right, sir?"

"I'm fine, Mario." He waved the thug out of the room.

"I had not expected," he said with another cough, "that our conversation would take this turn . . . What would you like me to do for you?"

"We would like to talk to Marie," Nuala said briskly. "Would that be possible?"

I hadn't thought of that, but, hell, I was only the spear-carrier.

"Marie?"

"Marie Kavanagh Sullivan . . . She must be still alive or you would not be concerned about the agreement her husband made with Mr. Capone and which you are vowed to honor."

The Angel looked at his sherry glass, picked it up, and drained it.

"Are you permitted a second glass, sir?" herself asked politely.

"On certain rare occasions," he said with a weak smile, "of which this is certainly one."

She poured him a second glass, this one filled to the top. She offered me nothing at all, but then, wasn't I out of the loop?

"I'm not sure that I can grant your request," The Angel said cautiously as he sipped from his glass. "I will have to consult. If I cannot do so?"

"Then we will have to wait," Nuala replied, shrugging her shoulders. "However, I expect that Mrs. Sullivan might want to talk to us."

"Perhaps you are right . . . I have your word that nothing will be written about these individuals, unless you have proper permission."

"Absolutely," she said.

"The dark ones never lie," he said as if to himself.

"They always keep their promises," Nuala agreed.

I had never heard this at all and I doubted that it was true in Irish folklore.

"I'll see what we can work out." He nodded his agreement. "I must thank you both for being so cooperative and so . . . candid."

It sounded to me like he meant it. Nonetheless, I would have Reliable Security keep an eye on us for a couple of weeks.

We returned to small talk, mostly about what a grand weekend it was, with both Notre Dame and the Bears winning.

Mario shook hands with me as he showed us out. "Good luck with the book, Mr. Coyne . . . and with the grand jury."

"Thanks, Mario," I said affably. "I'll need luck in both."

Outside, as the afternoon slipped away in quiet haze, Nuala asked me, "What do you think?"

"I think you scared the shite out of him."

"That's what I wanted to do."

"Will Marie agree to talk to us."

"Certainly. Didn't I say she wanted to talk to us?"

—21—

CINDY AND I waited in the antechamber to the grand jury room all morning, a wait designed to unnerve us, just as the waiting at Angelo Albergetti's house, a plan which in Nuala's case had no effect at all.

At all, at all.

I had told herself that there was no point in her coming down to the grand jury hearing. It was a ritual. No matter what I said or didn't say, I would be indicted. Moreover, most of the day would be spent in a windowless room furnished with a beige steel federal table and a couple of matching chairs. She most certainly could come to the arraignment later in the week. Better that she spend the day as she had intended—working on the last-minute details for the wedding.

I was amazed at how calmly I said the words "arraignment" and "indictment."

"How do we play it?" I had asked Cindy.

"There's two ways. One is to stonewall her. You have the right to come out and ask me whether you should answer a given question. She won't tell you that of course. But you have the right. You could come out often and frustrate her. Or you could let things go because the ritual doesn't mean anything anyway."

"What would you advise?"

"Let her know that she has a fight on her hands," she said, jabbing her finger at me as a sign that we were in a fighting mood.

"Yeah, that's what I feel like doing."

At noon one of Quade's subordinate amadons, same pinched

face, same lean and hungry look, same angry eyes, same studied rudeness, entered the anteroom.

"We're breaking for lunch," she said curtly. "Be back at 1:00."

Cindy glanced at her watch.

"One-thirty, Counselor. We're entitled to time for a decent lunch."

A spasm of rage crossed the woman's face. "Suit yourself, it's your funeral."

"Whose funeral it will be," Cindy said, gathering her purse and notes, "remains to be seen."

"Can we really nail them for malicious prosecution, Cindy?" I asked as we rode down the elevator.

"Certainly. They have pushed the envelope too far on this one. They've been getting away with more outrageous behavior each time they go after someone, so what they're trying to do to you looks like a gradual step, but it goes into a whole other area of depravity."

"Fine," I said with considerable lack of enthusiasm.

"With any luck at all, we can charge them with criminal conspiracy," she said, jabbing her finger again. "That will be a little trickier. We'd need some kind of special prosecutor and a confession from Jarry. A sympathetic judge might go along."

"That would be a nice irony, an informant turning informant."

"I'd love it."

"I'm sure you would."

She did not notice my irony. I mentally offered a prayer of gratitude to the deity that my bride-to-be had chosen accounting and music as a career instead of law. She would make my sibling seem noncompetitive by comparison.

About three in the afternoon, the witch de camp came into the windowless room again.

"OK, Coyne, your turn."

"Mr. Coyne," Cindy reminded her.

The woman's eyes burned.

"Very well, MR. Coyne."

On the way in I encountered Jarry Kennedy, a triumphant grin on his fat face.

"You're dead, Dermy Boy, totally dead."

I smiled affably. "No, Jarry, you're the one who's dead."

Inside, twenty-four men and women were distributed on a two-tiered grandstand. The walls were oak panels. The United States Attorney's staff sat in comfortable chairs behind an oak table. I stood in the front of the jury, most of whom seemed bored, even half asleep after their lunch.

It was a charade. Grand juries always indict.

(Excerpts from testimony of Dermot M. Coyne before the grand jury in the United States Court for the Northern District of Illinois.)

US: What is your occupation, Mr. Coyne?

DMC: I'm a writer.

US: You support yourself entirely from your writing?

DMC: From my writing and from my investments.

US: What proportion of your income does your writing support?

DMC: I'll have to ask my attorney whether I should answer that question.

(DMC: leaves room.)

(He returns.)

US: Well?

DMC: My attorney directs me to refuse to answer that question because it is irrelevant.

US: Is it not true that you worked for four years at the Mercantile Exchange?

DMC: Yes, it is.

US: Were you a very good trader?

DMC: No, ma'am. I was not.

US: Why were you not a very good trader?

DMC: I don't have the mind of a good trader. They must make decisions very rapidly. I like to take time to make decisions.

US: Yet you remained there?

DMC: Yes, ma'am.

US: Why?

DMC: It left me time to write.

US: About how much money did you lose during your years at the Mercantile Exchange?

DMC: I didn't lose money, ma'am.

US: I mean up till the time of your surprising windfall?

DMC: I didn't lose money, ma'am, even before that time. I didn't make much, but I didn't lose much either.

US: How much did you make?

DMC: I can't recall. I'm sure it's in my tax returns, which the Internal Revenue Service has examined very carefully.

US: Is it not true that you were thrown out of Notre Dame?

DMC: No, ma'am.

US: Why did you leave then?

DMC: I had failed all my courses during the second semester of my sophomore year. I could have remained out of school for a semester and then reapplied for admission. I elected not to do so.

US: Then you enrolled in Marquette University?

DMC: Yes, ma'am.

US: Where you also failed?

DMC: No, ma'am. I passed all my courses during my two years there but it would have taken several more years of school to make up for my failing grades at Notre Dame.

US: So you have been pretty much a failure at everything in your life?

DMC: I'll have to ask my attorney whether that is an appropriate question.

(DMC: exits room.)

"You must be driving her out of her mind, Derm," Cindy said to me.

"She does seem frustrated. The jury members like me."

"Poor, affable, honest Dermot, everyone's inept friend! Well, they'll still have to vote for an indictment, but keep it up."

"She is one sick woman. She doesn't look at you while she's asking her questions. Then suddenly she turns on you and stares directly into your face, her eyes glowing with revulsion."

"Oh yes, she should not be permitted to be a prosecutor. Poor kid, that husband of hers drove her round the bend, but that's not our problem. Maybe we can drive her over the top."

"What should I tell her?"

"Tell her that your attorney said she should know better than to ask a question like that."

I went back in the room and repeated Cindy's words. Some of the African-American women tittered. Quade's face turned crimson. She drove on relentlessly, taking apart my life and creating the image of an inept, hapless failure, an image which was, heaven knows, not totally inaccurate.

US: Is it not true, Mr. Coyne, that the commodity pits are nothing more than gambling casinos?

DMC: Socially useful gambling casinos.

US: How can gambling be socially useful?

DMC: All mature capitalist economies have commodity markets. Farmers can hedge against bad weather, companies that depend on oil can hedge against fluctuations in oil prices, investment funds against sudden changes in stock prices.

US: And traders like yourselves can make large fortunes out of those events.

DMC: And lose large fortunes.

US: But you made a large fortune?

DMC: Yes, ma'am.

US: Because of your skill as a trader?

DMC: No, ma'am.

US: How then?

DMC: Luck.

US: Luck, Mr. Coyne? Come now, that won't do.

DMC: It's true though.

US: Why don't you try to explain to us how your, ah, luck worked.

DMC: Well, it would be like someone wanted to bet on a horse and by mistake bet on the wrong horse and the wrong horse won.

US: And that way you won, if I may use the word, three million dollars?

DMC: That's right.

US: Do you think you earned that money?

DMC: (hesitates) When a person goes onto the trading floor he accepts all the risks, including bad luck. By so doing, he also opens himself—or herself—to the possibility of good luck.

US: Do good luck and bad luck occur in equal amounts?

DMC: It often seems that there is more bad luck than good luck, but over the long run the coin will come up heads as often as it comes up tails.

US: Very interesting, Mr. Coyne. So you think it is all right to accept good luck?

DMC: Yes, ma'am.

US: Even if you cheat to get it?

DMC: It is not right to cheat. Moreover, cheating is not luck. It's cheating.

US: Since you earned three million dollars in a single trade by cheating, you were not lucky after all, were you?

DMC: I did not cheat, ma'am.

US: Do you expect the grand jury to believe that?

DMC: I hope they do, ma'am.

US: Suppose you explain to the grand jury how you made your lucky fortune.

So I explained my good luck. The jurors seemed to understand. Yet I was a trader and therefore they would indict me.

US: So you made yourself a fortune?

DMC: Yes, ma'am.

US: With your client's money?

DMC: No, ma'am. He called at the end of trading Monday and said that he hoped I had enough sense to bail him out before he lost too much. I told him that he hadn't lost a thing. I explained why.

US: His reaction to that?

DMC: He was delighted that the two of us had been so lucky. He hadn't lost the money he thought he was going to lose. And I'd made a lot. He did advise me to get out of trading because he said I'd never be that lucky again. I had already made up my mind to do that.

US: You made money on your client's money, did you not?

DMC: No, ma'am. I made money on my own stupid mistake. If the market had gone up instead of down, I would have had to pay my client back, probably for the rest of my life.

US: That's a very charming story, Mr. Coyne. You might write a novel about it someday. But you can't expect the grand jury to believe it, can you? I'm sure that, like me, they will think you cheated your client.

DMC: He didn't think so. As he said in his testimony to the CFTC . . .

US: We're not interested in that right now, Mr. Coyne.

DMC: Yes, ma'am.

US: Are you acquainted with a certain Jared Kennedy.

DMC: I went to school with him.

US: Did you not have a recent conversation with him?

DMC: Yes, ma'am.

US: Do you happen to remember when and where that conversation was?

DMC: Yes, ma'am.

US: When and where was it?

DMC: At Grand Beach on the Labor Day weekend. On the beach itself in the afternoon.

US: You discussed this trading incident with him at that time?

DMC: No, ma'am.

US: Then you discussed it with him on August 27 at the Trader's Inn, did you not?

DMC: No, ma'am. I haven't been in the Trader's Inn in years.

US: Then when did you discuss this trade with Mr. Kennedy?

DMC: Never.

US: You can't expect us to believe that, Mr. Coyne?

DMC: I have no expectations at all about what you might believe, Ms. Quade. However, I repeat what I have said: I never discussed the trade with Mr. Kennedy.

US: You realize that you are under oath?

DMC: Yes, ma'am.

US: You realize that you could be charged with perjury for lying under oath?

DMC: Yes, ma'am.

US: I would like you to listen to this tape of a conversation between you and Mr. Kennedy.

(Conversation is played.)

US: Now, I ask you, Mr. Coyne, did you not admit to Mr. Kennedy that you cheated your client?

DMC: No, ma'am.

US: How can you say that, Mr. Coyne, when we just heard you admit it on tape?

DMC: That is not my voice on tape, Ms. Quade. I never had that conversation with Jarry Kennedy or anyone else.

"How did she react when you denied the voice on the tape was yours?" Cindy asked me.

"She laughed and then warned me again about perjury."

"Did it sound like your voice?"

"I don't think so. It sounded like someone doing a bad job of trying to imitate me. But I'm not sure what my voice sounds like."

"During discovery we will get a chance to listen to that tape.

We'll get someone to do voice analysis, and we'll blast them out of the water. They'll try to deny us a copy of the tape, but they'll have to turn it over eventually . . . She didn't seem shaken by your denial."

"Not in the least."

"I don't get it, Dermot. I just don't get it. She assumes we'll plead and the tape won't be an issue. But if we insist on proceeding with discovery, she'll have to turn it over to us. She should at least wonder about her informant."

"Unless she's really over the top."

"Which she might be. I can't help but feel sorry for her in a way. Her husband and those damn . . . You look like hell, but it sounds like you did a good job . . . How did the jury react?"

"She only needs a majority, right?"

"That's all."

"She'll certainly get that. There were enough people in there who were envious of my unmerited success and some who slept through the whole thing. But some of them don't like her and some of them seemed to like me."

"She'll browbeat them into handing down a true bill . . . Tomorrow morning she'll ask you about other traders that Jarry has picked up on wire. This is a signal about the people against whom you'll have to testify if we want to plea bargain with her."

"Perjure myself?"

"Certainly. That's what immunized witnesses are expected to do. First she'll ask if you are familiar with them. If you are, you admit it. If she asks questions about specific misdeeds on their part, you cannot recall. If she persists, you come out and see me and I'll tell you not to answer those questions. Got it?"

Another admonitory jab of her finger.

"Yeah, Cindy. I got it."

"Do you think it might be a good idea to postpone the marriage a couple of weeks, Derm?" she asked hesitantly. "At the present indecent haste, you're likely to be arraigned on Wednesday, the day Nuala's parents arrive."

"It might well be an excellent idea," I replied. "There is no way herself will agree with it."

She nodded.

"That doesn't surprise me . . . Traci has begun our media counteroffensive. May Rosen is helping her again. We'll be getting some good coverage in a day or two."

The media were waiting for me when I left the waiting room.

"How did it feel, Dermot?" one sweet-faced young woman asked me.

"Like five hours in Mother Superior's office!"

They had the decency to laugh.

—22—

Conversation Overheard in Lunchroom of
Chicago Bar Association

First Woman: I hear they're going to hand down the indictment of this Coyne kid today, Cindy Coyne's brother.

First Man: Poor kid. Who's the judge?

First Woman: Evil Elvira.

Second Woman: He's dead.

Second Man: Sounds like a pretty weak case to me. I don't think he did it.

First Man: Get real. Who cares whether he did it or not? Cindy's only hope is to get a dismissal of the charges. She won't get that from Elvira. No way.

First Woman: Either he pleads or they'll suck all his money on legal fees. Even if Cindy isn't billing him now, old W. W. Winthrop won't put up with that for long.

Second Man: They're vampires.

Second Woman: You got it. I shiver every time I think of them going after me, particularly Daffy Dale. Our money for the kids' college would go down the drain and they might still get me.

First Man: O.J. walks and Danny Rostenkowski is in jail. Figures.

Second Woman: Cindy may have something up her sleeve. Those complaints against the media sound tough.

Second Man: Look, even if she proves absolutely that the conver-

*sation with her brother never occurred, Daffy Dale will never move
to quash. The kid is dead meat.*

First Woman: They should lock her up.

*Second Woman: Oh, they will eventually. Too late for this kid
though. He'd better forget about getting married next week.*

Second Man: You ask me, it all stinks.

*Second Woman: Sure it stinks, but that's the way they play the
game these days. Still, I bet Cindy's got something up her sleeve.*

First Man: What in the world is the matter with Elvira?

*Second Woman: Poor Dale is brilliant but a little crazy now.
Elvira is an incompetent idiot who never tried a case in her life,
knows no law, got the appointment because of political clout and
thinks she's God. She's not the first federal Judge of that kind, as
I need not remind any of you.*

First Woman: There ought to be a law . . .

COYNE INDICTED

A federal grand jury today handed down an indictment charging
that novelist and commodity trader Michael Coyne engaged in multi-
ple acts of fraud and conspiracy to commit fraud during his days on
the Chicago Mercantile Exchange. If convicted on these charges
Coyne could spend twenty years in a federal prison.

Coyne's first novel, *Irish Love,* described by its publisher as "an
erotic Irish romance," is expected to debut on the national best-seller
lists next week.

(City News Bureau)

FIVE O'CLOCK NEWS

Anchor: We have a late-breaking story. The Federal grand jury which
is hearing evidence in the Operation Full Platter investigation has
handed down its first indictment. As expected, the indictment is
directed at commodity trader–turned-novelist, Dermot Coyne. Our
Laverne Meyer has the story from the Dirksen Federal Building.
Laverne?

LM: That's right, Michelle. Just minutes ago, Assistant United States
Attorney Dale Quade announced that the grand jury has leveled
seven charges of fraud, intent to commit fraud, and conspiracy to
commit fraud against Dermot Coyne.

(Cut to Quade, looking like a furiously angry novice mistress.)

DQ: The United States intends to prove that Mr. Coyne violated Federal law on the floor of the Mercantile Exchange. In a complex scam he earned illegally more than three million dollars. Moreover, he admitted this fraud and bragged about it to a government witness. We intend to make Mr. Coyne an example to all the young fast-living high-rollers in the commodity markets. This government will not tolerate your get-rich-quick schemes. If you try to become wealthy by cheating your clients, you will do time in prison at hard labor.

LM: We asked Coyne's lawyer, Cynthia Hurley, for her reaction.

CH: I have yet to see the indictment. It does, however, seem to me that it has been handed down with indecent haste. The Internal Revenue Service and the Commodity Futures Trading Commission reviewed my client's records in detail for months and found nothing illegal. Ms. Quade glances at them for a couple of days and seeks a solemn high indictment. We will reserve the right to charge false and malicious prosecution at a later day.

LM: It has been assumed around the Dirksen Federal Building that Coyne will plea bargain and testify against bigger fish who are allegedly caught in Full Platter's net. However, his lawyer's feisty response to the indictment suggests that there might yet be an explosive trial. Back to you, Michelle.

Anchor: Do you think Hurley is bluffing, Laverne?

LM: (with some hesitation) She may have a point when she says the indictment seems to be hasty. Around here they say that Hurley is the best poker player in the Chicago Bar.

COYNE LAWYER PROMISES "BIG SURPRISE"

Cynthia Hurley, lead lawyer for her brother, novelist Dermot Michael Coyne, said today that the office of the United States Attorney is in for a big surprise if it brings Coyne to trial. "The U.S. Attorney and Ms. Quade are in for a very unpleasant surprise if they pursue this hasty and sloppy indictment of my client," Hurley said. "They have pushed the envelope of conviction by leak and indictment pretty far, but this time they've gone over the line. When we are finished with them, they'll be lucky if they still have their jobs. Indeed they'll be lucky not to be in jail themselves. It's time that this charade come to an end."

Asked if Coyne might plea bargain for the lesser charge of simple fraud, Hurley laughed. "Not a chance," she said. "If anyone has to plead to avoid a jail sentence for criminal conspiracy it will be certain people at the office of the United States Attorney."

TV COMMENTARY

It seems to this commentator that Assistant United States Attorney Dale Quade, called by many the Wicked Witch of the Dirksen Building, is acting with unseemly haste in her feud with Chicago novelist Dermot Coyne. Just last week she subpoenaed Coyne's papers. Normally months are spent combing through a target's papers. But Quade subpoenaed Coyne himself with hardly any time to examine the papers and obtained an indictment yesterday afternoon. Why this unseemly haste? One theory is that Coyne is scheduled to be married a week from Friday and that Quade, out of pure spite, wants to block the wedding. Another theory is that she is worried that Coyne's lawyer, Cindy Hurley, might have a point when she says that the tape obtained by a federal informant is a fake. Whatever the reason, many Chicago lawyers are wondering whether the cause of justice is served by a high-profile legal crusader like Quade who turns every case into a personal vendetta. Moreover, if the tape is a fake, the lawyers of several Chicago media outlets, including this one, will have severe attacks of apoplexy.

—23—

IT WAS appropriately a cold and wet day when I was formally charged in the court of Judge Elvira Crawford with seven counts of fraud and conspiracy to commit fraud.

"Our luck has been terrible," Cindy whispered to me in the corridor outside of the courtroom. "Evil Elvira, as they call her, is incompetent, dumb, and arrogant. She doesn't do her homework. She had practically no trial experience before she was appointed and thinks her own personal opinions as a judge are law. She gets overruled and reprimanded routinely by the Seventh Circuit, but she doesn't care. She's only forty-five and is a judge for life."

"We can get another judge, can't we?"

"Eventually, but not today."

Nuala was with us, the only one in the clan whom I had not persuaded to stay home. She was wearing a black suit, appropriate for a wake. Her hair was tied back into a bun. She was grim and somber. Her greeting to me when we had met in front of the Federal Building was blunt, "There'll be no talk of postponing the wedding, do you hear, me bucko? If you try it, won't I be finding meself another man?"

"Clear enough warning," I said with a forced laugh.

Joe Hurley, my accountant, and an expensively dressed bail bondsman met us in the corridor and we entered the courtroom.

"I think we should get a release on his own recognizance," Cindy explained to us. "Dermot has never been charged with anything before, not even a traffic violation, and is a responsible citizen.

Daffy Dale will probably insist on some bond. Maybe we settle for a hundred thousand or so."

"With Daffy Dale and Evil Elvira isn't anything possible?"

Cindy frowned uneasily. "You got it, little bro."

The courtroom filled up quickly with media types, scavengers closing in for raw meat.

Judge Crawford bustled into her courtroom twenty minutes late, glanced around the courtroom, and shouted, "This is a courtroom and I want respect! If I hear any more noise I will expel all of you."

It was, I thought, going to be a long, hard day. I didn't know the half of it.

The judge was a short, ponderously overweight woman with darting eyes and a perpetual frown. Not Mother Superior anymore, but now Mother General.

THAT'S UNFAIR TO THE NUNS, the Adversary warned me.

"OK," I told him. "Now go away; this is bad enough without you hounding me."

I was numb, befuddled, in a stupor like I had been drugged. How could this nightmare be happening? I had done nothing wrong. Yet I was being subjected to malicious prosecution by the government of my own country. Land of the free and home of the brave indeed.

I promised myself that when it was all over I would destroy these people with my pen. Well, with my computer. They would never do something like this to anyone again. It is not a promise that I have withdrawn.

I was so distraught that I did not even feel erotic longings for the silent, implacable woman next to me. What would she do before the court session was over? I could not imagine her accepting it all quietly.

If we ever escaped from the *purgatorio* of this courtroom, we would go up to O'Hare to greet her parents who were to arrive at 4:55 on Aer Lingus flight 125. Hi, Ma and Da, me darlin' man was arraigned in a Federal courtroom this morning.

There were three arraignments before mine, two on drug charges and one on smuggling. The judge shouted at the men and berated their lawyers. In her view, it seemed, the accused men had already been convicted.

We waited patiently for our turn. The proceedings at the bench dragged on as the judge delivered angry lectures to her browbeaten victims.

Nuala took my hand.

"In the matter of the United States of America *versus* Dermot Michael Coyne," the bailiff intoned solemnly.

"Where is this Dermot Michael Coyne?" the judge demanded as we walked to the bench, as though she suspected I had fled to Tierra del Fuego.

"We're present, Your Honor," Cindy said easily.

"Hurry up, Counselor. You know I don't like to be kept waiting."

Dale Quade, dressed in a severe black dress with a white collar, read the charges against me in a flat monotone. Her narrow face was twisted in righteous rage. Once she turned on me her look of pure venom. I smiled back at her: my standard response to her venom.

She looks like a grand inquisitor, I thought. Dominican Mother General.

CUT THAT OUT! the Adversary demanded.

I saw behind the U.S. Attorney's chairs a child, perhaps third grade, dressed in crisp designer clothes and looking like a solemn and carefully burnished doll. What kind of crazy woman would bring a little girl into a situation like this?

"Well, Mr. Coyne," the judge screeched, "are you too busy planning your next novel to enter a plea?"

"Not guilty," Cindy nudged me.

"Not guilty," I said in a loud and firm voice.

"You may be a famous novelist outside this courtroom, young man. But in here you're a criminal before the bar of justice and I expect you to attend to my questions and answer promptly."

"I thought I was not a criminal until I was proven guilty, Your Honor," I said mildly.

Gasp from the courtroom. Next to me Cindy cringed.

I thought the judge would fly through the roof.

"In this courtroom, young man, I am the law. You'd better remember that."

"And the Constitution of the United States doesn't apply?"

"One more smart remark out of you and I'll hold you in contempt of court. Do you understand?"

As well to be damned as a goat as to be damned as a sheep.

I didn't answer.

"Answer me young man."

"Yes, Your Honor," I said with my most charming grin.

"Do you understand the rules of this court?"

"I think so, Your Honor," I said. "I'm kind of new in this situation."

A titter of laughter swept the courtroom and was quickly silenced by the judge's banging gavel.

"Incorrigible, Dermot," Cindy whispered. "But brilliant."

I hadn't been trying to be brilliant.

"You'd better learn quickly, Mr. Coyne," she warned me. "I don't like your attitude."

"I'll try, Your Honor."

"You'd better."

"This could be fun," I told the Adversary.

You're crazy, he replied.

The judge ordered that I be bound over for trial the following March.

"Your Honor," the Wicked Witch floated up closer to the bench. "I am going to ask that bail be denied in this case. The defendant is charged with a major crime. There is every reason to believe that he is dishonorable and will flee if he is released on bail."

Cindy blew up.

"Counselor, that is an absolutely absurd suggestion and you know it. My client has never been charged with any violation, not even a traffic ticket. He is a responsible citizen and a generous member of the community. There is no grounds for such a punitive motion."

"I'll determine what is responsible in this courtroom, Counselor. If you talk like that again I will hold you in contempt of court."

"I am only asking, Your Honor," Cindy said softly, "that my client be treated fairly."

"All right, I'll treat him fairly. A million dollar bond. He has all that money; let him put it at risk. Moreover, I forbid you, Mr. Coyne to leave this jurisdiction. If you as much as cross the Indiana line to go to your fancy house in Grand Beach, you'll be in jail the next morning. Is that clear?"

I nodded.

"A nod won't do, Mr. Coyne. Say 'Yes, Your Honor,' or I'll hold you in contempt."

"Yes, Your Honor."

"Thank you, Your Honor," La Quade said triumphantly. "I believe that is a reasonable arrangement."

The judge turned to Cindy.

"The matter is settled, Counselor. I won't tolerate another word from you. Understand?"

"Yes, Your Honor."

"I suppose you intend to appeal the bond."

"I believe that is my privilege, Your Honor."

"I just want to remind you that I won't forget it if you do."

Cindy looked startled. "You ought not to say something like that, Your Honor."

I wondered if the judge was either drunk or on some kind of drug.

"Don't you dare tell me what I should say . . . Now I want both of you back in this courtroom first thing Monday morning. I have a crowded docket and I will not clutter it with trials that are not going to happen. Understand? And remember that I don't automatically approve plea bargains. Ten-minute recess."

She struggled to her feet. I glanced behind me to see how my love was dealing with this show. She was glaring intently at the judge. The judge tripped and stumbled as she descended from the bench, losing what little dignity she had left. Nuala smiled faintly.

Had she put a hex on Judge Crawford? She ought not to do things like that.

You're hoping she did, the Adversary informed me.

"Shut up."

"Is she drunk?" I asked Cindy.

"More likely on drugs. Everyone in the building knows she uses them . . . Don't worry, Dermot, as she knows I'll get the bail cut this afternoon and maybe the restriction to the jurisdiction. If I don't win the latter, I'll be back to them on Monday with an emergency motion. Count on the honeymoon."

"We're not worrying about that," Nuala said firmly.

"I am," I said with a laugh.

"Wherever you are, me darlin' man, is honeymoon enough for me."

Before we could finish that potentially delightful discussion, Dale Quade swaggered over to us, a contented leer on her face. She ignored me and spoke directly to Cindy.

"Face it, Cindy, your brother will have to do time. If you plead him, we'll try to see that it won't be too much time. However, he'll have to cooperate in our further investigations."

"I don't know whether you or Elvira are crazier," Cindy said evenly. "And I think it is deplorable for you to expose your child to a courtroom like this."

The United States Attorney turned pale, her lips tightened, her eyes narrowed.

"You'll regret saying that, Cindy. You'll have to apologize to me before I am ready to consider a plea."

"I'll see you in hell before I plea," Cindy shot back.

Nuala intervened in the confrontation. Slipping in front of Cindy, she pointed at Dale Quade, stared at her with deadly eyes, and in a voice colder than dry ice spoke solemnly in Irish. La Quade recoiled just as Larry McGrail had.

"You're cursing me!" she said almost hysterically.

Nuala continued her imprecations. Sobbing, Ms. Quade turned and ran away. Somehow no one else in the courtroom noticed this scary little scene.

"Did you really curse her, Nuala?" Cindy asked softly.

"Och, sure, would I be doing such a terrible thing?" Nuala grinned and rolled her eyes. "Wasn't I just repeating the words of a lullaby?"

"You scared the shite out of her," I said.

"Wasn't I trying to do just that? The poor woman is about to go over the deep end and I thought I'd just give her a little nudge."

"I've never seen Dale react that way," Cindy said.

"She's never been cursed by a Druid princess before," I said.

"Druid goddess," Nuala corrected me.

SHE LOVED DOING THAT, the Adversary whispered to me. THAT ONE IS REALLY DANGEROUS.

"Now you tell me," I whispered back.

I would be held temporarily in a room in the building till bond was arranged. Cindy assured me that would be unnecessary because she would get a reversal in an hour or two.

Judge Crawford's bailiff, an officious wimp, led me out of the court to the holding room.

It took three hours for a judge in the appellate court to overrule the bail requirement and free me on my own recognizance. However, he refused to agree to let me leave the jurisdiction.

So we would honeymoon in Galena.

The media were waiting for us as I emerged from the holding room.

"Will you miss your honeymoon, Dermot?" one of them demanded.

I put my arm around Nuala Anne.

"Wherever my bride is, that will be my honeymoon."

I had shamelessly stolen her line.

"What about you, Ms. McGrail?"

She smiled modestly and said, "I'm not worrying about that at all, at all."

"What are you worrying about?"

"Who will play Judge Crawford in the movie."

EDITORIAL

We applaud the firm stance Judge Elvira Crawford has made on the granting of bail to indicted novelist and former commodity trader Dermot Coyne. In the past we have criticized Judge Crawford for her seemingly arbitrary style in the courtroom. In this case, however, she has acted properly. The commodity exchanges are and have been for many years a cesspool of trickery and corruption. Previous attempts by Federal prosecutors to clean up the commodity market mess have been frustrated by judges who have been entirely too soft on suspected criminals who exploit their customers. Mr. Coyne is accused of monumental theft. Moreover his lawyers have launched an assault on the freedom of the press in what we fervently hope will be a vain attempt to protect him from public scrutiny. We have no sympathy for Mr. Coyne. If he must give up his elaborate plans for a honeymoon, few will feel commiseration for him; most young people must be content with much less expensive wedding trips. We hope that Judge Crawford will bring him to a speedy trial and thus begin the long overdue reform of the gambling casinos at the foot of LaSalle Street.

TRADER DENIES HE WAS CHEATED

By Sean Cassidy

Sam Harris, the famous Chicago investor who is alleged to be the victim of Operation Full Platter target Dermot Coyne, denied vigorously today that he had been cheated by the novelist and former trader.

"It's an insult to my reputation to suggest that I would let a kid like Dermot put something over on me," Harris said.

"I can't understand why they didn't call me before the grand jury. Hell, I'm supposed to be the victim and they apparently didn't care about my version of the incident. Dermot made a mistake and he was lucky. Everyone knows that those things happen all the time in the trading pits."

Asked if he had made money on the trade, Harris replied, "You bet your life I did. Dermot delivered to me contracts at the going price on the day I ordered them. I held on to them and sold just before the market peaked out two weeks later. I made more than he did."

Asked if he would testify for Coyne in his forthcoming trial, Harris replied, "I don't like to go over to that jungle. It's a trap for innocent people. But if Dermot wants me to appear in court, I'll try to explain to those idiots how the commodities market works."

10:00 NEWS

Anchor: Channel 6 has learned exclusively that a plea bargain agreement has already been reached between lawyers for novelist and commodity trader Dermot Michael Coyne and the Office of the United States Attorney. Coyne will plead guilty to one count of simple fraud and will be sentenced to three years in federal prison and a fine of two hundred thousand dollars. With time off for good behavior Coyne could be free in twenty months. He could have been sentenced to twenty years in prison if convicted of all the charges against him. Coyne must also promise to cooperate with the government in its attempt to net bigger fish for its Operation Full Platter sting. One fly in the ointment is that the approval of Judge Elvira Crawford is required. Judge Crawford has a reputation for shooting down plea bargains.

— 24 —

I DIDN'T recognize Annie and Gerroid McGrail when they came out of the customs hall at O'Hare. Only when Nuala, with a whoop of joy, broke away from me and bounded like a frolicsome filly towards the well-dressed couple, did I realize that they were "Ma and Da."

She had been fretting nervously at my side as we waited for them. What if they had missed the plane? What if the INS was detaining them? What if they had landed at the wrong airport? What if they had become frightened and changed their minds?

After all, Dermot Michael, they've never been on an airplane before in their lives, never left Ireland, and rarely left the County Galway. Sure, shouldn't I have gone over and brought them back?

All her doubts and worries were swept away when she embraced the two of them in a mighty hug.

I also understood in that moment where Nuala had derived her ability to change roles instantly to fit the situation in which she found herself. If there were peasants left anywhere in Western Europe and poor peasants at that, they were the small dairy farmers out in the rocks and peat bogs of the Irish-speaking region of Connemara who supplemented their living by "giving teas" for busloads of tourists. Yet this smiling, well-dressed couple, both in conservative gray suits, looked and acted like experienced travelers and sophisticated cosmopolitans. They would fit in at dinner tomorrow night at the Oak Park Country Club like natives, though perhaps more handsome than most of the natives of their age. Supplied with money by herself, they knew how to play the game.

They hugged and kissed and praised me and told me that I looked, "grand, super, brilliant." They charmed my parents who, being what they are, responded in kind.

The trip over was brilliant, too. Everyone was so nice; they loved it in the first-class section; no one seemed to realize that it was their first time in an airplane and their first time out of Ireland. And, sure, isn't this a gorgeous city now, with all its big buildings and that wonderful lake? Weren't they looking forward to their month's holiday in America? And didn't Nuala Anne look lovely and herself already talking like a Yank?

Irish-American.

So she had bought them first-class tickets and arranged for a month's trip around the country. Good for Nuala. Frugal for herself, she knew how to spend money when it would do good for others.

They were to ride to my parents' home in River Forest with herself and meself in my car. Then we'd have a light supper—with all our family there of course—and they'd live in the coach house till after the wedding. Nuala had vetoed a hotel. They had to live where Nell Pat and Bill had spent the last years of their lives.

"Your generosity to them makes me fall in love with you all over again," I said to her as I helped her in the car.

She replied with tears.

She was, I realized again, really a shy child, a shy and poor peasant lass from the Gaeltacht. She was also a lot more, too.

They talked in soft, melodious Irish as I drove out of the parking lot and waited to pay the fee. I knew what was being said. Yes, Dermot had been indicted and arraigned. No, he wasn't going to jail. No, the trial wouldn't be for months. The case would probably be thrown out of court. Yes, the honeymoon was a bit uncertain. Absolutely not. No change in wedding plans. As for that amadon Laurence, he had better stay out of her way.

Ah, sure Nuala, we love you and himself very much and we wouldn't miss this wedding for the world. He's such a nice sweet young man.

Grand. Then we went into English and I played tour guide when we were able to escape the Kennedy Expressway rush-hour mess at Cumberland and wend our way down Thatcher eventually and into River Forest.

My future in-laws were appropriately impressed but not overawed. No wonder Nuala was who she was.

The supper, hardly light by any reasonable standards, was a huge success, enough Irish charm all around to melt the winter snows— and singing and telling stories and even a bit of dancing.

The little bishop had brought my uncle Bishop Bill out from the cathedral where he was staying. Retirement seem to suit him well. What a rotten job being a bishop had become.

Our little bishop, however, seemed to prosper. He drifted around the party, looking bemused as always, as if he were not sure where he was or why he was here, but enjoying himself nonetheless.

He kind of materialized in a corner where Nuala, Cindy, and Joe Hurley were marveling again about how young her parents seemed.

"Doubtless this regrettable unpleasantness will arrange itself appropriately early next week," he said during a lull in the conversation.

"It will take a lot longer than that, Bishop," Cindy said. "It may be a year before we go to trial."

"I would have thought that a comparison between Dermot's voice and that on the tape would have settled the matter."

"Sure it would, but they're not going to let us have a copy of the tape for a long time."

"Patently they will play it on television, arguably tomorrow night."

We were all silent for a moment.

"They wouldn't be that dumb, would they?" Cindy asked dubiously.

Nuala, thick as thieves as always with the little bishop, grinned happily.

"Sure, isn't your man right? Aren't they just that dumb?"

As much as I admired their joint detecting ability, I didn't think we could possibly be that lucky.

Much later, at our pub (our "regular," Nuala had come to call it), Nuala and I were both drinking caffeine-free diet cola and feeling dejected.

"Too much for one day," I said, head in my hands.

"Too much altogether," she agreed.

"I had almost forgotten about your brother. What's he up to?"

"Isn't the amadon flying all around the country, stirring up trouble? He'll be to see Pedar and Podraig in New York tomorrow."

"Paying his own airfare?"

"Unless he can find some way not to."

We both laughed hollowly. She laid her hand on my arm.

"I suppose he'll have a grand time with today's events."

"Won't he ever?"

"The man's mad, Nuala Anne."

"Aren't they all."

"Nuala, how do we attract the crazies?"

"Take your hands away from your face, Dermot Michael; I want to admire your good looks."

"I'm flattered."

Her affectionate smile made my heart skip a couple of beats and picked up my spirits for a moment or two.

"You know what me da says about crazy people?" She rubbed her finger along my lips, forcing me to smile.

"What does your da say?"

She said something in Irish and pounded the table. I assumed that the blow to the table was a required part of what her da would say.

"And that means fockmall?"

"It does not. My da never uses that kind of language, at least when I'm around."

"So what does it mean?"

"Isn't it difficult to translate?"

She was having me on, anything to make me keep smiling. The woman would be a grand spouse (super and brilliant, too) at any time in a life, but especially when the going was rough.

"Try."

"Well it means stay out of the way of the daft folk and when they get in your way, go around them."

"Sane advice."

"'Tis a lot better than advising a good punch in the jaw."

"I won't punch Larry in the jaw, not unless the provocation is intense."

"Och, Dermot, don't you have to go through them sometimes?"

"Speaking of going through people, did you put a hex on the judge this morning?"

She became the picture of injured innocence. "Dermot Michael Coyne! I don't put hexes on people, not at all, at all. Didn't I know she was going to trip and herself so pompous?"

"Didn't help her just a little bit?"

Smirk.

"She didn't need me help . . . Now that poor Quade woman is altogether daft. Isn't she going to be roaring insane before this is over?"

"And your mumbled lullaby will facilitate that process?"

"Sure, it might just, poor woman."

"Sociopaths are clever, Nuala. She may be round the bend, but she's been getting her way."

"Not for much longer."

Nuala seemed supremely confident that we would win. What did she know that I didn't know?

"Your ma and da were wonderful tonight. They acted like experienced world travelers."

"Where do you think I learned how to be such a terrible faker? When you saw them weren't they being the poor Galway peasants for your German tourists?"

She had finally made me laugh, a real laugh and not a hollow gasp. "They're on our side, aren't they?"

"How could they not be after they met your da and ma and the family? And didn't Prester George charm me ma?"

"Better her than you?"

"Now don't be jealous of the poor priesteen."

We laughed again.

Poor little priest indeed.

"But they don't like the prospect of a big family quarrel, do they?"

"They do not, Dermot Michael, not at all, at all. Laurence thinks me da is too old to be the head of the family and therefore he is the head. He just brushes them aside . . . But now, Dermot Michael, we have a major decision to make before we go to our respective beds."

"Do we now?"

"We do."

"And that is about?"

"Our wedding night."

"Are we getting married?"

"This is a serious issue, Dermot Michael Coyne. We have to resolve it now."

"Yes, ma'am."

"I assume that you're planning to disrobe me when we finally get back to our house?"

"I'll admit that thought had occurred to me."

"All you men think about is ripping off a woman's clothes."

"Not all by any means."

We were holding hands and giggling.

"There are two ways the matter can be arranged."

"Are there now?"

"The first is that I sneak off somewhere and put on some frilly and transparent nightgown and robe and then you take those off me before you have your evil way with my body."

"How transparent?"

She slapped my hand playfully. "That's an irrelevant question ... Transparent enough."

"And the other delicious option?"

"You take off all me wedding clothes, piece by piece. That'll be more complicated, and won't you be having clumsy fingers by then?"

"Piece by piece?"

"That's what I said. Slowly, of course, so as to embarrass and tantalize me."

"Very slowly."

"And very gently, mind you."

"Naturally."

I pretended to be thinking seriously about this difficult decision.

"The end result will be the same," I said.

"It will be that."

"Your radiant self."

"I don't know about the radiance. I'll be blushing, that's one thing certain and all yourself taking away all me modesty."

"A difficult choice between two delightful experiences ... Do I have to decide tonight?"

"Dermot Michael Coyne, this is no laughing matter!"

"We're both laughing."

"That's because I'm so mortified."

"Go long wid ya, woman, you love every moment of it."

"You must decide tonight!"

"Why?"

"Don't I have to decide on me lingerie tomorrow morning?"

"So that's what it's all about!"

"'Tis!"

Now she was blushing.

"Well, if it's all the same to you, I think I'd prefer the second option."

She smiled happily.

"Sure, wouldn't that be my favorite, too."

"Not that it's the last time I'll be doing such wicked things."

"I suppose you think you're going to undress me every night for the rest of me life!"

"And maybe a couple of times every day, too."

"I'll not tolerate that kind of lollygagging, not at all."

"Woman, you'd better get used to spending a lot of your time stark naked."

She was now blushing furiously, but grinning complacently. "That's a terrible thing to say to an innocent young woman like me, Dermot Michael Coyne!"

"You started the conversation."

"Tis true . . . Oh, Dermot me darlin' man, I love you so much."

She kissed me, despite Sonia and the other folks in the bar, none of whom were paying any attention to us in our dark corner.

"Now can we talk about the terrible, obscene things I'll do to you after I get your clothes off?"

"We certainly cannot . . . Tis time you get your sleep, you've had a long hard day."

"Fair enough."

"The first thing you'll do," she said when we were out of the tavern and on Southport Avenue, "is kiss me boobs for the longest time and set me on fire, but that will only be the beginning, won't it now?"

"Yes, ma'am."

"A lot more fire after that?"

"Sounds like fun."

Doubtless she had the whole scenario planned in her head and would tell me about it in due course.

Better to know what is expected of you than not to know, right?

RIGHT, the Adversary agreed.

"Go away," I told him.

SHE JUST WENT THROUGH THAT CONVERSATION TO CHEER YOU UP, he taunted me.

"Wouldn't I be knowing that without yourself telling me?"

—25—

 THE MORNING papers just about put me away in a federal penitentiary, probably but not certainly a minimum security camp somewhere. They reported that it was a foregone conclusion that a plea bargain was being worked out. Cindy's fierce denials were written off as part of the plea bargain process.

Daffy Dale must be leaking this stuff, I thought, but to what purpose? To put pressure on us to cave in? Surely she didn't think it would be that easy. Or because she had become such a monomaniac that she actually believed that it would happen?

Most likely she wanted to establish a public image of me as a crook on the edge of admitting his guilt; then, if there were ever a trial, the jury would think me a crook even before the evidence.

As I stared out at the low gray sky and the scudding clouds that were hurrying towards the lake just above my windows, I decided that she believed the whole scenario—from Jarry's tape to my departure in handcuffs for prison. All right, she was crazy. But wasn't there someone else in the U.S. Attorney's Office who could restrain her? Or in the Justice Department?

Apparently not.

A spokesman for the Feds had dismissed Sam Harris with the brusque comment that a man's belief that he had not been a victim of fraud did not prove that fraud had not been committed against him.

How could they say that stuff with a straight face? How could the papers repeat it as though it were a serious comment?

It was all a surrealistic nightmare, leavened by erotic tête-à-têtes with a delicious woman.

I should get some exercise today. Doubtless herself had run a couple of miles this morning before her venture to the lingerie shop. I should go over to the East Bank Club and engage in a furious workout. Over there, however, I would have to answer questions about my plea bargain. So I settled for a mile swim in the pool in my building. I assured two elderly women that I was not going to prison. I don't think they believed me.

Back in my apartment and not feeling one bit better I called my travel agent who had thoughtfully selected a hotel in Galena on the Mississippi as a substitute for San Diego. I told her not to cancel San Diego yet.

I then devoted some thought into what I should pack for the wedding trip, wherever it might end up. Actually I didn't put much effort into it.

The phone rang.

"Dermot Coyne."

"Mario, Mr. Coyne."

The Angel's pleasant thug.

"Yes, Mario."

"We had a message from a certain individual this morning, Mr. Coyne."

"Indeed."

"This individual is familiar with a request that you and Ms. McGrail made during your recent conversation with our mutual friend."

"Ah?"

"The individual will be happy to meet with you and Ms. McGrail."

"Good . . . When?"

"Today. At 1:30 a car will pick you up at the door to your apartment. The driver will stop at Ms. McGrail's apartment and pick her up if she is not with you at the time. He will deliver you to wherever you wish to go at the end of your conversation. Will that be satisfactory?"

"I'm sure it will, Mario."

"It is not one of our cars, Mr. Coyne. I assure you, however, there are no grounds for fear. But those individuals involved would not be offended if you had your friends follow you."

"Friends" meant Mike Casey's people from Reliable.

"Thank you, Mario, that's very reasonable of the individuals involved."

"We will be in touch with you subsequently to ascertain whether the conversation was satisfactory. Our mutual friend believes that it will be."

"Thank you very much, Mario."

"Subsequently" and "ascertain." Did Mario have an MBA?

I called Nuala. No answer. She was, naturally, at the lingerie shop. I guessed it would be Elegante across the street in the 800 North Michigan Building.

I had guessed right.

Herself, looking like the teenager she was only a year ago, was there in jeans and sweatshirt and carrying an umbrella. A huge pile of silky-seeming bags and boxes were piled up on the counter in front of her, doubtless a treasure trove of lace and other dainty materials.

"Hi," I said cautiously.

"Dermot Michael Coyne, whatever in the world are you doing here and yourself spying on me?"

She was more amused than displeased. Good for me.

"Pretty good detective work to figure out where you'd be, isn't it?"

"WHAT do you want?"

Patience slipping away.

I told her what I wanted.

"We'll have to go, Derm," she said grimly. "No choice."

"Certainly," I said, not clear why we had to go.

"The priesteen is taking me ma and da for a ride on one of them big cruise boats. We were supposed to go along."

"I can call your man and tell him that we won't be there."

She nodded her approval. "Tell him that I'll explain later."

Not "we will explain later." Long ago, like a year or so, I had become very angry at being relegated to my spear-carrier role. Now I took it for granted.

"I'll do that . . . Can I help you with these bags?"

"You certainly cannot, Dermot Coyne. Now get out of here. You have no business in a store like this at all, at all."

She was, however, grinning.

"Won't I be seeing them soon enough?"

She grinned more broadly and blushed.

I took my leave while the grin still lasted.

I called George and told him that something had come up which would occupy herself for the afternoon and that we would see him and the two sets of parents at supper at Oak Park Country Club. As long as I attributed the change of plans to Nuala, he did not object or even ask for an explanation.

Then I called Mike Casey of Reliable Security and told him about our planned ride in the country.

"Our people will be watching. Mario said it would be safe?"

"Yeah."

"I'd trust those guys more than I'd trust a lot of businessmen, at least on something like this."

Why had I said "ride in the country?"

I had assumed that Marie Kavanagh Sullivan would not be living in the city. But who would be alive in the city that might recognize her?

Promptly at 1:25 I was summoned to the lobby of the building, where a handsome and proper driver with silver hair, complete with the prescribed cap, was waiting for me.

"Good afternoon, sir; I'm Brendan," he said, with only the slightest hint of a brogue. "I'll be your driver."

"Grand, Brendan," I said, slipping into the patois unintentionally.

He ushered me politely into the vast Lincoln and asked whether there was another stop. I gave him our address on Southport. "There are refreshments in the fridge, sir," he said, and pushed a button which closed a thick window separating driver from passenger.

The refreshments were impressive, sandwiches, small cups of ice cream, Coke, ice, and a couple of different kinds of booze. No Irish whiskey, however.

Nuala was waiting for us in front of the house, perhaps having talked to God in Church before we arrived, as she was wont to do. In her very professional gray dress with black buttons, her hair pulled back severely, she didn't look very happy. Indeed, there was a trace of red around her eye.

"This is Brendan, Nuala, our driver."

"Good afternoon, miss."

"Good afternoon, Brendan."

Inside the car, I said, "There's refreshments in the fridge."

"Food!"

"Yes, ma'am."

She flipped open the door.

"Have you eaten?"

"No, ma'am."

"Neither have I . . . Four sandwiches. Shall we split them? You can have two of the ice-cream cups."

"Now?"

"After you eat your sandwiches, silly," she said with a very faint hint of a smile.

She put our sandwiches on plates, filled two tumblers with ice and diet Coke, and offered me a plate and a tumbler and a napkin.

"Now don't spill anything on your nice blue suit, Dermot Michael."

"No, ma'am."

"I'm acting like a terrible bitch, am I not?"

"I figure you had more trouble with your eejit brother."

"I excommunicated me whole friggin' family!"

Despite this catastrophic experience, she virtually inhaled her first ham and cheese sandwich.

"Not your da and ma?"

"No, not them. All the rest of the friggin' bunch. Well not Fionna, not yet anyway."

"What's happening?"

"Isn't your man having a family council in New York with Nessa and Pedar and Podraig? And don't they want me to fly down there tomorrow to defend meself? And didn't I tell them what they could do with that friggin' scheme?"

Her West of Ireland accent was now as thick as a peat bog.

"I bet you did."

" 'We're just so worried about you,' Nessa says, and herself friggin' weeping. And I says I can friggin' worry about meself. And doesn't she beg me to think about what I'm doing to Da and Ma? And don't I say that they're the ones doing it, not me?"

"Aha!"

"And I tell her I'll be marrying you a week from tonight even if they throw their friggin' bodies in front of our cars on State Street."

"Powerful image."

"And doesn't she say that she doesn't see how she can be in the wedding party? And so don't I fire her as me woman of honor and then hang up?"

"Nuala Anne?"

"I don't care! I don't want any long faces at me wedding, seeing that it will be the only one in me life."

"You'd better believe that."

"So then Pedar calls me with the same ton of shite and I tell him that I'm disinviting the whole lot of them from the wedding and I don't want to see their sniveling faces. And then I hang up on him."

"They keep calling?"

"Didn't they ever? And didn't I hang up on them every time?"

"You call your parents?"

"Didn't I have to? Me ma took it pretty well. All she wants is for us to be happy and she knows we will. I tell her not to let it ruin her cruise this afternoon and she says it won't. She knows what that asshole Laurence is like, though she doesn't call him that. But I hate to see them suffer. I don't give a good shite about the rest of them eejits."

Her fury was icy. No tears this time around. She turned her attention to her second sandwich, chomping at it like it was one of her siblings.

"It's all your man," she continued, clenching the fist which wasn't occupied with her sandwich. "Sure, if it were someone else, I'd probably be on his side. He's a grand troublemaker, especially when he has something to work with."

"Like he does now."

"'Tis not your fault."

She polished off her second sandwich and reached for an ice-cream cup.

"Me da says you should never drink when you're angry or sad, but I'd love a touch of something stronger than a diet Coke just now."

"No," I said firmly.

"I know . . . Besides, won't we need to be bright and quick when we finally meet herself?"

"You're sure we'll meet Marie?"

"No doubt about it."

Normally the hours between eleven and two are the best time during the day to navigate the Chicago Expressway system. Brendan ("A Mayo man," herself noted with approval) skillfully steered through the mess which Fullerton Avenue always is and then made rapid progress on the JFK. At the Eden junction, he took a right turn and headed north.

"Isn't the weather clearing up nicely, Dermot? Sure, themselves will have a grand time on your cruise boat. Maybe the day will clear up a lot for us, too."

"Do you think it will?"

She nodded slowly.

"I think she wants to talk to us as much as we want to talk to her. She's a smart one, you know? Wasn't the whole thing her idea?"

"How do you know that?"

"It was too clever for either of them male eejits to think up."

That settled that.

I amused myself during the trip by caressing some of the more delicate parts of Nuala's anatomy, a task facilitated by the shortness of her miniskirt. She sighed complacently as my explorations proceeded. A week from tomorrow night we'd be in bed together, no matter what Judge Crawford tried to do to us.

"I'm having meself a grand time," I remarked, "fantasizing about yourself in all those lacy things you were buying this morning."

She didn't rap my arm for this indecency. "Dermot, dear, darling Dermot, I can hardly wait."

At the end of the Eden we turned on the link to the Tri-State and continued north. We passed the exit for Libertyville and Mundelein, where Prester George had attended the seminary. Finally, only a few miles short of the Wisconsin border we exited at Highway 173 and turned towards the lake. I'd never been this far north of the city off the expressway system. We passed through wooded country with an occasional elaborate gate at the side of the road. These were surely the homes of the super rich. Finally, not too far away from the lake, I thought, we turned again to the right, went through a gate and down a curving lane with glorious red-and-gold autumn foliage towering above us.

Then we came to a large, neatly manicured lawn and, after one more turn, pulled up to a house that reminded me of Brideshead in the miniseries, an English manor house lifted from a film. All it lacked was a Rolls or a Bentley or maybe both parked on the gravel road in front of the door.

Brendan opened the car door for us. We stepped out of the car into a zone of almost unnatural quiet, no birds, no traffic, no wind, no sound at all, at all.

"Scary," Nuala whispered to me, taking my arm.

"You can hear the grass grow," I replied.

"If you ring the bell," Brendan said, "Gorman will see to you. I will be waiting here to take you back to the city when you are finished."

"Thank you, Brendan," Nuala said, now in her lady-of-the-manor guise.

"Waugh," I whispered to Nuala.

"Or Wodehouse."

I rang the doorbell. Deep inside the house a gong responded. The door opened almost immediately.

"Mr. Coyne and Ms. McGrail," I said briskly to the young woman, a few years older than herself, in a maid's uniform.

"Come in," she said. "I will tell Mrs. Mangan that you are here."

We were shown into a parlor just off the entrance corridor and invited to sit down. We remained standing.

"That one's a Cork woman," Nuala says to me.

"And our friend is now using the name of Mangan."

"Clarence Mangan was a grand Irish poet."

"I know THAT."

The maid, presumably Gorman, returned.

"Mrs. Mangan will see you now. Will you follow me, please?"

We were led through an immense parlor and a vast dining room towards the rear of the house. The place seemed dust-proof and stain-free. Yet I doubt that there had been any parties here in a long time.

In the parlor a large and tasteful painting of a nude hung over the fireplace. She held a flimsy garment beneath her breasts and looked enchantingly vulnerable. The painter must have worked with both adoration and respect.

Mrs. Mangan was waiting for us in a solarium at the rear of the house. Mums of many different colors filled the autumn garden outside.

Mrs. Mangan was a tall woman with perfectly coifed white hair. Dressed in a simple gray dress, almost the same shade as Nuala's, she awaited us standing up, cane in hand. Despite the network of wrinkles which covered her face she was handsome and apparently alert.

Marie Kavanagh Sullivan, almost seventy years later?

No doubt about it!

"Miss McGrail and Mr. Coyne, ma'am," Gorman informed her.

She inspected us closely for a moment, then fell back into the easy chair from which she had apparently risen.

"Bill!" She gasped. "It can't be! And Nell!"

She began to weep.

The quiet, pretty solarium quickly filled up with the uncanny. Or the Uncanny.

Almost instantly Nuala was kneeling at her side holding her hand.

"He's Bill Ready's grandson, Mrs. Mangan; I'm his fiancée and not half the woman she was. And I don't have her red hair, worse luck for me. But I am from the same town."

Gorman stood at the other side of the stricken woman, anxious and worried.

"Tis all right, ma'am, tis all right."

The Uncanny swirled around. I was surrounded by Druids. And ghosts.

Perhaps a few angels, too, but they weren't singing and dancing, not at all, at all.

Marie Mangan recovered her composure with surprising speed.

"Come closer, young man. So you're Bill Ready's grandson? Well, aren't you the spitting image of himself?"

"And isn't he gorgeous?" Nuala demanded proudly.

"Very much so, my dear. And you're from Carraroe?"

"I am, and didn't the two of us meet in a pub in Dublin?"

"Where else would you meet," Marie said with a laugh. "Well you're both most welcome. I'm very glad you've come. I wanted to tell someone our story. Bill and Nell's grandson has a right to know it."

"Thank you, ma'am," I replied.

"You know, child," Marie said to Gorman, "I think all four of us need a bit of a drink. Irish whiskey? Yes, I thought so."

"And you two are about to be married?" she continued.

"We are, ma'am," Nuala replied. "A week from tomorrow. At the Cathedral?"

"Might I come?"

"I hope you will."

"I'll smile when Brendan parks in that lot where it all happened so long ago."

We drank a toast to one another in Bushmill's Green.

Then the old woman said, "Well, I'd better begin telling my story if you two are to return home before dark."

—26—

MARIE'S STORY

Jimmy killed the first time when he was ten. A kind woman had given him two shillings because he was so polite when he delivered a couple of loaves of freshly baked bread to her house. He told his friends about the gift. One of them, a couple of years older and much stronger, cornered him in an alley with a knife and tried to take the money away from him. Jimmy fought back of course, as he always would. Fighting back was the only way to survive. In the scuffle he turned the knife around. He had no idea what was happening. The knife plunged into the other lad's heart. Jimmy never forgot how quickly the blood exploded from the poor boy's body. He dreamed about the expression of terror and surprise and the boy's face for the rest of his life. He'd wake up at night sobbing. I'd hold him in my arms like a little boy and sing songs to him till he went back to sleep. In many ways Jimmy was always a little boy. He never had a chance to grow up.

"All the shillings in the world are not worth a single drop of human blood," he used to say. "And I have shed blood, hundreds of gallons of it."

He didn't know who his mother or father were. He had no memories before Sullivan's bakery in Cork. He heard from some that he was the son of an English officer and an Irish serving maid and from others that his father was an illiterate countryman and his mother an Englishwoman from one of the "big houses." He loved to tell stories; I think he could have been a novelist. He used to make up stories about his parents and tell them to me and ask if they seemed plausible. I'd say that all I needed to know about him was that he was Irish and that someone had loved him very much when he was a small child; otherwise, he would not be able to love as generously as he did.

He was a bright, alert and hardworking little boy. One of the Sullivans' daughters, a few years older than him, taught him the rudiments of reading and writing. That was the only school Jimmy ever had. Somehow he managed to educate himself, mostly at the front during the Great War as he used to call it. If you had met him without knowing his background, you would have said he was a witty, well-educated gentleman. That role fit him like a glove. It became Jimmy Sullivan by the time I knew him. Everything else in his life was walled up behind it. Even I had a hard time getting beneath it to the real Jimmy. He'd only talk about his past in bed and only when I'd press him to tell me more.

There was so much agony, so much pain, so much grief locked up inside him. I never was able to do any more than touch the surface of it.

Survival was all that mattered to him, to stay alive for a few more days, a few more weeks, maybe another year. He admitted to me that he was a thief in Cork. He organized a gang of thieves his age. "We didn't steal much and only from the swells," he used to say. "As gangs went in those days we were rather harmless. We never killed anyone, thank God."

He joined the English army to escape from Cork and move up in the world. He did not want to talk about the war, not ever. He'd just say, "Ah, sure, love, wasn't it easier to be a company commander in Flanders than boss of a gang of street thieves in Cork?"

He did say once that at Paschendale when the Royal Tank Corps broke through the German lines for eight miles the English could have won the war if Sir John French and Douglas Haig, the British commanders, had the sense to exploit the breakthrough. He hated French especially, blamed him for the destruction of his company. I think that was the time he was recommended for the Victoria Cross. They gave him the

Military Cross instead because he was Irish. He told me that he threw it into the River Lee when he returned to Cork. His men apparently held the line for an extra day during the German counterattack and saved tens of thousands of English soldiers—"only to have most of them butchered later on," he said to me once.

I read a lot of Irish history, trying to understand my man. I asked him once if Michael Collins had really ordered the killing of General Maitland, who was Chief of the Imperial General Staff, during the "troubles."

"It was an execution of a criminal," he said coldly. "And please, love, I'll talk about it someday, but not today."

He never talked about it despite his promise, but I think he was involved in the killing. He liked to tell me about his past, especially after we'd made love, but only in bits and pieces.

"When I came back to Ireland after the war, with a few gold pieces in my pocket and nothing much else to show for five years of killing, it was either sign up with the Black and Tans who wanted me or join the Big Fella. So I did a little bit of both."

"You were a spy for Collins, Jimmy?"

He'd wink and kiss me and say something like, "Well, love, I was certainly not spying for the Tans."

He later broke with Collins after the peace treaty was signed and then, after they killed Collins, he quit the irregulars and came to America.

"I watched Emmett Dalton sweep those fools out of Cork that summer and knew we didn't have a chance—and the Cork Regatta going on at the same time as if it were the most important thing in Ireland. I thought the Big Fella might end the fighting, but when they killed him I knew it would be a fight to the bloody end, and I wanted a couple of more years of life."

That was a long speech for him. Sometimes it was hard to know which side he was on.

"On me own side," he'd say when I asked him, "just trying to survive for a couple of more days."

He took to Bill Ready the way he did because Bill had lived through the same confusion and had to leave Ireland for similar reasons . . . Jimmy wasn't twenty-five then and Bill, as you know, was barely twenty. That seems so young today . . .

He believed that we lived in a jungle, and heaven knows there was nothing in his life that gave him any reason to question that conviction.

"Maybe there was order under the Roman Empire," he said to me once, "though I'm not even sure about that. But it's the era of the barbarians now. Governments don't work. They never have, unless you're rich. They can't make proper wars or proper peace either. The police are corrupt, always, everywhere. If you're rich, maybe they can protect you. If you're not, they won't even try. Every man has to defend his own castle and his own people . . . whatever that involves."

There was nothing in the Chicago of the nineteen twenties to make him change his mind. Shortly after he opened his bakeshop with some of those gold coins from the war, a couple of punks tried to make him pay protection money. He laughed at them. The next day the windows of his shop were broken. They came back again. He threw them out of the store. He went to the police who, he found out later, were getting a cut of the protection money. They told him to wise up. When the punks came back to set fire to the place he was waiting for them. No one ever saw either of them again.

"It's a war," he'd say to me. "You defend your life and your property any way you can."

He had come to believe that killing was necessary to survive, but he never loved killing as they used to say back in those days. He brooded over every death.

"The man was no good," he'd say to me. "But once he was an adored little baby in his mother's arms. Like I was."

Bootlegging was a perfect opportunity for him. He knew how to organize an operation from his days in the army and he was smarter than all the rest of them. He thought the law was silly, as everyone in Chicago seemed to. He defended his own territory like a row of trenches in France, though he thought that the gang leaders were stupid to bother fighting one another.

"Al Brown is right," he told me before we were married. "There's more than enough for everyone."

He always called Capone "Al Brown" or "Mr. Brown" with

a wink in his eye. Or sometimes even "Your friend over in Cicero," with a nod of his head towards the West Side.

Some of the people who wrote about us said that I was a flapper, a dizzy deb without a brain in my head. I was young and inexperienced, God knows. But I was not dumb. I knew that he was a criminal and a killer, but I wasn't fascinated by that. I was fascinated by him. I did not think I would save him from his crimes. I wanted him. It was, if you will, a terrible schoolgirl crush, but it turned into a lot more than that and very quickly. He didn't seduce me either.

I knew nothing about where he came from or what he had done. I would learn something about that much later. It wouldn't have made a bit of difference if I had heard about his past before we were married.

He was the most wonderful man I had ever met, gentle and charming and respectful and funny and kind and generous. So he seemed then, and so he seems even today after all these years.

Excuse my tears. I miss him so much.

I realized that he adored me and that he would do anything for me, and eventually that he believed I was the best thing that had ever happened to him. "You're the only good thing in my whole life," he said to me, "the only grace God ever bothered to send me. I hope I can have you with me for a few more years."

He was a fantastic lover. I don't know and don't care how he learned about women. He knew me, knew what I needed and wanted before I knew myself. After the first time, I realized that I would belong to him forever. That part never changed.

We both liked the Readys—Bill, the big, smart, simple man that he was and Nell, the passionate little fireball that she was. Maybe Jim saw in Bill the moral integrity he would have liked for himself. I saw in her the gritty loyalty I hoped I would learn in marriage. They came to Jim's apartment to ask help against Klondike O'Donnell, who was trying to extort protection money from Bill's business. They were in deeper trouble than they realized. Klondike was the kind of man who killed on a whim. Jimmy warned him off and that was that. We invited them to our wedding. They fit in wonderfully. I wanted to keep them as friends. But Jimmy said to me, "Love, they're not our kind of people."

I said, "Are we too good for them?"

And he replied, "No, they're too good for us."

I knew what he meant and for the first time began to worry about our future.

When I fell in love with Jimmy, did I think it would last? Did I realize that most bootleggers died young? I was eighteen. I didn't ask such questions. Now is forever and tomorrow doesn't matter. I didn't care about the risks because I didn't think of them much.

But he did think of them, every day, especially after little Peggy was born. The system that Capone had imposed on the gangs and which Jimmy supported had worked at first. Then the thugs began to get greedy, the Genna brothers who were totally insane, Bugs Moran's gang, Klondike O'Donnell. They begin to kill one another and then kill Capone's men and Jimmy's, too. He did what to him seemed the natural thing to do, he fought back.

Then some people inside the Capone gang started to think that they could do a better job than Big Al. It was dangerous to think such thoughts as his two gunmen Anselmi and Scalise learned when Capone had them killed. The Genna brothers were behind the trouble, as they always were in the late nineteen twenties. They got themselves killed one by one but each one of them was tougher and meaner and dumber than the previous one. They were Sicilians, from Little Sicily or Taylor Street as we call it now. They resented the fact that a Neapolitan like Capone was running the mob. That was not the way it was done in the old country.

I found out about these conflicts only later. Jimmy didn't tell me and I didn't ask. I didn't read the papers much because I didn't believe anything they said. I did realize, however, after Ellen was born, that Jimmy came home each night more preoccupied and worried. "Nothing serious," he told me.

Then some of his men were killed by Capone people. Machine-gunned in a restaurant up on Fullerton Avenue. We went to their funerals of course. For the first time I was really scared. I was pregnant again and I realized that I could become a widowed mother of two children anytime.

"Is it ever going to stop, Jimmy?" I asked him one night.

"It's going to have to stop," he said. "One way or another."

The next event was the famous shoot-out in front of the Lexington Hotel, where Capone lived at the time. Jimmy's men drove down the street in ten cars and cut those three killers into little pieces. In broad daylight.

"I had to do it," he told me. "They killed my men and they would have killed all of us if we'd left them alive."

Then he told me all about what had been happening. I was petrified but I tried to act like an adult.

"What happens next?"

"I fight Al Brown. It's him or me at this point."

Then Frank Nitti, the one they called "The Enforcer," came to see us under a kind of a flag of truce. Jimmy let me listen to the conversation. Almost seventy years later I still remember it like yesterday.

"Our mutual friend says to tell you that he don't owe you nothing," Nitti begins.

"Ah," says Jimmy, as smooth and slick as he ever was. "I'm glad to hear that."

"Turns out," Nitti goes on, "you did our mutual friend a favor."

"Always happy I can do that."

"Them dopes were in with the Gennas."

"I have suspected as much."

"They were trying to make trouble between you and our mutual friend."

"They will never learn, will they?"

Nitti touches his head to his finger to indicate that the Gennas are crazy.

"Will you be so good as to tell our mutual friend that I am delighted there are no ill feelings."

"I will, Jimmy. He'll be glad you feel the same way he does. As far as he's concerned the old system is still in place."

They talked about the weather and baseball and then Nitti gets up to leave. He is very respectful to me as they always were. At the door, Jimmy stops him.

"Frank, will you do me a favor?"

"Anything, Jimmy. Anything. You name it."

"In a week or two I might want to have a confidential chat with our mutual friend. About the future."

Nitti looks at him with those cold expressionless eyes, and says, "Anytime, Jimmy. You know where to get me. I'm sure he'd be glad to chat with you. Some place you both agree on. Maybe out in Melrose Park."

"What do you want to talk to Al Brown about?" I ask him after Nitti has left.

"It's time to get out, love. This peace isn't going to last. Al Brown has made himself a worldwide figure. The killing will go on. The Federal government will have to put him in jail eventually. The fools have ruined the business, but what's done is done. I have three choices. The first is that I go to jail, probably on some trumped-up charges, the second is that I get killed, the third is that I get out. Now. While there is still time."

"I'll vote for the third," I say firmly.

He nods and smiles. "Funny thing, love, I was thinking the same thing. Johnny Torrio, who brought Al Brown along, was shot up by the Spike O'Donnells and decided to get out. He turned things over to Al. Maybe I should do the same thing."

"Turn all your business over to him?"

"Why not? We don't need any more money."

"And you'll survive, like you have always done."

"You got it, love," he said with another grin. "I'll have to see if Al and I can negotiate an agreement in which he and his successors take care of my men and my friends like Bill Ready, and the unions I've protected from the extortionists. I think we can do it."

"Then let's do it," I say.

"There's one problem."

"What's that?" I say, feeling the kid inside jump for the first time.

"Al Brown has often said he'd like to do the same thing Torrio did—get out while he was still alive. Only he says it's too late. There's too many people who want him dead and too many government people who want him in jail. He could never get away. I'm very much afraid, love, that I might have to say the same thing."

"No," I say. "You can't let that happen."

"I have to figure a way to do it," he says slowly. "There must be some strategy that would work."

I had been learning about the gangs and their wars only in the last few days. So I didn't know enough to keep my crazy suggestions to myself.

"Get yourself killed," I blurt out.

He looks at me like I'm crazy. Then he gets that slow smile which I always loved so much.

"Get Al Brown to rub me out?"

"If you're going to give him all your business, that's the least he can do."

So we begin to work it out. He was very proud of me, because I'm good at working out a lot of the details. I never thought I could be such a conniver. We figure out who we have to bribe. It turns out not to be that many people, some cops, the chief at the Chicago Avenue Station, the ambulance people, Doctor Herman Bundesen the coroner who later ran for governor and lost, the undertaker. We don't have to bribe the little priest at the Cathedral, because he likes us both and will be delighted that we're getting out.

Gorman, you must bring me another small drink. And for our guests, too. These memories excite me more than they should.

Those were very exciting times. Al Brown looks at us like we're crazy when we meet him at a little restaurant out in Melrose Park. First he's surprised that I'm there. They never bring the women, and he knows Irish women because his wife is Irish. And she stayed loyal to him like Irish wives do. Then he's astonished at our scheme. But before the lunch is over he accepts the whole plan and swears a solemn oath that he and his followers will never breathe a word as long as either of us are still alive. They've kept the promise.

So the whole plan works perfectly. No one, not even the stupid reporters, smells anything wrong. And no one ever says what happened. There are rumors but they don't mean anything. None of the guns are loaded. I don't know what happened to the cornerstone at the Cathedral, but it wasn't chipped that day. Even Anselmi's wound was faked. Jimmy is hiding in a house in Oak Park and I'm at our apartment until a few days after the funeral. Then we're ready to begin our new life.

We had new identities, new names, new papers, new bank accounts. We're now the Mangans, I'm still Marie and he's Johnny. We planned to move to Portland because the Outfit wasn't out there and no one would recognize us. We had even bought land out there which we thought was a good investment. It turned out to be a much better investment than we thought.

Then one thing goes wrong. Somehow the Gennas suspected that there was more to Jimmy's death than met the eye. They were too dumb to imagine something as elaborate as our scheme but they know something is going on in Oak Park, which in those days was solidly Republican and whose police force, astonishingly enough, is not corrupt. So they start nosing around. They find out about Al Brown's safe house out there and are about to close in on it, just when I arrive to join Jimmy with Peggy in my arms. In two days we're scheduled to get on the Empire Builder. It will take us to the Pacific Northwest and a new life.

Jimmy doesn't know what to do. Al has warned him on the phone that the Gennas are coming and that we should get out of the house while we can. We leave by the back door just as two Packards pull up to the front door. All we have is Peggy and some money and the tickets to Portland. But where should we go? We sneak down streets and alleys dodging the Genna cars. Jimmy says it's like running from the police in Cork when he was a boy. I am terrified, but I try to hide my fears for his sake.

Then I remember that the Readys have an apartment on Austin Boulevard. It's almost completely dark and we can hardly see the street numbers on the two flat buildings. Every car that passes on the boulevard seems to have a Genna brother in it.

Finally we come to their flat. We ring the doorbell. Naturally they're astonished to see Jimmy, but also happy. We tell them we need a favor. Can we hide with them for a few days?

This is a much bigger favor than they owe us. But they don't hesitate a second. They take us into their apartment and treat us like royalty. The Gennas trash the safe house, but they don't find anyone or anything. They give it up. We call Al Brown and tell him we're all right and we'll be leaving soon. He asks God to bless us, if you can imagine.

Two days later Bill and Nell—you couldn't keep that one out of the adventure—drive us over to Niles Center, where the Empire Builder stops briefly, and we say good-bye. We never see them again, though we did call them every year at Christmas while Jimmy was still alive. He thought it was unsafe to send Christmas cards. He was always very cautious, more cautious than I was. But no one ever found us.

There's not much else to tell. The rest of our life was peaceful. Jimmy was a very successful entrepreneur in Portland and we never needed money. We moved to San Francisco during the war. Jimmy became a colonel in supplies. He was such a brilliant organizer that they wanted him to stay in the army as a general. He knew better than that, at least after I told him not to.

He made good investments to take care of me and the children. We had three more children, fifteen grandchildren, and twenty great-grandchildren, though Jimmy didn't live to see any of the great-grandchildren. He missed the bakeshop, but we thought it was too dangerous to go into the same business again. He did a lot of baking at home. After a few years he turned to painting and became very good at it. You probably noticed the big portrait in the parlor? It flatters me more than it should, but it's good work. He went to Mass with me every morning. In Portland Jimmy finally found some peace, not as much as I wanted him to have but more than he had ever expected.

He died in 1961 of a stroke. Instantly and without warning. He was only sixty-four years old. I suppose all the stress of his early years took their toll. He smoked too much, too, as I always told him. He is buried in a cemetery in Portland and I will lie next to him when I die. I have missed him all these years. We'll be together soon, I think. I'm sure God loves him as much as I do and understands that his early life influenced what he did. I know how sorry he was for the men he killed, so God must know, too.

I thank God that I had Jimmy with me for thirty-four years.

I came back to Chicago in 1970. For some reason all my children and many of my grandchildren moved to Chicago.

They have never known that I was born and raised here. I see them often but I stay away from Chicago social activities, though there are very few people who would know me and none who would recognize me as the flapper deb who married the famous bootlegger.

You recognized me at once, my dear? That's very kind of you.

I have a small studio in Streeterville where I stay overnight when I have some reason to be in town. The ride back and forth on the same day tires me. I go to Mass at the Cathedral. They tore down our store and Brendan parks the car in the parking lot that's there now. When I get out of the car, I think about how we fooled everyone.

Jared Kennedy is my grandson? You are clever, my dear. Yes, he does look a little like Jimmy, though he's now much fatter than Jimmy ever was. He is clever like Jimmy too, but so twisted. His parents spoiled him terribly.

I owe it to your grandparents to make him tell the truth. Will he risk jail if he does? Since a very large inheritance might be at stake, I think he will. Jared is very clever, even if he is usually too clever by half. I suspect he won't have to go to jail.

I will see what I can do about him.

Come to your wedding my dear?

I'd love to. Thank you for the invitation.

Perhaps you are right; perhaps Nell would want me to be there.

As for my story, after I'm gone you certainly may tell it. Indeed I hope you tell it.

—27—

 "HE MUST have loved her even more than she realized," Nuala Anne observed as we rode back to Chicago. "He forced himself to change completely to keep her happy."

"You think that's what happened?"

"He loved the excitement of battle. He gave it up for her."

"Capone might have killed him."

"More likely he would have killed Capone . . . You saw the painting in the parlor?"

"I couldn't take my eyes off you."

"Go long wid ya, Dermot Michael . . . He adored her even more than she realizes. She was his salvation . . ."

"Women usually are."

"She idealizes him now, makes him seem almost innocent of his crimes. We don't know whether he used force to succeed in Portland. Maybe he did. There were, I think, no more killings."

I did not argue with Nuala's analysis. She had figured the whole story out before we had entered Marie's house, including her relationship with Jarry. Who was I to second guess the Great Detective?

"Do you think she will lean on Jarry?" I asked.

"She said she would, and I believe her."

"She didn't say when."

"Before the day is over, Dermot Michael," she said impatiently.

"Will he go along?"

"She didn't promise, did she now?"

"No. She said she'd see what she could do."

"She seemed confident that he would. There must be a lot of money involved. We'll have to wait and see."

I still felt powerful traces of the Uncanny which had filled that solarium while Marie told her story. Energies and dynamisms which I would never understand were unrolling in that room. Favors were being paid and repaid. My bride was riding the waves of the Uncanny as it swept through the house, directing them skillfully and wisely. How and why did I ever get involved with such a one?

"Were we at the edge back there, Nuala Anne?"

"You mean where the light begins?"

"Yeah."

"Sure we were. Couldn't you sense the angels all around us?"

"I certainly sensed something."

"Wasn't she the remarkable woman now?"

"Marie?"

"Her too. I meant your gram . . . I wish I were half the woman she was."

"You know what, Nuala love, I think I'm going to enforce a ban on that comparison. I don't want you making it anymore. Ma was a grand woman . . ."

"Super, brilliant," she added with a giggle.

"So are you, and it's wrong to make comparisons like that. Do you understand, young woman?"

"Yes, Dermot Michael," she said obediently. "Aren't you right, like you always are?"

I didn't want any comparisons between me and Pa either. I'd lose any way you looked at it.

The sun had already set. Night was chasing twilight out of the sky. We'd be late for the dinner schedule with our respective parents. I asked Brendan to drive us to the Oak Park Country Club. We'd take a cab downtown after dinner.

Huddling in the protection of the dark, Nuala laid out a scenario for our wedding night. She had obviously been reading a lot of books. The activities she proposed were all technically possible and every one of them would be delightful. It was doubtful, however, that either of us would have the stamina or the restraint to engage in all of them.

I tried to listen to what she meant instead of what she was saying. It wasn't hard to figure it out. Herself was confident about me and utterly insecure about her own performance. How should I respond to that fear?

"It will be brilliant, Nuala Anne, even if both of us are nervous and inept, as I know I will be. Everything will be grand. We don't need a touchdown on the first play, do we now?"

She was silent, perhaps upset because she couldn't say that I didn't understand what she was talking about.

"If you say so, Dermot Michael," she said dubiously.

"We love each other too much to worry if we don't make the touchdown."

"'Tis true," she agreed. "But we should at least make a first down."

"Or second and short."

She laughed happily, her fears erased.

"Och, Dermot, I'm such a worrywart. What would I do without you, me darlin' man?"

I had not done too badly in that little interlude, had I?

I thanked the angels who might have been lurking on the edges of our conversation.

You're going to have to spend the rest of your life playing the same game, the Adversary warned me.

"She's worth it," I told him.

So you say, he replied, and left the car.

We were only fifteen minutes late for dinner. Cindy, who was not to be one of the guests at the meal, was waiting for us in the lobby, pacing restlessly.

"Derm, wherever have you two been!" she said as she hugged me. "I've been searching all over for you. We were beginning to get worried."

"Didn't we have some investigating to do?" Nuala answered for me.

"I didn't think they'd dare do it, but they have. Dale must really be out of her mind."

"What did they do?" I asked.

"They leaked the tape to the TV stations. They all played it on the five o'clock news. We have them, Dermot, we have them!"

The ice, I thought, was beginning to crack. But we hadn't won yet.

— 28 —

"I'M HAPPY that all of you have been able to interrupt your busy schedules this Friday afternoon to attend our little conference," Wade Warren Winthrop said, caressing the diamond on the ring finger of his right hand. "I understand that some of you may miss planes up to Dorr County. I think you'll find that you've made a wise choice before our little conference is over."

We were in Winthrop's personal conference room. Floor-to-ceiling windows looked out over the Lake, McCormick Place, Soldier Field, the railroad tracks, Northerly Island with its Shedd Aquarium and its Adler Planetarium, and much of the South Side of Chicago, dull and somber on a cloudy October afternoon.

W.W. (as he was always called) was a large man, not quite fat, in a perfectly fitting dark blue suit with a trace of weave in its fabric. His hair was long and silver and carefully groomed. His voice was resonant baritone. He looked like a supreme court justice or possibly a very corrupt divorce lawyer. He was in fact the managing partner of Winthrop, McClaren, Donovan, and Epstein, a model of probity and perhaps the last influential WASP in the Chicago Bar. His prestige and his prestige alone had constrained the representatives of the Chicago media outlets to give up their Friday afternoon.

The other lawyers present were cut from the same bolt of very expensive cloth, senior partners all of them, and very heavy members (in both senses of the word heavy for the most part) of top-drawer Loop law firms, though none of them were anywhere near as shrewd as W.W. They did not seem very happy about being dragged to a "settlement conference" about which they were murmuring words like "premature" and "much too soon."

Three journalists were also present, probably because the lawyers were not able to keep them away—Jack Riordan, an anchor on Channel 6, Jena Lange, the news editor of Channel 3, and an assistant managing editor of one of the papers who apparently did not have a name.

Before the conference began, Riordan, a Black Irish charmer with perfect white teeth, engaged Nuala in conversation which was but a short step away from flirtation. I figured that herself knew what she was doing.

She was dressed in what looked like a leather suit (and probably wasn't) and a plum-colored blouse with one extra button open. Since she always looks wholesome no matter what she has on (or hasn't) the result was a devastating mix of sweetness and sophistica- tion. Again she doubtless knew what she was doing and why. Better that I not ask. Rather I should merely enjoy being devastated.

Lange for her part was content to murmur over and over again, as though it were a mantra, "This is all shit."

Completing the group were Cindy and a professor from the Uni- versity of Illinois at Chicago (still called "Chicago Circle" by the locals), and the plaintiff in the suit against the media. I said nothing to anyone. Rather I sat at the table looking like the cat who had eaten a shop full of canaries.

"My colleague, Ms. Hurley, will make our presentation," W.W. intoned solemnly.

"I think I speak for everyone here, W.W," one of the gaggle of lawyers interrupted, "to say that it is only because of your personal intervention that we're here. We believe the matter is not yet nearly mature enough to speak of settlement."

"You may well change your mind, H.H.," W.W. responded, "after Ms. Hurley's presentation. Would you please begin, Cynthia?"

"We are prepared to consider very limited settlement payments," my sibling began, her eyes flashing, "if apologies are forthcoming by Sunday. In the morning papers for the print media, and on the Sunday afternoon newscasts for the television media. We would require naturally that these retractions appear also on Monday. Anyone who does not avail themselves of this opportunity will find themselves liable for the whole amount of the plaintiff's demand."

There were murmurs of "preposterous" and "outrageous" from the assembled body, punctuated with several scatological observations from Ms. Lange.

"Hear me out, gentlemen," Cindy said sharply, her voice sounding like a rifle shot. "I wish to introduce Dr. Ralph Gunderson, chairman of the Department of Electrical Engineering at the University of Illinois at Chicago. Dr. Gunderson is a specialist on voice sounds and has often appeared as a government witness in trials in which voice has become an issue."

Gunderson was a little man with a lot of jet-black hair and an infectious smile. He unveiled a machine—which looked like a medium-size television set with some *Star Wars* add-ons—on a moving platform which he dragged to the center of the room.

"Thank you, Ms. Hurley. This machine is a somewhat complicated version of an oscilloscope. We use it in preliminary comparisons of voices. It measures two elementary dimensions of voice waves—amplitude or height and depth of the wave and duration or length of waves. Mr. Coyne, would you read this paragraph please into our microphone?"

"Yes, sir," I said as I took the paper from him.

"You bet I did," I read, "inside and out, backwards and forwards, real good. And he was too dumb to know what was going on."

I put the sheet of paper on the conference table in front of me.

"You will note," Dr. Gunderson said, "that the screen recorded Mr. Coyne's sound waves. Let me play it back for you."

He played it back. I was prejudiced but I thought the waves were kind of elegant.

"Now I'll print out a graph of the waves," he said, pressing a button on the back of the machine. A printer on the second shelf of the platform chugged out two pages, with approximately the same sound as that of an EKG printout machine.

"You may pass it around and inspect it," Dr. Gunderson continued.

The people around the table glanced uneasily at the output and passed it on. They were afraid that they knew what was coming and they did not like it. At all, at all.

"This is all shit," Ms. Lange muttered, doubtless trying to dispel evil spirits. Little did she realize that angels were congregating in the light at the edge of the room, pushing one another in their eagerness to get into the act.

Actually, I didn't see the angels at all. I was merely imagining what my bride might be seeing.

"Now," Dr. Gunderson said with an appealing smile, "let me play another recording of the same paragraph. This is taken from our recording of a clip broadcast on television during the ten o'clock news last night. We have filtered out the static and the extraneous noise from the clip. You are naturally perfectly free to work with your own tapes which, presumably, you received from the Federal Attorney's office."

"You bet I did, inside and out, backwards and forwards, real good. And he was too dumb to know what was going on."

"At first hearing, this sounds to the naked ear, if you will excuse my expression, something like the voice of Mr. Coyne, possibly his real voice, possibly someone attempting a crude imitation of his voice. However, when I play this tape again with the monitor presenting the waves, it appears, even at first glance, a very different set of waves."

Cold silence in the room. The angels were already in it, dancing and frolicking and having themselves one, you should excuse the expression, hell of a good time.

"I'll now turn off the audible sound and play the two tapes together, so you can compare the sound waves."

The second set of waves seemed to be shorter, more irregular and with less amplitude.

"I'll now play them again and activate the printer so that it will print out both sets of waves. It will actually produce two copies, so that we can make Xerox prints while you're examining one copy. Are there any questions? Ms. Hurley?"

"Can you say on the basis of this comparison that these are the same voices, Dr. Gunderson?"

Setup question, naturally. Nuala Anne slipped out of the room to make copies of the second set of output sheets.

"Quite the contrary, Ms. Hurley. They are evidently very different voices. Often in our work for the courts we find ourselves comparing voices that are far more similar than these two. Then we do more elaborate tests to confirm the similarities. However, in this case, since the voices are so dissimilar, such refined comparisons are unnecessary. I'm sure no student of voices in the world would conclude that these voices are the same."

The lawyers were now peering carefully at the graph which displayed both voices. Jack Riordan rolled his eyes. Neither Lange nor the nameless managing editor bothered to inspect them. Perhaps they knew that the game was up.

The angels were doing pirouettes.

"I see," Cindy said, as if she were surprised by the finding. "I note that Dr. Gunderson's wonderful machine is making copies of the first tape, which you may take with you if you wish. You have of course in your own possession the copies that the United States Attorney leaked to you. Thus you can make your own comparisons . . . Ah, Ms. McGrail, will you pass around those copies of the output and, yes, the tape copies, too."

"So what?" one of the lawyers sneered. "So they're two different voices? So that doesn't make us responsible for investigating either the tapes or the transcripts that the U.S. Attorney gave to us. If they're fakes, and mind you, I don't admit that, it's not our responsibility to find that out."

Fingering his diamond like a magic implement, W.W. rumbled ominously, "Come now, J.J., you can't be serious. First of all, it is illegal for the U.S. Attorney to give you either the transcripts or the tapes and illegal for you to accept them. Moreover, your TV channel could have with great ease obtained a recording of our client's voice and made a comparison before broadcasting that tape last night. Such care certainly is well within the boundaries of what the courts have ruled to be due diligence."

Jack Riordan pursed his lips in a silent whistle.

"Shit," La Lange said, returning to her mantra. The angels laughed.

"You will want to have your own people do voice tests," Cindy said smoothly. "You may also want to consult with your colleagues about due diligence. I am taking the liberty of distributing folders with prints of the relevant decisions which Lexis-Nexis has cleverly found for us."

More silence.

"What's the rush?" another lawyer snapped.

"No rush, F.F.," Cindy shot back. "Our client will find relief one way or another. If it's in the short run, the costs will be less prohibitive for you than if it's in the long run, much less prohibitive . . . Any more questions? No? I'll remain here in our offices till 5:00.

Our answering service will be instructed to give you my home phone, should you have any questions . . . W.W.?"

"Thank you, Cynthia . . . I want to express my gratitude to you all for coming here to our little conversation. I trust that by Monday we will have arrived at the broad outlines of settlement terms which will be acceptable to all. I think I can assure you that our client will be reasonable in his demands, made as you know, in the name of several worthy educational institutions . . ."

"What is reasonable?" one of them demanded.

W.W. made a face, hesitated, and then said slowly, "Well, we would certainly not require anything in seven figures. I would guess we might be somewhere in the lower end of six figures. Of course we'll have to see what happens between now and Monday. I don't believe that we feel any obligation to haggle."

Needless to say, this response had been carefully rehearsed.

Gathering their graphs, their tapes, and their folders of citations, the attorneys straggled out of the conference room and down the corridor towards the elevators, whispering to one another as they went. One of them remained to murmur into W.W.'s ear.

Nuala stood in the doorway in intense conversation with Jack Riordan. What the hell was she up to now?

And why were all those angels dancing around her?

"They know we've got them," Cindy said to me, *sotto voce*, "and they're furious at the newspeople for getting them into this mess."

"Well done, Cynthia," W.W. said as he joined us. "I have no patience with those people. They're far more pompous than their ability merits."

Jack Riordan drifted down the corridor after the lawyers. Smiling proudly, Nuala joined us.

"Haven't I just paid a deal, just like a real Chicagoan?" she asked us.

"A deal?" Cindy sounded skeptical: Nuala was adorable but not a lawyer. Only lawyers made deals.

"Didn't I suggest to that silly young man that they could have a great scoop, if they put our little act on the five o'clock news? And didn't I hint that if they did, wouldn't we consider dropping our suit against Channel 6 altogether? He'll be calling you Cindy in a half hour or so. And, Dermot Michael, I'll not let you go on television unless you buy yourself a blue sport coat that does not clash with your eyes. We can walk over to that nice Paul Stuart place in your building, can't we now?"

Cindy looked at me. Both of us laughed. We turned to W.W., who also laughed, something which, according to all reports, he rarely did.

"I believe you're an accountant, young woman?" he asked genially.

"Yes, sir," she said, quickly donning the shy child mask.

"She also sings," I added.

"If you ever grow weary of your present occupations, I think you'd make a splendid lawyer."

"Thank you, sir."

"And I'd like to hear you sing, too."

My magic Nuala would charm anyone, even WASPs.

"Would you ever like to have a copy of me first album?" she said, reaching into her purse and producing a copy of *Nuala Anne*.

"Thank you very much," he said with a gracious bow. "My wife and I will listen to it first thing this evening since we won't be flying up to Dorr County."

Cindy said, "Thank you very much, W.W."

"I wouldn't have missed it for the world, Cynthia."

Nuala Anne led us out to the elevator, her nose pointing in the general direction of the moon.

I did not dare offer an argument about a new blue sport coat.

A CLIP FROM THE 5:00 NEWS

(Setting is Channel 6 newsroom. Present are Jack Riordan, Dermot Michael Coyne—in new blue sport coat—and Arjay Douglas, chief sound engineer for Channel 6.)

JR: (looking at the chart of two voices which the magic machine has just generated) You're saying, Arjay, that these two voices are not the same?

AD: That's right, Jack. The first line represents Dermot's voice, which we have just recorded. The second line is the voice which is alleged to be Dermot's in the tape from the U.S. Attorney. Clearly they are very different voices.

JR: Then it could not have been Dermot whom the FBI recorded.

AD: If this really is their tape, absolutely not.

JR: So it looks like Dermot was framed?

AD: It certainly does.

JR: (Outraged) And the FBI used Chicago media to help frame him!

AD: It certainly looks that way.

JD: Do you have any comment on that, Dermot?

DMC: (Charming smile) I have said all along that I never participated in such a conversation. I am grateful that Channel 6 has set the record straight.

JD: Myles McLahren, our vice president and station manager has issued the following statement, Dermot (reads from statement): Channel 6 deeply regrets the embarrassment caused to Mr. Coyne and his family by the false tape furnished us by the U.S. Attorney. We should have checked on the tape before we played it and we did not. We apologize for this failure. We promise we will learn from our mistake. Furthermore, we call for a full investigation of this apparent conspiracy and prosecution of all those responsible.

DMC: That's a very handsome apology, Jack. Please tell Mr. McLahren that I accept it.

JR: Do you think this revelation will clear your reputation, Dermot?

DMC: It will help, I'm sure. I doubt that my good name will ever be completely restored.

JR: Now you and your fiancée will be able to go on your honeymoon without any worries, is that not the case?

(Camera cuts to said fiancée, who is smiling happily.)

DMC: That all depends on Judge Crawford.

We returned to Cindy's office after the news broadcast and waited for the phone calls. Joe Hurley joined us to help with the calls. They were already pouring in by the time we got there. Cindy decided to stay at the phone till all wards were heard from. By seven-thirty every lawyer had checked in with a proposed apology. Cindy grimly insisted on wording in which they admitted negligence. Eventually, they all caved in.

Nuala Anne leaned back in Cindy's "judicial chair" and beamed contentedly, taking credit, as well she might, for the speed of the deal.

"Didn't we destroy them altogether?"

"It looks like you're completely out of the woods, Dermot."

"We still have to contend with Dale Quade and Judge Crawford.

I don't think Quade will give up. Nor will the judge risk a chance to get her name in the papers again. The fight is not over."

Cindy glanced up from her yellow, legal-sized notepad.

"Possibly Dermot, but not even Dale Quade would refuse to move that the indictment be quashed in the present circumstances. The principal support for the indictment has been impeached beyond repair. She could go back to the grand jury and seek to indict you with other evidence, but my guess is that she'll forget about you and go after someone else."

Maybe Marie Mangan, as she called herself now, was our ace in the hole. But could she really force Jarry to admit his fraud? She was a nice old woman, but he was a twisted young man who would not easily admit anything.

"With Jarry's tape as evidence?" I replied to Cindy. "Operation Full Platter is dead. Her only hope to salvage something is to put me in jail."

"She'll never do that, Dermot," Joe Hurley insisted. "If Judge Crawford continues to be obnoxious, Cindy can ask for another judge. Anyone else on the Federal bench will throw out the indictment. Even Dale can figure that out."

"The woman's sick," Nuala interjected.

"Not that sick," Cindy insisted.

I could not be optimistic. We had only a week left. We would win eventually. There were worse things than a wedding with an indictment hanging over one's head—such as an indictment with a canceled wedding. My gut, however, told me that the web of evil which Jarry Kennedy had spun would not disappear easily. The bitter end was not just yet.

The phone rang again.

"Hurley," Cindy snapped at it—my sister the tough litigator.

"Yes. I assume that the indictment will be quashed on Monday morning. What! She said that! I am astonished! Yes, you may use that as my response. You may add that when this is over I am going to cite Ms. Quade to the Bar Association and the Ethical Practices Review Board."

She slammed down the phone.

"City News Bureau," she said glumly.

"They had a comment from Dale?" Joe asked.

"They sure did. She said that our dog and pony show—her words—was nothing but a clever media trick to strengthen our hand in plea bargaining. I'm sure she'll be calling her columnist friends to spin the story the same way."

"So," I said wearily, "the game goes on."

"We'll be shopping tomorrow for Dermot's trousseau," Nuala said. "Sure, won't we be keeping Galena in mind. I hear it's a lovely place in autumn."

—29—

NUALA AND I took our respective parents to the Yacht Club for lunch. Annie and Gerry marveled at the beauty of the city and the Lake on a crisp fall day.

"Sure," Annie said, "doesn't it put Galway Bay to shame?"

"Och, Ma, doesn't me darlin' man say that we shouldn't make comparisons like that?"

"And isn't he right when he says that?" Gerry agreed.

Nuala was uneasy about the coming week. Apparently the "family council" she had refused to attend was taking place in New York, despite our triumph the previous evening. The event had not been reported in the *New York Times* and thus had not officially happened.

"The gobshites are still going to make trouble, Dermot," she had confided to me.

"Maybe we're just shell-shocked after all that has happened, Nuala."

"We are that . . . Och, it was fun shopping with you this morning. I won't have to be ashamed of appearing in public with you!"

While our parents were walking along the lake shore before lunch, I had a moment alone with my soon-to-be bride.

"I suppose there were lots of edges of light yesterday, Nuala Anne?"

"Och, didn't you see them all, Dermot Michael? Wasn't light everywhere?"

Did she really see edges of light? Or was that merely a poetic metaphor? Or did Nuala Anne know the difference?

"And angels dancing in it?"

"Haven't they been on our side all along?"

After lunch we returned to my apartment to watch the Notre Dame game which was being played in Tennessee. My half alma mater seemed to have little trouble in the first half. But in recent years they had acquired the bad habit of falling behind in the second half. This time they didn't succumb to the habit and won easily.

After the game, just as we were preparing to leave for Gordon to eat supper, my dad turned on the television for the local news.

Anchor: There has been another development in the Dermot Coyne case. In a breaking story that we are covering, Jared E. Kennedy, the FBI informant who reportedly is the government's main witness in the Operation Full Platter investigation admitted that the conversation between him and Coyne was a fake. Our Angela Smith is with Kennedy. Angela . . .

AS: Well, Duane, I'm here with Jared Kennedy, who has just told me that he never interviewed Dermot Coyne in the Operation Full Platter investigation. Isn't that true, Mr. Kennedy?

JK. You know, Dermy Boy has always been a crook. Everyone knows that. I tried to get him to talk a couple of times, but he wouldn't do it, which proves he's a crook, doesn't it? So, you know, I figured that I might just as well get down on tape, you know, what he would have said. So I asked my friend, Porky Conway who, you know, is a really great mimic, you should hear him do the president, you know, I asked him to help me. Porky has always had Dermy Boy down cold, so we put together a great interview, you know.

AS: But it was a fake interview, was it not?

JK: It depends on your point of view. Like I say, you know, it's what Dermy did and what he would have said if I had a chance to get him to talk to me. It's his fault. If he had talked to me, I wouldn't have had to fake it.

AS: So it's his fault that you gave the FBI a fake interview?

JK: (Grinning broadly now that his argument has been grasped) You got it!

AS: Do you think this admission will weaken the case the FBI has against the other people you talked to?

JK: Why should it? They can do voice tests on all the others, you know. We faked only one of the conversations.

AS: So that's Jared Kennedy's story. Back to you, Duane.

Anchor: Thanks, Angela, and a strange story it is.

"He was such a nice little boy," my mother, who can always find something good to say about anyone, commented. "Too bad he's a borderline personality."

"A gombeen man," Annie added.

"Round the bend altogether." Gerry shook his head. "Dermot, you're a living saint to have put up with all of this foolishness."

"Ah, no," my bride concluded the commentary. "Aren't I the living saint for keeping your man sane?"

We all laughed and then left the apartment for dinner, now with two victories to celebrate, the triumph of the Fighting Irish only marginally more important than my good fortune.

Or, as I could not say because of our pledge of secrecy, the triumph of Marie Mangan—and Ma and Pa—over Jimmy "Sweet Rolls" Sullivan's look-alike grandson.

"She did it for us, didn't she, Dermot?" Nuala hugged me in the elevator.

"Marie?"

"Her, too, but I meant Nell Pat."

— 30 —

FED INFORMANT CALLED TRICKSTER

By Sean Cassidy

River Forest

There was little surprise in this upper-middle-class community over the confession yesterday by a neighborhood boy who admitted that he had faked a tape implicating novelist Dermot Michael Coyne in the Operation Full Platter sting. Jared Enright Kennedy, according to those who know him, was always "playing tricks" on people with the help of his friend Charles "Porky" Conway.

"Porky can imitate anyone," said one acquaintance of both men. "He's great at Bill Clinton. Jarry would put him up to calling a girl, imitating her boyfriend, and breaking up with her. They both thought it was pretty funny."

"I can't believe the Feds trusted him," said another man in a bar on North Avenue, safely across the street from this dry community. "Everyone knew that Jarry was a sociopathic liar. No one believed a word he said."

No one questioned Mr. Kennedy's intelligence or athletic talents. The men around the bar, however, pointed out that Kennedy had been thrown out of Fenwick High School and both Notre Dame and the University of Miami, each time because he was caught in a lie. The Notre Dame incident involved allegations of sexual molestation of a woman student.

Moreover, he was fined and suspended from the Chicago Mercantile Exchange for five years. He has never returned to the trading floor.

"He always hated poor Dermot because everyone liked Dermot and no one liked him," a friend of both men said. "All of us heard him swear that he'd get Dermot someday, one way or another. Looks like he might have done it this time."

"Yeah," another one replied, "but why didn't the Feds check him out?"

Here in River Forest that looks like a very good question.

I was running down the field towards the end zone. A crowd of women was chasing me—my mom, Annie, Dale Quade, Judge Crawford, Kelly, Cindy, Nuala. I was determined to score the touchdown, the only one in my football career. As I was about to cross the goal line, Nuala tackled me. She rolled over on top of me and demanded sex or a fifty-yard penalty for unnecessary roughness. I reached out with my arm and broke the plane of the goal line with the football. The referee threw up his arms just like the touchdown Jesus on the Notre Dame library. I tried to apologize to Nuala because I wanted sex more than the touchdown, but she vanished, to be replaced by Kelly, who was now a skeleton covered with dirt from the grave and smelling like a garbage pail.

I woke up, drenched in sweat. For a couple of moments the dream seemed more real than the reality of my bedroom. Then its pleasure and its terror slipped back into my unconscious.

I had not scored the touchdown after all. But neither had I lost Nuala.

I struggled out of bed and stumbled towards the drapes which kept out the city. Outside a hard rain was falling. Chicago looked morose and displeased. Perfect day for a Bears game.

What was my schedule? Pick Nuala up for church, drop her at my sister Meg's house for another shower. Talk to Cindy about affidavits for the hearing tomorrow.

Well, next week I wouldn't have to drive to the house on Southport. Nuala would be in bed beside me. Maybe we could engage in a little entertainment before Mass. I grinned at the image and permitted myself to enjoy it. We would have come a long way since my first lecherous fantasies about her in O'Neill's pub.

The telephone interrupted my lustful imaginations.

"Dermot Coyne."

"Marie Mangan, Dermot." A firm, crisp voice.

"Good morning."

"You saw Jared yesterday?"

"Indeed we did."

"The poor boy is truly twisted."

"With all respect, Mrs. Mangan . . ."

"Marie."

"Yes, ma'am."

"You were about to say that he was always twisted. I quite agree . . . I have two phone numbers for you. Do you have a pencil?"

"Just a second . . . OK."

"The first is for Jared's lawyer. If your sister calls him at noon, he will have an affidavit from Jared which she will find useful. The second is my number up here. I hope you will feel free to call me occasionally."

As I took down the two numbers, I wondered whether she had worked with her husband in their projects in Portland. She must have. Indeed she might have been a better businessperson than he.

"We will certainly stay in touch with you," I said in reply to her question. "I hope we see you at the wedding."

"Your young woman is a remarkable person, Dermot."

"Funny thing, I was just thinking that, too."

"You must be patient and kind with her."

"I know that."

"I assumed you did. God bless you both."

Cindy would be awake. Kids didn't let you sleep even on Sunday morning. Did I want that hassle? Too late to think about it.

"Yeah, I know the guy. Sleaze. Melrose Park. I'll call him at noon. Where did you get this, Derm?"

"Information received."

"You and that one have been doing some poking around of your own?"

"Who, us?"

"Well, it seems to have helped. Tell me about it someday."

"Sure."

I glanced at the clock next to the phone. No time for a swim. My exercise schedule had fallen apart.

After a hasty shower, I drove up to Southport, hungry for the sight of my woman.

She wasn't waiting for me. So I rang the doorbell.

The door opened slightly. The upper half of a face appeared.

"'Tis your self," she murmured.

"Would you be expecting another lover?"

"If I were," she said, opening the door so I could come in, "I wouldn't tell you . . . Sorry I'm not ready."

"And don't you look grand in your lime underwear and hose."

I seized her from behind, my fingers digging into the firm muscles of her belly, and kissed her neck.

"Dermot! Not before church!"

"I don't think God would mind . . . I don't know about your friends the angels."

I let my fingers drift upward so that my thumbs touched the bottom of her negligible bra. She sighed deeply and leaned back against me. I lowered the straps, peeled away the cups from her breasts and took possession of them. They were mine, she was mine. She sighed again in surrender.

"I should have put my dress on before you came in," she said. "Now aren't you destroying me altogether?"

"You'd better get used to being destroyed altogether."

She sagged against my chest.

"Dermot," she gasped, "your fingers are sending electric shocks through me whole body."

"Better get used to that, too."

Her nipples hardened against my palms. There'd never be any trouble turning this one on.

"'Tis a good thing we're getting married before next Sunday."

"I'll be doing a lot more than this next Sunday before Mass."

"Go long wid ya, Dermot Michael Coyne. You'll be so worn out I'll have to drag you out of bed."

"Put on your dress, woman, or we'll be late for Mass."

"They call it the Eucharist these days . . . How can I put on me dress with you holding me boobs?"

"That's true," I said, releasing her.

"Since you came in and violated me privacy," she said, readjusting the straps of her bra, "the least you can do is zip up me dress."

"That seems reasonable," I said, helping her on with the dress, a closely fitting lime creation with a turtleneck and a silver belt. Then I kissed her back in the process of fastening the dress. "How come you're not ready this morning?"

"I had to do a lot of thinking last night."

"You'd better wear a raincoat."

I helped her down the stairs and into the car. While we were away on our honeymoon the contractor would finish the modernization of the house, restore the first-floor entrance, and demolish the outdoor stairway, a relic of the days when Chicago was a swamp.

"What were you thinking about?" I asked as I started the car.

"I was thinking that I wasn't afraid anymore."

"Were you now?"

"I was. I'm not afraid of the wedding day or the wedding night or of marriage or even of you, Dermot Michael Coyne."

"Isn't that grand!"

"Brilliant, actually."

"And why are you no longer afraid."

"I didn't have enough trust in God or in you. I'm over that now. I'm sorry."

She was perfectly calm and matter-of-fact.

"Well, I don't know about God," I said, trying to be funny, "but you certainly should have trusted me."

"I won't do it again."

What did this conversation mean? She certainly seemed confident and self-possessed. But then she often seemed that way.

"We'll do fine, Nuala," I said, hoping that I was saying the right thing.

"We certainly will, Dermot," she said, patting my arm.

That settled that.

After Mass I drove out to River Forest to my sister Meg's house (she's the psychiatrist in the family) where the last of the showers would be. Cindy was waiting for me with her van. We were going hunting for affidavits. Nuala waved a forlorn farewell as we drove off.

"That one doesn't want to let you out of her sight," Cindy said.

"Really?"

"You saw the look on her face. I think she's in love."

"Really?"

"Almost as bad as you are."

We collected signed documents from Dr. Gunderson, Jarry's obsequious lawyer, and a very anxious Porky Conway.

"Honest, Derm, I didn't know he would do something like that."

"No problem, Pork, no problem at all."

Porky had certainly realized that Jarry was up to no good. At his stage in life Pork, however, once the life of every party, would do anything for someone who laughed at some of his jokes.

"Good day's work, little bro," Cindy said as we pulled up to my parents' house. "It will be all over tomorrow."

"Don't bet on it. Listen to what Dale's favorite columnist says this morning:"

COLUMN ITEM

Legal beagle **Dale Quade** is untroubled by the recent dog and pony show over the alleged forgery of a tape featuring novelist **Dermot Coyne** bragging about his tricks on the floor of the Merc. Sources tell us that Quade never considered the tape to be an important part of the government's case against Coyne. We hear that there are enough other gotchas in the Fed evidence to send him to jail for a long time unless he buys into the generous plea bargain that Quade has offered.

"Wow!" Cindy exclaimed. "It's the only evidence they cite in the indictment. She doesn't have anything else."

"She'll probably want to go through my papers and hunt for something."

Cindy thought for a moment.

"She'd have to go back to the grand jury to get another indictment. I doubt that her boss, even if he's besotted with her, would let that happen. Moreover, the Justice Department might finally wake up and figure out that it's collecting a lot of black eyes out there."

"What if Judge Crawford decides she doesn't need another indictment?"

"She couldn't do that," Cindy said, not sounding all that confident.

"Don't bet on it."

We pulled up in front of my parents' house to which Nuala had retreated after the shower. The Mercedes was parked in the driveway. An unfamiliar car was in front. Avis. Something was up.

"You let herself drive the Benz?"

"Doesn't she have a license and isn't she a better driver altogether than I am?"

Cindy laughed at my imitation.

"Is she really?"

"At least as good . . . Thanks for all the help, Cindy."

"Like I said, little bro, we're gonna cream them."

She poked her finger at me in reassurance.

"You'll go home to the kids now?"

"Not hardly. Joe and I are going to the office to prepare two motions, one to dismiss and the other asking for a new judge."

"When do you get home?"

"Midnight, if we're lucky. Don't worry, little bro, there'll be great stories about this case for decades. See you tomorrow promptly at nine."

I let myself into the house. Angry voices with strong Irish brogues were arguing in the parlor.

Thick, dark rage boiled up within me.

"What's the matter with a postponement for a week or two?" a reasonable male voice asked.

Not Larry.

So the whole "family council" had come.

"The matter," Nuala shouted, "is that I'm not going to do it. Not for you, not for anyone."

"But, Nunu, look at all the pain you'll be causing Ma and Da."

"You're the ones that will be causing the pain!"

Nunu? Cute name. For a baby. Just now she sounded like she had been sobbing and was but a step away from hysteria.

"Your sobbing doesn't help the discussion," said a third voice. "Why can't we talk about our suggestion reasonably?"

"Because it is not a reasonable suggestion. I will not postpone my marriage just to please you gobshites."

"There's no need to be vulgar, Nuala"—Larry now. "The young man is a criminal and you will disgrace us all if you marry him. Have you no concerns for your nieces and nephews?"

"Fuck me nieces and nephews!"

CAREFUL, the Adversary advised me.

I walked into the parlor.

"Nuala, who let these people into my house?"

It wasn't my house at all, at all. But I wasn't worried about technical truth.

"I did, Dermot," she said meekly.

"Get out!" I ordered. "All of you! Get out now!"

The three siblings were attractive, dark Irish young people, not as attractive as Nunu, but still appealing—black hair, pale skin, white teeth, slender, cute breasts on the girl. Larry, standing apart from them, his face glowing with triumph was as ugly as ever.

"Now just a minute," one of the men said. "There's no cause for acting that way."

I had not intended to lose my temper. However, the black rage within me exploded. The berserker within took over.

"Are you Pedar?"

"I'm Podraig."

I grabbed his shoulder and hurled him towards the doorway to the parlor.

"There's plenty of cause. It's my house and I don't want you in it. You too, Pedar," I grabbed the other one. "Out!"

"You can't treat us this way," he argued as I tossed him towards the door.

"Who's going to stop me?"

I grabbed both of them and pushed them to the door of the house.

"There's no need to shove," one of them said.

I kicked open the door, which I had left unlocked when I had come in.

"Out! Or I'll throw you down the stairs on your fat asses."

They stumbled out the door.

I turned to the parlor.

"You too, bitch!" I yelled at the frightened young woman, doubtless Nessa.

She scurried past me.

"Now as for you, Larry. I hope you stay. Because I'd love to smash your front teeth down your throat, you useless gobshite of a gombeen man."

I would have done it, I really would have.

He, too, scurried past me.

I glanced at Nuala. She was grinning. Fair enough.

"Now, listen to me, all of you," I yelled at the disorganized group at the bottom of the stairs. "I don't want to see any of you ever again as long as I live. Don't you dare come to our wedding or ever show your ugly, stupid faces anyplace I can see them. If you do, you'll need long-term medical care."

I walked down the front steps and faced them head to head.

"Do I make myself clear, or do I have to crack some heads for emphasis?"

They hurried back to their car and drove off.

"How about that?" I asked the Adversary.

YOU'LL TAKE THEM BACK INTO THE FAMILY WHEN THEY APOLOGIZE, he said nervously.

So I had scared him, too.

"Where are your ma and da?" I barked at Nuala.

"Gone to the Bears game," she said solemnly. "In a skybox."

I picked up the phone and punched in the guesthouse number.

"Annie, Gerry, tis meself. I had a minor disagreement with some of Nunu's siblings who were trying to talk her out of marrying me. They left the house in, ah, some haste. It will be all right in a day or two or three. Don't worry about it. And don't let them involve you in it. I hope you enjoyed the game."

"Och, Dermot Michael Coyne," Nuala flew into my arms. "Aren't you the terrible desperate man altogether!"

"Do you think they'll leave you alone for a while?" I held her close.

"They won't dare come near me."

"Grand. Now let's gather up your loot and take you home."

"I have a nice new swimsuit." She grabbed a few pieces of cloth from her pile of prizes. "Could we ever swim in your pool? I didn't have time to do me run this morning."

She would have been only somewhat overdressed in it at Cocacabana.

"Tis a grand idea. You'll raise the water temperature twenty degrees in that."

"Isn't that what it's for?"

I didn't care about the rain or the cold or even about Judge Crawford. I had rescued the maiden from the dragons and was very proud of meself. Myself.

—31—

AS WE might have expected, Judge Crawford kept us waiting till midafternoon. Cindy, sounding totally exhausted, called me at eight.

"Court call put off till promptly at one."

"Which means?"

"Which means she'll probably show up at two."

Nuala had dragged me off to play tennis at the East Bank Club.

"I'll not be going to bed with a man who is out of condition," she insisted.

We played inside because the cold rain was still assaulting the city.

Herself swept me off the court and then taunted me about being old and out of condition and probably a poor risk for any woman foolish enough to marry me.

She was in an exceedingly upbeat mood under the circumstances.

While we were waiting for the judge, Dale Quade, looking more like an angry Mother Superior than ever before, strode briskly into the courtroom and over to Cindy.

Patently she knew that promptly at one didn't mean promptly at one.

"Well, have you thought about my offer?"

"Offer?" Cindy, her face haggard from exhaustion, seemed surprised by the brazen attack.

"Three years in minimum security."

"Minimum security is a concession," I said with my most disarming smile.

Next to me Nuala began to move her lips as if she were uttering an ancient incantation.

"You're not going to move to quash?" Cindy asked as if she couldn't believe her ears.

"Why should I?"

"Your witness has been discredited."

"We don't need him."

"But his evidence is all that is mentioned in the indictment."

La Quade shrugged indifferently. "We have a lot more."

"Then you should move to quash and indict him again with the new evidence."

"A waste of time."

"How can we defend against charges that are not specified in an indictment?"

"Your problem."

Nuala's murmuring grew louder. It sounded like an Asian chant.

"This is most unprofessional conduct, Counselor."

"I'll be the judge of what's professional."

Joe Hurley, who had been quiet as the two women jousted, intervened. "Come on, Dale. Don't get yourself into worse trouble than you're already in."

"Don't threaten me, Counselor, or I'll have you up before the Ethical Practice Board."

"Have it your way."

Dale Quade finally noticed Nuala's incantation and hypnotic eyes. Again she recoiled and sped off quickly.

"Be careful, Nuala," Joe warned. "She may charge you with contempt for cursing her."

"And meself merely reciting words from an Irish lullaby."

Nuala was wearing the leather suit again, this time with a green blouse with enough buttons open to hint at black lace. Again I had no idea what the theme meant but I ached with longing for her.

Cindy's prediction had been optimistic. Judge Crawford entered her courtroom at 3:05, swaying just a bit as she climbed to her seat behind the bench.

Definitely on drugs this time.

"Well," she glared at us, as if we had been keeping her waiting, "have you agreed on a plea?"

"Your Honor," Cindy began, "I note that we have our own court reporter as well as the one appointed by the court. We exercise that right in order to have transcripts readily available."

"I don't approve of that."

"With respect, Your Honor, we do not need the Court's approval for that. Of course the transcript will not be the official one."

"It certainly won't . . . Now what do you have to say for yourself."

"Your Honor, I was expecting the United States Attorney to move to quash the indictment. Since she declines to do so, I have presented a motion to dismiss. I believe you have the motion and the relevant affidavits."

"I have no such thing," she replied. "If you're going to submit a motion, you should give it to my bailiff the first thing in the morning."

"I did, Your Honor."

"I'm sure you did not . . . Bailiff, you have no such motion, do you?"

"Uh, Your Honor, I believe that counsel did submit such a motion. I put it with your papers."

"Well, it's not here!" she said, irritably brushing the poor bailiff away. "You'll just have to submit it again before the next court date."

"Your Honor, I believe it is in that envelope with our firm's letterhead just beneath your left hand."

"What? . . . Oh, this? . . . Well, let me see."

She opened the envelope, glanced at the first page, and then threw it aside.

"Well, I don't need to read it. On what grounds do you want me to dismiss the case?"

"Let the record show," Cindy said, "that the Court refused to read the motion to dismiss."

"Expunge that from the record," Judge Crawford shrieked. "Counselor, I am very close to citing you for contempt . . . Now summarize your argument for me. Briefly, and I mean briefly!"

"Your Honor, the indictment which the United States Attorney has brought is based entirely on the testimony of an FBI informant. We have presented affidavits which demonstrate that the informant has been completely discredited, including one from the informant himself. Under the circumstances we believe that the Court should . . ."

"I don't care what you believe . . . Does the United States Attorney wish to reply?"

"Your Honor, we propose to present evidence in a trial to prove the defendant guilty beyond any reasonable doubt, evidence which does not depend on the allegedly discredited testimony of the FBI informant. We do not, incidentally, grant that the testimony has in fact been discredited."

"Motion denied . . . I expect to see you both back here, bright and early next Monday morning with a progress report."

"Just a minute, Your Honor," Cindy said firmly. "I'm afraid that I am going to have to ask you to recuse yourself from this case."

"What!" the judge shouted. "How dare you ask that?"

"Your Honor, with respect, we have the right to ask that."

"You must have grounds!"

"We believe we have grounds, Your Honor."

"What are they?" she demanded, hoarse with rage.

"That you have shown yourself to be consistently biased against the defendant and careless of his rights."

"You're in contempt, Counselor. I've warned you before. A thousand dollars or twenty-four hours in jail. Next time it will be a week in jail. Bailiff, remove counsel from my courtroom!"

"Your Honor, I ask that you defer the sentence, pending appeal!"

"I will do no such thing! Bailiff, get her out of here!"

We followed Cindy out of the courtroom. She made out a check in the bailiff's room with a broad grin.

"Joe," she said to her husband as the media swarmed towards her in the corridor, "call the bank and tell them to stop payment."

Joe was grinning, too.

"She really surpassed herself that time."

"Dead meat," Cindy said as she glanced at her watch. "Only four o'clock. My friend in the Seventh Circuit is waiting for me."

"Cindy, what are you going to do?" a breathless woman said, jabbing a mike at her.

"Do? Appeal. What else? Now if you'll excuse me . . ."

She pushed her way through the crowd of vultures towards the elevators.

"Dermot, what do you think of Judge Crawford?"

"She reminds me of Paul Newman playing Judge Roy Bean."

General laughter.

Joe and I restrained the vultures while Cindy and Nuala slipped into an elevator. We found Nuala waiting outside a judge's chamber on one of the floors occupied by the Seventh Circuit, a place as solemn high as the Pope's chambers in the Vatican, if not more so.

"Isn't she inside talking to your man?"

"She's asking for a suspension of the fine," Joe explained, "the appointment of an emergency panel to review the conduct of the trial, and an order for the appointment of another judge who will consider the motion to dismiss. Every judge in town is upset by Evil Elvira. This is their chance to do her in."

Cindy emerged from the chambers a moment later, her eyes shining with triumph.

"Got it all," she said. "Contempt sentence suspended and a panel to convene tomorrow at 11:00. They've informally set up the panel already. We'll have to get our transcripts to them by 9:00."

"They'll rule in our favor?" I asked.

"Minimally, we'll get a new judge. No question about that."

"Who?" Nuala asked. "Not another crazy one?"

"We won't know till late tomorrow afternoon, I'm afraid. We'll probably have a hearing Wednesday morning."

"And the wedding is Friday."

"I'll be there anyway," Nuala announced. "And you'd better be there, too, young fella, or I'll sue you right and proper."

We all indulged in a much-needed laugh.

Mine, I fear, was hollow.

—32—

EDITORIAL

We are increasingly troubled by the behavior of Federal Judge Elvira Crawford. It should be clear to everyone that the indictment of Dermot Coyne as a result of the now moribund Operation Full Platter sting was a serious violation of Mr. Coyne's rights. The indictment should have been quashed and the shameful attack on his reputation ended. Full Platter ought to be put mercifully to rest. Since the United States Attorney is unaccountably unwilling to admit a serious mistake, the Court should have dismissed the charges against Mr. Coyne. Judge Crawford's courtroom behavior when presented with a motion to dismiss the charges can only be called bizarre. In effect she refused to hear the motion or to read its documentation. Moreover she slapped a contempt of court fine on Mr. Coyne's attorney who exercised a defendant's right to seek a new judge. We are confident that the appellate court will reverse her rulings. Nonetheless, serious questions must be asked not only about the Full Platter fiasco, but also about Judge Crawford's behavior. We question whether she belongs on the Federal bench.

"Hmpf," Nuala snorted. "Last week they were praising her. Doesn't anyone keep track of what editorial writers say?"

"Nope," I said, digging into my second helping of pancakes.

"You'll have to swim another half hour to make up for that second helping."

"I look forward to a life of nutritional terrorism," I said, as I soaked the pancakes with maple syrup.

"I won't go to bed with a slob."

"I haven't put on a pound since I met you."

"You know what happens to men when they get married. I won't tolerate it."

She was talking half fun, and full earnest.

"Well, I'll not tolerate an overweight wife either."

"You've seen me ma?"

"Woman, I have."

"Same genes."

"Different diets."

"Fair play to you, Dermot Michael . . . Would you ever pass some more of that maple syrup?"

"We'll have to rely on each other's self-respect."

"You'll have to rely on mine. I'll rely on my own close supervision."

We both laughed again.

For a couple of reasons we were both in excellent spirits as we ate in the coffee shop of the Ritz Carlton in the lobby on the twelfth floor. Nearby the fountain spun water into the air and then dropped it in a pool.

Earlier in the year herself had characterized it as the sound of a herd of cows pissing on a rock—a metaphor around which I wanted to write a whole novel.

The news on our artistic ventures was better than we had expected. Both *Nuala Anne* and *Irish Love* were prospering, even though there was some negative criticism that there were too many Irish singers and too many Irish writers. One reviewer wondered how there could possibly be a market for a novel about such a small group as Irish-Americans.

Another reason for our cautious optimism was that the media, without so much as a look backward or an acknowledgment that they had changed their song, were now definitely on our side.

Finally, both Cindy and Joe were confident that Judge Crawford would be summarily dumped before the day was over.

After breakfast we were to conclude our shopping expedition for "proper" clothes for me, that is to say clothes of which herself approved. Then we were to have lunch with Cindy at the Bar Association. Finally we were to spend the evening with the little bishop, who proposed to give us "premarriage instruction."

"Me siblings are embarrassed altogether," Nuala said, after pouring my tea.

"They should be . . . You hear from them?"

"Not to say hear from them exactly. Hasn't Fionna come to town and didn't she chew the asses off them and hasn't she called me?"

"She's the second oldest?"

"Big sister."

"Tough?"

"Not as tough as I am, but tough enough . . . And hasn't me da had words with Larry?"

"In which he said?"

"He told him that he should go back to his wife and kids in Pacific Palisades and leave this wedding alone."

"In so many words?"

"I've censored out some of the words that might offend you."

"That's pretty direct for your man, isn't it now?"

"'Tis . . . I think herself put him up to it. When me da lays down the law, he lays it down . . . 'course he's never had to do it with me."

"And what did he say to the others?"

"Didn't he tell them that he was ashamed of them and yourself being such a nice boy from such a wonderful family?"

"So they're trying to find a way to apologize?"

"They are . . . They're terrified of you and yourself being such a desperate man altogether."

"A terrible dangerous man when the anger is upon him."

"So you're telling them that I'm not like that at all, at all."

"I am NOT . . . I'm hinting that it might take years for you to calm down. Let them be proper afraid of you."

"Like you are?"

"Just like I am . . . Now finish your tea. Don't we have work to do?"

Joe and Cindy were both grinning happily when we caught up with them at the Bar Association. They hardly noticed us coming in because they were so busy accepting congratulations.

"Just what we expected," Cindy said, hugging first herself and then me. "Contempt charge reversed, new judge to be appointed before the day is out, strong reprimand of Evil Elvira. New judge to hear motions to free you on your own recognizance, permit you to leave the jurisdiction, and dismiss the charges."

"So," Joe chimed in, "you won't have to go to Galena for your honeymoon."

"I kind of wanted to see it," I said.

"Who's the judge?" Nuala asked.

"We won't know till the end of the day. He or she will almost certainly have a hearing tomorrow morning and rule on the first two motions."

"The media are busy covering their behinds," Joe continued. "Elvira and Dale and even Dale's boss are in deep doodoo. There's a rumor around this place that Justice is going to ask Dale's boss to resign. No one's sorry about that. He was a dumb appointment in the first place."

"Me sister Fionna is being fitted with her dress this afternoon," Nuala said, changing the subject. "So we'll have two women of honor in the sanctuary anyway."

"She didn't cross the berserker, I take it?" Cindy said with a wink.

"Not yet, anyway. I think she's terrified of your man and himself having such a terrible temper, don't you know?"

Just then Dale Quade strode by our table, looking neither to the right nor the left.

"Shush," I said, "I think I hear Mother Superior's rosary beads."

On cue Nuala whispered her lullaby.

Quade tripped and almost fell on her face.

"You shouldn't do that, Nuala Anne," I said with notable lack of sincerity. "You'll drive her round the bend altogether."

"How will we know the difference, poor woman?"

"She's destroyed herself," Cindy said with some measure of sympathy. "She didn't used to be a true believer. If she had moved to quash yesterday and maybe apologized to you, she'd have come out smelling like a rose. But that wouldn't fit her tough image in the gossip columns of which she is so proud."

"As more women become lawyers," Joe added, "the macho litigator image we males love will fade. In the meantime some women will ruin their careers and maybe their lives as they try to pretend that they can be more macho than we are."

"As if," Nuala sniffed, "we were not the stronger gender all along."

After lunch we went up to our house to discuss the final plans for remodeling with our designer. I was forbidden access to the bedroom, which was to be a "grand" surprise.

"Depends on whom I must share it with," I protested.

For my troubles I was thumped, lovingly I admit, on my forearm.

At four-thirty we called Cindy's office.

"It's Rex Jackson," she said hesitantly. "Problematic. New appointee. Honest as they come and supposed to be bright. Cautious, however, very cautious."

"So?"

"So we are to be in his courtroom at 1:30 tomorrow afternoon. He'll have all the documents first thing in the morning."

"Bad news?" Nuala asked.

"Problematic news to quote herself."

At supper the little bishop insisted that all matters were arranging themselves well.

His principle injunction to us was that we should fight on every possible occasion.

"There'll be no problem about that, at all, at all," I said. "We're Irish and the Irish love to fight."

"That is the myth about us, but I fear it is not true. We argue about unimportant things and cover up the important. We hide the things we don't like, the offenses we think have been done to us, the violations that we resent, the habits that drive us crazy. We nurse them and treasure them and store them so that they fester. By the time we are forced to talk about them, it is usually too late to deal with them."

Dead silence for a moment.

"'Tis true," Nuala admitted. "We reckon it is better to absorb something we don't like than quarrel about it. Offer it up for the souls in Purgatory. Then forty years later we stick it to the one who has offended us. Sure, we never forget an insult, do we now?"

"Or an injury, real or imagined," I agreed.

"I hardly think your marriage will fail," the bishop said. "But arguably it will be much happier and richer if you don't let the sun go down on your resentments."

"No argument about it," I said.

"Well, now, Dermot Michael," my bride said with a vast and affectionate smile, "I've got a list here in my purse . . ."

In fact, she didn't. Not yet anyway.

Judge Rex Jackson was a handsome African-American who

looked like he might have been a cornerback in college. His square solid face was accented by a trim mustache. He spoke slowly and thoughtfully, as though he was pondering every word.

"I have read the motions and the supporting documentation this morning," he said softly. "I should like an opportunity to go over them again. However, I will address myself to the first motion this morning, that for the lifting of the restrictions on the movements of the defendant. Ms. Hurley, do you wish to add anything to what you have written?"

"Only, Your Honor, that the original bail was utterly inappropriate in the case of a man who has never had a traffic ticket and whose twenty-five years have been marked by exemplary probity of life. Moreover, he is no threat to the community, is certainly most unlikely under the present circumstances to flee this country to avoid trial; and his marriage and honeymoon ought not to be blighted by this restriction."

"The marriage is when, Counselor?"

"Friday evening, Your Honor."

"I see . . . Ms. United States Attorney?"

"Your Honor, defendant's motion is simply outrageous. He is under a serious criminal indictment. That he has never had a traffic ticket proves nothing except that he has been very clever. Given the seriousness of the charges against him, he has every reason to want to flee to Costa Rica or even to Cuba."

There was a gasp from the courtroom. The media folks could not believe their ears.

"Yes, I see. Well, I will rule now on this motion and, if you don't mind coming back tomorrow morning, after I've had another chance to read the documentation, I will rule on the second motion. Ms. Hurley?"

"We'll be here, Your Honor."

"Ms. Quade?"

"We disagree, Your Honor. A matter this important cannot be decided in twenty-four hours."

"It may be so important, Ms. Quade, that it must be decided in twenty-four hours. I will rule tomorrow morning."

"Yes, Your Honor."

La Quade struggled to control her temper. She looked like she might climb on a broomstick and fly around the courtroom.

"Now as to the first motion, I am going to free him to leave the jurisdiction. You will stay in touch with Ms. Hurley, won't you, Mr. Coyne?"

Cindy nudged me.

"Answer the judge."

"Yes, Your Honor, I certainly will."

"Excellent."

Another nudge, this time from my bride. "Tell him thank you."

"Thank you, Your Honor."

The judge smiled briefly.

"You're welcome, Mr. Coyne."

"Your Honor, I object . . ."

"Your objection is noted, Ms. Quade . . . Bailiff, what is the next matter before us?"

There was much hugging and kissing on our side of the courtroom.

"We've won," Cindy exulted. "Now I can go home to the kids and my estate work."

"She loved every second of this one, Dermot," Joe said. "Don't let her tell you any different."

"What if he gave us something today and feels he has to balance it off tomorrow?" Nuala said. "Doesn't he seem to be the kind of man who likes balance?"

The three of us turned to look at her. It was a very wise question from a very wise woman.

—33—

COLUMN NOTE

Despite what you hear, ace prosecutor **Dale Quade** has not yet lost the **Dermot Coyne** case. Informed sources at the Federal Building expect **Judge Rex Jackson** to refuse to dismiss charges against Coyne this morning. The fact that he lifted the ban limiting defendant Coyne to the jurisdiction of the Court for the Northern District of Illinois yesterday but reserved his decision on the motion to dismiss suggests that he will balance his prodefense decision yesterday with a proprosecution decision today. Coyne will be able to go on his honeymoon with his immigrant bride but he will have to come back to face a trial or a plea bargain which will force him to do time in a Fed pen. We hear that such a threat does not make for a good honeymoon.

"Did you see that shite in the column?" Nuala demanded. "Is that woman here? I'll scratch her eyes out! 'Immigrant bride,' indeed!"

"They never give up, do they?"

The courtroom was filled—media, families, curiosity seekers. My whole family was there, including a couple of nieces and nephews. Nuala's clan was there too, save for Larry, who presumably had followed Gerry's suggestion and returned to his wife and family.

Pedar and Podraig had both tentatively raised thumbs up to me as herself and I entered the courtroom. Desperate man that I was, I had grinned and returned the sign.

"You're a berserker with a soft heart," Nuala had whispered.

For this climactic event she was wearing a light green suit with dark green buttons and a V neck that ventured into décolletage. The young woman who had tried to be dowdy when she went to work at Arthur's was now into being spectacular.

"You look fabulous," I had told her.

"Thank you, Dermot Michael," she said complacently.

I was worried. The nightmare had gone on for so long that I could not really believe that it would end and just in time for the rehearsal dinner. Even if our motion was denied, Cindy had assured me, the Justice Department would drop the prosecution as soon as it discreetly could. The case and indeed the whole Operation Full Platter had become an acute embarrassment to them. In my head I knew she was right. Yet I did not want to depart on my wedding trip with the mess hanging over our head.

End it, end it, end it, I pleaded with God and with all the angels who might be skipping around in the fringes of light that the Indian summer weather had slipped into the courtroom.

Promptly at 10:00 Judge Jackson entered the courtroom.

"I will rule this morning," he began when we were all seated, "on defendant's motion to dismiss charges. If there is any oral argument, I will hear it."

"Your Honor," Cindy began, "my client has been subjected to malicious prosecution by the Federal Bureau of Investigation and the United States Attorney. The charges against him, which were spread widely by the media, were based entirely on a tape provided by an FBI informant who is an immunized witness. The tape was an obvious fraud, which the witness and his coconspirator admit, I might almost say cheerfully admit, in the affidavits I have submitted. Moreover, an analysis of the tape by professional experts has established that the voice on it was not that of my client. The United States Attorney, knowing the unreliability of her informant and hearing my client's repeated denials, could easily have performed a similar analysis. Finally, given the fact that the charges against him were entirely dependent on a fraudulent tape and a discredited witness, the United States Attorney had and has no case. If she wishes to submit more evidence to a grand jury, she certainly is free to do so. First, however, she should have moved to quash this absurd and, if I may say so, dishonest indictment. My client is entitled to freedom from the fraud the United States Attorney has perpetrated. He is also within his rights to demand that this Court begin the process of restoring his reputation to him."

"We are not hearing a case for malicious prosecution in this court, Ms. Hurley," the judge said mildly.

"I do not intend to suggest that we are, Your Honor. Rather I am making a flat assertion. From beginning to end this disgraceful episode can only be called malicious, a blot on the American legal system."

"I see . . . Ms. Quade?"

Mother Superior looked like she had just arrived on her broomstick, a woman about to explode. She turned her glowing eyes on me. Brr . . .

"Your Honor, I ask you first of all to instruct counsel for the defense to withdraw her charges of malice. Such words have no place in this courtroom and are clearly an appeal to the media."

Judge Jackson's face was unreadable, implacable.

"I will consider that request, Counselor. Please go on with your argument."

"Your Honor, the Office of the United States Attorney for the Northern District of Illinois has tried for the last several years to clean up the national disgrace in the commodity exchanges of Chicago. Our current investigation has uncovered evidence of massive and systematic fraud. We believe that we will be able to prove that the defendant has been an important part of this fraud. To dismiss the case against him without a trial will only encourage perpetrators of commodity fraud to continue to defraud innocent investors. We do not accept the defendant's description of the tape as fraudulent. Nonetheless, we are convinced that we can present a case that will be persuasive to a jury without that evidence."

"Then why did you not follow the procedure suggested by the defendant's attorney and move to quash the present indictment and seek a new one?"

"We did not believe it necessary, Your Honor."

Dale Quade was smiling, confident that she had won the argument. Once more she glared at me, now triumphant.

"I see. I fail to find any reference to any other evidence in the indictment as I read it."

"Your Honor," Quade said smoothly, "we believe that the terms of the indictment are aufficiently broad as to include the possibility of further evidence being produced. We do not accept the suggestion that the indictment as it stands relies entirely on the disputed tape."

"I see," the judge said softly.

The courtroom was silent. Everyone leaned forward. I felt my heart leap into my throat. Where were those damn angels?

"We win," Nuala informed me.

"I have one more question, Ms. Quade?"

"Yes, Your Honor?" she said triumphantly.

"Do you have a conscience, Ms. Quade?" Judge Jackson asked softly.

"I beg your pardon?"

"Do you or anyone at the Office of the United States Attorney have a conscience?"

"Certainly we do, Your Honor."

"I presume you would also claim that you have a sense of decency?"

"I fail to see the point of this line of questioning, Your Honor."

Dale Quade looked stricken.

Nuala was right, as always.

"Do you believe that the goal of the American justice system is the gathering of scalps without proving the guilt of the one scalped?"

Through this catechesis, Judge Jackson's voice remained soft and mild, as though we were discussing a matter over the lunch table.

"No, Your Honor," she said stiffly, "I do not."

"From beginning to end, Counselor, this case has been exactly what counsel for the defense said it was, a disgrace, one of which you and the United States Attorney and the Federal Bureau of Investigation ought to be thoroughly ashamed. I am going to notice you and the United States Attorney to the Illinois Review Board and to the Bar Association. Moreover, I am going to insist that a special prosecutor be appointed to consider the possibility that there has been criminal conspiracy in this case, a possibility that I consider to be highly likely. I want to remind you, Ms. Quade, that the desire to punish criminals does not permit a prosecuting attorney to make up the rules as she or he goes along."

"Your Honor, I must . . ."

"I want to hear no more from you, Ms. Quade, in my court-room . . . I grant the defendant's motion and dismiss the charges against him."

Cheers from the courtroom.

The judge banged his gavel once . . . All judges must bang their gavels.

"I have one more remark . . . Mr. Coyne . . ."

Both Cindy and Nuala nudged me. All three of us stood up.
"Yes, Your Honor."

"In this whole ugly affair you have behaved with dignity and grace. Your government framed you on a false charge, yet never once did you indulge in anger or self-pity. I congratulate you on your restraint and, in the name of the American justice system, I apologize to you. I hope that the charming young woman you will soon marry realizes what a superb gentleman you are."

Two more nudges.

"Thank you, Your Honor . . . I'll remind her often of your words."

Laughter, cheers, hugs, kisses.

None of which did D. M. Coyne deserve any more than he did the judge's words of praise. But one takes one's rewards where one gets them, including soon in the marriage bed with me naked woman.

At her desk on the other side of the courtroom, Dale Quade, head buried in her hands, was sobbing. Her three toadies ignored her.

The Coynes and the McGrails swarmed around us, I shook hands with Pete and Pat, both of whom assured me with charming grins that I was a desperate man altogether. I hugged Nessa and Fionna and kissed them both.

As we were celebrating our victory, I saw, out of the corner of my eye, Dale Quade, her face twisted with fury, rushing towards Nuala.

"Watch it, Nuala!" I cried.

She was watching it. A split second before Quade's claws sank into her face, Nuala swung her right arm out as though she were brushing aside a drape or a curtain. The Assistant United States Attorney, wailing hysterically, flew backwards against a row of chairs and then collapsed into a fetal position.

Duck, Dermot Michael Coyne, when you see that right arm coming your way.

Cries of horror broke out in the courtroom. Judge Jackson rose from his bench in dismay.

Then my Nunu bent over the poor woman and began to croon softly to her. The melody, I would have bet every cent, to the lullaby which had been the pseudo curse.

"It'll be all right now, Dale," she said softly. "You just need a couple of good nights' sleep and it will be all right. Come on now, stand up and we'll take you off to the women's room where we can put you back together again."

The judge, eyes wide in astonishment, pointed at the entrance to his chambers. Nuala, cooing reassurance, guided the weeping woman in that direction.

"Sure, all you need is some rest and then everything will be all right."

It wouldn't be all right, maybe not ever. Yet perhaps there was still a chance.

I found myself standing next to Judge Jackson.

"Astonishing," he murmured. "I've never seen anything like that in all my life . . . You are a very lucky man, Mr. Coyne."

"Tell me about it."

5:00 NEWS

Reporter: Do you have anything to say, Dermot?
DMC: I want to thank my attorney for her splendid work (hugs Ms. Hurley) and my family and my fiancée's family for their loyal support. I also want to thank the future Mrs. Dermot Coyne, my Irish immigrant bride, for her strength of character, which is as rock-solid as the mountains of her native Connemara. (Hugs her too.)
I would also like to point out to all those who are watching that what happened to me can just as easily happen to you. Perjured informants, politically ambitious lawyers, storm troopers with FBI warrant cards, publicity-seeking judges, and corrupt journalists can destroy your lives, too, even if you've never had even a traffic arrest. My freedom is your freedom, my victory is your victory, my enemies are the enemies of all of us.
And by the way, while tis true that the police never gave me a ticket, not even for parking, it is not true that the cops never stopped me! I guess I must have an honest face!

There is not much else to tell. We dropped charges against the FBI agents. David McAuliffe was reassigned to Anchorage. Martha Regan remained in Chicago. The United States Attorney resigned at the request of the Attorney General. His successor shook up the staff and Dale Quade was fired. She did two weeks of extensive therapy in a psychiatric ward. I'm sure Nuala sneaked into the hospital to see her, but I had the sense not to ask. When we returned from our honeymoon we found a silver plate she had sent us for a wedding gift.

The media made generous contributions to those institutions which had tried to educate me. The investigation which Judge Jackson had recommended is not doing much. Jarry Kennedy continues to live in his own half-light world of grand expectations and notorious failures; few people will speak to him.

The rehearsal dinner at the Four Seasons was "brilliant altogether," though there was more singing and dancing than that illustrious hotel had ever seen before; so the manager told me with a happy smile.

At the wedding the Bishop told us his famous strawberry story. Marie Mangan knelt in the back of the Cathedral. Nuala kissed her as we went down the aisle after Mass. The ghosts departed and left the scene to the cavorting angels.

Nuala's dress, I was later informed, was satin and lace with a very chaste high neck, long sleeves of lace, a headpiece of lace with a long veil of net and a long train (carried by a small Hurley child), and a tight waist with a panel of lace going down the front.

All I realized when I saw her coming down the aisle was that she took my breath away she was so lovely.

"Sure," she whispered in my ear. "There's almost nothing at all under this."

I gulped.

The reception was a grand success. Sean Cassidy, my friend from Marquette, met and fell in love with a gorgeous colleague of Nunu's from Arthur Andersen. He's so much in love that he forgot about my questions the day we had lunch at Berghoff's. The full story of Jimmy Sullivan's life and death and new life will be told someday but not now and I hope not for a long time.

— 34 —

 NUALA SANG at the wedding Mass, er, Eucharist. She sang at the dinner at the Drake. She sang too in our home before, during, and after the joyous—and comic— union which sealed the beginning of our new life together. The room was filled with light and I imagined that the prancing angels were singing with us.

Despite her promise that there was almost nothing on under her bridal gown, my fingers were clumsy as I tried to remove it.

She refused to help me. "Sure," she said, "take your time, there's no rush."

There was indeed not much under it, but all of it was delightful, and fun to remove.

A famous writer once said that the naked body of a woman was the most beautiful sight a man would ever see. He was right.

Then we became man and wife with surprising ease and great pleasure and joy.

"Ah, that wasn't so bad at all, at all?" Mrs. Coyne said when we collapsed into each other's arms at the end of our ride through the stars.

"Woman, it was not." My hand rested on her sweat-covered belly.

"Well, as I said to everyone, sure, when it comes to lovers, me Dermot won't be the worst of them!"

She moved my face to her breasts, kissed me very gently, and murmured, "Go to sleep now, me love. Tis fine altogether. Isn't the courtship over and our marriage begun? And won't I take good care of you always and sing you to sleep every night like I'm doing now?"

So I went to sleep to the tune of an Irish lullaby.

— NOTE —

JAMES "SWEET Rolls" Sullivan is a figment of my imagination, though to some extent he is based on Charles Dion "Dean" O'Bannion who was gunned down in his florist shop (Schofield's) across from Holy Name Cathedral. The rest of the atmosphere of the Prohibition era in Chicago is as authentic as I can make it. Of the many books about that time, the best I have read is *Mr. Capone* by Robert J. Schoenberg (William Morrow).

All the characters in my story are products of my imagination, including the lawyers and journalists. Alas, the abuse of power by prosecutors and media is not fictional. I agree with Dermot's final statement to the TV vultures.

Writing stories plays strange tricks on you. I was well into the book before I realized that O'Bannion was buried near my grandparents in Mount Carmel Cemetery. Moreover, my mother was married at the Cathedral and a wedding photo taken after the ceremony shows Schofield's in the background. O'Bannion was indeed killed among the flowers and his second-in-command, a certain Hymie Weiss (real name Earl Wojeichowski) was gunned down in the street outside the shop (probably the time the Cathedral cornerstone was chipped, if it ever was) because he demanded that Capone let him kill Anselmi and Scalise to even the score. Later "Al Brown" would have to kill them himself.

Is this the end of the "Nuala Anne" stories?

Well, now that's not for me to say, is it?
But, sure, wouldn't *Irish Cream* make a grand title?

Grand Beach
May 1997